Praise for *In Deep Water*

'A wonderful opening to the Rachel Harlow series. It's great
on the morality of police procedure, but it's even better on the
inevitable desires, embarrassments and joys of being a human.'
Abigail Dean

'Twisty and entertaining!'
Sarah Turner

'Original and dangerously additive (with relatable characters).
An exciting new voice in crime fiction.'
Will Dean

'A fast-paced, polished debut by a very talented writer which
will definitely make a splash!'
Trevor Wood

'One of the most confident and assured debuts I've read in
years. *In Deep Water* has it all – from laugh out loud moments
to heart-in-mouth cliffhangers. An absolutely cracking read!'
Robert Rutherford

'DI Rachel Harlow has a forthright swagger, and there's plenty
of tension to keep the blood pumping in this confident debut.
You'll dive into this book!'
Ellie Marney

'Oozing with northern charm and grit, this is a real page-turner
of a debut.'
Rebecca Philipson

'The scope is intoxicating, the characters compulsive, the pacing
and drama absolutely cracking. It's chilling, funny and
ultimately very moving.'
Henry Sutton

ELLE BLAIR has been an English teacher for over two decades, but always wanted to write. She completed her debut novel, *In Deep Water*, as part of the Crime Fiction MA course at the University of East Anglia, from which she graduated in 2025 with Distinction. Elle also writes children's fiction and her debut, *Robyn Hoodie*, is published by Andersen Press. She lives with her family by the sea in Whitley Bay.

In Deep Water

ELLE BLAIR

HQ
An imprint of HarperCollins*Publishers* Ltd
1 London Bridge Street
London SE1 9GF

www.harpercollins.co.uk

HarperCollins*Publishers*
Macken House, 39/40 Mayor Street Upper,
Dublin 1 D01 C9W8
This edition 2026

1
First published in Great Britain by HQ,
an imprint of HarperCollins*Publishers* Ltd 2026

Printed and bound in the UK using 100% Renewable
Electricity by CPI Group (UK) Ltd

My starting point for this character was her fringe. I dedicate this to two women with iconic fringes whom I greatly admire: Claudia Winkleman and Angela Rayner.

'Adrift! A little boat adrift'

Emily Dickinson

Prologue

She's being followed.

The corridor tightens with every step – bare walls, locked doors, no windows. Above, the strip lighting buzzes an urgent warning. Behind: footfalls. Quick. Closing.

Rachel clutches the paper to her chest. The evidence. Her last card. Proof that two men didn't just die – they were silenced. They knew too much.

She runs.

Back home, she'd have a warrant card. A radio. A weapon. She'd have a rank: Detective Inspector. But none of that counts here. Not in open water.

She can't stop now. Can't look back. She has to get above deck – to her family, to witnesses.

Every breath scrapes her lungs. The air down here is thick, recycled. No breeze, no escape. Just ocean pressing in on every side.

Anything can happen at sea.

It already has.

A red light stabs her vision. That tiny whir – another camera shifting on its axis. The crew can see everything on board. Watching. Recording. Deleting.

Her legs drag like anchors. Her stomach heaves.

But she runs. Because, right now, she knows too much.

Chapter 1

Sea

Thursday 20th April

The horn blared a guttural drone as the ship lurched from shore. Solid ground was gone. Anyone having second thoughts now would have to suck it up.

Or jump. That was always an option.

Rachel unclenched her hand from the cold metal rail and took a step back. From this height, the water below would turn to concrete and, in her line of work, she knew what a bloody mess that made of a body. It would have to be avoided, whatever the provocation on board.

She tried to look optimistically at the four members of her family squashed around her; it was only a week, and this was escape, not captivity. *Quality time.*

Jake and Jess were laughing in what almost looked like sibling harmony. Intrigued, she leaned closer as Jess pointed to the crowd waving from the dock. 'Her! She'd be your Snog.'

Jake squinted, then shrugged. 'Yeah. Fit.'

Jess raised one eyebrow. 'Punching. OK, one bullet – who's your Kill?'

She turned away, not wanting to jinx it. On her other side, she could hear snippets of the sort of bickering that could only come from forty years of marriage.

'The big one needs to be out of the way, Barb. We're blocking the route to the bar.'

'Well, you can't be lifting it. Doctor's orders. Rachel, tell him!'

It had started.

She closed her eyes momentarily, then gave her mum a tight smile, but Barbara was oblivious, tutting at Jake's backpack. The zip was beyond repair after he'd ignored all packing suggestions and rammed in a laptop, tablet and a spaghetti mess of cables and chargers. It hadn't been worth the argument.

Drifting from the two conversations, she scanned the bustling deck. Her DI instincts itched: there were crew everywhere in maroon blazers, but two waitresses caught her eye, almost hidden by cocktail-laden trays. Their corporate smiles were cracking, tense whispers just out of earshot.

Nausea was bubbling in the pit of Rachel's stomach now and the wailing sirens of home ringing in her ears. She shouldn't be here, the fifth wheel on board a floating old people's home. She should be at the station, addressing the team, banging the OT drum, doing whatever it took to stitch the case back together.

Her palm throbbed under the clear dressing, the scar raw, threatening to split. Even here, four hundred miles away, Operation Fever was still searing beneath her skin.

She'd always dismissed the medicinal properties of sea air as total bullshit, but could there be something in it? Maybe once they reached open water she wouldn't feel the DCI's white-hot anger banging around her brain anymore. Or hear each beat of the ticking clock counting down the seconds until the disciplinary hearing. They hadn't set a date, but she knew how it ended: unemployment.

Come on, *breathe*. At least in this version of rock bottom she had an all-inclusive anaesthetic wristband.

'Selfie?' she said, channelling calm waters. This could mark the start of a new era. No drama. The bruising at her temple was almost invisible now, after all. Obligingly, they pressed back against the railings for the picture – five links of one weathered chain, anchored together with gritted teeth.

'Oh, Bob – the T-shirts!' squealed her mum, breaking the pose and rummaging through her Radley shopper. Beaming, she pulled out a set of baby pink polo shirts.

Rachel blinked.

Jess voiced their collective bafflement. 'Are they for us, Gran?'

Like a magician eager to get to the prestige moment, Barbara dramatically crossed her hands for the big reveal of the back of the polyester top.

WILDE/HARLOWS ON TOUR

It was written in loopy Comic Sans, and by her parents' faces this was meant to be met with pleasure rather than horror. Jesus Christ.

She tried to express a complicated range of instructions to her children via eye contact, body language and mind control: *Yes, I know they're hideous. But, they're paying for this trip and it obviously means a lot to them. So just do it.*

Miraculously, some of this seemed to have landed as, after a seesaw-like silence, Jake cleared his throat. 'Mint. Have I got a pink one, though?'

'Of course you haven't, love! You and your grandad've got these!' Barbara thrust him a blue version.

'You've done too much for us already,' Rachel said, turning to her dad.

His cloudy eyes sparkled. 'Our pleasure. Not often we're all together, is it?'

Jess smiled reasonably nicely and took her top without a sarcy comment.

'Let's get another picture, a proper one!' Barbara trilled as they all pulled the bastards on. Now that Rachel could see the front up close, she noticed a clip-art icon of a boat with 'JUST CRUISIN' emblazoned in the same 'fun' font.

Gamely, they regrouped as the horn reverberated once more. Robert and Jake at the back, Jess and Barbara in front, and Rachel crouched awkwardly in the centre, hand shaking as she tried to get everyone's head in the frame.

With Southampton's shoreline gradually disappearing into the distance, all she could focus on were five words: *worse things happen at sea.*

Chapter 2

Sea

The Vegas vibes had shocked Rachel within the first five seconds. She'd thought she was well acquainted with all the cultural references: Jane McDonald belting out a big number; the sequel to *Speed* which Keanu Reeves must have declined to lower himself to; even that battered old Agatha Christie book.

But arriving on board was a gut punch of bling: a floating monument to capitalism in all its garish, Swarovski-encrusted glory. If there was a surface available that hadn't been polished to within an inch of its life, she was yet to see it.

They'd left Newcastle at stupid o'clock, reaching the terminal just in time for their four p.m. embarkation slot, but the stress of driving the full length of the M1 receded as the three of them stared up in awe at the mountainous white vessel, *The Synergy of the Seas*.

Now, the way the almost-entirely South East Asian crew were rolling out the red carpet for White Middle England was starting to make her feel uncomfortable. The stewards were actually bowing as they shepherded passengers through a gleaming atrium towards the retail outlets.

Even the air on board was obnoxious: eau de hand sanitiser

with top notes of box-fresh merchandise. But it was masking something beneath. Something sour that made her want to gag.

She looked at Jess and Jake, both taller than her, both wide-eyed, and gave herself a shake. They were slipping away. This time next year they'd be sixteen and probably wouldn't be seen dead with her in public, let alone agree to share a cabin. Though her DI salary plus Scott's sporadic maintenance payments kept them ticking over, holidays had been off the table for years.

Being here together had to be an opportunity – a chance to fix the fraying fibres still tethering them before the cord snapped for good. At the very least, with Jake out of school, she'd have a brief reprieve from calls from Mr Powell.

They followed the regal pensioner procession to the safety briefing, which everyone around them was nonchalantly referring to as the Muster Drill. Jake was immediately shot down by his sister when he mooted giving it a miss.

'It's part of our legal requirement as passengers.'

'Calm down, Jess,' Rachel said. 'Threat level's minimal.'

'Who knows what'll happen with *him*,' she said, nodding at Jake's glaiky expression. 'Are you sure he wasn't switched at birth?'

'Could've been. I was a bit busy with the haemorrhage in the aftermath.'

Jess rolled her eyes. 'Any excuse to dust off your *I Gave Birth to Twins* medal.'

Rachel resisted the urge to remind Jess that having unplanned twins at nineteen had seemed anything but medal-worthy at the time. And no one had been handing out anything other than NHS tea and toast.

They stood dutifully for twenty minutes on the dance floor of the Poseidon club, listening to Wikipedia: The Live Show. Who knew that the *Synergy* was equipped to carry up to 4,905 passengers and had had its maiden voyage in 2015? She was dismayed to hear that only sixteen lifeboats were available. Her shoulders tensed: hadn't this industry learned anything from the *Titanic*?

After running through arrangements in case of fire and terrorist threat with all the pizzazz of an ITV game-show host, the compere gestured to the senior crew members, seated on a raised stage: 'As you can see, we're a happy ship!'

They might be smiling, but all were dead-eyed, presumably having had to trot out the same lines for wave upon wave of new passengers boarding the ship over the afternoon.

The captain was a late-fifties, English-gent type and the compere's tone took on a nauseating reverence. 'Captain Miller has been circumnavigating the globe for two decades aboard HLC's fleet of vessels. His mastery of the sea is unparalleled.'

Rachel felt herself clicking into work mode, instinctively conducting a visual assessment. Miller had to be ex-services: classic Sandhurst material. With his stately posture and clipped accent, he was clearly innately comfortable with steering a thousand-tonne floating village across the continent.

The chief security officer, Simon Van der Wyk, was hailed as an industry shining star, with a background in the South African National Defence Force. He was square-jawed with biceps to spare, and his dazzling blue eyes locked onto hers for a moment as he outlined his role. She shivered, goose bumps rising in the chill of the air-con.

'It's my pleasure to ensure your vacation with us is plain sailing. Rest assured my team and I will be overseeing every aspect of your safety and security throughout the voyage.' Surely this was a change of pace, switching the mean streets of Joburg for squabbles over who'd put a towel on the last sunlounger.

Her phone vibrated. Lennon.

She'd been avoiding him since admitting defeat and putting in her leave request. Easy enough, when he'd been storming up and down the M60, doing her job, and she'd been confined to a desk, shuffling paper and trying to stave off the panic attacks.

The acrid tang that had been curdling in her stomach for two excruciating weeks started to creep up her throat. The way she'd lost control, lost herself up there, with *him*. And Lennon had seen it all. Swallowing hard, she squeezed the shame back down.

No. She couldn't let herself start thinking about the whole Gallagher/suspension clusterfuck or Lennon's reaction. Everything between them was still frosty. All messaging minimal: *OK. Fine. No bother.*

Maybe it wasn't even work-related. Maybe he was dating someone; he'd been quiet on that front for a while. And there'd been an atmosphere, even before Dalton Crescent. He'd had a succession of girlfriends over the years, though, and it had never bothered her in the slightest. The thought of moving slowly towards him, lips achingly gentle, brushing her tongue against his and feeling the heat of his neck close to her skin did absolutely nothing for her at all. Nothing.

JPG still in critical care. Merseyside made the arrests. You were bang on about Davison being a wanker but we've got enough to charge. 11erife obvs acting like he traced the Scousers single-handed. Enjoy the trip.

He still sounded formal. Too polite.

She craved his piss-taking. Dark eyes burning into her as he spoke; every word teetering on the edge of the unsaid. But it was entirely normal to feel that way about a close friend. She couldn't help that, objectively, he was an attractive man. There was no point denying the purely aesthetic appeal of his face. Or body. Or arse when he wore those black Levi's.

Years ago, sure, things could have been different, but that was fully behind them and she didn't spend any time thinking about him naked. Or sweaty. Or whatever.

Another message, like a PS:

Don't come back riddled from all your shagging.

She grinned; he was back.

Rachel made sure the phone was out of view of Jake, lolling restlessly at her side, before replying. Jess, further along, was alert, preparing for a non-existent exam on the content of the presentation.

As if. Only thing I'll be catching is norovirus. Or feelings.

Ugh. Keep me updated.

Straight away, three dots bounced underneath and she waited, feeling more positive than she had for weeks, despite the sting of the case – her case – being out of her hands.

If anyone's catching feelings, it won't be you. Stop texting and work on your tan.

The briefing reached its home straight, with the *Synergy*'s emergency muster points highlighted on a floor plan. They must be moving now; a coursing motion was dragging beneath her feet and the walls seemed to have tilted to an unnatural angle. She tried to steady her wedge heels on the floating floor, but there was nothing to grab onto. Whether seasickness or PTSD, this hadn't been in the itinerary her mum had circulated on WhatsApp.

'Upon accessing your cabins, please take a few moments to familiarise yourselves with the life vests provided.' The compere gestured towards the cruise director, a flamboyant American with an aggressively backcombed updo. 'Our very own Veronica Chase will now demonstrate how to tighten the straps.'

Rachel would swear under oath that several crew members at the edge of the dance floor exchanged pointed glances at these last three words. Her radar rarely misfired and she shifted to have a better sightline of the woman on the stage.

As the compere wrapped it up, Veronica seemed to recoil from the captain's hand, which was resting lightly on the arm of her chair. There was a flicker of something in her eyes. Unease. Or irritation? Consummate professionalism still shone from her blindingly white teeth, but Rachel clocked some context that told a different story.

They were released from the daylight disco room, safe in the knowledge that they knew what to do in case of piracy and/or food poisoning, and began their ascent up a marble staircase to the top deck for the full family rendezvous.

Everywhere, there were people.

But Rachel felt removed: an observer, not a participant. Snatches of chatter and wrinkled faces were bobbing around her, as if the whole ship was submerged and she was viewing this water world from behind a scuba mask. Panic set in and she scrambled for something, anything – a whistle, an air tank, an escape route.

She'd been drowning on land too, though, waiting for the disciplinary. This trip was her life raft. Cop-mode just had to be switched off for the next seven days. Surely, here, of all places, that was going to be possible?

Breathing deeply, assessing her surroundings, she conceded it was slightly more diverse than she'd given it credit for. A boatload of pensioners, granted, with their sensible slacks and combovers; but also harassed-looking parents laden down with designer buggies, and couples grinning smugly, stopping every five seconds to take loved-up photos.

It all reeked of money.

Suppressing a shudder, Rachel manifested a silent SOS as cruise life enveloped them in its shiny, sanitised embrace.

Chapter 3

Land

Three months earlier – Thursday 26th January

'The powers that be have decided to offer you the SIO position.'
DCI Bailey's mouth curved upwards a fraction at one corner. This
was the closest Rachel had ever seen to him smiling.

Her own reaction was just relief. She'd done it. All the prep,
the early starts and late finishes, transferring the kids twenty
quid to get another Dominos while she boxed off one more job:
it had actually paid off.

'Thank you, sir, for the opportunity.'

'Mmmm.' He was scanning a document on his desk and
sounded less than enthusiastic, but she continued, elated that
the hundred-day strategic plan she'd painstakingly put together
had got the nod.

'We can make a real difference in this pilot. Byker's been crying
out for this sort of focused policing for years.'

'Indeed. Your results and work ethic have certainly drawn
attention, Harlow, even if …' he looked at her, brow furrowed
'… there have been some *reservations* about your methods.'

Careful to maintain her poker face, she avoided delving into this pass-agg critique. Reservations or not, she'd got the job, hadn't she?

'When will I start, sir?' The notice period for Safeguarding could stall it, if DCI Murdoch was one of Bailey's fellow reservationists and wanted to throw his weight around.

'Arrangements are in process. Handover across the next fortnight, then straight into the NEROCU.'

NEROCU. The North East Regional Organised Crime Unit. She'd be leading a National Crime Agency brief to disrupt OCG activity across the three North East regions: Northumbria, Durham and Cleveland. The reality of Bailey's gruffly delivered message had started to seep into her bloodstream, a surge of adrenaline making her spine tingle. 'You won't regret th—'

'Damn right, I won't.' He sighed, organising his papers into a neat stack. 'Progress reported to me weekly and you'll be representing Operation Fever at the National County Lines Co-ordination Centre briefings.' His baggy eyes bored into her. 'A tight leash, you could say.'

She held his gaze without blinking. 'And my team, sir?'

'A unit of seven. I've had excellent reports of a GDP trainee, comes highly recommended. I'll get him moved across.'

Rachel kept her face impassive. Maybe he'd buck the trend of recent fast-track recruits, most of whom lasted less than a year before realising the job was a lot less glamorous than it looked on Netflix.

Bailey continued in his flat monotone. 'We'll need an analyst – Marianne Drummond's available for IO – but get me a shortlist by close of play Monday for the remaining CID and uniform roles.'

'Sir.' This was more promising. She'd worked with Maz before, and a canny intelligence officer would be the lynchpin of a team like this.

Rachel rose from her seat. DCI Bailey's office was much like the man himself: tired and full of stale air. Everything looked in dire need of a blast of Mr Muscle. The window had a border of frost around the edges, but the ice outside was thawing and she could see tiny buds on the bare branches of the tree at the edge of the car park.

'Oh, and Harlow—' He always had to have the final word, as a point of principle. 'Management advice. Trust no one. Give them a clear job and keep on comms. Got it?'

Out in the corridor, she bashed out a quick message with trembling fingers:

Got it!! Senior Investigating Officer for North East County Lines X

Dizzy with adrenaline now, she half walked, half ran, dodging officers, unable to stop the smile from stretching her lips apart. Diving into the locker room to splash some water on her face and regain her composure, she assessed her appearance.

Same pale face, same heavy fringe – cheaper than Botox – but the sparkle in her eyes was unfamiliar. Whatever it was, she liked it.

Her phone beeped. Jake: a thumbs-up emoji. For him, Shakespearean. In contrast, Jess was probably composing a furious takedown of the police force. Growing up with two parents who had worn the badge was, in her mind, grounds for lifelong therapy.

Before Jess could unleash her tirade, an insistent tone sounded: *Mum and Dad Landline.* She tapped green, suddenly breathless.

'You both OK? Did you see my message?'

Her dad's voice was thin and wheezy, but with each word leap-frogging the last. 'We did, love. How about that, eh? Serious investigation official!'

'Thanks – I'm absolutely buzzing.' She didn't bother to correct the job title; he'd got the gist. 'Thought I'd messed it up in the panel interview as well.'

'Ask her if it's desk-based, Bob.' Her mum's voice was faint, further away, then becoming louder, taking charge. 'It'll be a management role, will it? Off the street, as it were?'

'Kind of. Depends on the progress of the operation, but I'll still be on the arrests, dealing with the CPS and all that side of—'

'Oh.' Her mum's tone was flat, squashing her bubbling excitement with a single syllable. 'But it's for the whole county?'

'Across the three North East forces, but starting with a local Northumbria pilot.'

'Like when she used to run the eight hundred for the county, Barb!' her dad added cheerfully, although on completely the wrong track. 'Round that final bend like a whippet you were, love.'

Operation Fever couldn't be further from her brief spell as a junior member of Winchester Athletics Club, twenty years ago. Was this even worth explaining? 'The county bit means the way the drugs get in and out of region; remember I told you before? Monitoring the phone line and the children the dealers are exploit—'

'Well, heading in the right direction,' her mum said, each word a blunt pinprick. 'I daresay you'll be spending your time with more respectable people at least.'

Rachel said nothing, but felt her air slowly deflating. This again.

'Colleagues, I mean. You'll be operating at a different level to the likes of that dark-haired one. Took you out over Christmas.' She sniffed. 'Lennon, was it? All those dreadful tattoos.'

'He didn't take me out, Mum.' Rachel's energy for this conversation was expiring rapidly. 'We're just friends. He was giving me a lift. And you barely said two words—'

'Barbara,' her dad cut in, 'don't be lecturing the girl. Policing's what she's gone for; it's a noble profession and she's got our full support. Wouldn't have been my first choice for a woman, particularly of her height, but that's by the—'

'Right. I need to go.' She could picture them both so clearly: M&S stalwarts. Her mum winding the phone cord round and round her finger, her dad with his vest tucked firmly into his slacks. Both had fine, fair hair, if faded now to silver. Her own wild, dark mane in the mirror looked nothing like either of them. The odd one out.

'Send our love to the children.' Barbara couldn't help herself from one more attempt to pop the celebratory balloons. 'If you cross paths, that is. They seem to be fending for themselves somewhat—'

'Battery's dying,' Rachel said, stabbing the screen and leaning back against the locker. She closed her eyes.

There was a sudden bang as the door opened and she could sense him before she felt strong arms encircle her and spin her off her feet.

'She's only gone and done it! What's Bailey thinking?'

For a moment, she kept her eyes shut and savoured the sensation of being pressed so close to his chest. Just for a moment.

'Had a book going, y'know?' Lennon murmured, into her hair. 'You owe me a tenner.'

Normally any touch was a joke, just banter – an elbow to the ribs, a hip knocking the other off their stride as they walked side by side down the corridor. This was different. It took her straight back to faded fragments from years ago: that hazy glow, the heat of his body. One night that had almost changed everything.

'Your loss.' Her mouth was mushed into his shoulder, words barely audible, but from his squeeze she could tell he'd heard. She opened one eye and was horrified to find him looking back. Too weird.

Quickly, they shook each other off, untangling limbs, overplaying it for a non-existent crowd.

His nose was wrinkled for added effect. 'What's that perfume? Smells like rat's piss.'

'Says the man still using Lynx Africa.'

He held his hands up. 'Haven't had any complaints.'

She rolled her eyes. 'Please. You're tucked up on your tod every night watching Sky Sports highlights.'

'And? Stress of the job, pet. It's called self-care.'

'When's the last time you actually went on a date?'

'None of your business. Not everyone's a raving nympho.'

She feigned a yawn. 'Get some new material. And it's ma'am to the likes of you from now on – strictly professional.'

Lennon was a natural charmer. He could get a conversation going with a corpse and was referred to in certain departments as MTM, or Milk Tray Man, for his penchant for a fitted polo neck. But he was exactly the same around whomever he spoke to: from the commissioner, to the cleaner, to the spice-addled charvers he spent much of his working life rinsing for intelligence.

He was quiet now though, looking at her with a strange expression. 'What?' she said, turning to the mirror and smoothing her fringe down. 'Do I look a right clip?'

'That's nothing new.' He smirked behind her in the glass, but she could see red creeping up his neck from the collar of his shirt.

'What then?'

'Just – it won't change, will it? Us being mates. You'll be mixing with the top brass, but we can still – y'know, get a cuppa.'

She snorted. 'The top brass?'

'Don't sound like you, does it.'

She turned back. 'We're not going to change. Not getting rid of me that easily.'

'You've proper smashed it, Rach.' His smile was infectious. 'SIO!'

'And I was all over the place when we started.' She reached out and prodded him in the stomach. 'So were you, mind.'

'You always had a spark. You knew what you wanted.'

They were inches apart, but she could still feel the glow radiating off him from the way he'd held her before, hot and hard. She had known what she'd wanted back then – but, right now, was he thinking what she was thinking? How it could have been …

This was stupid. He'd just said it. They were *mates*. Nothing more.

'How'd you find out, anyway? News travels fast.' She leaned against the locker, still flushed, the cool metal a relief. 'I was on my way to find you.'

'Doppa said he saw you, proper coat hanger mouth, so I put two and two together.'

'Well. It's genius like that I'm looking to recruit to Operation Fever.' She raised her eyebrows. 'Fancy it?'

'Under you? Fate worse than death.' He put his head in his hands. 'You're going to be an absolute nightmare.'

Chapter 4

Land

Two months later – Monday 27th March

Rachel leaned over Tariq's desk, trying not to get too close to the old coffee cups, and refreshed the screen. It was pointless and they both knew it. For a Monday morning kick-off briefing, this had the potential to involve holes actually getting kicked in the walls.

She faced her team. 'Right, the 4-3-5 line's dead.' A shitstorm of epic proportions was imminent. 'I know—'

The feed had gone from everything to nothing overnight. They'd been inching forwards for six weeks and now, here they were, kicked back to the kerb, trying to monitor a phone line with zero activity.

Tariq, her usually mild-mannered analyst, slammed his fist into the desk and slumped back, kneading his knuckles in immediate regret.

'So, we're back to square one?' Coates said, indignant. He'd learn. Seven months into the Graduate Detective Programme and didn't they all know it. Full of suggestions on how long-established CID processes could be amended to increase efficiency, Lennon had renamed him Elevenerife on about day three.

'No.' God, he was more of a hindrance than a help. 'Not square one. They've just clocked we're on to them somehow. It happens. Once we get up on the new line, we'll transfer all the intel over.'

He nodded, somewhat pacified because he'd been addressed directly by the senior investigating officer which, presumably, gave him brownie points in his reflective training journal, or whatever bullshit document he was always asking people to sign off.

He made to speak, but she continued. 'It'll be the same users all over the new number so primary objective remains putting an ID to the line holder. Rossy, where are we on that?'

'Still NFI, boss,' DS Natalie Ross said, nodding at the evidence board. No Fucking Idea. Brilliant.

Rachel turned to the grainy A4 printouts: fifteen faces, arranged in a pyramid across one wall of the office. These ranged from surly teenage boys at the bottom, invariably snapped with hoods up, to older individuals, all known to the police, all with sizeable records. Each image was labelled with its corresponding mobile number, DOB and any additional information on their role within the OCG. As it stood, the pattern faltered the further you travelled up the tiers towards the ceiling.

Her focus, as ever, was drawn to a face at the mid-point. Strong jaw, shaven head, green eyes, snapped covertly while smoking a tab outside the Raby. Jo" Paul Gallagher. She'd stared at his face so much lately she was seeing it in her sleep. They even had the same fucking birthday. She quickly looked away.

'Not an answer, Rossy. Without an ID at the top, there's no way the court'll authorise the DDTRO. We need that board fully marked up. NFI's not good enough.'

The process of obtaining a Drug Dealing Telecommunication Restriction Order was like swimming through a shoal of piranhas; every time you thought you had enough to meet the criteria, the court nibbled off another piece of your case until it was reduced to a ravaged carcass.

There were muffled murmurs, but she didn't back down. She'd

been in teams where they'd all known the boss was a waste of space, hiding in their office with the blinds pulled down, duping the stats to alleviate pressure further up the chain of command. That wasn't going to be her.

Operation Fever had sounded the absolute bollocks in the interview, with free rein to pick her team. On reflection, that optimism might have had more to do with Dry January than the actual hospital pass she'd been handed. Bailey's face had certainly been tripping him up in every meeting since.

'We've still got multiple lines of enquiry open,' Rossy said. She could be bolshy and liable to sulk, but she was a good officer. 'Before this shit—' she gestured to Tariq's stone-cold feed '—the cell site analysis was dead close.'

'Still all the ANPR footage to trawl through,' chipped in Maz, the unit's intelligence officer. 'Someone's making weekly trips up the M60, but we've got so much activity from the bando it's getting too much to track.' Her Glaswegian accent made every update sound like she was laying down a challenge.

'Speak for yourself,' said Chris Chambers, her cherry-picked DC. 'Spending that much time watching charvers pissing around doing wheelies, I'm gannin' bong-eyed.' He nodded wearily to the screen in front of him, showing rolling surveillance from the camera they'd got into the bando, an empty flat opposite the corner shop in the Byker Wall estate.

Rachel gave him her patented DI death stare. 'Save us the sob story or I'll get you put straight back on the nonce squad.'

'Those were the days.' He smiled ruefully. 'Posing as a fourteen-year-old lass on Snapchat all day – started believing my own cover story.'

'What about Chambers getting on the exploitation side?' Rossy said. 'Respond to some of the Insta stories, see if we can set up a meet?'

Rachel shook her head. 'Just back to the old issue. Yeah, we can pick up a few young'uns, have them in custody in the next ten minutes. But then what? Minor inconvenience for the OCG. They'll lose, what? An eighth? No one's talking.'

People around the room were nodding. Coates was twitching to contribute, but everyone had learned to avoid eye contact wherever possible.

'Blades of grass,' said PC Ian Bradshaw. 'This lot get mown down, there's plenty more coming up behind.'

He'd been the hardest to sweet-talk into moving over, content to ride out his last few years before retirement in the Byker neighbourhood team and organise the station ski trip every year, but they had history. When she'd first joined the police, walking the beat on Shields Road, Bradshaw had shown her the ropes. He had an encyclopaedic knowledge of the entire community, as regular a presence as the paint flaking off the Tyne Bridge in the distance. Unlike the rest of the team, Bradshaw never kicked off and he spoke with the gravelly voiced purr of Aslan. The Alka-Seltzer to her heartburn.

'I know it's not easy,' Rachel said, looking around. The mood in the drab office was on the floor, and, with foreboding clouds at the only window, the whole room felt grey. This was meant to be the best the North East had to offer: Chambers practically horizontal in his swivel chair; Rossy scrolling on her phone; Tariq still messing on with his knuckles. She'd probably get more energy from whatever was growing in his Sports Direct mug. 'Fuck's sake, this is why you're not a copper. Go and get a plaster or something.'

Shouts of 'way aye' and 'soft lad' came from the assembled cops. Everyone knew their role in the banter and no one got away without a jibe or a nickname.

Tariq raised the middle finger from his injured hand in response to this standard slight on his civvy status. 'This one's working fine.'

She smiled, glad the bubble of tension had burst. 'Look, we're nailing jelly to the wall here most of the time, but we've got to keep pushing forward.'

Clicking the remote, she turned to the PowerPoint on the screen beside her, the next slide in two columns. 'Still two strands, right? The deal line – back on it, IDs, cell site analysis, track the Scousers' cars, Maz – follow the money. We keep on that and we eventually get who's holding the line.'

She eyeballed Rossy, who grudgingly put her phone down. 'CCE side – social media leads, liaise with Safeguarding, absolutely everything on record. We need to be ready to go on the exploitation charges as soon as the OCG's fully marked up.'

Coates jumped in, tapping his pen. 'They're all engaging in criminal activity though, aren't they? The teenagers aren't innocent. Why we going easy on them?'

He might have a degree in psychology or whatever it was, but he had a hell of a lot to learn. 'There's kids as young as twelve knocking around in this footage,' she snapped. 'They get offered twenty to keep a package under their bed, why would they say no? And then they're fucked. They're locked in.'

'Where's Lennon, boss?' Chambers said. She could see his weren't the only eyes to have wandered to the unoccupied desk in the corner.

It was first come first served for space, with DS Lennon as the sole exception to the hotdesking policy. For reasons best known to himself as a thirty-six-year-old man, he had steadily filled every available surface of his commandeered corner position with shitty Marvel bobble-head figures which he'd Blu-Tacked haphazardly into submission.

She appraised her team, still lolling in their seats. At least Coates had been taking notes, although that was more than likely just going to be his basis from which to knock on her door later, deconstruct their strategy and offer his own alternative. 'Out on CI contact. Something that the rest of you should be considering rather than sitting here whingeing about the 4-3-5. Local knowledge. Community ties. That's what's going to get us up the line.'

Some of them had the good grace to look a little sheepish.

'Few calls to follow up on since the Crimestoppers bit on *Look North*,' said Maz, picking some Post-its off her laptop. Her words hung in the air: these were thankless tasks. Pensioners ringing to complain about someone nicking their bins, usually passed down to the neighbourhood beat team, but Rachel had negotiated a segment on the local news last week and specifically requested for anything relevant to the Wall to come straight to the NEROCU.

'I'll do a few doorknocks,' Bradshaw said. 'Tag along if you want, Coatesy lad. Probably tick some of your boxes for you.'

Coates looked over, unsure if he was having the piss taken out of him, but Bradshaw's offer was genuine and Rachel was once again reminded why he was worth his weight in gold. She smiled at him gratefully. 'Plain-clothes though, OK?' Last thing any of the residents needed was a uniform turning up at their door.

'You told Lennon about the deal line?' Rossy's question was directed to Rachel, but played to the crowd. Sounds of mirth and a few comments of the 'rather you than me' variety abounded. He was always the epicentre of any team she'd worked in, even in his absence.

'Thought I'd leave that to you,' she said, sweetly, to Rossy, who rolled her eyes. 'I'm non-contact this afternoon, meeting with the NCA, so expect yet more good news this time tomorrow. In the meantime, fingers out of arses and get me something we can work with.'

Chapter 5

Land

Before the pleasure of a three-hour National Crime Agency Teams call reared its head, Rachel had another matter to deal with.

She sat, straight-backed, in one of the waiting room chairs and tried not to feel like a naughty schoolgirl. She had actually been impressed with Mr Powell's last contact, finding out Jake had been building a small retail empire selling protein bars from the Cash & Carry to kids in the yard at an extortionate mark-up. It had showed a level of entrepreneurship she wouldn't have thought him capable of, based on his usual monosyllabic interactions.

This time didn't sound so hopeful.

It was hard to put a positive spin on the news that he'd refused to attend a detention on Friday, calling the teacher a 'fucking bellend' before storming off the premises. She'd tried talking to him over the weekend, but hadn't got beyond a few grunts and a slammed door.

Her phone beeped loudly, earning a disapproving look from the receptionist. Hopefully this was Scott, with his standard, *soz 5 mins*, ETA. It was galling enough they were being called in to discuss their son's 'continued defiance to adhere to school rules' without having to turn up on her own, carrying a neon 'Broken Home' sign into the meeting.

She glanced at the screen, heart sinking to see Mark Matthews' name.

Just checking in. How's it feel being on top? x

A classic CID Billy-Big-Bollocks, he'd also interviewed for the DI job she'd got a year ago. He was matey with Scott, which made it somewhat less than ideal that she'd slept with him a few times, though, as far as she knew, this had not been communicated to her ex-husband.

Ignoring Matthews' unsubtle come-on, she focused on Scott, trying to summon him by sheer force of will: *FFS. You need to be at the school NOW.* He worked regular hours these days, not police shifts. Given he'd been on the same brusque email chain to arrange this day, this time, where the hell was he?

The phone on the desk gave an angry buzz and she was ushered into Mr Powell's office, resigned that she'd failed at the first hurdle of presenting them as a united front.

'Good afternoon, Mrs Harlow. Thank you for coming in …' he looked at the paperwork in front of him '… er – again. And Mr Harlow is—'

'On his way,' she said, too quickly. 'We've both spoken to Jake over the weekend, and he's written a letter of apology.' There was no need to mention that she'd dictated this through his bedroom door. 'And he's assured me he'll be back on track from now on.'

Mr Powell said nothing, but turned the sheet over to view the long list of recent incidents in their entirety.

She jumped in, disliking the heavy silence. 'He's struggling – he really lacks confidence. I mean, it can't be easy having a straight-A student like Jess for a sister.'

'Grade 9.'

'Excuse me?'

'The key stage four metric of achievement is now numerical, Mrs Harlow. You should have received a parents' pack on the

GCSE curriculum at the start of the academic year?' He left the question hanging, and she nodded, trying to look like someone who would have diligently read this information rather than leave it, drowning, under the sea of random shit on the kitchen bench.

He continued, 'Yes. That could certainly be a contributing factor, which brings me to the reason for this meeting.'

She gulped.

'As educators, we have a responsibility to act in the best interests of our entire student cohort. After discussion with the faculty, we see one path ahead being what we call a *managed move*.' He unclasped his hands to make air quotes. 'We try hard to avoid negative labels like "exclusion".'

Rachel had to sit on her own hands to stop herself slamming the desk. She was reeling: exclusion? As in, kicked out of school permanently? OK, the year ten detentions were racking up, but this hadn't crossed her mind for a second.

Mr Powell was still talking and she tried to concentrate on the words, not the tightness in her chest, or the roaring in her ears. 'Jake could have a fresh start, in a new environment. We believe this could work very well for all parties.' He crossed his arms and sat back on his ergonomic chair, as if to signify that the matter was settled.

Her stomach dropped. 'I'd be keen to avoid that. I wouldn't want him to lose the positive relationships he does have here. I mean, PE, that's a strength – Mr Rees said some good stuff at parents' evening? And ICT. He's doing OK in that, isn't he?'

'As I said, we need to consider all parties.'

'He's not that bad!' Her hackles were rising now. In the real world, Jake's misdemeanours were barely scratching the surface. She knew for a fact there were kids his age selling drugs, stealing cars and stabbing each other within walking distance of this office. 'Yes, we've been in here a lot, but they're all pretty minor incidents. I get it, he's sworn at a teacher, but that can't be exclusion level? And, what if he didn't settle at a new school? What would happen then?'

'In that case, Jake would go on the waiting list for the pupil referral unit.'

Fuck. This meeting was veering down a path she couldn't have Jake on, under any circumstances. She knew from her time in Safeguarding that the PRU, for all its noble aims and dedicated staff, was a sinking ship. The kids were only in for a few hours a day and could usually be found roaming Newcastle city centre, falling through the cracks in the system faster than rainwater down a drain.

Rachel stared at Mr Powell and took a deep breath. 'Can we just give it one more chance before you put any of that into place? I'll talk to him again. And his dad will. Please.'

He gave a grudging sigh. 'Last chance, Mrs Harlow. I'll need to see real change from Jake or I'll be left with no choice.'

Chapter 6

Land

Rachel's laptop screen had turned into Guess Who: the Police UK County Lines edition. The objective of this meeting, ostensibly, was to disseminate key findings from the regional units after the first month of Operation Fever. However, it was already clear from the message chat that this was really a chance for each unit to pull a wedgie on someone else before the assistant chief constable noticed the skid marks in their own pants.

She'd raced back from the school with a sense of dread. Scott had been a no-show. And she had no idea how she was going to get the urgency of the situation across to Jake.

With no home-office space, she'd set herself up on the kitchen table, shifting the laptop several times to find a background that didn't reveal just how much of a shit tip the room was.

The meeting was being chaired by the national county lines lead, ACC George Armstrong, with representatives from each of the ten regional units, as well as the Specialist Cybercrime Unit, Regional Fraud Team and Regional Intelligence Bureau. This was also the official launch of yet another new initiative, with Detective Inspector Alex Brand, whoever he was, having been appointed as the lead for TOEX, the Tackling Organised Exploitation programme.

Rachel's head was swimming with the sheer number of acronyms being bandied about. Drowning, as they all undeniably were, in the riptides of organised crime, establishing new units and giving them snappy titles seemed to be the main strategy.

'Thank you all for your attendance at this first monthly information sharing and collaboration point.' The ACC's face had now taken centre stage, with the sizeable grid of attendees shunted to the side. He was an imposing figure, even in virtual form: broad-shouldered, with rank insignia across both epaulettes. 'I'll now share my screen to begin the introductions. Slide please, Diana.'

There was a slight pause whilst the anonymous Diana made the switch to slideshow mode. As with all Teams meetings Rachel had ever attended, there was someone present who had neglected to turn their mic off, meaning they were all pretending they couldn't hear a dog barking somewhere in the ether.

'Can I ask everyone to ensure their camera remains on and microphone off until such time as you are invited to participate. If you have a pressing need to speak, I would invite you to use either the hand-up function or the message chat.' His voice was brusque. Even though she knew it wasn't her and she didn't even have a dog, Rachel immediately rechecked her own settings.

The next slides outlined each participant and their role in the overall National County Lines Co-ordination Centre structure, with four strategic values reiterated, as if the ACC was saying grace at a formal dinner table before letting them loose on the prawn cocktails. 'We remain resolute in our mission to pursue, protect, prevent and prepare for disruption to organised crime. Our goal is to successfully target those organised criminals causing significant harm in our local communities and establish a reputation as a co-ordinated set of highly professional specialist units.'

It was boggling her mind how much time and effort had

been put into the wording of these values, and how much more likely success was deemed to be now that they all began with the same letter.

'Each of our regional co-ordinators will now give a brief overview of their situation at ground level, giving us some context to your strategic priorities. I'll then open the floor for questions. As stated on the agenda, we'll begin with Detective Inspector Marie Connor for East Midlands.'

Rachel took notes as each of her counterparts presented their bleak but familiar pictures. Communities decimated by a decade of austerity; cuts to public services in addiction and youth work creating a perfect storm of supply and demand with a seemingly unlimited pool of vulnerable recruits ready to be exploited. Of course, the abuse of children as part of the drugs trade was nothing new, but social media was making the threat ever more difficult to control. Analysts like Tariq were dealing with rapidly changing goal posts of encrypted 5G networks virtually impermeable to police monitoring.

'Even five years ago, recruitment still meant hanging around the school gates.' The third speaker, DI Julie Adams, Met Police, sounded wrung out. 'Where now, they're in these kids' pockets 24/7. We've got twelve-year-olds touting for work on the socials, watching their mates get new trainers, wads of twenties handed out like sweets. It's desperate.'

'If I could jump in there,' a voice cut across. DI Josh Davison, North West. 'Just to make you aware of our strategic response to this issue. I've been piloting a parental education seminar to make carers aware of the ways apps like Snapchat are being utilised by OCGs to recruit young people and communicate on end-to-end encrypted software. We've had a ninety-five per cent positivity rating from the first sessions. Just one way Merseyside are delivering on the *prevent* element of the overall operation.'

'Thank you for that, Inspector,' said Armstrong, evidently impressed. 'This is exactly the purpose of these monthly check-ins

– the chance to share good practice and disseminate new operational tactics.'

'Can I just ask,' DI Adams said, seeming – like Rachel – to smell the unmistakable aroma of bullshit in the air, 'just to get a slightly fuller picture. How many parents were you able to actually engage with?'

Rachel waited for the inevitable bristle from Davison. They'd crossed paths before he'd transferred out of region, but there'd been something dodgy. Relationships with informants rang a bell. Lennon would know the details. Whatever it was, must have been swept under the carpet as, for now, Davison was in pole position as official arse licker of the NCA. 'Certainly, DI Adams. I don't have the details to hand, but I'd be amenable to arranging a follow-up call, if you feel that our approach might be something you'd want to emulate.'

In adherence to the agenda, her own slides were called at precisely 15.20. She was already waning and they weren't even at the halfway point. This was important though. She downed the dregs of the Red Bull next to her and shared her screen.

'DI Rachel Harlow, North East.' Not naturally comfortable with addressing this many high-ranking officers, she could feel her hand trembling slightly as she brushed crumbs off the IKEA table. She was determined to present authenticity though, rather than a highlights reel of immediate breakthroughs à la Davison, and this resolve instilled her voice with some power.

'After analysing the initial intelligence reports, we made the decision to prioritise one East-End estate as our pilot locality.' Without the assistance of her own personal Diana, she brought up her next slide, with several images of the imposing concrete and red-brick landscape.

'This is the Byker Wall,' she continued. 'Built in the Seventies to replace the shipyard terraces, it's got six hundred and twenty properties, and we've got about nine thousand officially listed residents. But the reality's much higher. Families of five, six living in one-bed homes and a high proportion of sub-letting so even the council don't have an accurate picture.'

She switched to the next slide, a map. 'The physical challenge of policing the Wall is its geography. We know it's Grade II listed and apparently of some great architectural importance, but it's your basic policing nightmare. Spans more than a mile and it's just as much of a mishmash as this map suggests. No through roads so our neighbourhood team patrol on bikes. And that's before you gain entry to the residences. The taller blocks, like Tom Collins House, here, are twelve storeys, and these exterior walkways make pursuit on foot a risk assessment in itself.'

A memory catapulted itself into her mind, one of her first shifts as a uniform officer. After pursuing a probable DUI down Shields Road at speed, she and Bradshaw had abandoned their vehicle in a bitter January flurry of snow. The suspect had played the terrain like a game of Screwball Scramble, flying through alleys, up and down stairwells and then away, shielded behind someone's locked door. When they'd returned to the squad car, they'd found both wing mirrors kicked off and a stark message written across the snow-covered windscreen: POLIS CUNTS.

She continued speaking: 'We had CI intelligence that the focus of local dealing is the Brinkburn Store, conveniently hidden away in the centre of the estate, so we've worked with the NCA surveillance techs to install a cam in an abandoned property. Current priority is IDing the line, from the kids running the stash to the individuals managing supply in and out of region.'

'Can I ask how many arrests you've made in the first operational period, DI Harlow?' DI Adams this time. This was classic David Attenborough fodder. Having been outmanoeuvred by Davison earlier, she was clearly looking to throw off her position as the weakest member of the herd. 'Seems like you've got criminal activity in plain sight. What sort of message does that send out to the community about Northumbria's commitment to safer streets?'

'I get that,' Rachel said. 'It's something we've weighed up. We've got youth workers interacting daily with the young people and there's the neighbourhood team and PCSOs as visible deterrents. But we've made a tactical decision to avoid criminalising minors unless we have clear safeguarding concerns for their immediate wellbeing.'

She was exhausted, with a numb bum and blurred vision when the meeting eventually wrapped up at five p.m. The kids had separately, but equally noisily, bundled in and she'd had to turn the camera off so they could grab some food. She had no idea how her debut at this first gladiatorial event had landed. She'd listened to the contributions of the other forces and found a few nuggets of possibility amongst the self-aggrandisement, but her pragmatic approach might have been a clanger of an own goal.

As she logged out of the secure system, trying to remember which day this week was her dad's appointment with the COPD consultant, she couldn't shake the visceral pressure still seeping from the device. The haze of buzzwords in the air. Those snappy acronyms and values just seemed to be compounding the enormity of real-life misery, not even three miles from where she sat, into manageable bite-sized chunks of jargon. Too much and not enough.

The SIO position of responsibility was quickly becoming a noose around her neck, pulling tighter with every week they made no progress. How long would she get before Bailey demanded results? It was Lennon more than anyone who'd encouraged her to go for it. Screw him and his bastard pep talks.

For now, her mind was stuck on a doom loop of the four Ps – Prepare, Prevent, Protect, Pursue – and the absolute bullshit they represented in reality. The only *preparation* she felt capable of strategically managing right now was shoving a couple of pizzas in the oven.

Chapter 7

Sea

Thursday 20th April

Now officially in open water, the top deck Sailaway Party was heating up. A band was playing, although Rachel's view of where the distant tones of 'Copacabana' were coming from was impeded by the sheer number of passengers already living their best lives.

Waiters circulated smoothly as if on wheels, refilling prosecco glasses and proffering trays of tempura king prawns. She took one, but couldn't stomach it. Her appetite over the last fortnight had been non-existent, just waves of panic sloshing around the empty void inside.

'They've had more than their welcome glass of fizz,' Barbara said, voice lowered, nodding at a group of women in their sixties with 'Spending the Divorce Settlement' T-shirts.

'I'd make the most of the freebies, love,' her dad said, leaning over to chink glasses. 'Drinks are a pretty penny the rest of the trip.'

Rachel held up her wristband. 'Upgraded to all-inclusive when we checked in.'

'Didn't take long,' Barbara said, raising her eyebrows.

'Makes sense, so I'm not giving these two cash to lose during the day.'

'Well, don't be overdoing it. You're here for some R&R, not more damage to your liver.'

'We're on holiday,' she said, tightly. 'I'm obviously going to have a few drinks.'

'A glass of wine over dinner doesn't need to turn into something you'll regret in the morning though, does it?'

Rachel rolled her eyes, but said nothing.

'There's a kids' club on Deck Ten, Jessica,' Barbara said.

'I'd rather stick needles in my eyeballs.'

'Yeah, Gran. We're fifteen, not five,' said Jake, putting in his AirPods.

'You're still children.' She sniffed. 'This is what comes from too much freedom too young.'

Rachel clenched her jaw. They'd been on board just over an hour and, already, it was becoming unbearable. She needed a distraction: maybe she'd message Lennon again. But her mind was racing. *He'll just annoy me … and I'll pretend I'm above it. Yep, totally professional. Definitely not grinning like an idiot.*

Jess broke into her spiralling thoughts with a heavy sigh. 'Can we go for a wander?'

She shrugged, accepting a top-up from a passing waiter. 'Fine by me – I can take this, can't I?' She held up her glass.

'Luggage should be in the cabins shortly,' Barbara said. 'I assumed you'd want to spend a bit of time settling in. The standard of accommodation on the *Synergy* really is second to none. You've even got a virtual balcony!'

'A *what* balcony?'

'Virtual. Brand new, apparently – some sort of video-device on the Deck Seven promenade. Jenny at Destinations said we were lucky to get another cabin at all at such short notice, never mind all the bells and whistles.'

'What'll they come up with next?' her dad said wheezily, shaking his head in cheerful disbelief.

The ship rolled, making passengers grab handrails with shrieks of excitement. Rachel's glass slipped from her grasp, soaking her palm with prosecco and sending jagged shards scattering across the deck. Almost immediately, the Muster Drill cruise director – Veronica Chase – appeared at Rachel's elbow, clicking impatiently for a minion to sweep up the debris. Up close, her rigid French pleat seemed to have been sprayed into submission with a full can of Elnett.

'Allow me to personally welcome you aboard the *Synergy*. It can take a short time to adjust to the movement on board.' Veronica flashed that lukewarm smile, which didn't quite ring true. 'Are you returning passengers?'

'First time for us,' Rachel said, trying to salvage the wet dressing on her hand whilst gesturing to herself, Jake and Jess, 'but my parents here are pros.'

'How fabulous!' Her well-practised spontaneity was almost believable. 'A special occasion?'

Barbara waffled a lengthy response, but Rachel could see that the cruise director was scanning the crowd and no longer listening.

'I think she's had enough,' she heard her mum say, shaking her head to a waiter holding out another glass.

Rachel took it anyway, forcing a polite smile. 'I'll manage,' she said, the fizz cool against her still-stinging palm.

Veronica clasped each family member with tepid enthusiasm. Her hand was limp, like a pale carp. 'I do hope to see you all again. Helping guests make memories is our greatest pleasure.'

A sharp whine of feedback from the band reverberated through the air, making Jess put her hands to her ears. 'Mam, can we go?' She grabbed one of Jake's AirPods. 'You coming?'

'K,' he said. 'I'm starving.'

'Dinner reservation is eight o'clock at the Riviera restaurant,' Barbara said, tapping her watch. 'We need to eat promptly – the opening night show starts at nine thirty, and it's always a must-see, isn't it, Bob?'

'Certainly is—' His raspy voice dissolved into a coughing fit.

'You OK, Dad?' Rachel reached out to him, wondering when he had become an old man.

He just gave a merry thumbs-up, which in no way matched the rattling sound emanating from his chest.

Barbara tutted, passing a bottle of water from the hand luggage. 'Wouldn't bring the oxygen mask. I've told him 'til I'm blue in the face, but he wants to struggle on – head in the sand—'

'Right,' she snapped, unable to bear her mum's incessant negativity a second longer. 'See you at eight.'

'It's dress to impress!' Barbara called after them. 'A nice frock for you both would be lovely. And no trainers,' she said, wagging her finger at Jake.

'Why does anyone care what I wear?' said Jess, barging through the exit door. 'This is the patriarchy,' she added darkly.

'Just chill out, OK? Your brother's getting bossed around too.'

'It's only his shoes he's held captive to. I'm getting told I have to fit into a feminised ideal for the sake of a corporate machine. It's just like that time—'

Rachel took a gulp of prosecco and tried to focus on the Muzak piped into the stairwell. Maybe she should copy Jake and ram something into her ears for the duration of the trip to drown out Jess's hyperbole.

They located Deck Ten, and their corridor, easily, although she could feel nausea building as they descended. The long window-less stretch of doors and garish carpet swam in front of her eyes and she leaned onto the wall for support, but it felt flimsy: MDF, not bricks and mortar.

The cabin was bigger than she'd imagined, with two king-size beds. The much-heralded virtual balcony was a white screen, taking up an entire wall, and currently switched off. Jake sprawled across one of the beds, calling out, 'Mine,' then closing his eyes.

Jess started busily opening cupboards and drawers, while Rachel tried to visualise solid ground beneath her feet. She pulled out her phone – one bar of signal – and opened Outlook, checking if she'd put her out-of-office on. One message from HR, received this morning, had a red flag.

Dear Detective Inspector Harlow

Following a complaint in reference to your conduct on 6th April whilst on Case Ref 1560a, you are invited to attend a disciplinary hearing with Northumbria Police Professional Standards. This is your opportunity to advise us of any mitigating factors to be taken into consideration. You are reminded that you are entitled to union representation. The meeting will take place at 10 a.m. on Friday 28th April …

Rachel downed the dregs of her drink and placed it, unsteadily, on the bedside table.

'This is outrageous!' Jess's voice rang out from the en suite. Nobody answered.

Friday 28th. Were they even back by then?

'Mam!' Jess had appeared by her side and, incandescent with rage, was thrusting a small envelope in front of her face.

'What?' Rachel said, distractedly. They would be back, just. She picked at the sticky residue on her hand, wondering if Lennon would be required to give evidence in person as the key police witness. She'd been hoping for longer to get the CPS file away and show that the arrest had, at least, started well. They'd have to speak in the meantime, go over the statements again and make sure it all tied together. Shit.

'Do you even care that people are having to support themselves on less than minimum wage just to be slaves to capitalist bullshit?'

'For God's sake, what are you talking about?'

'This extortion racket. The reliance on tips in lieu of fair wages. It's just corporate greed, pure and simple. We should take a stand.'

'Show me.' She snatched the envelope and read the handwritten message from their steward, Oksana. 'Right, get a pen. You can write back explaining that you'll be cleaning our cabin for the whole trip. Then Oksana'll still get her minimum wage and you'll be giving her the gift of time. Sorted.'

'I'm not cleaning it!' Jess yelled. 'This is my holiday! And what about him – he's just sparked out like he owns the place. Why does he get his own bed anyway?'

'As if I'm sharing with one of you,' Jake shouted back, eyes still closed. 'That's called incest.'

'I need another drink.' Rachel shoved her phone into her pocket and binned the useless dressing. 'Fight it out between you and call me when the luggage gets here.'

She strode out of the room without a backwards glance. It was only when she was halfway down the corridor that she realised she was still wearing the bastard pink polo shirt.

Chapter 8

Sea

Rachel stared at the map of the *Synergy*'s fifteen passenger decks, each with their own entertainment facilities. But that email was overriding everything. All she could see was trouble ahead and the pounding in her ears had become a ticking time bomb. It was now imperative to inhale a double shot of something in the next five minutes: was that really too much to ask? Focusing on the cocktail icons, she made for the Midship stairwell.

Emerging onto Deck Six, her senses were assaulted by a myriad of busy bars and restaurants. This was like being on holiday in a shopping complex, if the building itself had been pumped full of amphetamine and all the staff had been forcibly subjected to a spray tan and makeover.

Pushing through the crowds, desperate for sanctuary, she spotted a smaller place, Bionic Bar, in a darker, windowless stretch of the deck. One seating area was occupied by a couple sipping mojitos, but apart from them, and a man alone at the bar, the place was empty. Where were the staff? Glad of a reprieve from the forced merriment elsewhere, Rachel took a stool and tapped her nails on the granite counter.

'Robots.'

'Excuse me?' She looked around, confused.

'The bar.' The man had all the joyful energy of a Ben Affleck meme, but grudgingly slid an iPad towards her. 'Tap your wristband.'

He was dressed casually, in a black vest and tight jogging bottoms, light brown skin glowing in the dim light, and, even via side-eye, she was struck by the combination of perfect features on his high-cheekboned face.

His voice, however, was pure Essex. In her current mood, the nasal twang was more grating than feedback from a faulty comms radio. She wondered if it would be rude to ask him to just sit there and look pretty without opening his mouth, but, instead, she prioritised the more pressing issue: her thirst.

'An AI bar?' she said, holding her wristband to the iPad.

He shrugged, as if he really couldn't be arsed to elaborate. 'All be out of jobs here soon.'

'You're crew?'

'For my sins.'

'Sounds ominous.' She tapped for a double rum and Coke and stared in admiration as a glass descended from behind the bar and the optics jerked into operation. 'What d'you do on board then, when you're not knocking back the whiskies?' She nodded to his collection of empty glasses.

'Entertainment.'

The machine beeped to check if she wanted ice and she immediately hit the red button to maximise the alcohol ratio. 'Sounds better than arresting smackheads.'

'Really? Don't look like police.' His eyes lit up, assessing her properly. 'Cute as they come for a copper.'

'Detective,' she said, giving him the finger.

He sat up, moodiness gone. 'Fair enough, babe. Hot as fuck, detective or not.'

Rachel didn't know whether to be insulted or flattered. There was no denying his own physical credentials. 'Why you not out entertaining, then?'

'Don't start 'til later. They have their meal, then I'm the dessert. Chew me up every night and spit me out.'

'You and your tiny violin?' She reached for her drink. His *work pressure* wouldn't even scratch the surface of her concerns. But he did look strangely familiar – could she have arrested him?

He smirked. 'All right, babe. Start again. I'm Tyler.'

'Rachel.'

'First cruise?'

'Yep. And last.'

'They're not what they were. It's all fake.'

'Why d'you do it, then?'

He shrugged. 'Money's good. I work in a pair, so it's complicated with contracts and stuff. And … well, we're sort of a big deal.'

Rachel laughed out loud. 'Oh, really?'

Tyler waved his hand dismissively. 'You wouldn't understand.'

'Try me.'

'Nah. Tell me about arresting people and that. The thought of you with someone in handcuffs …' He gave her a gross wink.

'You're the first person to ever give me that line.'

'Really?' He looked stupidly chuffed.

'Er, no. A favourite of pissed-up morons.'

He reverted to sullen brooding while slugging the last of his whisky and she wondered if she had, perhaps, gone a bit far. But it was fun, pretending to be sassy and carefree. A single woman enjoying a bit of banter with an attractive man.

'Fair enough, Sherlock,' he said. 'Same again?'

She smiled while he tapped the iPad and added another glass to each of their line-ups. This was exactly what she needed. Already, she could feel her edges blurring as the rum hit the spot.

Clinking her glass, he moved his stool closer. 'Who you here with, then?'

'Parents and kids. But they're doing my head in already.' She gestured to her marshmallow top. 'I mean, look at the state of this.'

'Not your usual style?'

'Absolutely not.'

'No husband? Boyfriend?' He unsubtly checked out her naked ring finger.

'Nope. Young, free and single.' She raised her glass and downed half the contents. 'Though depends on your definition of young, I guess. And how free can you really be when every direction here hits a hard wall and then a splash?'

He laughed. It was a genuine, throaty sound and seemed to dissipate some of his dickhead energy. 'One out of three ain't bad.'

'True. You?'

'Same boat. I'm here for a good time, not a long time, babe.'

Rachel shuddered at his repeated use of 'babe'. In the real world, this guy would be high on the ick-scale, but here, in the cool darkness, pleasantly fuzzy-headed as she was, he was strangely alluring. Even his Essex twang was being drowned out by the undeniable vibe of sex in the air.

She raised her glass to her lips, eyeing him over the rim. 'What's your idea of a good time, then?'

Tyler said nothing, but winked again.

'OK. Let's play a game.' She picked up the iPad and scrolled to the list of spirits. 'Heads or tails. But shots. Heads I pick yours, tails you pick mine.'

He checked his watch. 'My tech run's in half an hour, but all yours 'til then.'

A coin was located and Tyler tossed it into the air, holding her gaze in preparation for the result.

Heads.

'Get in,' she said, triumphantly tapping the iPad. 'Hope you like tequila!'

He put his head in his hands in mock pain. 'Dying.'

'Don't be a baby!' Marvelling again at the AI optics, Rachel passed the shot and swivelled her stool to face him, duel-style. His hand around the glass was smooth and steady, face only becoming more attractive as she watched him throw his head back and grimace at the harsh blast of liquid.

'You're a bad influence,' he said. 'Game on.'

They continued, knees almost touching, eyes locked on each other, for five more rounds. Anaesthesia was kicking in nicely. Each shot she slammed seemed to cancel out one of the weights she'd brought on board.

Aftershock. The looming disciplinary. Her career in tatters. Gone.

Tequila. The Gallaghers – always there in the back of her consciousness, like white noise. The injustice of their hold over that community. Over her. Gone.

Absinthe. Her fractured relationships: Mum. Jess. Jake. Lennon. That was a harder one to swallow.

Rachel and Tyler's increasingly raucous laughter echoed around the dim interior and the couple in the corner looked over, disapprovingly.

'What sort of entertaining d'you do then?' she said, ignoring their snooty expressions and brushing his leg with her arm. 'Got any magic tricks?'

He licked his lips, slowly. 'I can turn my hand to most things, babe. Been round the block a bit.'

'You must be making decent money doing this, though,' she said, nodding at the bling-bling TAG Heuer on his wrist.

'It's a good pay packet, if you know your way around the industry. But I'm sick of it all, to be honest.' He gestured to the watch. 'Just a bit of sparkle, innit? Brand-new Range Rover on shore but what's the point when I'm never there to drive it?'

'Can't you just move on?'

His face fell slightly, and for a moment she thought she saw his eyes well up.

'You OK? Touched a nerve?'

'Nah,' he said. 'Just, got myself tied up in a lot of stuff here.'

'Well, if you could click your fingers, what would you want to do?' she said, surprised that she actually cared about the answer. Getting a glimpse into someone else's problems, however shallow, was helping.

'Write songs,' he said, words muffled as he rubbed his mouth with the back of his hand. 'Embarrassing really, but I've got all these lyrics. I write it all freehand, y'know, pen and paper. Like, from the heart.' He reached for her hand and slid her fingers under his Lycra vest.

'Jump ship, then,' she said, properly turned on from the sensation of the steady rhythm from his taut chest against the scar on her palm. 'Follow your passion.' The mutual attraction was so strong now she was surprised that sparks weren't flying off the bar.

'You've got something about you. Not just that you're fit.' His eyes were intense. 'You make me want to tell you stuff.'

'Another round?' she said, wiping sticky absinthe off her chin.

'Winner takes all.'

'What's the prize?'

'Nine inches of pure pleasure.' He looked smug, which was intriguing and gross in equal measure.

'I'm getting a ruler?' Rachel said, poker-faced. 'Don't know if I'm in the mood for underlining stuff right now.' She hiccupped, slightly undermining her delivery. Jesus, how many had she actually had?

'I'm in the mood for a bit of you.' Tyler bounced off his stool and grabbed her hand.

'Screw the shot, Sherlock. Come on.'

They ran, giggling like teenagers, into the bright atrium. Tyler ducked and dived through the holidaymakers, keeping a tight hold, fingers intertwined with hers. They clattered against hand luggage, sending strangers careering into each other and ignoring the disgruntled voices in their wake.

'What about your tech thing?' she called as he raced ahead.

'Done this show a hundred times. Piece of piss.'

He pulled her through a side door marked 'CREW ONLY',

impatiently slamming his key card against the shabby-looking lift. Doors closing behind them, they banged into the wall, hands everywhere, lips clashing, bodies pressed hard into each other. She could feel him rock solid against her leg as she hastily unzipped her jeans and shoved his hand down the front. She gasped as his fingers slid inside her and the lift plummeted down and down.

'Fuckin hell, babe,' he said.

The bell pinged and they broke apart, gasping with lust. Tyler pressed a finger to her lips and exited cautiously, looking left and right while Rachel straightened her jeans and caught her reflection in the mirror.

Was this a good idea? Probably gone far enough. She should make her excuses, head back up to her family.

But then again – what was the harm? A fling. A release. A bit of holiday fun. Jess and Jake would be fine in the cabin for a little longer, her parents just down the corridor. And where was safer than a cruise ship? There was literally nowhere for them to go.

Her cheeks were flushed, green eyes bright and sparkling. For the first time in months, someone desirable stared back – not a frazzled mum, not a black-sheep daughter, not a DI on the edge of dismissal.

Rearranging her fringe to cover the faint bruise, she followed him.

'Gotta be careful,' he said. 'Guests can't be down here.'

Rachel raised one eyebrow. 'Now who's the bad influence?'

Chapter 9

Sea

They raced down the corridor, no longer laughing. She wanted the oblivion of sex with a stranger and she wanted it now. Noticing movement ahead, Tyler sped up and pushed Rachel gently into Cabin H656. He pulled the door and stood in the entrance as footsteps approached. She held her breath and scanned the space.

Cramped was an understatement. It was about the size of the en suite in her own cabin, the ceiling low and dingy with a chequerboard of grey tiles. There were bunk beds and every available surface seemed to be piled with sequinned clothing. She wondered if the alcohol was making her hallucinate.

'Alright, Doc,' she heard Tyler say through the door. 'Thought you'd gone to the *Oasis* this season.'

'Not correct,' came a Scandinavian-sounding female accent. 'What would my favourite patient do without me?'

'Changed man this year, I swear.'

'No more antibiotics, Mr Tweedy. Invest in some condoms please.'

The voice chuckled and the footsteps faded away as Tyler opened the door, cringing slightly as he met Rachel's enquiring expression.

'I take it you heard that?'

'Certainly did.'

'Yeah,' he said, rubbing his nose with the back of his hand. 'That's crew life for you.'

'I'm clearly no angel myself,' she said, 'although, I actually don't make a habit of getting fingered by randoms in lifts.'

'Me neither, babe.' He turned and began scooping armfuls of clothing off the lower bunk.

'So, bunk beds? This must be … cosy.'

'Right. I stop noticing to be honest. Just wish Danielle would stop leaving her shit in here.'

'What is all this stuff?'

'Business she runs. Well, one of. Sort of on the side. Sells costumes at the dance workshops.'

'Oh right.'

'That's her all over – starts something, then I get roped in and all of a sudden it's my arse on the line.'

'So, she's your dance partner? Is this her room too?' She had a sudden vision of having been lured down here for a threesome.

'Officially. On the manifest.' He shrugged. 'She never sleeps here. Promised the stock would be gone as soon as we had the security check. But then, she's promised me a lot of things.'

Rachel joined him in clearing space on the bed, before sinking down and kicking off her wedge heels. Tyler stood over her and slowly took off his black joggers and vest. He was beyond fit, like he'd been formed with a hammer and chisel from the finest marble. Jesus Christ. There'd been no underwear to remove and, as her eyes drifted downwards, she saw that he hadn't been exaggerating about the size of the prize on offer.

'Hang on a minute, babe,' he said, turning away and giving her a perfect eye-level view of his ass cheeks. They hadn't been mentioned on the High Life Cruises website, but would definitely have scored a five-star TripAdvisor review. Normally she'd be staring at an incomplete evidence list at this time on a Thursday afternoon or interviewing some local charver off their head on spice to try and establish how a debt dispute had escalated into GBH.

A blast of music came from an unseen speaker as Tyler reached out both hands and pulled her to her feet. He smoothly lifted the polo shirt over her head leaving her black, lace-trimmed vest on underneath, cut to a deep V.

He smirked. 'What's this, pass the parcel?'

'If I never see that again it'll be too soon. Honestly, burn it.'

'It's cute,' he said, holding it up for size. He could probably have got one arm in. 'I'll sign it for you later if you want.'

'What, because you're *kind of a big deal*?'

'Fine, take the piss, but it'd probably sell for a few quid on eBay. Maybe when I'm a number-one singer-songwriter, eh?'

She tried, and failed, to dial down the sarcasm. 'OK. I'll keep it as an investment.'

Reaching up, he knocked one of the ceiling tiles loose. 'This is where I keep it all,' he said, withdrawing reams of loose paper from the cavity, scrawled in black pen. 'Never shown anyone this stuff.'

Without her heels, he towered over her. Stripping off her remaining clothes, she looked up at him, piss-taking gone. 'To be honest, I'm here for more than an autograph.'

He didn't seem to hear, but pulled her closer and moved her hands to his bum, swaying his hips to the beat of the music now booming from the speaker.

'This is the backing track I use. I'll give you a bit of my latest one, right? It's called "They Don't See Me".'

She had an almost uncontrollable urge to laugh, but managed to stifle it. What the hell would Lennon say if he could see this? It suddenly felt beyond cringe to be in this stranger's cabin, gripping his ass while he prepared to serenade her. The intro swelled, and Tyler's movement intensified, crotch grinding against her body.

'Let yourself go, babe,' he whispered huskily into her ear. 'Feel the rhythm.'

His vocal performance kicked off with a note so flat it actually made her wince. The ick-siren in her head was deafening now. A minute ago, she'd been ready to jump his bones, but if he talked – or warbled through his masterpiece – she was going to be drier than a sandpit.

There was something fragile about him, though. She couldn't just do a Simon Cowell and cut him dead mid-performance. There must be another way, more subtly, to stop this weird sex/karaoke mash-up.

She smiled. Teasingly slow, she kissed down his Greek-god chest, trying to block out the bizarre bunk bed set-up and his shitty lyrics: '*They want my body, They kiss my lips, But they don't really see me.*'

Kneeling on the carpet now, trying to find space amongst the nylon gowns, she took him in her mouth. He moaned appreciatively and held her high ponytail in his hands as she picked up the pace, pressing a finger hard against his lips to halt the second verse. She paused and looked up slowly, eyes meeting his, feeling a rush of pure desire. Fuck the weird room and his misguided vocal dreams: he was lush.

Suddenly, the door crashed open, hinges reverberating with the force of entry.

'What the fuck, Tyler! You've missed the whole tech run.'

Rachel didn't flinch, but put her top on and calmly catalogued the abrasive intruder, dressed in a neon version of the dresses strewn around their feet. Radioactive tan. Face like a smacked arse. She knew the type.

'Who d'you think you're talking to? And knock, OK? We're fucking busy.' Tyler remained, unashamedly, stark bollock naked.

'I don't give a shit about your little slut backing dancer, whoever she is. But fuck me, this is a quick start, even for you.'

'Definitely not a dancer,' Rachel said, evenly. 'Wouldn't wear that if you paid me.'

The banshee gave her an acidic stare, insofar as her rigid

forehead would allow, and addressed herself to Tyler. 'Guest decks again? You're a disgrace. We're on stage in forty-five minutes and you'd better get back to your normal limp-dick state before the opening number.'

'She's a copper, OK, so *you'd better* treat me and her with a bit of respect.' There was an edge to his voice this time.

Wrong move. Rachel clocked the woman's stance shift a second before it came.

'You're a fucking liability,' she screamed, lunging forwards and slapping him hard round the face, before strutting out on her four-inch heels in a blaze of fury and sequins.

There was a moment of silence. The tension in the room crackled, even after the door had slammed.

'Wow. That was an extreme reaction.' Rachel looked at Tyler, feeling a sting of outrage on his behalf.

'Yeah. Wasn't you.' He rubbed his cheek where Danielle's nail had pierced the skin. 'She always does a few lines before the show then acts like a total diva.'

'You could press charges. That's ABH. Unprovoked. She's drawn blood.'

'Not worth it, babe.'

She pulled on her jeans, removing the hard weight from her back pocket. 'Is that the first time she's assaulted you?'

Tyler shrugged. He looked vulnerable, despite his six-foot frame and chiselled physique: simultaneously world-weary and innocent. Rachel recognised the quiet defeat from countless domestic cases. A flat acceptance of the status quo. 'I just want out,' he said. 'I've had enough.'

Rachel's phone lit up.

Nine p.m.

Seventeen missed calls.

Holy shit.

Chapter 10

Sea

Head pounding, Rachel slunk into the bright Riviera restaurant. The air outside as she'd raced across the ship had felt far too close, with storm clouds gathering and darkness drawing in. She scanned the relaxed faces at the white-clothed tables. Queasy with self-loathing, and most of Bionic Bar's spirits menu, she took a deep breath before approaching her family.

'Mam!' At least Jess and Jake looked pleased to see her.

Her dad stood up. 'You had us worried, love.'

'Sorry,' she said. 'No reception. Totally lost track of time.'

'For three hours?' Barbara's face was tight and pinched. Her lips were non-existent, clenched in an icy chokehold.

'Have a seat,' her dad said. 'We're just finishing, but you'll need to eat.'

'No, no,' she said. 'I had something downstairs.' Her stomach rumbled, as if to draw attention to the fact that she was a liar as well as a complete and utter disappointment.

Rachel sat in silence, watching her family eat the remains of their celebratory first night dinner. She was hot with shame. Knives and forks scraped gently on square plates and conflicting smells from people's meals in all directions made her want to heave. All she could do was accept a glass of Sauvignon Blanc from the bottle on the table and self-medicate with frequent, anxious sips.

The excruciating tension was eventually broken by Barbara. 'Come along, then. Let's see if there are still any seats. We'll be right at the back, no doubt. Tyler and Danielle always draw a huge audience.'

'Tyler and Danielle?' she said, words catching in her throat. 'That's who we're seeing?'

Her mum sighed. 'The headline act, Rachel.'

It was all coming back to her now. That YouTube audition. A ludicrous name – TyD? The judges' comments. The tan. The Turkey teeth. Up close, they had both aged on their meteoric rise to D-list celebrity status, but she understood now why he had seemed familiar.

'Feeling OK, love?' her dad asked. 'You've gone a funny colour.'

'Perfect,' she said, swallowing her panic. 'Let's go.'

Grabbing a bread roll from the basket on the table, she took a furtive bite, like some sort of feral animal, then stuffed the rest in her pocket: that riotous concoction of spirits was going to need to be absorbed by something. Not that she had any intention of slowing down after Barbara's bombshell. You could take drinks into the theatre, surely? She caught her parents exchanging a look, but refilled her wine glass to the brim and just kept walking.

As they made their way across the room, she registered a cold voice in her ear: 'Your top is on inside out.'

Rachel turned and met her mother's icy gaze. Barbara's look of disgust said more than a thousand words.

The house lights were dimming in the auditorium as the usher showed them to the few remaining seats. Walking behind Jess, Rachel noticed that she had defiantly stuck to her screw-the-patriarchy dress code; she looked great in her high-waisted jeans and crop-top, but stood out a tad against the older, more refined passengers. She was surprised that Barbara had entertained Jess's anti-regulation ensemble, but presumably, in the maelstrom of her own MIA status, they'd had bigger fish to fry.

Her lanky, gawky Jake had actually followed Gran's instructions and scrubbed himself up for the occasion. That made her want to cry. He was wearing his one and only pair of smart trousers and the deck shoes she'd forced upon him in Next before they'd left Newcastle. She wanted to reach out and squeeze his hand, but he had already taken his seat.

Rachel had dived into the restrooms en route to recoup the last of her dignity and put her top on the right way round. It wasn't much, but it would have to do. At least she wasn't wearing the pink monstrosity any longer. Where was that, actually?

Her head pounded as the band crashed into action. The metallic thunk of the bass drum felt like it had been wired directly into her brain. To add insult to injury, the entire audience was clapping along with this overture. It was too much. She took a gulp of wine: a last-ditch attempt to dilute the horror of watching the virtual stranger she'd just had balls-deep in her mouth, now perform live for her multigenerational family.

Rachel was one row back from the rest of them, hiding in the warm, dark anonymity. A chorus line of showgirls flounced around the stage, making patterns with oversized ostrich feathers. She watched her mum crane her neck along the row of seats to say something to Jake. Those pursed lips must have thawed out.

A wave of tiredness washed over her – maybe she could just rest her eyes for a moment. But, as the band reached a volume that could surely be heard back in Southampton, the dancers took their positions, feathers pointed inwards, shielding the middle of the stage. A booming voice emanated from the PA system, jolting her back to life:

'*Ladies and gentlemen, boys and girls, for the fourth consecutive season on board the* Synergy, *we welcome our award-winning Latin American and ballroom duo; the stage sensation, who Amanda*

Applause erupted. Young girls screamed. A pair of women really old enough to know better, on the other side of the aisle, were holding a 'We LOVE You, Tyler!' banner. Jess turned round in her seat and gave her a sarcastic jazz-hands wave. Rachel did one back, trying to make up for her earlier disappearing act.

The ostrich feathers parted to reveal the 'incomparable' Tyler and Danielle, eyes and teeth gleaming, in a classic Latin hold, displaying the split in Danielle's neon outfit to its absolute max. Her legs, it had to be said, were extremely impressive. As were Tyler's rock-solid abs, his Lycra shirt cut down to the tightest pair of black trousers she had ever seen.

The band launched into Tom Jones's 'Sex Bomb' and Rachel blinked, her reaction to this glitter bomb veering between belly laughter at the cringetastic aesthetic and admiration for Tyler's incredible body moving in a blur of flicks and hip rotations. She took in the sea of captivated faces. Only a few hours ago, she'd smirked at his assessment of his status on board as 'kind of a big deal'. If anything, he had undersold himself. Tyler and Danielle were clearly very big fish indeed.

The cha-cha-cha opening number climaxed with an explosion of glitter. It rained down from the ceiling like the fallout from Hiroshima. Even from her position at the back of the auditorium, Rachel could feel herself ingesting sparkly particles of dance magic. She covered her wine in alarm, then reassessed her priorities and downed half the contents.

Tyler and Danielle swished off stage to rapturous applause whilst the ostrich girls returned, featherless, for some more filler. After an astonishingly tight turnaround time, the stars were back, dressed in completely different costumes, accompanied by the opening notes of a pared-down, moody version of Sting's 'Roxanne'. Danielle was in an eye-wateringly tight red floor-length number this time; Tyler all in black, a waistcoat covering his rippling muscles, but still allowing access to his defined biceps and shoulders.

Rachel felt herself flushing at the thought of what she could have been doing downstairs, below the water line.

The room was pitch-black, save for a single spotlight, which followed Tyler and Danielle around the floor as they tangled and untangled their limbs seamlessly in a series of sharp, staccato beats. This was actually good, she conceded, the two bodies a passionate blur of skin on skin. On the edge of her seat now, she held her glass unsteadily between her knees as the routine ended with a dramatic drop, Danielle caught by Tyler, their faces intensely aligned, almost in a kiss.

Swept up in collective euphoria, she joined the roar of the crowd, almost spilling her wine with the force of her clapping. The lights lifted, illuminating Tyler and Danielle, arms raised. They smiled at each other adoringly without a trace of the anger and threat that had characterised their interaction downstairs.

Rachel knocked back the remains of her wine, trying to stave off the sensation of the room spinning. If she just kept drinking, she would at least have a distraction: that should be her approach to the whole holiday. In fact, it was probably sensible to sneak out as soon as possible and get a refill.

Each holding a microphone, Tyler and Danielle faced the audience.

'Thank you so much for your incredible reception!' Danielle said, hand theatrically on her heart. Her voice was nothing like the shrieking banshee of an hour ago.

'We're so excited to be here with you tonight on the *Synergy of the Seas*!' Tyler boomed. His energy seemed more appropriate for a sell-out arena tour than a floating theatre somewhere between Southampton and Seville. Perhaps, like Danielle, he was partial to a chemical boost before a show. From her experience of policing taxi queues, she would have put money on the cause of his gurning.

'If you're enjoying the show, we wanted to remind you that we have our extremely popular *Dance with Tyler and Danielle* workshops running throughout the voyage. But spaces are limited, aren't they, Tyler?'

'They certainly are, Danielle. And we wouldn't want anyone to miss out, so get it booked!'

'Should we give them a sneak preview?'

'Let's do it!' Tyler blew a kiss into the crowd and took his microphone off the stand. 'Danielle and I pride ourselves that we can teach *anyone* to dance at one of our workshops. You might think you've got two left feet, but don't let that put you off!'

'That's right, Tyler. And you can book as a couple or just come along solo – remember strangers on the *Synergy* are simply friends you haven't met yet. Isn't that right, guys?'

The audience whooped and clapped enthusiastically. Rachel glanced at her family, scattered across the row in front but they were all watching intently, even Jake. These two had them eating out of the palm of their hands. It was like a cult.

'Shall we get a couple of guests up here right now and show everyone what we can do in only ten minutes?'

Each holding a microphone, the dance sensations strode down the steps at the side of the stage and into the auditorium. Rachel shuffled further down in her seat.

'So many eager volunteers!' Danielle trilled. 'However, what we really need is two slightly more reluctant performers. If you don't know your quickstep from your rumba, this is the moment to learn—'

'That's right, Danielle, it's a once-in-a-lifetime moment to shine!' Tyler was walking dangerously close to her part of the room now. She craned her head away and tried to make herself morph into the red velvet chair.

'I've spotted a perfect dancer-to-be!' called Tyler. 'She's trying her best to avoid eye contact, but here she is. Ladies and gentlemen, please put your hands together for our first volunteer!'

Rachel closed her eyes tightly, bracing for catastrophe. And there it was: Tyler's hand, stretching forwards from the aisle, gripping her arm. She tried desperately to stay seated, but, rallied by the ear-splitting applause, the strangers around her demonstrated almost-criminal levels of coercion and physical strength that belied their ageing limbs and previous decorum.

She was shunted forwards, legs feeling like they belonged to someone else, until she stood, horrified, next to Tyler. Jesus fucking Christ. Instinctively, she scrambled for her handcuffs, determined to regain control, but the relief of cold metal rings at her fingertips was gone. She was defenceless.

Tyler whispered into her ear, 'Couldn't resist, Sherlock.'

Booming again now, into his microphone, he addressed the audience. 'Our first dancer! Shall we find out her name, guys?'

As the crowd sounded their approval, Rachel looked desperately to her children, hoping they might stage an intervention. Jake shrugged, looking highly embarrassed, whilst Jess – the traitor – was creased over, hysterical with laughter. Her parents looked bemused, but again, offered no help whatsoever.

'It's Rachel,' she said, through gritted teeth, into the microphone. Her voice sounded hollow and far away. Maybe she was having an out-of-body experience. Up close, Tyler looked manic. His pupils were pinpricks – tiny dots jumping in front of her as his eyes darted around the crowd.

'Right, Danielle, let's get Rachel ready to dance!'

Defeated, she let herself be led to the stage behind an obese fellow volunteer, who was practically sprinting towards his five-minutes of 'fame'. The house lights dimmed and she was thrust into the spotlight next to '*the Gorgeous Kevin*', whose shirt buttons strained as sweat dripped from his shiny head.

Danielle looked her up and down slowly and flashed the fakest of fake smiles.

'So, can we teach them to dance, guys?' Tyler called into the crowd.

'YES!' came the deafening reply, accompanied by whistles and cheers.

Gripping with knife-sharp talons, Danielle embraced her rigid shoulders. She breathed into her ear, 'Stay away from, Tyler, you slutty polis bitch,' before squeezing her warmly for the benefit of the audience and speaking into her microphone. 'A lady this beautiful needs a dress to dance in, do we agree?'

Danielle snatched a white, diamond-encrusted gown from the wings and skipped back into the spotlight where she held it aloft, 'Stunning!'

Rachel swayed on unsteady feet as the nylon encased her body. The full skirt skimmed over her tight jeans, transforming her into a replica of the ostrich girls she had foolishly smirked at earlier. Dear God, when would this nightmare end? It didn't help that the whole room was now spinning at a worrying speed.

Up close, she could see the deep scratch on Tyler's cheek, despite his heavy make-up. As Danielle arranged the skirt to its crystal-light-catching perfection she saw a look of fury pass between them. Tiny, contained, but full of rage.

Tyler grinned, escorting her to the left of the stage, whilst Danielle and her victim moved to the right. His hand felt clammy, or was that coming from her own skin? The band kicked into a high-energy blast of something that sounded like Abba.

'With a bit of support, even the unlikeliest of dancers can become an elegant partner!' Danielle said, her empathetic tone juxtaposing with the death stares she kept flashing in Rachel's direction.

'Just follow my lead, babe,' Tyler said to her, unmic'd and intense.

She said nothing, mouth filling with saliva as she concentrated on not tripping over the hem of the dress. Tyler spun her around so her back was pressed into his body and she felt his hand snake up beneath the long skirt. She blinked blindly in the glare of the lights, the audience invisible, and felt something slide into her back pocket, a hard edge against her bum.

Tyler's voice again, low and muffled. 'Let yourself in later. I want out. I'm gonna give you all of it, OK?'

Rachel swallowed, desperately trying to stop the rising nausea, but it fought back against her clenched throat, uncontrollable now, as the music surged to its crescendo. A powerful motion rocked her body and she felt vomit explode into the air, landing with a splat, centre stage, spraying Danielle and the Gorgeous Kevin with six hours' worth of all-inclusive drinking.

It could have been her imagination, but she was sure she heard her mother's scream as the music stopped abruptly and she fled the decimated stage.

Chapter 11

Sea

Rachel couldn't see straight as she ran through the wings, tripping on the trailing hem. Lungs constricted with humiliation, she could hardly breathe as she willed herself forward. Now in the backstage corridor, all she wanted was a silent corner where she could lie down and black out for the foreseeable future.

But the small voice in the very back of her mind knew she needed to get outside, to fresh air, to a place where she could expunge the rest of the liquid in her stomach.

After what felt like a marathon of patterned carpets and strangers' stares, she burst through the double door onto the top deck. Wind and rain smacked her in the face. She stood there, still, just letting the water fall, then grabbed the railing and felt sweet relief as the remaining alcohol thundered into the waves below.

The last time she'd been sick from drinking was the CID Christmas party, where she'd had to be forcibly removed from a karaoke bar by Lennon to save the general public from a third Whitney Houston number, murdered in her own unique style. He'd put her to bed in her clothes and slept on the floor just to check she wasn't about to choke on her own bile.

She missed him. His warmth, a million miles away.

Clumsily, with fingers that wouldn't follow simple commands, she located WhatsApp and pressed Call. She waited, stomach clenching, not knowing what she wanted to say, but aching for the comfort of his voice.

A crackle and then his unmistakable laid-back tone. 'Rach – what's up?'

'Are you there?' She snorted back the sobs that were threatening to come rushing out.

'You OK? It's – hear—'

'Did I wake you up? What time is it?'

'S'alright. Yeah – early night – worry about – though.'

'You sure? Sorry. I'm sorry for everything.'

'—talkin' about? Sorry – what?'

'Gallagher. The job. The hearing.' She winced. 'I need to tell you—'

'—man – bother. You sound – sure you're—'

'The worst night. Made a total fool of myself. I've let everyone down, Lenn.' Her voice sounded thick and slurred; she couldn't get her lips to catch up with her tongue.

'You're breaking up – didn't catch – say again—'

'I'm a mess.'

The line clicked back into clarity. 'You're always a mess, man. A beautiful mess. That's why we love you.'

Her eyes inexplicably filled with tears. 'Do you, though?' He didn't mean *beautiful*. Not in that way. She couldn't read too much into this classic Lennon throwaway charm. Certainly not when he'd seen her at her very worst.

'—didn't – say again—'

'I'm scared to tell you the truth.'

'Can't – anything – standing in – hurricane?'

She breathed in, trying to control the pain in her chest. In for three, out for three. The way they did with people who'd been stabbed.

'—chel? —chel? You OK? You – the kids?'

'I'll be OK. Go back to sleep. I'll find some better reception tomorrow.' Her voice was small and caught in her throat.

'—off the deck – inside. It – be late where you are – yourself to bed.'

'OK. Bye.' The line went dead.

She looked down at her phone, water bouncing off its cracked screen. An interminable stretch of time accumulated as she stood fixed to the spot, holding tightly to the only connection she had to her real life, to him.

It was no good. She had to go inside. However long she'd been out here, the white dress was now sodden, dragging across her numb toes as she eventually turned to follow Lennon's advice. But, as if she'd un-paused a movie, this step seemed to accelerate her into another unwelcome climax.

Her mum.

Barbara came clattering through the entrance, red in the face and wild-eyed and Rachel died a little inside. This couldn't be happening. She had been hoping to make her apologies and start picking up the pieces after a few hours' sleep. By then, her reaction might have receded somewhat on the Richter scale.

'Rachel – why? What makes you behave like this?'

Right, they were going straight into it. No preamble.

'I don't know what you want me to say. I know I've fucked up, OK?'

'Your language! The children just mimic you. Your dad's had to take them back to your cabin. Breathing's worse than ever, after all the upset. And I've been high and low, looking for you.'

'Have we not got bigger issues than me swearing? I mean, for fuck's sake, Mum. Pick your battles.'

'I don't know where we went wrong. We tried our best.' Barbara's voice cracked. She pulled a handkerchief from her sleeve and dabbed her eyes.

'You were fine.' Rachel wiped her mouth, still sour and sticky.

'You *are* fine. I'm just going through a rough patch. I wanted to forget about everything, just for one night.'

'But you've got responsibilities! Two children. Bills to pay.'

'I know!' Her head pounded, rage building. '*I'm* not a child. We get by.'

'Straight back up north. As soon as you turned eighteen, you were off.'

'Why d'you always bring that up?' This again. For the millionth time. 'You know I wanted to find out where I came from. Who I was. Why can't you accept that?'

'I *tried*, Rachel. I tried to make you mine. Tried to protect you from it all.' Barbara's voice rose to a wail. Her carefully made-up face and respectable demeanour were falling apart.

'You shouldn't have to try though,' she bit back. 'Loving your daughter shouldn't be a fucking effort.'

'And neither should loving your mother!'

She fought to hold it back. But it was coming. It had been coming for so long and there was nothing she could do now to stop it. 'You're not my mother, though, are you? You're not anyone's mother.'

She watched Barbara stumble as if she'd been slapped and clutch the railing for support.

Oh God. Her face was crumpling, and Rachel hated herself.

She stepped forward, holding out an unsteady hand. 'I shouldn't have said that—'

Barbara lifted her chin and busied herself with brushing the rain from her linen trouser suit. It was drenched to a completely different shade from its original biscuit tone, worn out and shapeless.

Rachel's hand shook in her fragile attempt at reconciliation. Barbara said nothing, her own hands rigid by her sides. The row had burnt itself out, leaving only silence and rain. With a final wounded look, Barbara walked away, handkerchief trailing like a white flag with no use anymore.

Rachel watched the door shudder to a close and allowed the full force of misery to engulf her. She'd ruined this trip, on top of everything else. Nothing could repair the damage she'd inflicted.

All she did was drag people down. Her poor mum. The kids. What sort of toxic example was she setting? Professionally, she was finished. Operation Fever back up and running without her. Lennon thriving.

She was dead weight. Taking up space she didn't deserve.

The lashing rain knifed her like a thousand tiny incisions, but she kept her feet moving mechanically, one in front of the other, until she found herself at the very back of the ship, leaning over a railing, hardly able to tell what was sea and what was sky.

It was all oily blackness. A void in every direction.

Clambering higher, wedge heels slipping on the rungs, she felt unexpected relief at the spray of the crashing waves. The sights and sounds of the abyss swirled in dark symmetry to everything in her head.

Calmer now, numb with cold, Rachel swung one leg over, then the other. The dress caught on the rail but she didn't care.

She was right on the edge. Arms twisted back. Wind whipping her knuckles.

All she had to do was release her grip. Then the ship would continue, leaving her in its wake. No future to battle through. No past to keep at bay.

Rachel lifted one finger. Then another. Her muscles trembled, exhausted beyond measure.

One shuddering breath.

She let go.

Chapter 12

Sea

Friday 21st April

Gravity was taking over.

But a sound broke through. A firm American voice.

'Would all passengers please return to their cabins. We are currently experiencing a period of inclement weather, and, for health and safety reasons, we ask all passengers to return to their cabins immediately.'

Suddenly lucid, Rachel could feel her heart banging against her ribs as she scrambled for the rail: what the fuck was she doing?

Her fingers were slipping, clawing for purchase.

It was too late.

But it couldn't be too late – she had to hold on.

Heaving with some sort of primal force, dragging the weight of the dress, she grasped the top barrier and hauled herself over, every sinew screaming as she slammed against the deck with a heavy thump.

Pain tore through her body. She curled, foetal-like, cradling her head with both hands. Images kept coming – crashing and colliding behind her eyes.

Jess and Jake, shadowy and much younger, sinking into the blackness, somewhere far away in her mind.

She willed herself to reach out to them.

It felt real: Jess holding her hand tightly, Jake's outstretched fingertips just brushing her own. Clinging to that almost-touch, she forced her body upright, inch by agonising inch.

Finding her way back, with regret oozing from every pore, was a Herculean effort, but the windowless cabin was a relief, once she was inside, protected from the elements.

Jess and Jake were still awake, but muted. Neither asked where she'd been. They turned on the virtual balcony and sat, huddled tightly, watching grey sky battle grey water. All the furniture was nailed down. Only the cups and spoons clattered as the ship rolled, in sync with the motion on screen.

Jess's phone beeped: Grandad checking that their mum had returned.

Rachel's own phone was silent.

The relentless assault of the storm lost its hypnotic appeal and Jake put the TV on despite it being nearly one a.m. They found *The Incredibles* and settled into the nostalgic comfort of the superhero family fighting baddies.

Rachel felt her lip wobble. Pathetic. No superpowers here – just her own inadequacy and the weight of the night. As the credits flickered, she reached for the remote. Both kids were asleep: Jess with her mouth slightly open, Jake curled on his side.

A lump caught in her throat and she tucked them in tighter. Those moments on deck, the near descent into crashing water. She'd let them down. But she was here now. And maybe it wasn't too late.

The Tannoy woke Rachel, its velvety tone making her open one eye groggily, wondering where she was.

'Due to the ongoing adverse weather conditions as we cross the Bay of Biscay, we request that passengers remain inside and do not

use the outdoor decks. A further announcement will be made in due course, when we will be delighted to reopen the full facilities.'

She pushed her fringe out of her eyes and looked around. The room was unfamiliar, with a strange rumble coming from behind her back. She shivered, and yanked at the duvet. Picking up her phone from the floor, she checked the time: 9.15. The windowless box was dark and warm; if she hadn't had a clock, it would be impossible to tell if it were night or day.

Sitting up, she surveyed the scene. Jess, lying beside her and hogging three-quarters of the duvet, appeared unconscious until another snore emanated from her open mouth, shaking the mattress. Jake, in the adjoining bed, was face down on the pillow.

A dragging motion was pulling in the pit of Rachel's stomach – a rollercoaster with the speed dialled right down. The sensation seemed to rise and fall at regular intervals, though, and she was relieved to find that, for now, the nausea of last night had abated.

More clues were needed. Gingerly testing her hangover, she tiptoed around the room, picking up discarded clothes. The white gown was still damp, her jeans also not looking their best. She felt a key card in the pocket and was rapidly transported back to Tyler's words in her ear, urging her to let herself into Cabin 656, his hands everywhere under the dress. A twang of regret reverberated. It could have been good, if she'd managed to stop him singing and put his energies elsewhere.

'Mam?' came a croaky voice. 'How you feeling?' It was Jake, rubbing his eyes and yawning.

'Not too bad,' she said. 'You?'

'Yeah. All right. What time is it?'

'Half nine. We've got to stay inside though 'til the storm blows over.'

His eyes widened. 'Is that normal?'

'Sure the captain's got it covered. And I'm not dying to get back out there.'

'You weren't that bad.'

'I was. I'm really sorry you saw me in that state.'

'What d'you mean? This is mint. You can literally never have a go at me in the future for getting mortal.' He gave her a lopsided grin.

Another rumble from Jess shook the room and Jake grabbed his phone to film his sister making the inhuman noises.

'Careful. She'll kill you.'

'Bit of insurance for the bank.' He nodded sagely, then dived onto the bed and squished his face right into his sister's. She let out a scream as she opened her eyes.

'Get him off me! His breath stinks.'

'Your snoring's going viral.'

Jess sat bolt upright and tried to snatch the phone. 'You wouldn't dare.'

'Try me.'

The morning of captivity crawled, with hours of channel hopping, playing cards and listening to Jake's increasingly plaintive requests for food. Rachel realised she'd forgotten to pack a book. Jake seemed unfamiliar with the concept of reading something not on a screen and, although Jess had a small library in her case, her taste was niche. She eventually accepted *1984* and left her daughter to *The Communist Manifesto*, wondering if they were all likely to be red-flagged by HLC management.

At the point where cannibalism was seeming like a viable possibility, another Tannoy sounded and they were given the all-clear.

Rachel had already sent her mum a short but apologetic message, intending to clear the air and start her penance. The double blue tick had appeared immediately, but so far, no reply. She also messaged Lennon, embarrassed about her outpouring of emotion, and grateful that the line had been so bad that he wouldn't have heard much. At least, she hoped he hadn't.

Jake was only interested in eating, while Jess wanted to find a hot tub so they compromised on filling their faces in the all-day buffet before locating an array of jacuzzies looking out to sea.

After skulking around for five minutes on the periphery, eyeballing people, a couple got the hint and vacated one of the pools. Rachel claimed the small patch of peace, until a voice cut through the bubbling white noise.

'It *is* her! Jon, I told you. How *are* you, baby doll?'

Unsure to whom this was directed, she wafted a hand through the steam, and unwelcome memories hit her like a shower of shit. It was the rotund man from the hellish stage fiasco, still sweaty – but now dressed in ill-advised speedos and a kimono, flanked by a slimmer figure she assumed must be Jon. They stared at her, clearly awaiting an update.

She squirmed. 'Not my finest hour.'

'We've all been there, Queen,' Jon said, hand on hip. 'You keep that head held high, hear me?'

'I'll try,' she muttered, praying they would now move along.

'I told Kevin, afterwards, you could see the state of her, why didn't you sashay over and help her off the stage?' That was it: Kevin, or the Gorgeous Kevin, to give him his full title.

'Honestly, it's fine. I'm over it.'

'What's a bit of drunk and disorderly between friends!' The Gorgeous Kevin forced a fist-bump. 'Room for a small one?'

Before she could protest, they were dropping their silky cover-ups, and plunging into the water.

Rachel turned to Jess and Jake with a silent scream. They, however, seemed fascinated. As the larger man lowered himself beneath the bubbles, half the contents of the pool sloshed over the edge and Rachel grimaced – probably now eighty per cent sweat.

'Family trip?' The Gorgeous Kevin peered closer, examining them.

'She's our mam,' said Jess.

'No way!' Jon gasped. 'Goddess!'

'It's our first cruise. And our gran and grandad are here too.'

'Kevin! They're virgin cruisers. A-DOR-A-BLE.'

Rachel tried to pivot. 'What about you?'

'Pros, baby girl! Ex-crew – met on the *Princess of the Seas*, 2004 – and the rest was history,' the Gorgeous Kevin said, sweeping a hand to emphasise.

Jon nodded to an eyes-and-teeth crew member, collecting glasses nearby. He lowered his voice, theatrically. 'All smiles now, but we've seen some sights.'

'Trust us, the real stories aren't up here!' The Gorgeous Kevin guffawed, throwing his head back. '*Below Deck* gave people a sniff, but viewers don't want scripted reality – they want genuine BTS cruise content.'

Rachel narrowed her eyes. 'What's—'

'Mam!' Jess interrupted. 'Behind the scenes. Everyone knows that.'

Jess and Jake leaned forward, slack-jawed, as Jon launched into their influencer origin story. Their YouTube channel, *Crewz Secrets* – 'crewz with a z' – had blown up post-Covid: sponsorship, subscribers, five times their old salary.

'You've just gotta know the industry,' the Gorgeous Kevin said, smoothly reclaiming the narrative. 'Cruises are for specific types of people—' he held up three fingers, wrinkled from the hot tub '—newlywed, overfed, almost dead. And now *Crewz Secrets* can't get the content out quick enough!'

'See, Mam,' said Jake, piping up. 'YouTuber *is* a serious career option.'

'Maybe,' she said, smiling. She leaned back against the powerful jets and tried not to think about last night. From here, they could watch the now-calm sea stretching to the shimmering horizon, but she didn't feel relaxed: she felt restless.

She'd dropped Tyler's key card into her bag when they'd left the cabin, and as she sat, stewing in the bubbly water, she wondered whether to just rip the plaster off and apologise. At the very least, she could fish out the repellent polo shirt from where it presumably lay camouflaged by glitter.

Leaving Jess and Jake deep in conversation with the influencers and assuring them she'd be back in half an hour max, she threw a sarong over her bikini and took a deep breath. Yes, she'd vomited on stage right next to a minor celebrity she'd just sucked off, but that was all water under the bridge. What was the worst that could happen?

And besides, nine inches was nine inches. It was always good to leave your options open.

With access to the crew lift, it was easy to retrace her steps down to the lowest echelons of the vessel. Pausing for a second outside his cabin, she knocked and waited. There was no answer, so she knocked again, louder. Three o'clock now, so, surely, he wouldn't be asleep.

She considered the legality of just popping her head in. Given her possession of his key card, there would be no use of force required, negating the potential of a breaking and entering accusation. That left only trespassing, and – as she'd had a very enthusiastic invitation only twelve hours ago to let herself in – she decided to take that as permission granted. A tiny click was all it took.

'Tyler?' she called quietly, as she took a couple of steps into the room. 'I just wanted to—'

The word expired on her lips. He was on his knees, body slumped forwards. The acrid smell of shit in the air, along with the unnatural position of his head told Rachel more than half the contents of any coroner's report. She dropped to her knees, pressing two fingers to his wrist.

Nothing.

His eyes were open, but unblinking: dilated, blank pupils stared into the distance of the otherwise empty room.

Come on – *think.* CID training. Assume nothing; believe no one; challenge everything. Position of the body suggested a sudden loss of consciousness. Grey pallor and stench in the air pointed to a time of death nearer yesterday than today.

In the absence of gloves, she wrapped the sarong around her hand and carefully raised Tyler's head a few inches from the floor. His lips had a horrible blueish tinge. The dried foam at his mouth and powder remnants in the plastic wrap beneath his body were unsurprising. The colour, though, was odd. A brownish shadow. He'd been the headliner – surely, he wouldn't have been snorting any old shite.

There was something stuck to the outside of the plastic too. A clear disc, folded over on itself, barely the size of her smallest fingernail. A contact lens. She followed a trickle of blood backwards from the corner of his mouth, peeling back his cold lips to find a savage laceration at the front of his tongue. A fit, then? Some sort of seizure?

Decisively, she pulled out her phone and took pictures of the key exhibits, Tyler's body and a wide shot of the cabin. It was bare. Anonymous. Not a single lurid gown remained. Avoiding touching anything more to preserve the scene as much as possible, she ran into the corridor, hammering on doors and shouting into the ether for backup.

No one came.

Tyler was dead.

And now she was going to have to explain why the fuck she was down here, first on the scene, with a body on her hands.

Chapter 13

Land

Thursday 30th March

Crawling to the end of the week, Rachel was almost ready to put herself in a body bag. It was glaringly obvious that the operation was floundering and any glimmers of progress had been short-lived.

She'd arranged to meet Lennon for a canteen coffee, craving an escape hatch from the intensity of the office. Even thinking of him twisted the pressure valve back to a manageable level. Although still part of the same unit, she was seeing a lot less of her DS since she'd stepped up to SIO. He was always on the move, always following up on the whiff of a lead, or meeting one of his dubious informants for some off-the-record intel.

She spotted him straight away in the bland open-plan Northumbria HQ canteen, leaning on the till and making the new blonde laugh.

'You want to watch him,' she called. 'Make sure he's using the hand sanitiser. Spends his days with all sorts of wrong 'uns.'

'Who asked her?' Lennon addressed the woman, giving Rachel a dismissive side-eye. 'Louise and I were having a perfectly pleasant conversation.'

'Yeah, well,' she said. 'Now you're not. I'm saving Louise from your pitiful excuse for banter.'

'Can you believe this?' he asked, mock aggrieved. 'It's all an act. One drunken fumble back in the day and she can't get over it.'

Louise giggled and aimed an exaggerated pout at Rachel, filler and all. But Rachel knew the script: Lennon charmed, she cut him down. They had this routine nailed – a double act, not an ensemble cast.

'Yeah, still crying into my pillow,' she said, rolling her eyes and picking up a cardboard cup from the tray. 'Cheers for this – can I drag you away?'

They'd sat here countless times over the last decade. The canteen coffee was rank, but the ritual was its own relief. She filled him in on the kill-or-be-killed vibe of the NCA meeting while his low, easy tone worked the knots from her shoulders.

'That Davison's a special type of wanker. Can't remember the details – some relationship he hadn't disclosed. Must've got it binned off somehow.'

'He can talk, mind. Kept piping up with all sorts they've got on the go.'

'Load of shite. Operation's hardly even up and running. Slow and steady wins the race.'

'Not too slow, though,' she said, thinking of the blank evidence boards in the office, 'or I'll be out of a job.'

'Just chill out. Bailey's never getting rid of you.' Lennon gave her an affectionate punch. 'You broke records in response for most overtime accrued – no one wants to lose that sort of freak in the force.'

'Cheers for the confidence boost.'

'Any time. Someone's got to tell it to you straight …' He paused, a glint in his eye. 'You've let yourself go, pet.'

'Still way out of your league.'

He pointed at himself, then her. 'Premiership. Sunday League pub team.'

She laughed, in spite of herself. 'You need to get back out there. Play the field.'

'I'm all right.' He gave her the finger. 'Don't *need* to do anything.'

Rachel glanced back towards the till. Louise was wiping already-clean tables, bending too low. 'Looks like she wouldn't say no.'

'Nah,' Lennon said. 'Not my type.'

'Come on. Men don't have types.'

'Course they do. She's not …' He looked moody, like he couldn't be bothered to explain, more interested in the sugar he'd spilt on the table.

She held up her hands. 'Fine. Won't show an interest.'

He flicked a few grains of sugar at her, eyes still down. 'I'm trying to set an example. Don't shit on your own doorstep.'

'That would be silly.'

Rachel and Lennon smirked at each other. Her propensity for shagging questionable colleagues was a source of regular amusement.

They spoke at the same time.

'Who's more your type, then?'

'Heard about Gallagher?'

She abandoned her previous question – his love life was a dead end. 'Which one?'

'Michael. HMP Durham. Wounding with Intent.'

That family spawned like locusts. They'd been out in full force a couple of months ago when Carl, one of the OGs, had kicked the bucket, lining Byker's pavements like it was a state funeral. Most of that generation were either serving long-term sentences or dead, but policing the next layer down was Whack-a-Mole on speed.

'Out?' She braced herself. That was all they needed, already struggling to keep a lid on Jo" Paul, plus multiple cousins and hangers-on.

'Hoyed acid over his cellmate Sunday night.'

'Jesus.' Prison was normally a holiday camp for the Gallaghers. Flexing their muscles, in with the guards, and always out quick for good behaviour.

Her stomach clenched at the horror of being inside with a member of that family. Just the two of you in close proximity, breathing the same air. She swallowed the bile rising in her throat and entered into the spirit of it. Gallagher-bashing was practically in the Northumbria training manual: they were universally despised and everyone had a story.

'You'd be begging for an acid wash, just to get the stench off you.'

Lennon's eyes lit up. 'That's dark. Even for you.'

He'd said worse. 'Any reason?' she asked.

'Nah. Animals, the lot of them.'

She downed the dregs of her coffee, but there was grit at the bottom of the cup and it left a bitter taste in her mouth. She held her hand out; Lennon always had gum.

'How's your dad?'

He shrugged, sliding a half-full pack across the table. 'Is what it is. Pop in a few times a week, but, y'know.'

She took one and pushed it back. Chewed for a moment. Sometimes he said more about his family if you left it hanging. Not today though.

'Messaged Jake last week about the Sam Fender tickets and he's never replied.' He was messing on with the gum packet on the table, flipping it up and stopping it dead between finger and thumb. 'Ask him if he wants one or he's getting ditched.'

He was infuriating, always rebounding from one topic to another. Nothing stuck. He had made it his personal mission to educate Jess and Jake in what he called 'The Music' ever since Rachel had disgusted him by taking Jess to a Little Mix concert.

'Currently grounded till he stops calling teachers bellends, but I might use that as an incentive.'

'Give him a break. He's a canny lad—'

'—who's about to be kicked out of school, according to the head.' She blinked back tears, which had been threatening to make an appearance every time she let her mind go there. Crying wasn't going to sort it out. Apart from anything else, what if someone saw her? A decade of building a professional reputation would be eroded in the time it took for one rogue drop to trail pathetically down her cheek.

Lennon didn't count. There'd been times over the years when she'd really leaned on him. They never discussed it afterwards, and the insulting texts, put-downs and eye-rolling continued unchanged, but they both knew.

He squeezed her hand. 'Come on, let's get back on it.'

They stood up, Lennon binning their empty cups and giving Louise a flash of his straight white teeth. Invisalign. Embarrassing.

His familiar, musky smell was suddenly irritating. And that bastard heat radiating off his neck. She'd never met anyone with a body temperature like his.

She wrinkled her nose. 'Why don't you just flop it out and show her what she'd be working with? Don't let the poor lass get her hopes up.'

'Jealousy doesn't suit you,' Lennon whispered into her ear as he held the door open and let her walk ahead.

You could practically fry an egg on him.

Jealous? As if.

'Any joy from those Crimestoppers leads?' she called to Bradshaw, as they re-entered the fray. Time was ticking on. She had an epic to-do list, which she'd barely scratched the surface of and flagged emails stacking up in her inbox; how was it already after four? The office, however, was half empty. Bradshaw was typing at speed as she and Lennon surveyed the daily whiteboard of who was where.

'Actually yeah,' he said, turning his head without dropping pace. 'Always worth a knock.'

'What you got? Did you take Coates?' Elevenerife was nowhere to be seen, and Rachel rejoiced that she might actually get an hour's work done.

'Two reports on the same property. Information syncs up – no obvious reason they'd grass without cause. One of the Dalton Crescent perimeter flats. Third storey.'

She knew it well. On the edge of the estate, halfway between Shields Road and the Brinkburn Store. The Wall was colour coded and the part Bradshaw was describing had bright red doors and balconies, visible from the road like foreboding no-entry signs. It snaked across the East End of the city, twisting and turning, towering over the ebb and flow of the urban landscape below.

'What's the crack?' Lennon peered over Bradshaw's shoulder. His enthusiasm for the chance to kick a door down was legendary.

'People in and out at odd hours, stinks of weed, noise late at night. One of the fellas thought he'd heard a lass screaming, but he wouldn't be drawn. None of them know who officially lives there.'

This level of recalcitrance was standard for residents' contact with the police. *Mind your own* was the general mentality; people kept their heads down and avoided involvement with other people's drama as much as possible. There were plenty of absolute diamonds in that community who'd give you their last quid, no questions asked. People who volunteered at the community centre, checked in on elderly neighbours, worked on the shared gardens and picked up the litter and dog shit. When the blood hit the pavement though, even the gobbiest would go to ground.

'Which number?' she asked. 'Don't the council use some of that block for care leavers?'

'Rings a bell,' Lennon said.

'Step ahead of you.' Bradshaw tapped the phone on his desk, which she now noticed was on hold to Housing Services.

'Keep me in the loop,' she said. 'Any idea where Coates is?'

'Probably took himself for a full hose-down and uniform change.'

She was surprised to hear this criticism from Bradshaw who never usually had a bad word to say about anyone.

'Hard work, that one,' he continued. 'Must've been born with a silver spoon in his gob. Way he went on you'd think a full Hazmat suit was standard issue for a house call.'

Lennon shook his head. 'Prick. Can't you get him moved over to Traffic or something?'

She rolled her eyes. 'No, more's the p—'

Her response was cut off by Tariq. 'Putting this through to your desk,' he called, from the other side of the office. 'Came through the switchboard.'

This was unlikely to be good news. Please, not another complaint from the school about Jake. Her dad had had a hospital appointment sometime this week – could he have been admitted? She'd meant to call her parents last night and get the details, but instead had woken up, groggy and confused, on the sofa at two a.m.

'DI Harlow.'

'PC Dan Holmes, British Transport Police.' She felt momentary relief at this being a professional matter. 'I'm looking for whoever's heading up North East county lines. Would that be yourself?' His Scouse accent rang out like a bell.

'That's me, Constable. How can I help?'

'Sorry to throw a curve ball in your day, Inspector, but we've picked up a lad at Lime Street Station – might be of interest to you.'

'OK,' she said. 'You've seen the marker?' Maz had put an Intelligence note on the Police National Computer for anyone they'd already IDed on the line or traced from the bando surveillance in case they were stopped by another copper.

'Yep. Right little scally – McKenzie Jackson? Member of the public reported to a PCSO that he seemed distressed. We've had the wellbeing team with him for an hour and they've eventually got a name and DOB. Refusing to give any more, but looks like day-tripping.'

'Backpack?' Her voice was hopeful, but expecting the worst.
'Nope.'

He'd be plugged, then. This was going to be grim.

There were about five Jackson kids as far as she could recall, all known to social services and youth offending. There'd been something with McKenzie last year. Possibly possession. Or he'd gone for the stepdad when he'd put the mam in A&E?

He'd be acting the big man now, return ticket and a few grubby twenties in his pocket, but Jesus Christ, the kid was fourteen; he shouldn't have made it on the first leg of this trip without raising suspicion from Newcastle Central Station staff. If he was the one they'd picked up last year in Safeguarding, he was five-foot-nothing and looked about twelve.

'Shite. What's your timeframe?'

'We'll book him in round the corner at Canning Place and get him examined. Can you organise a car your end to pick him up tonight?'

'Leave it with me. What sort of state's he in?'

'Kid's only wearing a T-shirt. Demolished some scran – twenty chicken nuggets like he hadn't eaten in a week.'

'Have you pulled the CCTV?' She held her breath: if they could track his movements throughout the day, this might be a breakthrough in establishing where the Byker packages were coming from.

'Got him arriving on the 11.05 on Platform Five, but the cameras on the main exit are knackered so no eyes on him leaving the station or returning, unfortunately.'

Her fleeting hope of the whole operation igniting in a blaze of glory smouldered. It would still be worth pulling the footage from around the station, though; she'd get Chambers all over that tomorrow. An awful job, jigsawing the separate feeds together to carve out a timeline, but worth a go nonetheless.

She hung up and scribbled down the immediate actions needing to be taken. Uniforms to collect McKenzie. The mam would need to be informed; from memory, Rachel was fully expecting Tiah Jackson to be hard to get hold of and likely to simply hang up when she heard the mention of police. That would leave her floundering to find a registered appropriate adult who'd be willing to come to the station at stupid o'clock in the morning. She wanted McKenzie interviewed the minute she had legal clearance.

'Lenn – pull Rossy off whatever she's doing and meet me in the incident room in fifteen minutes. And cancel any plans you had for tonight.'

Chapter 14

Land

By ten thirty they'd been through McKenzie's lengthy file backwards, forwards and upside down. From his PNC record, Rachel was half expecting him to rock up in a few hours, swaggering around the custody suite. He'd been in the cells on several occasions and, from his mam's reaction when they eventually got a response, this wasn't going to go down as a major family turning point. Rossy had made the call, which she then played back to Rachel and Lennon, open-mouthed.

'This is DS Natalie Ross, Tiah, Northumbria Police. I'm afraid your son's been arrested in Liverpool.'

'The fuck? Who's in Liverpool?'

'I'm calling about McKenzie. Had you been informed he wasn't at school today?'

'Dunno, maybes. School's always callin' about one of 'em.' There was shouting in the background, a dog barking, a slammed door. 'Fuckin' pack it in, Aleesha!'

'We're going to need someone to come in, once he's been collected and brought here to the station.'

'Is he breathin'?' Her voice was flat, barely questioning his status as alive or dead.

'Definitely breathing. He's had a traumatic examination though and the medic at Merseyside Station recovered a significant quantity of cocaine inside a condom from his rectum.'

'Right.' She sounded bored.

'Obviously, we need to speak to him as soon as possible to ascertain exactly who's recruited him to carry these drugs back to Newcastle. He's been arrested so we'll be interviewing him under caution.'

'Well, I've never seen him for a week and I'm not comin' in nowhere. You can send him back in a fuckin' taxi.'

Tiah's voice was replaced with the dull hum of the dial tone. Rossy shook her head as she looked at Rachel and pressed stop on the recording. Her shock at this reaction from the mother of the fourteen-year-old was still tangible, despite this being the second time she'd heard Tiah Jackson's side of the conversation.

The hours ticked by, frustration setting in as the night shift took over. There'd been a delay in getting a couple of response officers freed up after an onslaught of 999 calls. Premier League Darts on at the arena always meant a load of pissed-up punters stumbling into kebab shops to finish their night with a few punches and a chase. Added to this, the last Thursday of the month, Universal Credit pay day, invariably led to a spike in call-outs, and tonight was no exception.

Rossy looked at her watch resentfully and pushed the paperwork away. It was now after one in the morning. 'Left a message for the Jacksons' social worker and called the out of hours,' she said. 'Nothing back. I know they've got caseloads coming out their ears, but fuck's sake, man.'

'Try the duty team again,' Rachel said. 'Priority for now is we need an AA. Squad car's sent an ETA of 4.10 and I want him fed and sat in the interview room by half past.'

'Won't get it.' Lennon yawned loudly. 'They'll enforce a rest period.'

'Keeping you up?' She raised her eyebrows. 'Thought stamina was your middle name.'

'Come on, boss, we're on, like, hour twenty of this shift,' Rossy said, crossing her arms.

'You'll get the OT.'

'February's claim form's still on your desk so I won't hold my breath.'

That was true. 'My bad. I'll get them both signed off tonight.'

Rossy muttered something else under her breath.

'Wind your neck in, OK?' Rachel's patience had snapped. 'I get enough of that at home. I said I'll sort it. Take this and do a coffee run.' She slid her bank card across the table and watched as Rossy took it and slumped off down the corridor.

'What's her problem?' she asked Lennon. She knew she was taking her frustration out on the pair of them; he was right about the likelihood of a couple of hours' sleep being mandated before they could commence an interview, but she just didn't want to hear it right now.

'Hayley keeps calling. Meant to have their scan tomorrow.' He shrugged. 'Twenty weeks or something.'

Shit: she did know that. There'd been chat in the office about some big gender reveal. And she'd clocked the side-eye glances Lennon and Rossy had given each other during the night. Maybe she was acting like an arsehole, but the need to control the uncontrollable was weighing down on her shoulders. Everyone knew that CID wasn't a nine to five when they were working a job like this, and at least Rossy and Lennon were actually getting paid for the overtime. Being here was pretty inconvenient for her too, but OT claims didn't exist at inspector level and no one was going to hear her wanging on about it.

The hum of the strip lighting was heavy in the recycled office air, a nostalgic throwback to all the night shifts of years gone by. Rachel was rarely in the station overnight anymore, with scheduled CID hours more regular, giving her a fighting chance of being able to put something resembling tea on the table.

She'd had to swallow her extreme irritation with Scott's no-show at the school meeting, and ring him with a galling request to have Jess and Jake for the night. Unfortunately, she'd failed to factor in his CrossFit schedule, which evidently held more weight in his calendar than dad duty.

They're not kids, Rachel. And your chaos isn't my problem. They can sort themselves out for one night.

She'd messaged them, explaining the situation at work, promising to be back before they left for school in the morning. Not for the first time, she considered the irony of her work-life balance. Pumping ninety per cent of her energy into protecting other people's kids from harm, whilst essentially phoning it in for her own, a fact that certainly hadn't gone unnoticed by Jess and Jake themselves.

They'd both read it, but, whether out of annoyance or indifference, Jake had left her hanging.

Jess's reply said it all.

And 'Parent of the Year' goes to …

If she really thought about it, the imbalance between her and Scott in their kids' lives boiled her piss. Jake had muttered recently about him seeing someone, so obviously she'd done a full Instagram trawl – Holly, a nurse, two lads under five. From past experience, Scott playing happy families elsewhere would make him even more unreliable in his contact with his own children. But what could she do?

Heavy rain against the window pounded like a steady drumbeat.

She was itching to lead McKenzie's interview herself. The aluminium table. The hard chairs bolted to the wipe-clean floor. The smell of bleach and unwashed bodies.

But, instead, she'd be handing the buzz of the interrogation over to Lennon and Rossy and either watching the remote monitor, or hearing the highlights when they emerged from the ring, victorious or empty-handed. Her choice to swap the part of CID she'd excelled at most for data, paperwork and a few hundred quid more a month seemed like the shortest of short straws.

It was after four a.m. when McKenzie was eventually deposited at the custody desk, the two uniforms looking surprisingly chipper after their eight-hour round trip.

At least they'd been out of the rain. There were far worse jobs you could get as a response officer than a pick-up, drop-off. Manning the perimeter tape around a critical incident and fending off nosy passers-by took some beating.

She'd inadvertently got her sergeant's back up in her first year on the beat, and subsequently been stationed at a hit-and-run scene from dawn till dusk without a break. She could still remember a member of the public taking pity and handing her a Costa, which had felt like liquid gold in her hand.

The same upbeat mood could not, unfortunately, be said of McKenzie.

He was a train wreck.

Rachel's instinct, on seeing him, dazed and bedraggled, was to give him a hug. He was shivering, dressed only in trackies and a T-shirt, a scraggy blanket around his shoulders.

He looked even younger than she'd remembered; a bony scrap of a lad, head shaved like he'd had nits, dead-eyed gaze fixed squarely on his Nike Air Jordans. Were these the initial down payment on his services? Or was he working off a manufactured debt of his own weed consumption?

Rossy had ploughed her way down the approved AA register, getting a hard no from each request. They were all volunteers so the appeal of bouncing out of bed in the middle of the night to sit with a surly teenager who'd recently had five grand's worth of coke pulled out of his arse was, understandably, minimal.

She'd finally got a yes from Dean, one of the youth workers at the Byker Community Centre, but he had to take his own kid to nursery so couldn't get there 'til at least eight thirty.

Rachel sat on one of the benches around the custody desk with McKenzie, explaining what was going to happen next, while he devoured a dry sandwich. His eyes never lifted from the floor and she was surprised he managed to swallow from the vice-like tension in his jaw.

She reached out to take the plastic sleeve, trying to shield him from the shouting and bawling of the adult detainees waiting to be booked in. This had been a bumper Thursday night by the looks of the cuts and bruises, and the stale alcohol fug that hung in the air.

The custody sergeant led them to the only empty cell, where he'd sleep for a few hours until Lennon and Rossy could start digging into the specifics. She was dying to give him a shake, make him see that the people he was working for weren't his 'crew'.

But realistically, what else did he have going for him?

It wasn't like there was anyone at home ready to scoop him up and wrap him in cotton wool. He was staring down the barrel of two equally desperate options: snitch up the line, probably get taken into care and spend the foreseeable looking over his shoulder, or stay silent, suck it up and get back in the game.

Rachel watched him through the hatch, a heaviness in her bones that was more than tiredness. He lay still, facing the wall on the thin blue mat. Face rigid with the effort of holding in an avalanche of feelings he probably couldn't even name.

'Everything's going to be all right, McKenzie,' she lied.

Sliding the grate closed softly, she turned away, each of the stifled sobs seeping from the cell an incision to her heart.

Chapter 15

Sea

Friday 21st April

'Yes?' A gruff bark echoed from behind a half-open door.

Rachel ran towards it.

'Can you help me?' she garbled, averting her eyes from the state of semi-undress. 'There's a man – Tyler, he's dead. His cabin's this way.'

'Give me minute,' he said, shutting the door in her face.

What the fuck?

She paced on the spot, adrenaline surging. If he didn't reappear in five seconds, she was booting the flimsy piece of shit down and dragging him to the body.

True to his few words, though, the door reopened and the man emerged, dressed in a beige short-sleeved shirt and pressed chinos. The hairy paunch was gone, tethered tightly now with a leather belt. He huffed and puffed beside her as she sprinted back to 656, where her bag was wedging the door.

'There's no pulse,' she said, struggling to remember her professional skill set. 'What's the protocol?'

He looked dispassionately at Tyler's crumpled form for a moment. 'You kitchen? Why you find him?'

'No, I'm a guest. Look, it's a long story. You need to take me to the captain or whoever's in charge of security. Or the doctor? Is she along here?' Rachel yearned for the amused voice in the corridor of last night. Tyler wouldn't be needing those condoms now.

'Why you not press?' he said, gesturing to a red wall-mounted button clearly in view outside.

Rachel registered its significance for the first time. How could she have failed to see an alarm when emergency response took up most of her CV? 'Shit, I don't know. I panicked.'

After muttering something in another language, which sounded disparaging, he turned and began walking heavily to the lift. 'I take you to bridge.'

'What's your name?' Rachel said, following. 'And your role on board?'

'Andre,' he grunted. 'Security.'

'Oh great, perfect – what's the procedure for this sort of situation? How do you arrange for police to come on board?' Her words tumbled out breathlessly: the gradient of this long windowless expanse felt a lot more challenging than a flat corridor should be. Maybe the ship was rolling. Or whatever they called it.

'No police.'

'Sorry?'

He stopped abruptly and repeated himself in flat, heavy syllables. 'No po-lice.'

'What? It's an unexplained death.' A sharp pain in her chest made her wince. But he'd already started moving again and she had to hurry to keep up, voice rising. 'He'll need forensics, toxicology, a post-mortem, everything.'

'No.'

Rachel glared at the back of his head. That couldn't be right.

Surely this prick was about to be severely reprimanded by the senior-level crew.

The lift carried them upwards in tense silence. Rachel drummed her nails on the mirrored wall and considered how she was going to explain her presence in the staff quarters. It was disorientating to be on this side of a critical incident, the one expected to give answers, not ask the questions.

The lift juddered to a halt with an incongruous bing and they stepped out into the set of *Star Trek*. Screens were everywhere, with enough flashing red and green lights to power the national grid. There were floor-to-ceiling windows on three sides, looking out onto an endless horizon with impeccably uniformed personnel calmly observing wavy lines on digital monitors.

An imposing wooden sign hung on the wall with huge letters etched into its surface in hard black lines: *Eternal Vigilance is the Price of Safety*. The juxtaposition of this Old Testament–style warning and the hyper-tec"ology all around was stark.

Northumbria Police HQ this was not.

Andre had wordlessly deserted her when they exited the lift and so she stood awkwardly, very aware that she was wearing a bikini covered only by a thin sheet of material, waiting for someone to acknowledge her presence. Tugging the sarong down as much as she could, her hand brushed something stuck to her thigh. She lifted the material and was dismayed to see the single contact lens from the coke wrap.

Perfect. Now she'd have to add evidence tampering to her list of misdemeanours.

She considered its significance; presumably Tyler's, although she hadn't noticed any lens paraphernalia in the room. Her skin had an oily sun cream sheen and it lay there, stubbornly defying gravity. Immaterial as it seemed, she was loath to discard anything associated with a potential crime scene.

Opening her bag and removing a wad of euros from their polythene envelope, she dropped the tiny piece of plastic into her makeshift evidence bag and shoved the notes into a side pocket.

She remained standing in the vast space, squirming, for what felt like an eternity until her gruff escort returned, walking beside an aristocratic figure she recognised from the safety briefing. He held out a hand and encompassed hers with both palms, squeezing with just the right degree of firmness to be reassuring, but not painful.

'Captain Richard Miller. I understand you are here to report a fatality.' He looked grave.

'Yes. Downstairs, H656. One of the entertainment staff. I just found him. He's … dead.' Her voice trailed away. She'd lost the thread of how much she should be relaying.

Miller raised his eyebrows. 'And you are?'

'Rachel Harlow. I'm a passenger. I was a … friend … of his.'

He turned to Andre, sharply. 'Excuse us a moment – is it Miss or Mrs Harlow? It will be necessary to make an announcement.'

She could feel her cheeks flaming. 'Actually, it's Inspector – I'm a detective with Northumbria Police.'

'Detective?' His eyebrows almost disappeared into his salt-and-pepper hair. 'Well, well, Inspector Harlow. How fortuitous.'

Not quite reading his tone, Rachel waited while Miller leaned over one of the desks and pressed a switch. His voice rang out over the ship's Tannoy system.

'*Crew announcement: Code Rising Star. Dr Larson and Simon Van der Wyk, please report to the bridge immediately. Repeat Code Rising Star.*'

'Rising star?' Rachel said.

'The code we use in the event of a fatality on board, Inspector. Unfortunately, given the average age of our guest population, sudden death is not entirely unheard of.'

'So, what happens now?'

'I have a few questions for you whilst we wait for our doctor, Anna Larson, and our chief security officer, Simon van der Wyk, and then you will be free to return to … the pool?' His upward inflection contained the merest hint of condescension, but it was enough for her to mentally assign him Strike One.

'Can I quickly make a phone call?' she asked, remembering the kids, still in the hot tub, adamant that last night's disappearing act would not be repeated.

Miller gave a curt nod and turned his attention back to the security guard. A quick WhatsApp call reassured her that Jess and Jake were where she'd left them and she briefly relayed that an actual bona fide emergency had held her up, but didn't elaborate further.

There were also two missed calls from an unknown number. Who'd be ringing her while she was on holiday? They'd left a voicemail, but, with the captain tapping his foot impatiently, this wasn't the time to dial in.

'Now, Inspector Harlow, if you'd kindly follow me into my office. Andre, please show Dr Larson and Simon in as soon as they arrive.'

Rachel followed Miller away from the *Star Trek* switchboard to a mahogany-panelled room, with *Captain* etched on the door in the same hard-lined script as the Eternal Vigilance maxim of doom. He indicated that she should sit in one of the upholstered chairs and took his place behind the desk.

'Firstly, allow me to extend my sincere condolences. It must have been deeply upsetting to find your *friend* in these regrettable circumstances.'

She perched, uncomfortably, on the overstuffed seat. 'I'm obviously not here professionally, so – yes – to find Tyler dead … was a shock.'

'Indeed. May I ask how you came to be in his cabin, Inspector? Our crew accommodation is strictly out of bounds for guests, at all times.'

Rachel swallowed. She had steeled herself to withhold the substance of her interaction with Tyler, and her possession of the key card, but now, in the interests of professionalism, she cracked.

'I got talking to him yesterday in one of the bars,' she said, forcing herself to keep her head up and meet his eyes, 'and, well, one thing led to another. He gave me this for after the show.' She reached into her bag and passed the small rectangular piece of plastic across the desk. 'But … it didn't happen.'

'I'm afraid I'm not following,' he said, frowning.

She paused. Was he really going to make her spell it out? 'I was unwell, during the evening. So, I – er – didn't take him up on his invitation.' Her cheeks were burning now. 'I – er – went down this afternoon to return the card and collect something I'd left. And that was when I found him.'

'I see.'

'There's a witness, if that helps. His dance partner saw me yesterday so she could vouch for why I had the key card.'

'Danielle Paige?' His tone softened, sounding almost reverent in the way her name rolled off his tongue. Strange. They looked and spoke like they inhabited different planets.

'That's the one. She was off her face on something, though, so her memory might be hazy.'

His eyes widened. 'I can assure you that none of our crew would be *off their face on something*, as you put it. Standards on an HLC line are rather different to what you'll be used to. The North, wasn't it – your police division?'

She bristled, instinctively, at this. Strike Two. 'One of your crew *has* just overdosed though, haven't they? In my experience, drugs find their ways into the most unlikely of holes. Not just in the *North*.'

'Of course, we'll be conducting our own internal investigation into Mr Tweedy's death. Our security team is highly trained.'

'You'll be searching Danielle's cabin, then? Whatever that batch was needs to be out of circulation.'

'I can assure you that will not be necessary.'

She stared at him, taken aback by his complacency. 'What exactly is your procedure for examining the scene and conducting the post-mortem? I've got some concerns from my initial impressions.'

'Yes?' Miller's right eye was twitching, and Rachel could sense his discomfort in the direction the meeting had taken.

His irritation was quelled by a sharp knock on the door and the arrival of Andre plus two people who she surmised to be the doctor and chief security officer. The former looked to be a similar age to her, attractive in an unmade-up, Scandinavian milkmaid sort of way. The latter she also vaguely recognised from the muster drill. He was wearing heavy square glasses this time though, framing his startling blue eyes, which gave him an air of Clark Kent, pre-Superman transformation.

'Thank you, Andre – that will be all,' said Miller, waiting until the door closed before continuing.

'I'm afraid I have to inform you both that we have had a crew member fatality. Tyler Tweedy. Andre has reported evidence of an accidental overdose, but I'll need you to verify and complete the paperwork.'

'I saw him only yesterday,' said Larson, the doctor. 'This is terrible news.'

'Indeed,' said Miller. 'A tragic loss.'

'We will need transportation to the morgue, of course, and the certification will be made in Vigo?' Larson looked to the security chief, who had thus far remained silent.

He cleared his throat before speaking. 'Might be best to leave him in situ, Captain, given the attention it'll attract in the press? Only a week. Vigo's not ideal, right?' The South African seemed to defer to the weight of Miller's colonial rule for instructions. Or maybe he was just unused to being called away from his usual security concerns: OAPs arguing over who called 'House' first in the Bingo, or whatever was equally pressing.

'As far as optics goes, given his prominent position, yes, I'm inclined to agree,' Miller said, nodding. He looked at Rachel, seeming to remember there was an outsider within their ranks.

'This is Rachel Harlow, the unfortunate guest who found his body.' She noted his use of her full name rather than title, clearly an attempt to reinforce his own authority rather than recognise her credentials.

What was it they had said in the muster drill about the law whilst at sea? She couldn't recall the details, but it seemed that, in terms of policing, they were floating in the Wild Wild West.

'Does an overdose seem credible in your experience of Tyler?' she asked, deciding to get her concerns out in the open, despite her bikini and non-inclusion within the chain of command. 'Is this not unusual that crew would have access to drugs whilst on board?'

'Certainly unusual. Unheard of.' Miller bristled. 'We have stringent security measures for crew and guests on all HLC lines. Our crew accommodation is inspected prior to embarkation and we have a zero tolerance policy on illegal substances anywhere on board.'

'Checks were completed by myself, Andre, Tomer and Subash,' the security chief said. 'Nothing to report.'

'Very good.' Miller nodded, addressing himself to Rachel. 'Employee standards across our entire fleet are unparalleled.'

'So, there's no previous history of Tyler's drug use or any medical red flags—'

She was cut off abruptly, the captain now openly displeased. 'It is not company policy to share details of staff appraisals or medical records. I have included you in this meeting as a courtesy, given that you found Mr Tweedy's body. However, your input into the incident is now completed and I will be happy to escort you back down to the guest decks.' He stood up. 'Doctor Larson, Simon, can I ask you to make your way to Deck Two. I will, of course, make the arrangements in terms of his internment and next of kin.'

'Has anyone informed Danielle?' said Larson, looking from Miller to Van der Wyk.

'That, I will also handle personally,' Miller said, smoothly. 'It is imperative that all information be kept entirely confidential.'

The two crew members left the room to carry out whatever duties were required as part of the elusive Operation Rising Star. An apt name, thought Rachel, for a personality like Tyler. He had set that dance floor alight. Before she'd doused his flame with vomit, anyway.

Miller narrowed his eyes, weighing her up. He drew a document from one of the desk drawers and passed it across the polished surface. Rachel glanced at the heading: *High Life Cruises LTD. Non-Disclosure Agreement.*

'It is company policy, Inspector,' he said, 'in regrettable situations such as these, for guests to make a commitment to maintain the privacy and reputation of our brand. I'm sure, in your esteemed position, you are familiar with such concerns. If any unsubstantiated information were to be leaked, you can imagine the distress this could cause.'

'Of course,' she said, meeting his steady gaze with an unflinching look of her own.

He slid a Mont Blanc fountain pen across the desk and watched as she didn't pick it up. 'Of course, you are welcome to sign and return at your convenience, if that is your preference.'

'I'll do that. I'm sure in *your* esteemed position, Captain, you would never sign a document without proper due diligence.' She folded the paper and placed it into her bag, noting the makeshift evidence bag she had filed away earlier. She decided to refrain from disclosing the contact lens, for now; it was probably nothing.

'As you wish.' He reached out a hand again, and gave her palm another squeeze, this one forceful enough to make his feelings abundantly clear beneath his upper-class manners. Strike Three.

That's what thousands of pounds in public school fees bought you, thought Rachel, as they made their way back out of the ship's tightly organised control centre: an ability to polish your arrogance with charm.

It didn't wash with her, though. She had a sinking feeling that vigilance, eternal or otherwise, was going to be required to silence the faint alarm bells now ringing in her head.

Chapter 16

Sea

The loudest alarm bell was, obviously, Danielle. Her involvement, whether before or after Tyler smacked out, resounded with an insistent pulse.

Rachel ran, cursing her inappropriate footwear as she slipped, almost falling on the polished floor of the deck, which the staff lift had dispatched her onto.

Deciding that her best course of action was to approach Danielle on the pretext of returning the dress, she went through her options of which cards to play and which to keep close to her chest. It was important to have a legitimate reason for tracking her down, with any luck before she would have received official confirmation of her partnership now being a solo act.

She had no doubt, though, that Danielle would already be well aware of her dance partner's demise. The bare room. The conspicuous absence of any of the garish gowns. You simply couldn't pick up and remove that amount of cheap glittery clothing without leaving a stubborn scattering of sparkle behind.

After grabbing the Lycra abomination from her cabin, she made for the theatre. The dress was now dry, though slightly crusty, its torn hem scraping the floor like a sorry excuse for a bridal train. She stopped short of sniffing it, but – even at this distance – registered an unpleasant, sour odour. Fuck it. Danielle would have seen and done worse.

The door to the auditorium wasn't locked and, without an audience, it was a cavern of nothingness; the particles of dust dancing through the air a lame echo of Tyler and Danielle's complex choreography. Adrenaline coursing, Rachel pushed the heavy curtain, searching for a gap in the black fabric.

She emerged centre stage and quickly exited, not wishing to reminisce. The dark backstage area had props and costumes arranged haphazardly on rails, out of view of the audience, ready for the illusion of a quick change and big reveal as the dancers stepped back into the applause.

She found the fire door and looked along the corridor. Framed, autographed photographs lined the walls: the *Synergy*'s questionable Hall of Fame. She recognised a few washed-up has-beens and TV talent show contestants amongst the copious images of Tyler and Danielle, clearly top of the bill.

Faint noises intrigued her – a tinny hum of music and the sound of something being sprayed. Rachel made her way towards the source and stood for a few seconds, unnoticed in the open doorway of a dressing room.

A black thong carved a deep line between Danielle's arse cheeks as she applied another layer of what appeared to be Ronseal over her skin. Cloying vapour billowed around the room and, although Rachel attempted to shield her face, she was unable to avoid inhaling the fumes. She coughed, revealing her presence, and Danielle snapped round, full of hell.

'Get a good eyeful, did you?' It took a moment, but once the penny dropped, her reaction to Rachel's identity scaled new heights of fury. 'What the fuck are you doing back here?'

'Came to return this,' she said, tossing the dress onto a table to the right of the door. 'Thanks for the lend.'

'Don't be thinking you're something special. He was always

doing that. Bringing slags up on stage, parading them round. You're the only one that ever puked though.' Her laugh was a bitter scratch of disgust.

Ignoring Danielle's words, but registering her use of past tense, Rachel leaned against the doorframe, 'Getting ready for tonight?'

'What's it got to do with you? Fuckin' mouthy polis bitch.'

'I think you've got something of mine. And I want it back.'

'Oh yeah?'

'I left a top in Tyler's cabin.'

'And?'

'You might've picked it up. With your *merchandise*.' She relished this sort of confrontation, back in the ring, actually doing the questioning rather than sorting out logistics for other officers.

'You're fuckin' cracked.'

'You haven't been in Tyler's cabin then, since the show last night?'

'I'm not answering shit. Don't care who you are on land, you cunt. You're at sea now.'

A drone of hard dance music pierced the tension. Danielle's phone buzzed on the chair beside her, and Rachel saw the caller ID: Rich.

'You should probably answer that,' she said. 'Might be important.'

'Off you pop, then.' Danielle jabbed a sharp talon at the door.

'Don't mind me. I'll just wait.'

Caught between the insistent ringtone, her view of the caller ID and the presence of a police officer, Danielle glared before answering with a sharp: 'What?'

Unable to make out the voice on the other end, Rachel watched Danielle's unnaturally smooth face register neither grief nor shock at the lengthy message being delivered.

'Right. I'll come up,' she said at last, throwing the phone back onto the chair.

'Bad news?'

'None of your fuckin' business.'

'I beg to differ,' she said. 'Criminal activity and unexplained death is bang on my business.'

'What fuckin' criminal activity? And I don't know nothing about a death.'

Her tone was impressively outraged. She should branch out into acting, thought Rachel. If she could hold a tune, she'd be a full-on triple threat.

However, she was avoiding eye contact and the repetitive brush of her finger against her nose was either a telltale indicator of her lie or an attempt to make sure all traces of white powder were gone from both nostrils.

Rachel gave her a slow handclap. 'Decent. I'd give your little performance an eight, maybe even a nine if you sort out your nose in advance next time. But your vocab needs work. Past tense at this stage is a bit of a giveaway.'

'Get the fuck out, you tramp.' Danielle grabbed a neon pink stiletto and took a step forwards, heel raised like a knife.

Rachel didn't flinch. This was schoolyard stuff.

'Where I come from, that's basic bitch level.' She seized the outstretched four-inch spike and snapped it off with a twist of her wrist. 'Embarrassing. Geordie girls graduate from fighting with heels and hair-pulling at half your age.'

Danielle's eyes roved around the room for something else to use as a weapon.

'Look, unless you're going to spray-tan me to death,' Rachel continued, 'I'd suggest you calm the fuck down. Fortunately for you, OD victims don't have a lot to say for themselves, but don't worry, I'll keep asking questions 'til I get the answers I need. Or you could do the decent thing, of course, and just tell me what was in that coke?'

'Rather shit in my hands and clap.'

'Nice. In the meantime, I want the top. Pink. Polo shirt. Do I need to draw you a picture?'

'Haven't seen it.'

'Well, when you do, send it along to C709. Deck Ten. I've already recommended that your accommodation be searched – that batch is another OD waiting to happen. If there's anything else you want to tell me, you can knock on my door like a civilised human being and we'll have a conversation.'

Danielle's mouth twisted, but Rachel had had more than enough of the vile-smelling air. She threw a final warning over her shoulder:

'Otherwise, watch your back.'

Chapter 17

Sea

The family's second try at a pleasant evening passed without major incident, until Rachel broke the bad news about everybody's favourite ballroom dancer.

They ate as a semi-unified party of five, before Jess and Jake dived off into the arcades, leaving her and her parents to have a tense stroll around Deck Seven. Its central covered section had been designed to resemble a manicured park, complete with piped birdsong and a bandstand. To either side, the outdoor promenade stretched the full length of the ship, fore to aft, open to the sea.

Rachel noted how low the barriers really were. Laddered railings, perfect for little legs to climb – or for a mortal-drunk woman to see as a way out. A shiver ran through her, despite the warmth. She knew exactly how fast someone could vanish over the edge.

Too close. Far too close.

She turned to leave, but froze, eyes locking on to a red light. It was a camera.

Discreet. Much like the one she'd watched a tec"ician affix to the bando in the Byker Wall. This was in plain sight though, if you knew where to look, trained on the deck and water beyond. The same one that fed the cabin's virtual balcony.

A cold sweat flooded her skin. The thought of her private collapse captured on film made her stomach flip.

'Even better than Jenny's photos!' Her mum's shrill voice half jolted her out of her panic. She'd been miles away from here, hadn't she? Right at the back of the ship. Surely not caught on any sort of camera.

'Sorry, what?'

'Jenny,' Barbara repeated, with an edge this time. 'Jenny from Destinations. Booked the whole trip.'

On the surface, mother-daughter relations had been disinfected and stitched together. Although she still hadn't acknowledged the apology message, Barbara had fallen back into civil conversation during the meal. It was only when Rachel had tentatively relayed her grim discovery that the stitches threatened to snap.

'Tyler Tweedy?' she gasped. 'Dead? What on earth, Rachel?'

'I know.' She coughed, adding vaguely, 'I was, sort of, there when he was found.'

'You were there?'

'Yeah, sort of.'

'Well, you either were or you weren't, so which is it?'

'Barbara,' said her dad, putting a hand on her shoulder. 'Let's not interrogate her. She's clearly alerted the right people, so it's not her who'll be dealing with this. Tragic, though it is,' he added.

'Thanks, Dad. Although it's not as simple as that. I'm not convinced they're dealing with it professionally. It was an overdose, and—'

'Drugs?' Barbara interrupted, eyes on stalks. 'Never in the world. Tyler and Danielle? They're not that type; it said so in that *OK* article, didn't it, Bob? Into organics and the like – don't even drink! It was in the magazine – full three-page spread! Drugs?'

'Mum, keep it down. This is all meant to be confidential.'

'Well, I still don't understand how you're privy to all this information. I mean, you wouldn't know him from Adam, except of course, the … *incident* on the stage.' Barbara shuddered, her memory of the family's collective shame still raw.

'I didn't know him,' Rachel said, trying to dodge the obvious holes in her prepared story. 'I just, sort of, bumped into him, before the show, when I'd lost track of the time, and I – er – left something with him so I popped back. And that was when I found him.'

Barbara exchanged a pointed glance with Robert, as if she had already given him a thorough run-down of her suspicions regarding yesterday's MIA window. She shook her head and tutted under her breath.

Rachel felt her jaw automatically clench. That audiovisual combination had been a mainstay of her youth: a chisel of disapproval chipping away over years, rarely rising to an outright bang, but building up incrementally, forming a pattern that she was loath to fall back into, at the age of thirty-five.

She forced herself to breathe.

This whole Tyler debacle was making her decidedly uneasy. Far from her usual role in upholding the truth, she had now withheld information to two separate parties and was starting to feel disorientated. Experience from the other side of the interview room had taught her that it was better to say as little as possible if you were straying from an honest recount of events.

Much as she wanted to stick to a simple 'no comment' for the rest of the trip, Rachel made reluctant arrangements to spend the next day all together, sightseeing in Vigo.

An idea occurred to her, as she detached Jess and Jake from the slots, and she darted down the aft staircase to the guest services desk, booking an appointment at the medical centre for the following evening. A conversation with Dr Larson might be enough to allay the concerns still hovering in her periphery.

She had barely met the guy, and this wasn't on her caseload: an overdose was an overdose. But something told her she owed it to Tyler, however random their liaison had been, to check a few details.

When they got back to the cabin, their stewardess, Oksana, was just leaving. They were greeted like old friends, the well-groomed blonde woman giving no sign of the exploitation-identity she'd been assigned by Jess. Far from it, if Oksana's Pandora bracelet and Gucci watch were anything to go by, her wrist heavy with beads and pendants as they shook hands.

'You're Ukrainian?' Rachel said, noticing the blue and yellow stripes of a flag on one of the baubles.

Oksana nodded, putting her hand to her chest. 'Yes. Several in crew. This company – we are grateful for HLC support of our nation.'

Jess immediately launched into a monologue on the Russian-Ukrainian conflict and her various theories surrounding its conception.

Rachel put a hand on Jess's shoulder. 'I'm sorry. My daughter has very strong views on most issues. We hope you're being looked after well here.'

'Of course. Captain Miller looks after my husband Andre and myself as if his own family.'

'Your husband – he works in security on board?' That bloated, grumpy troll was married to this angelic vision? Not for the first time, Rachel castigated herself for judging on first impressions. That was what police work did for you. Once you'd acquainted yourself with the worst humanity had to offer, it was difficult to take your cynical shades off.

They said goodnight to Oksana and Jake led the way inside. The room was immaculate. A paper schedule had been delivered, with timings for the next day's arrival and departure, suggested points of interest on land and an itinerary of activities for those electing to remain on board. A small text box on the back caught her eye: *We regret that, due to unforeseen circumstances, Tyler Tweedy will not be performing for the remainder of the voyage.*

She passed the paper to Jake, who scanned it before flopping on his bed. 'Looks boring. Just old buildings and stuff.'

'What were you expecting?' Jess piped up. 'Alton Towers?'

'Do one. I'd rather be at home. Haven't even got proper Wi-Fi.'

'Great,' Rachel said. 'Well, let's have another look in the morning. Try and pick a few things to do.'

He reached for his laptop. 'I'll just stay here and play Champ Man.'

'Not a chance,' she said. 'I told the school you'd be getting exposed to some culture. Why don't you google it – see if there's anything takes your fancy.' She felt pleased with her measured response as he grudgingly prodded the keyboard.

'Get in,' he said, suddenly animated. 'It's the drugs importation capital of mainland Europe. Let's get Gran smacked off her tits.'

'Jake, man! Not an image I want in my head. And mind your language.'

'It's not a joking matter,' came Jess's voice from the bathroom. 'Probably means the whole city's under a corrupt authoritarian influence.'

Rachel exchanged a glance with her son. Jess's ability to have a strident angle on every single issue was wearying.

'Right,' she called out, taking some control. 'We're not involving ourselves in any drugs deals on this trip. I get enough of that at work. I keep telling people – This. Is. Meant. To. Be. A. Holiday.'

The sound of the toilet flushing as Jess emerged seemed a fitting finale to her speech. They both looked a bit guilty and didn't backchat, which she resolved to take as a full apology.

Jake smirked. 'Get it, no class As. We'll just get Grandad started on something recreational. Like poppers.'

Lying in bed an hour later, listening to Jess's snores, she found herself reverting back into investigation mode. She couldn't help it.

Some cases were more consuming than others, but there was

always a physical reaction when she'd been around a body. A tingle in her spine.

She'd worked with CID colleagues who understood, who kept smelling the stench of death in their nostrils, long after leaving the scene. Lennon would get it. Lennon always got her.

She shifted onto her side, trying to twist the unease out of her bones. But there it was, still fizzing under her skin, reminding her that there was something she'd overlooked, waiting to be uncovered.

She tried a few pages of Jess's book, but it all felt too close to home: characters crammed into bleak flats like Dalton Crescent, as cramped as cabins, under the coercive control of a PA system. Wasn't reading supposed to take you away from real life rather than holding up a mirror to it?

Snapping the paperback shut, she closed her eyes, but her thoughts had already toppled into Operation Fever. The scar on her palm was throbbing and all she could see was Gallagher. His green-eyed gaze. The weight of his words.

I know who you are.

She could still feel the spit on her cheek, as if he were here now, pressing in.

As quickly as she tried to stop her thoughts spiralling, to break the sentence down and assess it at a distance, she was being dragged under, submerged in icy blackness.

The wind on the balcony had whipped her hair and she'd felt the progress of his polluted DNA seeping insidiously into her flesh, coursing through her bloodstream, staining her from the inside out.

Stop. Breathe.

She wasn't drowning. She was safe, on a ship, moving steadily towards land.

But even here, she couldn't shake the pull of policing. Putting the pieces together in the right order, until a lifeless body on the floor started to make sense.

Accepting that she wasn't falling asleep any time soon, she reached for her phone. She scrolled, slowly, through the images she'd taken in Cabin 656. Earlier, she'd been unprofessional, emotional. Now the shock of her grim discovery was fading, she could assess the photos analytically.

Pinching her thumb and forefinger, she zoomed in to the dried white froth around Tyler's nose. It smacked of some sort of opioid. He hadn't struck her as a junkie, though, and she saw enough of them in Byker to recognise a likely candidate. He was definitely on something by the time he was performing last night, but he'd seemed in control. Flying, not fading.

Thinking there was no harm in enlisting reinforcements, especially as she hadn't signed the NDA form still crumpled in her beach bag, she fired off a couple of quick emails. First, Lennon.

> Just a hypothetical question, don't take this in any way that I'm failing to have a normal holiday, but if you had a situation off-duty where you found an OD victim and it seemed a bit suss, would you investigate or leave it to the ship's weird kangaroo court?

Even as she typed, she knew his answer: he'd dive in headfirst. And she'd be right there with him. On shift or on holiday, she couldn't shake the code she'd signed up to.

Her second message was to her friend, Saira, for a pharmaceutical opinion on cause of death. She weighed up whether to send it momentarily, knowing Saira was on maternity leave, but — from what she'd been saying over cocktails a few weeks ago — she could do with a diversion from nappies and colic. She cringed, remembering the way that night had come to a cataclysmic halt.

But, here, tonight, she could officially let the tension in her shoulders relax, now that she'd flagged her concerns. She yawned and closed Gmail; the fizzing sensation was subsiding. Landing back on her photos, she swiped one more time to the whole-room shot, and caught something glinting in the image, just to the right of Tyler's crumpled form. It must have been behind her as she'd knelt down.

Trying to enlarge that part of the screen just made it blurry. It could it be a metal straw, something he'd snorted the powder with. Or a pen? That looked more likely the longer she examined its pixellated shape.

Her pulse quickened. A pen.

What the hell had he been writing? And where, exactly, was it now?

Chapter 18

Land

Friday 31st March

Peeling herself off the desk, Rachel tried to get a grip on how long she'd been asleep. She'd sent Lennon and Rossy home at five to get turned around, and from the pen imprint on her cheek, must have crashed out herself soon after.

With nothing more to be done until McKenzie's rest period elapsed, and Dean the AA arrived, Rachel left the station to sort Jess and Jake's breakfast. Dashing through the car park, a blast of freezing puddle water seeping into her shoes made her swear, each step now a soggy slush. She slammed the door of her Audi, and let her head rest on the steering wheel. The rain had stopped, but it was dark and bitterly cold. Her whole body ached with exhaustion, and she was struggling to remember what day it was.

She opened one eye to check the dashboard. Friday, 5.33 a.m.. This really meant 6.33 a.m. because she hadn't put the clock forward last weekend. The car was still fairly new, a promotion present to herself, but she'd already lost the manual and hadn't found five minutes to google how to adjust the setting. There was probably time to grab a shower before they woke up if she put her foot down, but she hesitated, waiting for her mind to stop racing. She was starving. Rummaging in the glove compartment, she pulled out half a Twix she'd secreted at some point and inhaled it.

The adrenaline of last night was wearing off, and she knew she was likely to take the crash into her interactions with the pair of them if she didn't get it out of her system. She felt more and more these days that her resting state was a standard six-out-of-ten pissed off, quickly escalating to a nine if anyone breathed loudly, crunched crisps in her vicinity or used the word 'pacific' when they meant 'specific'. Chuck in a complex safeguarding concern for a child being exploited by a criminal gang and she could very well combust with the pressure of it all.

Pulling out of the car park, and attempting to steady her rapid breathing, she joined the Coast Road. A memory seeped into her consciousness of noisy family breakfasts with Scott and the twins, before things had soured to the point of venom. The logistics of shift work were always a challenge for the family. Breakfast had been one of the few points in the day when the whole quartet crossed over: either Rachel or Scott on the come-down from nights, the kids bleary-eyed, but sometimes chatty about school or gymnastics or Pokémon.

She flicked the indicator on impulse and pulled off to the twenty-four-hour Tesco. The twins used to love one particular type of cereal, always fighting to be the one to open a new box. What was it called?

Swiftly, checking her watch, she made her way down the cereal aisle, scanning each shelf for the nostalgic brown packaging. Triumphant, she grabbed a box of Choco Pillows and was just racing for the till when her attention was diverted to a security guard gripping the arm of a young woman by the freezers. She looked like shit, her face a mask of numb shame, turned away from a baby throwing stuff out of the buggy. Rachel could see her knuckles, white and sharp as icicles, holding on to a toddler who was straining to escape, as she faced the security guard.

'Everything OK?' Rachel asked as she approached. The burly security guard assessed her with disinterest.

'Shoplifter,' he said, gruffly. 'I'm escorting the *customer* to the office.'

'She hasn't left the premises,' Rachel said, taking her warrant card out of her bag. 'And I'd take your hand off her arm. Probably more than your job's worth to get a complaint from me as a witness.'

He bristled. 'She's barred. Tries this regular when we're quiet. All sorts under that buggy.'

'Can I take it from here?' Rachel said, making eye contact with the woman and picking up a four-pack of toilet roll, which had been chucked near to her feet.

'I'm only doing my job,' he said, releasing the woman's arm. 'Getting stupid, like. People just helping themselves.' He stalked off towards the back of the store, still muttering and shaking his head. 'We're not the bloody foodbank.'

'What's your name?' Rachel bent down to help the woman pick up items from the floor.

'Ashley.' Her eyes darted everywhere, except the police officer standing in front of her. 'Am I getting arrested?'

'Not today,' Rachel said, reaching out to tickle the baby's bare foot. 'You're going to need to show me what you've got though I'm afraid.'

Mutely, eyes downcast, Ashley drew out the contents, hidden beneath a blanket: two packs of super tampons, extra-value nappies, a roll-on deodorant and a box of own-brand formula milk.

'I can't make it last. Once I've got a bit food in and a few quid on the meter, there's nothing left. And I've just come on and I can't keep putting the washer on if I've leaked.' Now she'd started, the words spilled out of her mouth and her posture slumped, leaving her looking even more defeated.

'You working?' Rachel glanced at the kids, noticing that despite the barefoot baby and unorthodox shopping time, they both looked well cared for, with warm coats and gummy grins.

'Bits and pieces, but I've got no one to watch them.'

Rachel nodded at the buggy, her voice gentle. 'How many times you done this?'

There were a couple of beats of silence.

'A few,' Ashley said eventually. 'Got stopped last time though by him.'

The jobsworth security guard was marching towards them again, accompanied by a manager. Both looked officious, probably keen to hit some sort of store target for crime reduction. 'Come on, I'll get it today and I'll give you a number of someone local who can sort some of this for you.'

'I'm not getting put on some list,' Ashley said, voice rising. 'I'm a good mam – I am, honest. No one's ever said I'm not looking after them right.'

'I know. I can see that. But you can't keep doing this or you'll be put in the back of a car and taken to the station. That's not what you need, is it?'

Rachel led the way to the tills, Ashley trying to placate the toddler, mid-tantrum, and carry a massive bag of extra-value pasta.

Outside the store, the darkness was receding, but a grey haze of rain clouds still cast a shadow over the early morning. Rachel passed Ashley her other plastic bag, which she hung over the buggy handles.

'Thanks,' she said, moving her mouth upwards in a tight smile that didn't reach her eyes. 'I won't do it again.'

'No bother. And ring Lynne – she's been there; she's got some good contacts.'

She took her own single box of Choco Pillows and watched Ashley for a moment, manoeuvring the buggy through the car park, whilst holding the toddler back from running into the road.

It was nearly half seven now, just enough time make it before Jess and Jake left for school. She made a mental note to give Lynne a ring herself and get some information for the hygiene bank put up where people like Ashley might see it. This was both the problem and the privilege of living locally to the area she worked in; she was one of them, but removed. She could see the gaps that people were falling down, but there just weren't enough hours in the day to fill them all or even put up warning signs.

Chapter 19

Land

The streets of Heaton were heaving as Rachel approached her house. Buses trundled through the inner-city suburb and hordes of teenagers ambled along Chillingham Road, taking up the whole pavement. She turned onto the terraced street they'd lived in since she and Scott had sold their old semi.

Relations between Jess and Scott had faltered over the past few years, coinciding with her refusal to eat capitalist, factory-farmed meat products. Scott seemed to see this form of dietary self-expression as a personal attack on his working-class Geordie roots, and passive-aggressive memes had become their only, occasional, form of communication. He and Jake had an easier dynamic, focused around Newcastle United. Rachel wasn't sure how much they actually talked, other than player stats and transfer speculation, but it was better than nothing.

She ignored an ominous crunch as she wrestled the car against the kerb and briefly manifested the sort of quality time she could conceivably hope for in the next ten minutes. Her toes were pinching after twenty-three hours in pointy-toed heels and she was dying to ditch the damp tights. Key turning in the lock, she was immediately hit by a wave of angst as she stepped into the hallway.

'Mam, today's the last day for filling in the Germany form. Why don't you check your emails?'

Rachel scanned the room, taking in her daughter's peroxide bob, the dishes piled in the sink, a random bike propped up against the wall and her son, sitting on the sofa in his pants, headphones glued to his ears and GTA burning his eyes from the Xbox. Please say he hadn't been on that all night.

'We hadn't decided – it's, like, £800 for three days,' she said to Jess, whilst shedding her coat, heels and bag. 'Why would you voluntarily sit on a coach for twelve hours anyway?'

'Everyone's going,' came the wailing. 'It's a counterculture hub. And Berlin's LGBTQ club scene's, like, really important.'

'Wise up – you're not going clubbing on a school trip. And why the sudden interest in the LGBT community?'

Jess's face twisted in disgust. 'Er, I'm an ally.'

'You can be whatever you want, but I'm not paying the best part of a grand for it.'

'Gemma and Lex are going! I never get to do anything.'

'Right, OK, noted.' Rachel sighed, holding out the box of cereal and shaking it. 'Look what I picked up on the way home – remember how you loved this stuff …'

Jess regarded her blankly.

'Choco Pillows! Blast from the past!'

'For God's sake,' Jess said, rolling her eyes. 'It's totally full of sugar and Tesco are really bad for using palm oil – you don't listen to anything I say. We're only meant to be shopping in Morrisons now.'

'Jake?' she said, turning to her five-foot-ten behemoth. 'Quick bowl of this before you get your uniform on?'

'Nah, Mam,' he said without removing his headphones.

'What d'you mean, "Nah, Mam"? It's almost eight and you're not even dressed.'

'No one cares if I'm late. We're on flexi.'

'You're what?' He didn't answer, so she looked to Jess in confusion.

'Not my class.' Jess shrugged, pushing past with disdain and picking up her iPhone. 'He's in Set X; they're just happy if they turn up at all.'

'What's Set X?' Rachel said, infuriated now by Jake's glazed expression. 'Mr Powell didn't say anything about a new class.'

'Just leave it,' he said. 'Doesn't matter.'

'Bye then,' she said to Jess's back, stomping across the wood floor in her DMs. 'Nice chatting to you.'

The slam of the door signalled her exit. Standing in silence amongst the mess and still-flickering screen, Rachel wondered why she actually bothered.

'I'll drop you if you get dressed now, but I need to get showered 'cos I'm back in work soon.'

''K,' Jake said, unmoving.

'Jake!' She grabbed the headphones. 'Get up the stairs.'

'This is bullshit. I'm going to stay at Dad's.'

'Brilliant. Let's see how long that lasts.'

'You're never here anyway,' he said, slouching out of the room.

'It's called a job! We're not all on bloody flexi—'

His voice echoed, loud and clear, from above, 'Stop pretending you give a shit.'

She surveyed the scene around her, screen still turned on and headphones blaring in the Jake-shaped dent in the sofa. She perched on its green velvet arm and ripped open the box of cereal. Digging her hand into the bag, she munched quietly and reflected that manifesting was a total pile of shite.

Driving back to the station an hour later, she reasoned that, as she was already feeling emotionally battered, she might as well make use of this dead time and give her parents a call. Steeling herself for the inevitable blend of guilt and irritation, Rachel tapped their landline with a heavy finger.

'Hi, Mum.'

'It's Rachel,' came a muffled whisper, presumably covering the receiver and relaying the news from one end of the sofa to the other. 'We've been wondering if you'd gone into hibernation. I'll pop you on speaker.'

'OK,' Rachel said. 'Nope, just flat out on this job.'

'They work you too hard up there, love.' Her dad's voice was distant, but still audible. He sounded breathy.

'How you feeling? Any update from the consultant?'

'Discharged with the mask,' her mum said, already off on one. 'Oxygen on tap when he needs it, but will he have it? He'd rather struggle on, against medical—' Rachel zoned out, catching only odd words.

'How are the children?' she made out, concern brimming in her mum's voice. 'What's Jess protesting about this month?'

'Hard to keep up,' said Rachel. 'Erm … sportswashing, fracking was a big one for a bit … something about a *hypocritical Tory levelling-up agenda*, whatever that is.'

'Well,' Barbara sniffed. 'I just don't know where she gets this all from. It seems to be rife, though. I was talking to Diane at the bowls club, wasn't I, Bob? And she's got a neighbour who's got a son who's transgendering himself. Apparently, they're at their wits' end.'

'Right.' She tried to let the nonsense wash over her. But she could sense her mum auditing her weaponry, choosing an angle.

'And how's Saira?' Her voice had audibly defrosted. 'I knitted a few extra things for the baby and she sent ever such a thoughtful card.'

'I'm supposed to be seeing her tonight.'

'Tell her I was asking after her. Such a good girl. Pharmacy. That's the sort of profession you could have gone into. You had the grades, didn't you.'

'Yep.'

'And *she's* done things the right way round, hasn't she? Career first, then a lovely husband and now a baby to top it all off.'

Shots fired.

Rachel stared straight ahead and visualised how much she would like to rip her phone out of the hands-free and chuck it out the window.

'When are they giving you some time off, then?' her dad interjected, seeming to register the weight of her silence. 'We haven't seen you for months.'

'It was only Christmas five minutes ago,' she said, too quickly.

'It's the end of March, Rachel. I've left you message after message – is your voicemail still not working?' Her mum always went for the guilt trip; whatever time she carved out was never enough.

She started to speak, but was interrupted by Barbara's close-range sniper fire. 'And can you open the *Daily Mail* links now? Ever so useful, those parenting tips.' Her mum had abandoned the pretence that this was a conversation, instead sensing weakness and going for the headshot. 'Were you planning on coming home *any* time this year?'

Rachel gritted her teeth. Their bungalow wasn't her home. Had it ever been? She was almost at the station and would soon be able to legitimately end this torture. 'Depends on the job. Maybe at Easter.'

'What are the school holiday dates?' Barbara's voice had taken on a steely efficiency. She'd be reaching for her diary, eager to lock in a concrete arrangement. 'Only, we're trying to book another cruise trip. Jenny at Destinations is getting back to us with options for April and May. She's ever so good – isn't she a godsend, Bob?'

'Very helpful.' She could visualise her dad nodding solemnly in agreement.

Imagine having so little to worry about that *Jenny at Destinations* booking you a five-star holiday qualified as a godsend. Who the fuck even used a travel agent these days? 'I haven't got the dates to hand – I'm driving to work, but I'll message when I've got a sec.'

'You could come!' Her mum sounded like she'd just split the atom. 'All of you. Our treat! We could get Jenny on the case – an HLC cruise really is the *ultimate* in terms of relaxation. A real personal touch. It'd do the three of you the world of good.'

'I'll think about it. Got to go.'

She killed the call and turned the radio up, drowning out intrusive thoughts of the utter horror of a family holiday with her parents and children. A cold day in hell was the only viable departure date she'd consider.

Chapter 20

Sea

Saturday 22nd April

Thoughts of Tyler's prostrate body, secreted in the ship's freezer, were hard to shake as they docked in Vigo the next morning.

Surely it wasn't standard practice, cruise ship or no cruise ship, for a body to be held in transit for seven days. She could just about understand the reluctance to announce to the legions of fans on board that their idol was no more, but surely the man deserved a dignified onwards journey to the big ballroom in the sky.

She still felt a coursing pull. The dirty coke. The thorough clean-up. The discarded pen. Something didn't add up.

His whole dynamic with Danielle had been odd and he just didn't seem the type to have been using to that level. His complaints about his employment also seemed to echo differently now in her mind. What was it he'd said about trouble behind the scenes? She racked her brain for more than a vague recollection of his words in her ear up on the stage. Something about wanting to fill her in, but was that the prelude to a disclosure or just a come-on?

Their first glimpse of Vigo, as they queued to disembark

the ship, was somewhat underwhelming. A shitload of noisy activity: crates being loaded onto forklift trucks and port staff standing around observing the never-ending line of passengers making their way like animals two by two off the ark. At least it was sunny.

Through the early morning haze hanging over the dock, she could make out a rugged green panorama in the distance with stone buildings nestled high into the white rocks. After consulting the trusty paper schedule, they had arranged to meet Robert and Barbara at ten thirty in the city centre.

As they swiped their key cards through the security kiosk, Rachel considered the logistics of tracking the *Synergy*'s four-thousand-odd passengers. They had been informed via the Tannoy over breakfast that it was essential to log in and out of the ship in order for the manifest to scrupulously record the correct details of those on board at all times.

She watched the comings and goings with interest as they waited in the gangway crush. Obviously, there wouldn't be a flashing sign with 'Dead Body' being wheeled off the ship on a stretcher, but, since her dismissal from the proceedings on the bridge, she was intrigued to know exactly what had been decided regarding Tyler's official registration of death. As far as she could make out, the crates and containers were all transporting supplies onto the *Synergy* rather than off.

It seemed absurd that the passengers could have made a big enough dent in the ship's cargo to necessitate a restock after only two days, but, as the waiters made a big show of HLC's commitment to local produce, she supposed regular fresh supplies were needed.

She had been checking her phone obsessively all morning for replies from Saira or Lennon, but so far, nothing. A proper conversation with him about the Gallagher hearing next week couldn't be avoided much longer, but – as they followed the line of passengers towards Galician dry land – she resolved to give herself a rest from policing, whether home or away. At least for the time being.

She had the appointment with Dr Larson at five forty-five. If that interview gleaned any leads, she could always clock back on to Tyler's case this evening. Right now, she needed to be present. Today's excursion was all about #makingmagicalmemories, whatever that meant.

She peered over Jess's shoulder at the map of Vigo and motioned for Jake to take his AirPods out.

'Give your eardrums a rest for today, eh?'

He reluctantly put them back in their case and glared at his sister. 'Tell her to wind her neck in, then.'

Jess wasn't listening. She seemed to be counting, mouth moving wordlessly as she scanned the disembarking passengers. Rachel and Jake looked at each other and he shrugged.

'Right, let's go. Which way, Jess?' said Rachel, relishing these first steps onto Spanish solid ground.

'Sixty-four people there, all carrying plastic bottles, and that's only a sample in, what? Fifteen minutes? Extrapolate that across the whole passenger capacity. It's disgusting!'

'Yeah, really bad,' Rachel said, taking hold of the map.

'Not just bad, it's a serious issue. A ship this size has a responsibility to move away from single-use plastic. I mean, come on, it's 2023!'

'We should probably call Greta Thunberg,' said Jake, with mock urgency. 'It's the end of the world.' He rolled his eyes. 'Mam, I'm putting them back in. She's gone mental again.'

'You're the mental one, you div,' said Jess. 'Gawping like a lemon while the ice caps melt around you.'

'Let's talk to someone about it when we get back, yeah?' Rachel said, hoping the day of sun, sea and sand might distract her in the meantime.

An army of passengers from the numerous other ships docked alongside their own in the Muelle de Transatlanticos were making a steady advance on the city, so they put the map away and followed the flow of ageing invaders.

Vigo old town was full of character, with narrow lanes and steps connecting the hidden streets. Intricately carved dark wooden doors were a welcome contrast to the faux-splendour of the ship, with the city's fortress, El Castro, looming over them, high on the hill.

They met Robert and Barbara at an upmarket café, with outside tables overlooking Vigo's famous statue, Puerto del Sol. It was a strangely beautiful sight – half-man, half-fish – positioned high above street level on a stone plinth. Barbara was eager to act as tour guide, having already taken full advantage of the pamphlets available at the Tourist Information Office.

'Fluid amalgamation of man and sea,' she read, nodding knowledgably, 'representing the city's maritime heritage and respect for sea life.'

'Overfishing to the point of extinction, you mean,' mumbled Jess.

'Looks cool though, right?' Rachel wondered if she was going to have to keep up this cheerful referee role for the full day; being on constant mediation duty was already wearing thin.

'Above all, Vigo is renowned for its oysters,' continued Barbara, undeterred. 'Its famous open-air dining experience, Calle de las Ostras, or *Oyster Alley*, is a must for any visitor.'

'Ugh – no way,' said Jake.

'Well, there's the *Synergy* Oyster Experience this evening,' Barbara said. 'Veronica was telling us all about it. Came round all the tables this morning at breakfast. So attentive. It sounds quite the spectacle. How many oysters did she say they were loading on board—'

'Isn't that the dancer, Mam?' interrupted Jess, pointing to a couple inside the café, perched on high stools, sipping from champagne flutes. 'Danielle?'

'Don't point, Jessica!' tutted Barbara. 'Height of rudeness.'

'Danielle, as in, the fit one Mam spewed on?' said Jake, straining to see.

'Everyone – sit down and stop making a show of yourselves,' said Rachel. It couldn't be Danielle, surely, living it up less than twenty-four hours after her professional partner had been found dead. But it was. Even without a thigh-high split and diamantes, her hard features and tango-tan were unmistakable.

'Well,' said Barbara, elbowing Robert and making a discreet pointing motion of her own. 'You think you know a person.'

'Since when did *you* know her?' Jess asked, one eyebrow raised.

'Not personally, of course. But unofficially. Through the media. We'd read up on them, hadn't we, Bob, since we first saw them on the *Voyager*.'

'Think your gran had a bit of a crush on old Tyler.' He did a little wobbling motion in his chair, which made Jess snort her drink out through her nose. 'Always partial to a bit of a hip jiggle.'

This was too much information, on many levels.

Shuddering at her mother's attraction to the same person she had been embarrassingly up close and personal with, Rachel forced her attention back on the pair ensconced inside. Danielle was with an older, Spanish-looking man, black hair pushed back in an oily-looking quiff. His hand was dangling proprietarily over the back of her chair, and they were deep in conversation, heads close together and thankfully unaware of being spied on by the motley crew outside on the pavement.

'And she's drinking!' Barbara added, aghast. 'After all that talk of organics. It's not even midday, Bob.'

'She's had bad news, love. Let's not judge the poor girl.'

'Tyler Tweedy not even cold in his grave,' Barbara said, pursing her lips.

Cold in the ship's freezer, thought Rachel. Rather than join in the frenzied speculation, she remained quiet, eyes fixed on Danielle. Subtly, she snapped a photo, thinking she'd examine it later and see if she could identify the man with his hand so far up the dancer's thigh she could probably charge a fee per view.

Maintaining her covert surveillance, she zoned in and out of the family conversation: Jess describing the single-use plastic outrage to her grandad and Jake giving mostly monosyllabic replies to Barbara's inane questions. After finishing their drinks and examining the map, a plan was made to decamp to the beach.

The view from the Playa Samil promenade out into the Atlantic was worth the taxi ride. Fine white sand, cobalt water – uninterrupted, but for the peaks of several small islands dotted in the distance.

Rachel noted her dad's insistent offer to take Jess and Jake for a stroll while she and her mum found some sunbeds. By the meaningful glances exchanged, she could tell this was a preformulated strategy. Reconciliation incoming.

The kids followed their grandad, surprisingly enthusiastic at the prospect of finding some snorkelling gear. Left alone for the first time since Thursday night's blow-out, Rachel and Barbara appraised each other awkwardly.

They wandered, unspeaking, towards the shore, zigzagging through the rows of sunloungers and parasols. After finding some free beds and paying the extortionate charge to a man with a bumbag, they sat down.

'This is nice,' said Rachel, breaking the silence.

'Very well maintained.'

'Do you think Dad'll be OK with the walk?'

'He'll manage.'

'It's good for the kids. Being away, like this.'

'And you?' Barbara's voice was stilted. 'Are you finding it a break – from work?'

Her mum hardly ever acknowledged her job. The rare times it was mentioned, there was always an undertone of disapproval.

'In a way,' she said, carefully. 'Operation I've been leading was

… intense. And then, you know, I messed it up, and, well …'
She trailed off.

'I'm sure there was more to it. You're being hard on yourself.'

Tears unexpectedly pricked the backs of her eyes. Not used to this show of support, she felt unsure how to respond, eventually just landing on: 'Thanks.'

'Quite something, having a detective inspector in the family. Not an easy position by all accounts.'

'It's not,' she said, 'it's hard. And frustrating. You feel like you're not getting anywhere most of the time. Not making a difference.'

'You will be. More than you know.'

They sat, companionably for a minute or so, taking in the view of happy toddlers splashing in the waves.

'I really am sorry, Mum. For what I said – the other night.'

'You meant it, though.' Barbara's eyes were fixed firmly on the water.

Rachel took a deep breath. 'Bits of it. I can't blame it all on the drink. But most of it's my own issues, not you.' She continued, shakily, 'I'm still dealing with it all, you know, in my head. That probably sounds stupid. You never hid it – either of you. But we've never really talked about it – it's all just … blank, before I was three. There's part of me missing. It still feels – I don't know – a lot.'

Barbara nodded slowly, but said nothing, seeming to know she hadn't finished. That there was more.

'There's stuff I need to know … about what happened before I came to you.' It was so hard to get these words out. 'It's … affecting everything – and someone said something … on the job. I've … started, sort of … making enquiries, but I feel—' she sniffed '—you know … to you and Dad. You're the ones who brought me up. The ones who love me. Not—' Her voice cracked and she wiped her nose with the back of her hand, not wanting to say it aloud.

Barbara turned her head and Rachel could see her blue eyes

were also teetering with feeling, a cascade held back with repeated blinks.

'You might not like what you find. We've always been worried about you getting hurt. That's all.' She reached out a soft hand, met Rachel's and held on. 'You might be miles away, and grown up, with a career and teenagers of your own, but we're always going to see you as that little scrap we were handed. You'd already been through the ringer, and we wanted to give you everything. Make it all OK.' She squeezed her knuckles. 'We still do.'

'I know.'

She thought of the dark spots in her mind, the gaps in her history. If Children's Services were anything like the police records department, the process could take months. If they even had anything to give her. There could be more, that her parents knew. More they'd held back?

She let go of Barbara's hand and dug her fingers into the sand, trying to scoop out a handful. 'I know you've said the paperwork, pre-adoption, was sketchy. But they must have given you some details … *something* to go on?'

Barbara put her sunglasses on, eyes no longer visible. Her voice was steadier now, gentle and reassuring: 'I wish I could give you that. But I can't. Newcastle upon Tyne and your date of birth – that's all I know. You'd been moved from pillar to post by the time you came to us.'

They both watched as the sand escaped from Rachel's closed fist, tiny grains pouring from the cracks between her fingers until nothing remained.

'Maybe the key,' her mum continued, slowly, 'is to focus on who you are now – today – not who you were?'

'I don't know that either, though. That's the problem—'

The arrival of Robert, Jake and Jess, loaded down with flippers, masks and ice-creams, pressed pause on the conversation, but the words continued to wash over her. Like lying in a bath, water just at the right temperature, her mum's reassuring hand and acceptance had started to ease the tension she carried continuously in her chest.

It was a blistering tension. An icy chill, with half-formed suspicions that lurked in the shadows at all times, day and night.

Those had been tentative steps they'd made towards understanding each other, though, in the warmth of the midday Spanish sun. After everything that had happened, whatever lay buried, she needed to know.

The world seemed brighter. It was a race against time to stem the flow of white goop melting in the heat and making her cone go soggy, but she could handle it. The haze had lifted, and at this moment, all the darkness was bathed in sunlight.

Chapter 21

Sea

They were greeted with pleasantries from every crew member on their return. Even Andre, the sullen Ukrainian security guard from yesterday, nodded at Rachel as she made her way through the checkpoint and took her card after he'd swiped it.

Everyone was sun-kissed and relaxed from their afternoon at the beach, Barbara not having drawn breath on their return taxi ride with anticipation for the oyster night. The constant prattle of information made Rachel feel pleasantly drowsy, like being lulled to sleep on a car journey by the reassuring hum of the engine.

While the others headed back to the cabins to freshen up, Rachel readjusted to the syrupy on-board air and made her way to the medical centre on Deck Four, mentally cataloguing her lines of enquiry. She had heard from both Lennon and Saira during the afternoon and was eager to press the doctor on the official cause of death, and any context that might shed light on Tyler's state of mind.

Dr Larson's waiting room was about a thousand times nicer than her own Newcastle GP practice, décor all on-brand for the HLC juggernaut. Framed prints of tanned passengers gave the impression that any ailment could be cured with a dose of sea air or a gentle jog around the running track. She was the only patient, and the receptionist demonstrated an exemplary level of concern at her waffle about the scar on her hand needing to be re-dressed.

This was nothing less than she'd come to expect from the crew. Ferrari-level service to the point of obsequiousness, she'd already wondered at points if they were taking the piss.

'Dr Larson will see you now,' the receptionist said, ushering her through.

The doctor's office was a glorified cupboard, but furnished to clinical perfection.

'We met yesterday, I think?' Larson looked at her intently as they both sat down. 'Not a good circumstance for your vacation.'

'No,' said Rachel. 'I was very sorry to find him. He was a friend of yours?'

Larson shrugged. 'Tyler and I had known for some years. Always a big personality in the crew.'

'Can I ask what's been decided, going forward – has his body been released after your examination?'

'I'm afraid I am not able to give these details.' She looked confused. 'You have booked a medical appointment for yourself, at this time?'

A pause. 'Yes.'

'So how can I help you, please?'

There was another loaded silence for a few beats.

'Look, to be entirely honest, that wasn't why I made the appointment.'

The doctor blinked. 'I see.'

'I'm a detective, off the ship, I mean. That's what I do. And I just don't feel right about what I found. I was hoping you could help me.' She took her warrant card out of her bag and laid it softly on the desk between them.

Larson didn't look surprised at this explanation. 'Captain

Miller did mention something about your background.' She drew the card towards her and examined the photo and text.

'I know you were on good terms with Tyler. I understand you have to follow HLC policy, but is there anything about what you saw, that – worried you?'

Larson met her eyes and Rachel felt a chink of connection that, in her experience, gave hope of a witness opening up. If she was going to ask her to leave, it probably would have happened it by now.

'Off the record, of course,' Rachel added. 'I just want to understand a little more about Tyler. I care about what happened to him and I think you do too.' She swallowed her mortification. 'I was there last night, behind his door, when you were speaking to him. I heard what you said about the antibiotics. I won't be passing anything you say on to Miller.'

'You heard this?' Larson said, amused. 'Well, this was Tyler. He was full of life, always with the women. He made people feel something, you know?'

'Yes, I understand.'

'More recently, he seemed troubled. He was trying to arrange a transfer to another ship. I know he wanted to leave the *Synergy*.'

'But his partnership with Danielle. That made it difficult to leave?'

'For sure.'

'But, *troubled* – would he have been using drugs regularly on board? It looked like an opioid overdose, but does that fit with what you saw of him?'

'He liked to party.' Larson shrugged. 'For some it is a normal part of life at sea. We are miles from home, working hours are long, and the lifestyle is fast-paced. But no, not opioids. Not Tyler.'

'Will his body be examined, here in Vigo? He'll need a post-mortem, surely, to establish cause of death?'

'I do not know,' Larson said. 'His body remains in the mortuary on board.' Her eyes darted around the room. 'I cannot say more.'

'But that can't be normal practice?' Rachel pressed, not wanting to lose the fragile connection. 'What's happened with other deaths at sea?'

'This is my first experience of a crew member losing their life,' she said, voice lowered. 'When a passenger passes, it will depend on our itinerary. Sometimes it has happened, yes, on our Caribbean sailings, where the islands are small and not equipped, we can keep a body on board for a number of days.'

'And Captain Miller – he has the authority to make the decision?'

'Of course. Whilst at sea, we operate according to maritime law. If we are twelve miles or more from land, we are ruled by the legal system of our flagged nation. So, at the time that Tyler – in this circumstance – it is Panama law which applies.' She shrugged. 'They are the police.'

Rachel stared. Had she misheard? 'Panama?'

'Clearly it is not standard to contact Panama if we need to deal with minor incidents. We rely on the expertise of Captain Miller, and our own security staff.'

'Wow, OK,' said Rachel, mind blown at the concept of four thousand passengers, plus crew, being policed by a couple of ex-naval officers and a force five thousand miles away in Central America.

'I have said too much,' Larson said, looking at her watch. 'And I have other appointments.'

'Can I just ask one more question? I really am grateful for your help.'

She sighed. 'I hope I have been able to reassure you. I was very saddened to see Tyler. He was, how do you say? One of a kind. Many people here will miss him.'

'Including Danielle?'

'I'm sure Danielle will be reacting in her own way.' Larson's soft features darkened and Rachel got the distinct impression that she was not well regarded by the doctor.

'I saw her today, in Vigo.'

'Yes?'

'Let's just say she wasn't wearing black and weeping.'

'Nor would I expect this. Danielle is Danielle.'

'So, the last thing I wanted to ask, and then I promise I'll leave you in peace – you're equipped to prescribe medication, I assume?'

'Of course.' Larson nodded. 'We have many passengers with chronic conditions and there can be accidents which require treatment.'

'Where would that be stored?'

'There is a small pharmacy next to the medical centre reception. Accessed only by key card, of course.'

'And who would have access? Do the crew key cards open every door on the ship?'

Larson shook her head. 'Key cards have varying levels of privilege, and access to restricted areas, such as the pharmaceutical store, would only be myself and the most senior crew members.'

'OK. So you, plus the captain, cruise director – those would be the only people who could get into that room?'

'And Simon Van der Wyk, our chief security officer.'

'Would it be possible to see the pharmacy? Then I promise I'll go back to just being on holiday.' She gave the doctor a steady smile and reached for her warrant card, replacing it in her bag.

'Very quickly,' Larson agreed, 'but then I must return to my work.'

The receptionist watched, a frown disrupting her pleasant expression, as Larson and Rachel crossed the waiting area. Back in the corridor, the doctor looked around cautiously, glancing up towards a CCTV camera, before touching her card to an unmarked door that beeped and opened. She turned on the light to reveal floor-to-ceiling shelving on three sides with an array of white boxes, neatly labelled.

'What do you carry in terms of opioid pain relief?' Rachel asked, looking around.

'Not so much,' said Larson. 'Only this small area on the right.' She knelt down and traced her finger along the row nearest the floor. 'HLC stocks American branded products – a small supply of oxycontin for passengers with terminal conditions.'

Her finger stopped, and she looked up, confused. 'But, I don't— It is not here.'

Rachel's internal barometer in assessing the circumstances of Tyler's death had fluctuated since she had found his body, just over twenty-four hours ago. She had wondered whether she was overreacting, treating a grown man's misadventure with undue suspicion. Several comments the doctor had made, however, had done nothing to silence the siren ringing in her ears. And from the look on Larson's face, this was a situation she was equally concerned by.

The doctor stood abruptly. 'I will need to report this to Captain Miller immediately.'

They parted at Deck Five, Rachel watching Larson disappear into the crowd, straw-coloured plait bouncing as she hurried away.

Her head was battered. She was throbbing with adrenaline, itching to launch into action. But what to do? It was almost seven o'clock and, from the sheer volume of passengers around her, they must be at full capacity, soon to depart Vigo.

Larson had insisted on taking her findings from the pharmaceutical store to Miller alone, adamant that further evidence of Rachel's involvement would adversely affect the situation.

'Captain Miller protects the HLC brand at all costs,' she'd said. 'He will not allow you to know of any discrepancy. And it will put my job at risk if he knows I have spoken to you.'

Judging by last night, the Wi-Fi would crash once they reached open water, so she positioned herself in the centre of the crowded atrium on the edge of a marble fountain and called Lennon. Here she had a vantage point of crew and passengers in every direction. His phone went straight to voicemail, so she left him a hushed account of the day's events.

'*Call me when you can. I've interviewed the doctor and there's loads that just doesn't sit right. OD victim was a casual user, but nothing that would've made him smack out. And a load of oxy pills've gone walkabout from the medical centre. Only senior crew get access, but anyone could have used their card.*

'*Can I have an update on Gallagher too? Where's Maz with the DDTRO request? Sounds like you're back in business now you've got the Scousers. Think we're leaving this port approx. 20.00 so might keep cutting out after that. Oh, and I need a background check. First name, Danielle. Surname, Paige. Papa-Alpha-India-Golf-Echo. Cheers, Lenn.*'

She could hear trouble before she got halfway down her corridor: a frenzied screech accompanied by what sounded like missiles hitting the walls.

'What the hell's going on?'

The scene before her as she stood, gobsmacked, in the doorway to her cabin, was bizarre. Jess, still caterwauling, was whacking Jake, surrounded by what must have been twenty water bottles, all empty and twisted out of shape, discarded on the carpet.

'Mam! He's deliberately provoking me. Tell him!'

'What?' said Jake. 'I was thirsty.'

'Get fucked!' Jess screamed. 'You're just tipping all the water out and stamping on them.'

'Jess! People can hear you.' Rachel quickly shut the door.

'Why would I do that, you freak?' said Jake.

'Why wouldn't you? You obviously enjoy tormenting me for some sociopathic reason.'

'Right. Both of you.' Rachel raised her voice above their clamour. 'Jesus. Are you trying to finish me off?'

'He's an arsehole, Mam—'

'Language!' She pointed her finger as a redundant warning, ignored by both of them, and bent down to start picking up the crushed bottles.

'Whatever,' continued Jess. 'He's so arrogant. Doesn't even care that the planet's on the brink of collapse! Doesn't need qualifications. Just happy arsing around and failing all his mocks.'

'I'm arrogant? That's a joke. You think just 'cos you're the *oldest* by like seventeen minutes you know it all. And we haven't even done our mocks, you absolute melt.'

'Er – revision? You can't just turn up and get your predicted grade. Or stand around while millions of tons of plastic get put in landfill.'

He sat down heavily on Jess's pillow and farted. 'Bothered.'

'Oh right,' Jess drawled. 'You're going to make millions with your hacking skills, aren't you?' She stopped, and looked at Rachel, smirking. 'Sorry, was I not meant to mention that?'

'What?' Rachel said, standing up, arms full of plastic debris.

'She's just shit-stirring,' Jake said, jumping up to get Jess in a headlock. 'Aren't you?'

'No,' came her muffled response, arms flailing.

'Get off your sister!' Rachel shouted, properly losing it now. 'Both of you, what the fuck is going on?'

'Language,' both said flatly in unison, reluctantly separating, but still throwing murderous looks in the other's direction.

'Sit down, both of you. And don't say anything 'til I ask you a direct question.'

With a pointed lack of urgency, they both sat, facing her, from separate beds.

'Right.' She looked at Jake, trying to breathe normally. 'Where did you get all these bottles?'

He twisted his face and stared at his intertwined hands. 'Oksana. Room service.'

'Twenty of them? And you're kicking them round, because …?'

'She's doing my head in with this plastic shit,' he mumbled. 'Wanted to piss her off.'

'Well, mission accomplished. Great. What a totally meaningless point you've made.'

He lifted his eyes a fraction to the bottles still littering the floor. 'Sorry,' he said eventually. 'I'll take it all to the recycling.'

'And Jess. You're not in charge of him, OK? You've got different strengths – exams aren't the be-all and end-all. And don't make stuff up to get him in trouble. That's really childish. Of course he's not going to be hacking into anything, now or in the future.'

Jess was silent, but Rachel could tell from her foot, which was tapping furiously, that she was fighting the urge to say more.

'Fine,' she said at last, looking Jake square in the eyes. 'Sorry I lied.'

From the looks on their faces, there was something lingering that she hadn't got to the bottom of. The resemblance between them here was uncanny, despite their very different features. Two sets of furrowed brows and narrowed eyes. It wasn't an expression she recognised from the mirror, or even from Scott, but it had a familiarity that hovered in the back of her consciousness. Despite their antagonism, it must be reassuring to have someone else around with the same DNA – a sibling to share the load.

Rachel sighed deeply. 'Come on, let's get this place shipshape and make a move. There's about a million oysters out there for your gran to force-feed you, whether you like it or not.'

Chapter 22

Sea

The much-hyped *Synergy of the Seas* Oyster Night™ was exactly the mix of ostentatious glamour and mass-catering efficiency that Rachel had come to expect from High Life Cruises.

There was a complicated ticketing system, accessible on the app, through which they'd had to book a time slot to meander down Deck Seven's central thoroughfare. It had been transformed during their day's absence into an extravagant imitation of Vigo's Calle de las Ostras, with enormous hoardings, depicting the city's stone buildings and carved doorways, now masking the internal walls.

The vessel's formidable store of fairy lights had presumably been dusted off from the Christmas season. Strung across the ceiling, they cast a soft romantic light that blurred the wrinkles and liver spots of the majority of passengers and gave everyone a healthy glow. The wonderment of lighting and décor was heightened further by the sound of flamenco guitarists in the bandstand.

It was an exceptional display, but – yet again – Rachel was struck by how fake it all was. She was pissing herself off by this point in her cynicism though, so kept a lid on her critique. Why couldn't she just accept life at face value rather than picking at the cracks until they split and revealed the ugliness within? This was her curse, she supposed. The curse of the detective. Once you'd seen the hard drive of a respectable-looking father's seized PC, you were never the same again.

Veronica Chase was doing her rounds, dolled up to the nines. She glided through the space, dropping into group conversations, shaking hands and motioning to the oyster waiters to keep their service moving. Rachel was paused at a comparatively quiet spot within the menagerie when she felt a cool hand touch her arm and the hushed tone of the woman herself in her ear: 'Could I have a word?'

She stepped away from her family, still mesmerised by the pop-up transformation.

'Yes?' she said, half an eye on Jake who was gagging, holding a small plate with two open white shells sitting proudly in the centre. Rachel and Veronica were standing to the side of the walkway now, out of the glow of the twinkling lights and partially obscured by an ice sculpture.

'I understand you've had a distressing experience whilst on board.' Veronica's expression was solemn. 'In my role as cruise director, I wanted to reassure you that if you have any further concerns, you are, of course, free to raise them with me.'

'Right,' Rachel said, after a slight pause. 'No bother.'

'And, if there have been any … *oversights* … in your dealings with the crew, I would urge you to report these in order for me to gather all the information and reach a positive resolution.'

'I see.' Rachel was curious now at her lack of subtlety in digging for information. 'I'll bear that in mind.'

'*Whoever* you've spoken to,' Veronica reiterated. 'Please don't assume that anyone is exempt, regardless of position. I'm keen to build up a full picture of the recent tragic event. After all, your experience on board reflects on all of us.'

There was a chill in the air and Rachel shivered, scrubbed up as she was in one of the 'dressy' outfits her mum had insisted were required.

Veronica was standing so close, she must be able to see the goose bumps on her skin. The cruise director placed a business card in her hand and stepped back into the warmth of the ambient lighting and smiling guests. 'Don't hesitate to contact me with anything at all. You have my cell number.' And with that she was gone, straight back into professional mode, working the room with all the charm of a leading lady on the red carpet.

Rachel studied the dark red card, and recalled the frigid animosity she had detected between Veronica and Miller at the muster drill. And now, here she was, seemingly encouraging her to dig him out. Her radar had been right: so much for the '*we're a happy ship*' pretence. Filing the card carefully in her bag, she returned to her family, who were entering into the spirit of the oyster experience in varying degrees of enthusiasm.

'They're actually all right,' said Jess, wrinkling her nose. 'Just a shame they look like snot.'

'Jessica!' said Barbara, exasperated.

'Well, they do. Obviously, *he's* still refusing to even try one.'

Jake gave his sister a death stare, but kept his mouth closed, perhaps protecting himself from a possible force-feeding attempt.

'Very good, they are,' said Robert. 'Come on, love, get yourself a plate before they run out.'

'They're not going to run out, Bob!' Barbara fussed. 'We're only the second time slot and you can see how many they've got on ice back there. Must be an absolute gold mine for the Vigo economy.'

Rachel accepted a plate from a nearby waiter and helped herself from the display, but had to agree with Jess that raw oysters did not look attractive. She'd only had them once before: the night she and Scott had got engaged. He was a man for whom no gesture could be classified as heartfelt unless it was a cliché straight out of *Romance for Dummies*.

She'd been knackered and consumed with the needs of their

eighteen-month-old twins. None of her 'out out' clothes had fitted her, but they'd had a babysitter organised and he'd taken her to a fancy restaurant with views over the Quayside for oysters, champagne, roses and a very unexpected down-on-one-knee climax.

Twenty-one, barely at the starting blocks of adult life, but that night had felt like the midpoint of a marathon, with her ready to collapse at the side of the road. She'd sipped the champagne, put the strange salty snot in her mouth, and said yes. The roses had been taken home, put in a vase and neglected until only the dead buds remained and the water turned stagnant.

Determined to set a good example now to Jake, she swallowed both oysters on the bounce. Eyes watering, she coughed and gave the four expectant faces around her a thumbs up.

'Faking it,' said Jake. 'No way she actually enjoyed them.'

'I did! I'm with Jess,' she spluttered. 'You've just got to block out the look of them. And the texture. And the taste.'

This time, even Barbara smiled, eyes twinkling in the soft glow.

'What did *she* want, anyway?' Jake asked, nodding towards Veronica Chase.

'Trying to get me to make a complaint about how the Tyler stuff's been handled. At least, I *think* that's what she was doing.' Rachel shrugged. 'It was all a bit shady.'

'I'm sure she was just keen to maintain standards,' Barbara said. 'That's her role, after all, ensuring the *ultimate experience* for every guest.'

'Get that from the brochure, Gran?' said Jess, grinning.

'I may have read it somewhere, yes,' Barbara conceded.

'She's a chip off the old block, that one,' said Robert, ruffling Jess's hair. 'Future detective right there.'

Rachel was proud of her daughter's razor-sharp acumen herself, and surprised that the comparison wasn't immediately batted off, but seemed to be taken as a compliment. Could this alien concept of quality time together as an extended family actually be paying off?

'I was thinking,' she said hesitantly, looking from her mum to her dad. 'How would you both feel about a small undercover assignment? Nothing serious, just a bit of observation and a little chat with someone?'

They looked at each other, waiting for concrete information. It wasn't an outright no, so she continued, 'I think we need to find out a bit about Danielle's reaction to … you know, recent events.'

'Well, I've a good mind to give the little madam what for,' said Barbara. 'She's playing a good game, mark my words.'

'You couldn't do that,' Jake said, seriously. 'Undercover means you've got to get in with them. Like, just watch and listen.'

'Exactly,' said Rachel. 'Eyes and ears only. Then report back.'

'Sounds doable. We could give it a go, Barb, couldn't we?'

'Where are you suggesting?' her mum said, cocking her head in thought. 'We can't very well just go marching into her dressing room.'

Rachel recalled her own last interaction with the dancer. 'I think I've got that bit covered. Don't go mad, but I was having a look on the app when I sorted our slot for this business—' she waved her hand around the extravaganza surrounding them '—and I – er – noticed there were a couple of tickets available for the dance workshop tomorrow. So, I … booked them.'

Expecting this confession to act like a grenade, she was relieved to see her parents smirking in what actually looked like good humour.

'Yes, Rachel,' Barbara said with a merry eye-roll. Both looking excited by their mission and its responsibilities, they launched into an in-depth discussion of the likely dance style coverage.

Rachel averted her eyes from her mother's shuffling '*one, two, cha, cha, cha*' practice steps and noticed that the twins had shifted away and were now chatting animatedly with their influencer pals, Jon and the Gorgeous Kevin. As around the pool, the men were both in outfits that were trying hard to be edgy, but, instead, giving a lot of mid-life-crisis energy.

Jon had accessorised his ginger barnet with a pink beret. This, she could have overlooked, but not the crushed-velvet shorts suit and shiny brown brogues. The Gorgeous Kevin was rocking a more traditional all-white ensemble, with a pashmina draped around his shoulders, almost-but-not-quite hiding the gaping sections where his shirt buttons were refusing to come together quietly.

She sidled over and was immediately accosted by Jon.

'These two are going on the payroll,' he said, pointing to Jess and Jake, on either side of him.

'Absolute huns,' agreed the Gorgeous Kevin. 'They've brought us up to date, at last.' His final vowel drawled for approximately five seconds longer than was standard.

'Really?'

'Bang up on the socials and that's what we've been lacking. YouTube's dead; even TikTok's peaked. We're kidding ourselves if that's where subscribers are going to be in two years' time.'

'Whisper,' said Jake, knowledgeably. 'There's others, too, we can get you going with.'

'And we've negotiated a fee,' said Jess.

Rachel was impressed. Maybe all that time spent staring at screens wasn't killing their brain cells after all.

'Have you worked on this ship before? Before the career shift, I mean?' she asked, trying to focus on the Gorgeous Kevin's face rather than his straining shirt.

'Not the *Synergy* – that's why we're test-driving this trip. But the other HLC lines, we were all over them.'

'You know the crew, then?'

'Know them?' He snorted and leaned forward to get Jon's attention. 'Asking if we know the crew!'

'Queen, we've seen everything. You wouldn't believe some of the stories we could tell,' Jon deadpanned.

'Go on,' Rachel said. 'Spill.'

'Not for innocent ears,' Jon mouthed.

'We can handle it!' said Jess.

'Hmmm. Could make it part-payment, I suppose?' the Gorgeous Kevin said, looking at Rachel. She shrugged, doubting that there was much that would shock her offspring.

'Let's just say *she* wasn't always the model professional she's painting herself as these days,' he said, nodding over at Veronica Chase.

'Really?' Rachel's radar was now buzzing at max volume. She wished she had a pen to get the details down.

The Gorgeous Kevin deferred to Jon, who mouthed one word: 'Filthbag.'

Instinctively, everyone shuffled a little further in, shielding the gossip: five sets of shoulders pressed together, heads bent inwards, relishing the drama.

'Her and Miller. Open secret. Shacked up like Lord and Lady HLC. Wild. Some of the stories, honestly, they'd make your hair fall out.'

'You said, *were*,' Rachel whispered, drilling for detail. 'Not anymore?'

'She's been replaced,' Jon said, exaggerating each syllable. 'Ditched.'

'Who for?' Jess asked, captivated.

'Still waiting for visual confirmation,' the Gorgeous Kevin looked around dramatically, and lowered his voice even further, 'but multiple sources have given us the same name. And you and I, Rachel, have been in her direct vicinity very recently …'

'Danielle? No way!' She recalled the captain's shift in tone when the dancer had been mentioned. 'What's he thinking?'

'Apparently,' Jon whispered, 'she pursued him. Rat up a drain-pipe. And he was powerless to resist. Follows her around like a puppy and she's milking him for all he's worth.'

'What about Veronica? What's her reaction?'

'Fuming,' he replied, 'but nothing she can do. Outmanoeuvred.'

'Standards are slipping all over the HLC lines,' the Gorgeous

Kevin added, shaking his head. 'I mean, the *Sin-ergy*'s always had a reputation for being naughty behind the scenes—' he turned to give Rachel a pointed look '—but crew could *always* maintain decorum on deck. Some of the Europeans they're employing these days, though – didn't I say, Jon, these locals—'

'What's all this whispering?' Barbara's voice trilled through the gap between Jess's and Jon's shoulders.

'Nothing, Gran. Just ideas for what to do in Lisbon.'

'Well done, Jessica,' she said, impressed. 'We'll need to have a proper look at the schedule, won't we, Bob; then we can make a plan.'

Their allocated time slot was drawing to an end, with groups of passengers starting to drift away and crew refreshing the food for round three. As they left the impeccably crafted pop-up experience, Rachel spotted a discreet bin behind one of the oyster stands. She glanced at the contents: imperfect specimens that hadn't made the grade, whole shells where the waiters must not have been able to prise the contents open.

Had Tyler been an imperfect specimen, a blot on the overall flawless HLC service?

Giving herself a shake, she reminded her overactive imagination that it would have been perfectly possible for the cruise company to simply not renew his contract. For God's sake, they'd have an HR department. He wouldn't have been bumped off, like some dramatic mafia hit. Glad she had kept these thoughts to herself, she followed her family away from the glamorous utopia and back to the real(er) world.

They'd only been in their cabin for a moment when there was a light tap on the door. Oksana. Rachel raised her eyebrows, confused that she'd already tracked their return. Where was it that the stewards stationed themselves whilst not cleaning cabins?

Maybe they had CCTV access. Certainly, it seemed that any time the room was unoccupied, even for a brief period, it was given an immediate once-over, waste bin emptied and toilet roll returned to its state of perfection. Rather than inducing relaxation, this hyper surveillance was making her uneasy.

'I bring this,' she said from the doorway, bowing her head slightly, 'of Captain Miller.'

Rachel said goodnight, ripping opening the embossed envelope with interest.

Inspector Harlow, it read.

I have spoken this evening with Dr Larson, who informed me of your appointment and subsequent conversation. Please be assured that we have resolved the missing items and no medication is unaccounted for.

I have now had reports from two of my crew that you have approached them whilst on duty with matters irrelevant to your position as a valued guest. I would ask you to refrain from all future contact with any crew members, other than those serving you directly on this sailing. It is essential that my staff are able to carry out their duties without interference.

I would additionally ask you to return your signed NDA document to me via your stewardess as soon as possible.

Kindest regards,

Captain R Miller RN

She screwed the letter into a ball. Absolutely no chance, on either count. She had no plans to cease her investigation or sign his paperwork unless she was made to at knifepoint.

As for the miraculous rediscovery of the hardcore opioids, which could so easily be cut into a wrap of coke, turning it into an instant death sentence, she had one word for his story: dodgy.

Her experience in CID had taught her many things. The most important one being: never underestimate a hunch. If something looked a bit too shiny, it was probably because it was actually a steaming pile of bullshit, sprinkled with glitter.

Chapter 23

Land

Friday 31st March

'Your hunch was right,' Bradshaw said, pulling his grey Corsa next to her Audi at the car park barrier. She could see Coates craning forwards and nodded in acknowledgement. 'ID on the Dalton Crescent tenant. Seventeen-year-old lass. Care leaver. Still officially looked after so we're calling on the foster; see if she knows what's happening in the flat.'

'Good shout,' Rachel said. 'Keep me posted.' Another car was waiting behind so she left them to it, grateful for Bradshaw's initiative, but not sure if her heart could take another bleak story of a young person dragging themselves through their childhood today.

After showing her face in the office and registering the weight of admin on her desk, she hurried to the remote monitoring suite. Lennon and Rossy had already started and she could tell from the body language it wasn't going well. Rossy was leaning forward, appealing to the slumped figure of McKenzie, staring blankly at the metal table between them.

Dean, the AA, had an arm stretched across the back of

McKenzie's chair. He could have been intimidating. Scruffy hair in a ponytail. Heavily built. Full sleeve of tattoos up both arms. But from this real-time view on the screen, he reminded Rachel of a shaggy Newfoundland, curled around one of its puppies, guarding it from harm.

'We can't help you, Kenzie, if you're not going to give us anything.' Rossy's voice was weary. 'Those wraps didn't get there by themselves. Someone's exploiting you and they don't deserve your silence.'

'How much you get?' Lennon said. 'Fifty quid and a packet of Haribo?'

McKenzie's eyes snapped up to meet Lennon's. 'Wouldn't dare,' he muttered.

'What, more? You on the big bucks, sonny?'

Lennon was clearly trying to get a reaction. Whether McKenzie realised this or not, Rachel could feel the emotional intensity rising in the room. They'd planned this last night. With emotion, came results. She made a mental note to give him some credit, then swiftly reconsidered. They functioned best, professionally, on a put-down-only level.

'Earnin' more than yous.' McKenzie surveyed the two officers with contempt.

Dean put a hand on his shoulder. 'Remember what we talked about, Kenzie. Try and answer their questions. They're on your side.'

He laughed. A hollow, joyless sound. 'They can aks, but I ain't snitchin'.' He crossed his arms defiantly: two bony limbs intertwined. His scuffed elbows looked raw, protruding from the sleeves of his oversized T-shirt. Had they held him down – she shuddered – as they'd plugged his rectum with a bulging condom?

'You've got a little brother and sister at home, haven't you?' said Rossy. 'What's their names again?'

The hatred on the kid's face was palpable. 'The fuck's it got to do with yous?'

Rossy held her hands up. 'Nothing to do with us, Kenzie.' She glanced at the file in front of her. 'Aleesha and Rio. Just wondering how you'd feel if this was them. These people you're working for, don't think they won't be lining them up in a few years.'

'Younger the better, eh?' Lennon added. 'Less chance of getting picked up by us.'

Again, Rossy checked the notes they'd painstakingly compiled last night. 'Your Rio's eight, isn't he? This'll be him soon enough.'

McKenzie's already pale face drained further and he kicked out at the table leg.

'We can put them away, Kenzie,' Lennon pressed. 'Keep Aleesha and Rio safe. Charges would carry significant custodial sentences. You'd all be out of this permanently.'

McKenzie turned to Dean and breathed heavily through his nose for a few seconds without speaking. Rachel could see the flimsy cotton of his T-shirt trembling as his shoulders rose and subsided. 'Not goin' into care,' he said flatly. 'We'd get split up. That's what'd happen, innit?'

Dean swallowed hard before answering. 'You'd need to speak to the social worker. But at least this way you're taking some control?'

'Control?' He let out a bark of misery. 'Fuck yous. I'm done.'

By the afternoon, the mood in the office had flatlined. McKenzie had no-commented like a card-carrying gangster and been released back into the care of his social worker. They couldn't keep him in custody beyond twenty-four hours and, travel time notwithstanding, that deadline was looming rapidly. With no CCTV, no evidence and no comment there was sweet FA point in applying for an extension.

Bailey had put a Teams call in her calendar for a strategic update on Tuesday, and she could already foresee the way the meeting with the DCI was going to go. Nothing to show for their efforts so far but the removal of a few grand's worth of coke from circulation. A drop in the ocean. She could play the *disruption to OCG activity* card, but they'd both know it was one step forward, two steps back.

Maybe if she assigned it clearly to one of the four Ps it would land better. What would it be though, *preventing* Class-A distribution? Certainly not *protecting* McKenzie from the hiding he was bound to receive. She'd had Chambers *pursuing* CCTV footfall outside Lime Street Station all day. He'd got precisely nowhere, but she could sell it to the DCI as a work in progress. That would have to do.

She pulled her phone from her puffer coat pocket, desperate for distraction. The corner was cracked, a small web of faint lines making barely perceptible progress towards the centre of the screen. She'd been meaning to take it to one of the dubious tech shops in Heaton for months, but, just like getting her fringe cut and renewing her car insurance, it had fallen off her to-do list.

Thirty-six unread WhatsApp messages. Fuck's sake.

Unlocking the screen, she scrolled through the selection of requests, info and banter she'd been ignoring for the past few hours and sent Rossy a quick good luck for the scan this afternoon. There was some work night out happening, but she swiftly muted that group. No one wanted the boss turning up to kill the mood. And, she'd already made plans with Saira.

What time tonight? Lola's poo's been this weird green for last few days – is this normal? Should I ring 111??

Rachel deleted the picture without looking at it. This was the third or fourth time they'd tried to meet up recently and she could sense her laying the groundwork for another no-show. Saira had had her first baby nearly nine months ago and seemed to have morphed from the foul-mouthed, tequila-loving uber-babe Rachel had met way back in their halls of residence to this washed-out, excrement-obsessed version of herself.

She knew she was being unfair. She wanted to get on board and embrace Saira Khan V2. But it was hard finding shared ground.

Thinking back to her own first year with the twins, had she also been full of tales of shitty nappies and vomit? Probably.

She remembered crying to Saira in their second-year house-share when she'd found out she was pregnant. Saira had run down the street to buy her four more tests after she'd got the first positive result and they'd sat huddled on the bathroom floor while the blue lines developed slowly but surely across the blank white windows.

She bashed out a quick reply:

Gross but normal I reckon. Pic of her face next time

8pm – Osborne Road? X

Hopefully there'd be a chance for a micro-nap before then. Adrenaline had pushed her through longer periods without sleep, but heading straight out on the back of this epic shift wasn't exactly ideal.

Bradshaw and Coates re-entered the office, their brisk strides a welcome contrast to the dense fog of negativity hanging over everyone else. They made straight for her and she said a silent prayer for good news.

'Your mate, Jo" Paul Gallagher.' Bradshaw's expression was grim. 'Up to his old tricks.'

Rachel's heart sank. She had no wish to be associated with the Gallagher family, even if her arrest history said otherwise. 'Oh yeah?'

'We've had a fruitful conversation with the foster carer, Lorraine Hall,' Coates butted in, eyes bulging as he consulted his notebook. Rachel and Bradshaw looked at each other.

'I managed to establish an excellent rapport with the inter-viewee from an early stage and this elicited a full and frank disclosure of information in relation to the Dalton Crescent property. The IC1 female has been given tenancy of the aforementioned flat due to a breakdown in the foster care arrangement.'

Coates sounded like an AI detective. He was either ignoring the fact that Bradshaw had a twenty-year head start on his experience or considered himself an automatic cut above with his trainee CID status. Either way, her patience with him being an arrogant little tosser had officially run out.

'Coates,' she interrupted, 'before I forget, the super asked if you could submit a few pages of your training log as an example for other officers. Run that along to his office, OK?'

He bustled away, and she was left alone with Bradshaw. 'So, Gallagher?'

'Taken over the flat, according to Lorraine, the foster. She's worried sick, keeps trying to get through to Gaby, but her mobile just rings out.'

'You thinking that's the trap house?'

'Might explain all the coming and going.'

'Jesus. How old is she again?'

'Not long seventeen. Been in care a few years, doing canny according to Lorraine, but started talking about a new boyfriend a couple of months ago. Suddenly she's got all these new clothes, perfume, jewellery, the works. Then starts going AWOL for days at a time.'

'Don't tell me. The boyfriend's Gallagher?'

Bradshaw nodded. 'Boyfriend. Shitbag. Abuser. Say what you want about Tony and Carl – that generation – but they kept to a code.' He looked personally offended by the deterioration of the family, one of the only officers on semi-respectful terms with the few originals still knocking around the East-End.

'Really?' Some of the stories she'd heard about Tony Gallagher in the Eighties made her skin crawl.

'Well, social services've dealt with this Gaby lass by rehousing her – told Lorraine she'd requested an independent flat.'

'Did they know about Jo" Paul being on the scene?'

'Said she'd warned them, but it went ahead.'

Rachel was torn between raging at the sheer incompetence of housing a vulnerable seventeen-year-old alone in the Wall, thus accelerating her grooming by scum like Gallagher or jumping for joy at this major gear change in the operation's momentum.

'I'll put in the concern referral and go back round,' Bradshaw said. 'See what's—'

'Just hang fire,' she said, putting a hand on his arm. 'This is our chance to get higher up the line.'

He frowned. 'Yeah, but the risk's off the scale. Sounds like she's being cuckooed. No one's seen her in weeks.'

'We can manage the risk. We go charging in, asking questions, he's going to know we're onto him. He'll just scarper.' She couldn't lose this opportunity to get Jo" Paul Gallagher locked up for a proper stint.

'But the kid. That's not right, leaving her in there with him.'

'I just need a few days.' She looked at him with a steady gaze, which did not reflect the rattling cacophony in her brain 'OK? Lennon can ask around, find out more. If there's anything concrete, safeguarding-wise, we'll get the warrant and move.'

He whistled through his teeth.

'I owe you on this,' she said, grabbing on to his silence as agreement. 'And taking Coates under your wing – above and beyond.'

'Someone's got to show him the ropes. Be eaten alive out there otherwise.'

She grinned, exhilarated by the swell that now promised to sweep them forwards, like the sweet spot of a breaker. 'Let's see if he comes back from the super with a few limbs missing.'

'He didn't ask for him?'

Rachel shrugged. 'Dunno. But no one talks over you like that on my watch.'

Chapter 24

Land

By eight fifteen p.m., Rachel was two gins down, foot tapping a frantic rhythm on Spy Bar's wooden floor. She'd driven straight to Jesmond from the station, doing a botch job on her hair and switching her work outfit for the emergency heels and jeans she kept in the boot.

Crossing her legs to squash the nervous energy, she tried not to picture the people she'd left drowning these past few days. McKenzie. Ashley. Gaby.

The circling sharks. Gallagher, *Jaws*-like, rising again every time you thought the water was safe. A wave of either panic or exhaustion swept over her: what a bloody mess.

Quickly, she picked up her phone, mindless scrolling the only option. Saira was apparently on her way. Rachel replied with a thumbs up and continued to swipe. Insta, Tinder – there must be something here to distract her. Jess, blunt as ever:

Staying at Lexi's

Her mum had sent a link to the High Life Cruises website with what she evidently considered to be a persuasive message:

Seven nights cruising the Med departing April 20th? Food and entertainment second to none! Tell J&J there's a

BIG act from 'Britain Has Talent'.

As if. That would be a hard no. The kids would rather die than watch terrestrial TV. She thought about replying with *Britain's Got*, but it wasn't worth it.

Two messages from Mark Matthews caught her eye:

U ok? Why u not out? Heard operation's on its arse x

Who'd he got that off? Good to know the rumour mill was as supportive as ever. Then ten minutes later:

Wanna talk about it? Or not talk

She considered his offer. At least someone from work had noticed her absence. He was relatively fit. The sex was fine. It might take her mind off things.

Before she could engage her brain, she spotted Saira.

'Sorry I'm late.' She bundled in, dropping her car key as she tried to take her wet jacket off.

'No worries. You need to catch up though – I'm two down already.'

'I can't be out long.' She put her head in her hands, muffling the rest of her words. 'This sleep regression's sending me over the edge.'

'God, you're properly in the trenches. Come here.' Rachel folded her into a hug. 'Hard bit's done, though – leave the car and get an Uber. You know you want to.'

'I can't. Yusef's freaking out – Lola's bedtime routine's gone to absolute shit. Waking every hour.'

Rachel leaned back and took her in: dark shadows, mascara on one eye only, black silky shirt buttoned up wrong. But she was here.

'Ignore me, just excited to see you.' Rachel squeezed her hand and forced a grin. 'Do bars even *do* soft drinks?'

That got a laugh. 'S'all right. I can have one,' said Saira. 'Something classy.'

At the bar, Rachel gave the barman's cocktail shaker routine a slow handclap. 'Impressive.'

His eyes skimmed over her tight top. 'What can I get you?'

'I've had a request for classy. Beyond your capabilities?'

'Very much my skill set.'

'Right, make it two.'

'I'll even bring them over. How's that?'

She walked back to the booth, knowing that he was checking out her arse. But she'd seen his footwear over the bar. Crocs: red flag.

Her phone vibrated and she saw Scott's name flash up, but quickly cancelled the call and put her phone face down on the table. Whatever was going on there could wait.

'So, what's up, other than no sleep?' She sat down across from Saira, who had sorted her buttons out and was looking more herself.

'It's just relentless. Why didn't you warn me?'

'About what bit?'

'Everything. You were practically a child when the twins were this age. How did you actually manage?'

'I honestly can't remember most of it,' Rachel said. 'Scott was decent about the nights. I packed the breastfeeding in early. Fuck that shit with two of them.'

'Yeah, maybe it's time to reclaim my tits.'

They both looked down and assessed Saira's boobs. She'd always had a good pair, but currently they were another level.

Rachel smirked. 'Ten minutes, max, before a button gives up.'

That laugh felt better. Familiar.

The barman arrived, placing their drinks with fifteen per cent too much eagerness. Keen had tipped into desperate. Plus the Crocs. Definitely ick. Rachel smiled politely and tapped the reader, then turned back to Saira.

'It does get easier. But then you're just into the next phase – food, nursery, blah, blah, blah. Before you know it, you're communicating mainly by WhatsApp and wondering where it all went wrong.'

'You've done an awesome job.'

'Don't. Got to keep the image on-brand.'

'Which is what? Kicking ass in the daytime …'

Saira had always viewed Rachel's job like she was an Avenger, decked out in Lycra, getting baddies in headlocks. What would she think of her decision to leave a vulnerable teenager with a man who was likely to be exploiting her? *Risk*, though, she reminded herself. This was about managing risk, temporarily, for the benefit of the bigger operation. She had her reasons.

'Hardly. More like data and meetings. Big calls, not enough information.' She bit her lip. 'My team think I'm a total bitch.'

'Shit.' Saira grimaced, possibly at the strength of her espresso martini. 'Sure they don't all think that. How's the fit one? Dark hair, all the tats.'

'Lennon?' They'd met a few times over the years. He'd claimed she was '*terrifying – like you, but ramped up three levels*'.

'Hot-As-Fuck Lennon.' She grinned. 'Still pretending you don't fancy the pants off him?'

'Gross. He's like my brother.' Rachel shifted slightly in her seat, guilty heat prickling. She'd never told Saira the truth. That night. The forehead kiss. The sorry. She shuddered: it never should have happened. She'd still been married – barely talking, but still. Not an excuse. It was buried for good reason. And Saira would only have ripped him to shreds.

'If you say so.'

'He's going through a dry spell. Lost his touch.'

Saira raised her eyebrows. 'Make your move. He's obviously into you.'

'It's not like that. He's had a shit year. His mum died and there's issues with his dad.'

Saira's eyes lit up. 'Yes! It all kicked off at the funeral? You were there – a fight or something?'

'Did I tell you about that?' It felt disloyal to be discussing him like this. 'Yeah, his family are a bit nuts.'

'You want to get a jump on him.' Saira raised her glass. 'Won't be single for long. Walking wet-floor sign.' She let out exactly the sort of cackle that had made Rachel gravitate towards her in freshers' week.

Saira's phone rang and she grabbed it, hurrying to the doorway.

Rachel turned her own handset over on the table. Another missed call and a message from Scott:

J's been kicking off. Eaten everything out the fridge and left shit all over.

She tapped out a sharp reply:

FFS you've had him 3 hours. Talk to him about school. Please.

But almost immediately, another beep:

Just goes radge. He can't be here long-term. I've got Holly here this weekend.

Hitting Call, to take him and his shitty attitude down, felt like the obvious reflex, but she held herself back. Sometimes no response was a response. He'd see the blue ticks. Let him sweat.

She reverted to Instagram to calm down, but it was all reels from her colleagues, already on the Jägerbombs. Rossy with her arm round her partner: big bump, both of them holding blue balloons. Even the bastard canteen staff were out.

She zoomed in to one group shot. Lennon, holding a Guinness. He hardly ever drank. He'd definitely be away soon, trapdoor exit, hangover free.

Matthews had messaged again, half an hour ago:

Only came out to see you x

She replied quickly, before she could think better of it:

OK – fancy not talking at mine or yours? x

Saira returned from the toilets, looking shifty. 'Sorry, love. She's hysterical. Yusef sounds like he's having a breakdown.'

'You're officially lame,' she said. 'But I love you.'

Saira exhaled gratefully. 'Love you too, ass-kicker.'

'Let me know when she's on the bottle and I'll come and

babysit. Poor old Yus needs to remember what a knockout he's married to. Get yourselves out and remember why you're together.'

'You mean apart from the combined pressure of our families and *commitment to the traditions of our cultural heritage?*'

'Yep. What else was there again?'

'Erm, he's got a massive knob and goes like a sewing machine.'

They both cackled this time and Rachel waved as Saira clattered away.

She called back, one hand on the door, 'I mean it, with Hot Copper. You're mental keeping him in the friend zone. You'll regret it. Tell him you want him.'

Rachel cringed. People were looking. And it wasn't like that at all.

She decided to round off the night with one more and held up her glass to the offensively shod barman with a smile. Same again.

Another beep and this time Matthews's reply came with a photo: semi-erect.

Rachel wasn't a fan of dick pics. It always struck her as a weird male quirk, like a down payment on sex. She yearned for the simplicity of her pre-smartphone relationships – anticipation not transaction. But look where that had got her.

She cocked her head. Squinted. Kind of appealing:

Talking def not on my mind. Yours in 20 mins? x

She downed her drink, dashed for the taxi rank – and froze. Scott's name on the screen:

WTF?? Don't even want to know who that was for, but hope you have a great night ignoring your kids and acting like a total slag.

Rain hammered. A car sent splay up her legs.

Rachel stepped backwards, trying to recalibrate. How had she done that? An absolute rookie error. It was half nine. No chance she could spin this to Scott as some sort of early April Fool's. His words stung because they were true.

The appeal of Matthews vanished. Just more issues piling up.

Maybe her mum was right; what she needed was to get away and lie in the sun, away from all the pressure and those hard eyes staring at her from halfway up the evidence board.

And this cruise? Tedious, obviously. But how bad could it really be?

Chapter 25

Sea

Sunday 23rd April

Cruising had settled into a rhythm, which wasn't exactly bad, but more logistically complicated than the website had suggested from its airbrushed images of attractive people in different receptacles of water.

Breakfast in the Pancake Stack the next morning was a mixed bag. Each member of the family seemed to be tunnel-visioned in their own priority for the day. The *Synergy* was to be docked in Lisbon from eight a.m. to eight p.m., with the schedule again giving comprehensive suggestions for the Portuguese capital and a range of 'fun' ship-based activities.

Robert and Barbara's booking at the swiftly rebranded *Dance with Danielle* workshop began at ten, leaving them the afternoon to potter around the city. Jake had been surly since opening his eyes, but the few noises he had made involved finding somewhere to watch the Toon game, which kicked off at two.

Jess was still intent on proceeding with her one-woman campaign to outlaw single-use plastic, adamant that anything less than a written commitment to reducing non-recyclable waste by half on future sailings would be a failure.

For her own part, Rachel was content to go along with her teenagers' plans, even if that meant splitting herself in half, as, much like the previous evening, they were still barely talking. Her only personal goal was keeping well away from the prying eyes and ears of Captain Richard Miller until she'd had a debrief on Danielle and a clear phone line to Lennon.

Lisbon would have a lot to offer, culturally. Should she try and drag them round some museums and art galleries? Mr Powell probably wouldn't approve of their only planned excursion being the dark interior of whatever sports bar they could find screening English Premiership games. However, she resolved to give fewer fucks about what the headteacher would think. Watching the game meant something to Jake, and this holiday was meant to be about finding common ground – with both her children.

'Maybe we should tap up Veronica Chase for your plastic thing?' she suggested to Jess, thinking of the business card. 'See if she can sort something.'

'Yeah, OK.'

'Sure? You don't sound that bothered?'

'Just got a headache.'

'Let's just chill out here, then; or head to the pool.'

'No, see what she says. I'm just knackered. Probably a build-up, you know, from all the *lies* I've been telling.' She glared at Jake across the table, but he was busy overloading his fifth pancake with salted caramel and gave no reaction.

'Come on, you two. Draw a line under whatever that was yesterday.'

'K,' Jess mumbled. Unenthusiastic as this was, it was a step up from her brother who merely grunted thickly through a mouthful of saturated fat.

Turning to the other side of the table, Rachel attempted to

go over some of the basics of undercover ops and interrogation with her parents.

'The main thing is to establish how Danielle's responding to Tyler's not being there. There's some HLC corporate spiel about him being unavailable so she's not going to want to go into details.' She lowered her voice. 'Most of all, you can't let on what you already know. We don't want her to trace you both to me.'

'Say no more,' said her dad, tapping his nose with his index finger. 'We'll keep schtum, won't we, Barb?'

'No reason she should make the link,' Barbara said. 'Different surnames, and we certainly won't be bringing up the first-night incident. Luckily, we weren't sitting together so there's no danger of us getting drawn into *that* sorry business.'

'Cheers, Mum.'

'Well, we've all moved on now, haven't we. Fresh start.'

'And you think you can keep your disapproval of her drinking down to a low grumble?'

Barbara sniffed. 'I'm a very positive person.'

'No comment.'

'Bob! Tell her! She won't suspect a thing.'

'Shall we have a debrief at five-ish? We'll watch the match then meet you.'

'Good plan,' said Robert. 'Keep it all off the ship, on the "down-low".'

'Grandad!' Both kids snorted, momentarily forgetting their feud, then instantly reverting back to whatever sullen grudge they were feeding and watering. Rachel sighed. Hanging around with these two mardy arses was going to be a challenge. Her phone beeped.

'Jess – she's replied.'

'What's she said?'

'*Of course,*' she read aloud. 'Clapping-hands emoji *to your daughter. If you can come to the Guest Services desk in an hour,*

*I'll have Miguel Fernandez, our Environmental Services Manager,
give you a tour of the facilities.'*

'Get in. Thanks, Mam.'

'No bother. Nothing says holiday more than walking round
a floating dump.'

'Where you gonna leave him?' Jess nodded dismissively at her
brother, still shovelling pancake crumbs into his mouth.

'We're all going. That's the deal. Jake, you come to Jess's thing
and she'll come to the match later. No arguments.' She set her face
in the I-take-no-shit expression she normally reserved for hostile
arrests. It seemed to land as neither uttered a word.

She knew this strategy was a gamble. Either an empathetic
insight into the other's driving interests, leading to a mutually
beneficial ceasefire. Or, a bloodbath.

Lennon was next on her list. The kids had drifted off in opposite directions in search of snacks and stationery and, although
there were a few guests milling around, carrying newspapers and
coffees, the *Synergy* was almost deserted in comparison to its
normal hustle and bustle. She took up her hiding-in-plain-sight
position, perched on the edge of the fountain and was relieved
to hear his voice after a couple of rings.

'Alright, boss.'

'Well, y'know. Trying to enjoy the facilities.'

'As you step around the bodies?'

'Yeah. Bit of that.'

'Who was it, like? How come you found him?'

'Erm …' She tried to muffle her admission with a cough. 'My
dodgy shag-dar strikes again.'

He'd heard fine. 'Fuck me – that was fast work.' His voice had
gone up about an octave and she could imagine him shaking his
head, gleefully.

'Don't, OK. I'm well aware of the irony.'

'You must be absolute dynamite in the sack. Or awful. Can't
decide.' She almost corrected his use of 'must' – he knew exactly

what she was like – but stopped herself. And she was struggling to hear as he was laughing so much. 'He's either thinking he's never getting it that good again and wants to go out on a high. Or it's so bad. Like *so bad* he can't take the flashbacks.'

'You finished?' she said flatly, playing her expected part in this well-worn routine. Part of her wished she was there to deliver the whole story in person. The bit she hadn't told him about the snake hips and seduction routine might actually make him combust.

'Not even started, pet.' He was almost crying now and she could picture his dark hair flopping across his forehead. 'What was his name? This needs a deep dive.'

There was no way she could withhold the details. Assistance was needed. 'Tyler Tweedy.'

'How d'you do it, Rach? Please come home with more of these stories.' He gave a long sigh, attempting to get his breath back.

'What's the latest on the job?'

His tone switched: the detective was back. 'Breakthrough. Meant to message you actually, just been that busy.'

'Yeah?' It was unsettling, being this out of the loop. Not involved. She tried hard to sound supportive. 'Nice one. What's happened?'

'Possible ID on the line holder. Turns out Michael Gallagher's had a burner in his cell. No activity after that acid GBH on the cellmate, which ties in with the 4-3-5 going down.'

'So, he's been running the line from inside?' Rachel felt her jaw involuntarily clench. Everyone knew the Gallaghers got an easy ride from the screws, but this was a new low.

'Got himself a spell in solitary, then he's been transferred out of region. Need as much boxed off now for the CPS file as we can.'

'Who's pulled that together?' The urge to roll her sleeves up and get back into the fray was rising. Rattle some doors and get a hefty stint added on to his sentence.

'Rossy. Your tip-off though, remember?'

'Was it?' It was hard to think back, now, to the aftermath.

Two weeks she'd been on restricted duty, and Operation Fever certainly didn't seem like it was missing her management. Quite the reverse.

'Yeah – shitbag's been all over Facebook. New profile but Rossy ran the pic through facial recognition. Absolute cretin. Shooting his mouth off under the Dalton Crescent video.'

Her stomach lurched. That twenty-second clip, face mangled into the concrete, lived rent-free in her brain.

'Anyone questioned Jo" Paul, yet?' she asked.

'No access. Hopefully the morphine drip'll work in our favour, though, if he's too off his tits to remember what he shouldn't say about his relatives.'

She closed her mind to the dark possibilities of what might get coughed up whilst he was mainlining hospital-strength opioids. 'Sounds promising. What about Gaby?'

'Still with the foster. For now, anyway. Rossy's been out twice, but she's not saying much.'

'I take it you got the same email as me from Professional Standards?'

'It'll get chucked out. Stronger we can get the case for you before Friday though, the better.'

'Could go either way.'

'Nah, don't stress. I've got your back. Just stick to the basics. He flobbed on you, you got him outside to calm it down, he jumped. Nothing you could do.'

'Shit you've been dragged into it as well.'

'Just one of those things. Not like it was personal. You've got no more reason to want to shove Gallagher off a balcony than any other clampet.'

There was a beat of silence, but she knew it probably wouldn't register, given the slight delay in the international call. She shifted gears, getting back to events on board.

'Did you get anything off the database, by the way? For the one I left the message about?'

'Danielle Paige? Not a sausage.'

'No bother. It was a long shot.'

'She's a dancer, right? Wasn't shagging him an' all, was she?'

'Don't think so. Not recently, anyway. They were dance partners. But she's a definite POI.'

'Nothing on the records check. Clean as a whistle. Did a bit of digging on the socials too. It's all *Get Ready with Me* shite from the cruise and "wellness" brand partnerships in minimal clothing.'

Rachel could picture his withering disdain and suddenly ached to imitate the air quotes he'd be making. The desire to make him reach out to stop her mockery was as strong as it had ever been. Even after everything.

'Oh right,' she said. 'Sounds like you've done some thorough research.'

They had swapped roles. It was her turn to berate him, but on this occasion she couldn't remember her lines or play up her exasperated routine to her usual standard.

'Checking out the collagen powder for you, pet. Now you've embraced this OAP lifestyle—'

'Get lost – you're officially late thirties; I'm still mid.'

'I'd need to see your birth certificate. Always had stage age written all over you.' She didn't bother rising to this one. Especially as she didn't even have an original birth certificate.

A thought struck her. 'Could Danielle Paige be a stage name? Gloss over a murky past, sort of thing? Their big break was *BGT* years ago – called themselves TyD.'

'Worth a look. I'll check it out.'

'Only if you've got time. You must have Bailey breathing down your neck.'

'S'all right. But he does look like he wants a one-way ticket to Dignitas.'

Lennon must be playing this down. She had no doubt he'd be getting the brunt of the DCI's rage at the impending IOPC investigation. 'Well, prioritise Fever. I've got nothing concrete on Tyler or Danielle. Maybe he just overdid it, but something doesn't sit right.'

'Trust your instincts, then. Never let you down before. Anything else you need, I'm only a phone call away, right?'

'Cheers, Lenn. You too.'

'Miss ya, Rach,' he said, upbeat and throwaway. He wouldn't mean it. Not like that. But it was reassuring to hear they'd fallen back into the norms of their friendship. Mates – nothing more, nothing less.

Just mates.

'Yeah,' she said. But he'd already gone.

She found her offspring propping up the Guest Services desk, spaced as far as possible from each other's orbit. Jess was holding a notebook and clicking the end of a ballpoint pen in an irritating manner.

Plugged-in Jake was back and there was no mistaking his feelings as he stood, gazing into the middle distance, avoiding eye contact. Rachel resolved to just let him be. Setting the bar at ground level, she prodded him in the torso and gave him a sarcastic thumbs up. At least he was here.

The always-glamorous Veronica Chase approached the desk with a mega-watt smile, accompanied by a black-haired crew member in navy trousers and a white short-sleeved shirt with gold epaulettes. Nodding tightly at Rachel, he gave the impression that he was looking forward to this addition to his duties about as much as she was.

'Good morning!' Veronica said, brightly. 'And this must be the young environmentalist.' She put both hands on Jess's shoulders and held her at arm's length, beaming.

'Hi,' said Jess, nonchalantly. Rachel felt defensive on her daughter's behalf, not wanting her age and stature to be reasons she was not taken seriously.

'I'll leave you in the very capable hands of our environmental services manager, Miguel Fernandez.' The man gave a stilted nod of his head, but remained silent. 'Miguel is one of our local crew members, resident of Vigo when not at sea, and will be very happy to fill you in on all our exciting plans to meet our green targets ahead of schedule.'

From the look of Fernandez, brooding and bored, happiness was not an emotion he was familiar with.

Veronica gave her another crocodile smile. 'Anything else I can do for you during your trip, any information you need to pass on, *please* don't hesitate.'

She left the comment hanging in the air as she moved away, its meaning so unsubtle it might as well have had a tec"icolour hologram of Captain Miller's face attached.

'So,' Rachel said, awkwardly. 'Jess, did you want to ask some questions or …'

'Follow,' said Fernandez. 'I show you, and then questions.'

'Oh, OK.' Rachel was suddenly in pursuit as he strode away, across the marble floor. She shrugged to the kids, who followed. Catching up by the crew exit, she glanced at him, side-on, for the first time as he held open the door and was struck by a wave of recognition. She'd seen that haughty profile before.

'I think we saw you, yesterday, in Vigo? You had a day off the ship?'

He shook his head, firmly. 'I remain on board throughout this sailing. You are mistaken.'

Or you have something to hide, she thought, itching to zoom in to the photo she had taken of Danielle and her mystery man. Now, no longer a mystery.

The tour started strongly with the news that food waste on a cruise ship was compressed into bricks, meaning that the area didn't smell as bad as she had feared. Then they were shown down to Deck Zero, the lowest level.

Jess held out her phone to video the functional stainless-steel corridor, but their guide put his hand swiftly over the screen and glared at them. 'This is the I:95. Private. No filming.'

Awkwardly, they walked in stony silence down the busy highway, taking in the loads of laundry, provisions and food being transported along the full length of the vessel.

The Filipino crew members looked confused at the sight of guests straying out of their allocated luxury, into the hidden nuts and bolts of the operation. It was cold and echoey down here, a world away from the polished marble and sunshine mere metres above their heads. Whether due to the grinding background chorus or the industrial view in every direction, Rachel felt an intense heaviness washing over her again. She forced herself to keep moving, further and further along the metallic tunnel.

This was for Jess.

Eventually, Fernandez ushered them through a bolted door and gestured, tersely, to the mountainous store of packaging, which would be discarded following this week-long journey. The amount of waste was eye-watering, even to Rachel and Jake, who were not fully paid-up members of Extinction Rebellion.

Countless polystyrene crates were stacked in the darkest corner of the storage room, blindingly white and destined for nothing but landfill. The reaction in Jess was nuclear. In a voice hard enough to dent the reinforced steel decor, she let their tour guide have it with both barrels.

'This is an absolute disgrace,' she said, motioning to the floor-to-ceiling tower. 'From only three days!'

A vein in Fernandez's temple twitched. 'I can assure you, *señorita*, the HLC has a better record than many other cruise lines.'

'That's not good enough. It takes years for polystyrene to break down, meanwhile your ships are just perpetuating the cycle.' Jess stepped forwards, phone raised to capture the evidence.

He moved to block the crates. 'These were for the experience night, yesterday. You were there, no?'

Jess coloured slightly and her attempt to reply was immediately interrupted.

'We bring fresh produce on board from Vigo and it is important for safety it be kept at the correct temperature.' He looked Jess up and down with a sneer. 'This process, you call *disgrace*, I call it economics. This is what feeds my people in Galicia.'

Jess started to speak, but he waved his hand dismissively. 'You *joven*,' he spat the word as an insult, 'you have all the answers, but you offer no solutions. You, *nina binita*, how you English say? You are the white? The snow? You understand nothing.'

They stared, shocked. In the cold silence, one voice cut through like a machete. 'Don't call her *pretty girl* like she's just talking crap. She's got a point and she's not a *snowflake* if that's what you're trying to say. Talks a lot more sense than you.'

Rachel and Jess swivelled their heads in one whiplash-inducing, synchronised movement. Dumbstruck, they saw Jake, unplugged and irate, glaring at Fernandez like he was about to knock him out.

Chapter 26

Sea

Miguel Fernandez stepped forwards, arms swinging with just the right degree of swagger to emphasise the taut muscles beneath his uniform. 'We have problem here?'

'Yeah.' Jake was uncowed. 'A big problem.'

Rachel gaped, torn between admiration for Jake's loyalty to his sister and a professional reflex to de-escalate the situation. Policing won and she shifted to block the Spaniard's approach on her fifteen-year-old son.

'Let's calm this down, OK.' She forced him to meet her eyes. 'I don't think your manager would approve of the way you're addressing guests here.'

'Come on, we'll just go,' said Jess, regaining her voice. 'I need someone with more authority. There's nothing for us down here.'

As one, the twins stalked out of the oppressive space, leaving Fernandez with his polystyrene packaging, and Rachel followed, a searing bolt of pride hammering in her heart.

'The biggest revelation,' she said, as they left the dock a short while later in search of a Brits-Abroad pub, 'is how good your

Spanish is! That teacher at parents' evening was tearing her hair out with you.'

'Yeah. Sort of surprised myself.' He grinned, the three of them still buzzing with the unexpected drama.

'I still don't get it, though,' Jess said, giving her brother an affectionate shove off the kerb. 'You think I talk absolute horseshit!'

'You do,' Jake said, 'but I'm allowed to say that. Hearing some skanky bin-man patronising you hits different.'

'I knew you loved each other really,' Rachel cooed, getting in the middle and putting an arm round each of their shoulders.

'Deep down, maybe,' Jake said.

Jess smiled. 'Yeah, like a crumb of feeling.'

They continued in companiable silence, enjoying the warmth of the Lisbon sun on their shoulders. No map or plan, but it was freeing just to walk in a straight line, away from the ship's solid barriers in every direction.

'It's a twin thing,' said Jake, out of nowhere. 'I know you were born first and that, and you're the clever one and I'm thick, but we should stick together.'

Rachel's heart ached. 'You're not thick, J.'

'You're not,' Jess agreed quickly. 'I'm rubbish at languages. I'm only on a 7 in German. And …' she paused, the words seeming to cause her pain '… I shouldn't have tried to get you in shit with Mam yesterday. That was … harsh.'

She watched them side-eyeing each other as they walked. Was it comprehension? Or the elusive 'twin thing'? They would have communicated without words for the first instalment of their shared lives; maybe twins never lost that bond.

Jake stopped on the pavement. 'Nah.' He took a deep breath. 'Right, you're gonna go off it, but just remember how I was really nice to Jess before …'

'Yes,' she said, warily.

'Keep that in your mind, OK?' He bit his lip. 'She wasn't lying, what she said. I've – er – been, sort of, changing a few things on the school system.'

'Sorry, what?' This felt like an April Fool. But it was weeks late for that sort of nonsense, especially from Jake who rarely even knew what day it was. 'What d'you mean *changing a few things*?'

Jess nodded to him, in what looked like sisterly support. 'You might as well just tell her everything. We're in a public place, so she can't actually kill you.'

'Don't be so sure of that,' Rachel said. 'I know all the loopholes, remember?'

Jake had gone bright red. 'I was sick of getting in bother all the time. Like, from school, from you, from everyone. You're always so busy, I was just making your life more complicated. Every time you had to go into school, or whatever, I was messing everything up.'

She let his words sink in. 'Go on.'

'I got into SIMs and started changing the register – like, late marks. Just a few at first, to see if anyone noticed. But they didn't. No one did. So I carried on. And—' he cringed '—I changed some test results and stuff.'

'What?' Rachel stared at her son. 'I mean, *hacking*? It's a criminal offence, for a start. I still don't get how you even managed to do it.'

'It's easy.' He shrugged. 'There's this podcast about a guy in Australia, right? He got into NASA, just messing around on his laptop. So, I read more about it and, yeah ...' His voice trailed away and he stood rigid, braced for impact.

Rachel was struggling to form a coherent sentence, looking around in case she was being filmed for *Punk'd*. 'I actually don't know what to say.'

'That's a first,' Jess said.

'Shut it, snowflake,' Jake said. 'She's taking this a lot better than she could've.'

'Might be sunstroke. She'd definitely've gone supersonic by now if we were at home.'

'There's still time for that,' Rachel warned. 'Look,' she said, pointing to a dingy pub with a sign for *All Day Full English €10*. 'They've got a Sky dish. That'll do.'

Chapter 27

Sea

The pub was busy, but there was respite from the heat in its gloomy interior. Apparently, they weren't the only people in this dubious area of Lisbon who wanted to watch the Newcastle game; Jake, however, was the only one in a black-and-white shirt. Cockney accents filled the bar, giving Rachel a visceral callback to Tyler's voice in her ear; those last few words of private conversation whispered softly, in full view of the *Synergy*'s hyped-up audience. Something clicked in her memory as a Spurs fan shouted, gesturing to the big screen, 'He wants out, mate – look at 'is face. On 'is way.'

'Kane,' Jake said, reading her confused expression. 'Wants a transfer.'

'Why, though?'

'They're shit,' he said, simply. 'Wants to win something.'

Clearly, Tyler hadn't been focused on Harry Kane seconds before she covered the stage in partially absorbed alcohol. *I want out*, he'd said, *I'll fill you in later*. Shit. What had he wanted to say?

'I thought Tottenham were decent,' she said, trying to show some enthusiasm for her son's number-one interest. Or previously declared number-one interest, aside from unauthorised access into cyberspace. She was still processing whether she should be appalled or impressed by that revelation.

'Not this season,' he said. 'We'll win this, no bother.'

'Typical Newcastle fan,' came the cocky voice from the bar. The white-shirted speaker had evidently overheard Jake's optimism and was shaking his head authoritatively, like an ex-pro pundit. She had a hunch from the beer belly stretching the AIA logo on his shirt out of shape that he was anything but. 'You're a mid-table club, mate. Always have been. Just 'cos you've got a bit of coin – gettin' ahead of yourselves.'

'We'll see.' Jake had a quiet confidence about him that belied his gawky frame. He seemed older all of a sudden, and more self-assured, both in the way he met this Cockney geezer's sneer and standing up for his sister an hour earlier.

'I'm gonna FaceTime Dad, OK?' he said. 'Before kick-off.'

'Go for it,' said Rachel, turning to Jess, who was scribbling furiously in her notebook. 'Want to talk to your dad as well?'

'Maybe later.' She gave her pen a few hard clicks.

'What you writing?' Rachel asked.

'Just some notes.' She looked defensive. Rachel tried to keep her face neutral and, after a pause, Jess continued. 'I found last year's High Life Cruises AGM minutes online. So, I'm using their environmental data in an email to the CEO. I'm never going to get anywhere with the crew who deal with the waste. They're just cogs in the machine. I need to take this higher up.'

'Makes sense,' she said, impressed. 'Let me know if you want it proofread or anything.'

'OK.' Jess shrugged, determinedly casual, but she'd sat up a bit straighter and had stopped assaulting the pen.

On her other side, Jake had propped his phone against his Diet Coke and, against all odds, was managing to have an intense discussion about Eddie Howe's team selection, despite the lag from the 5G connection and the fact that Scott was currently seated amongst forty thousand fans at St James' Park. She leaned over, head now in view.

'Alright?' he bellowed. 'Good trip?'

'Interesting so far. You OK?'

'Aye, not bad. New deadlift PB. Work's been chokka, like, but can't complain.' Scott had quit the police a few years ago to manage a pub chain, after a decade of whingeing about positive discrimination and being overlooked for promotion.

'Jake's just been filling me in on an "extra-curricular" project he's been doing.' She made inverted commas with her fingers, to which Jake, out of view, made a swiping motion across his throat.

'Oh yeah? Well as long as he's not getting any lasses pregnant, he can keep his bollocks.'

Rachel laughed and gave herself a few credits for not being the only bad influence on her children's vocabulary. Barbara had never had much time for Scott – *common as they come, Rachel* – and this would have prompted the tut to end all tuts.

'Almost kick-off, Dad,' Jake said, drawing the phone back towards him. 'Speak later.'

'All right, son,' Scott shouted. 'Enjoy the sunshine.' His voice was overtaken by a roar as 'Local Hero' blared from the speakers at the ground, followed by an echo of the same music five seconds later from the multiple TVs in the bar.

Rachel glanced at Jess, who had paused her writing and was looking over to the phone, feeling stung on her daughter's behalf that she hadn't got a mention. Even when parents drove you insane with nagging and attempts to involve themselves in your life, it must be worse if you felt like they'd just tapped out.

Her own phone buzzed. Lennon. Sunderland fan, so he'd be doing anything but watching this game. In Jake's eyes that was his only, albeit significant, character flaw.

'Twice in one day? I'm honoured.'

'Did a bit more digging on your dancer. Good shout on the name change.'

'Oh yeah?'

'Started life as slightly less-glam Dannii Paggot. And she's got a very tasty PNC list.'

'Wait a sec,' she said, 'let me get somewhere quieter.' She motioned to the kids that she was going outside, but with Jess's pen moving at pace again and Jake's eyes on the screen, it barely registered.

She leaned against the wall of the pub, pushing her sunglasses down to shield her eyes from the glare. 'Go on. I'm gagging for this.'

'That what you said to this Tyler lad?'

'Fuck off and spill.'

'Strange one. So, she's twenty-nine, right? The last eight years nothing, nada, not even a speeding ticket.'

'OK. Cut to the good stuff. What about before that?' A sudden loud noise came from inside the building. Rachel ignored it.

'List as long as your arm. Youth justice, shoplifting, possession, intent to supply, affray. Cautions, convictions. You name it, basically.'

'Bingo.'

'I know. You impressed with my detective skills?'

She grinned. 'Yeah, almost like this is your job.'

'Thanks, boss.'

'That always sounds gross. Like it gives you an erection.'

'In your dreams, pet.'

'So, the cut-off – she would've been, what, twenty-one? That probably ties in with *Britain's Got Talent*. It was only the name of the act you saw on screen. So she makes the switch to Paige. Slippery little fucker.' Another, louder roar reached her ears. Sounded like it could have been Jake. 'Sorry, Lenn, got to get back inside. Something's kicking off.'

'Got it. Keep me updated though, I'm invested in this now. And tread carefully—'

Rachel cut the call and barged back through the heavy door. Jake was on his feet and singing at the top of his voice. She looked at the screen, surrounded by dumbstruck white-shirted punters: nine minutes in and the Toon were 3–0 up.

It didn't stop there. Rachel and Jess were swept up in Jake's euphoria as the goals kept coming. The Tottenham shirts were no longer worn with the arrogance of their pre-match predictions, ice-cool cockiness long gone. Jake's favourite player, Longstaff, backheeled the ball to the striker, Isak, who slammed it home, making it five–nil at twenty-one minutes.

A crowd of Cockneys left the pub in disgust and those who remained sat agog, heads in hands. Jake looked boyishly thrilled, like all his Christmases and birthdays had been delivered in a big fat gift drop. Kane's desultory goal in the second half did nothing to dampen his spirits, or rouse the few remaining Spurs fans drowning their sorrows at the bar.

'If we get a seventh, can I have a pint?' Jake asked, wide-eyed.

'That would be a no,' said Rachel. 'Nice try though.'

As the full-time whistle put the visitors out of their misery, Jake did a victory lap around their table. He was still doing a skippy jig rather than his standard head-down slouch as they emerged into daylight: three magpies flying high, wings stretched to their fullest, slicing through the clear blue sky.

Rachel let herself enjoy the moment, though a single shadow kept Danielle dancing at the back of her mind – case not yet closed.

Chapter 28

Sea

If she hadn't known better, as they walked into the swanky Lisbon restaurant, she would have said her mum and dad were on something.

'We've got intel,' Robert said, speaking out of the side of his mouth in a strange half-whisper.

'He's got the knack, all right,' bubbled Barbara. 'Blood out of a stone, this one.'

'Get in, Grandad,' said Jake. 'What you got?'

'Well, for a start, she was highly unprofessional.' Barbara tutted. 'Never off her phone. If she wasn't taking calls she was tap-tapping with those awful synthetic nails, sending messages every five minutes. Barely demonstrated the basic waltz steps, did she, Bob?'

'Very sparse coverage of the fundamentals,' he agreed.

'But what did she say?' Rachel pressed, quickly ordering drinks from the hovering waiter. 'The dance element is kind of surplus to our operation.'

'I was just setting the scene,' Barbara said. 'We were coming to that. You tell them, Bob.'

'We asked her, like you said. Asked her whereabouts Tyler had disappeared to. Acted like we had no—'

'Your dad's a natural,' Barbara jumped in again. 'Oscar-worthy.'

They looked at each other, giddily. This was the happiest she'd seen her parents in years. Maybe ever. And who knew a bit of light espionage was all it was going to take?

'What did she actually say?' Jess said, leaning over the table eagerly.

'She said …' Robert paused while the waiter delivered the drinks, then looked around for maximum dramatic effect '… that he had a personal situation and was having some time off.'

'Permanent time off,' Jess added, darkly.

'So, she's outright lied,' Rachel said, taking a sip of the local Douro. 'Not unexpected. She was hardly going to come out with it when they must have made a company decision to delay the announcement. Did you get anything else?'

They looked at each other again, savouring their information like the final suck of a Werther's Original.

'She's a fraud,' Barbara said, lips pursed in her signature knowing-disapproval expression. 'There's always been something in her eyes – didn't I say, Bob?'

Jess snorted. 'Gran! A couple of nights ago you were bigging her up to anyone who'd listen.'

'I had a niggling doubt,' Barbara said, eyes narrowed. 'She's good. Hides it well. But there was always a question mark.'

'How d'you mean a fraud?' Rachel was starting to lose patience with this pantomime style of delivery.

'The workshop. We were short-changed. It was billed as ninety minutes – ten 'til eleven thirty.'

'And it wasn't pennies,' her dad interrupted. 'We saw what you paid, love. Small fortune.'

'It was barely even five past,' Barbara continued, aghast. 'We'd only been in there an hour. And with all her tap-tapping and phone calls, we'd barely got to grips with the first eight bars. Tricky shift of weight on the off-beat, so *that* was taking its toll on proceedings.'

Rachel rolled her eyes at these irrelevant tangents and motioned to the waiter for another glass of wine. 'Go on, what happened at five past?'

'So, a man swans in. Bangs the door open and marches straight over to Danielle like he owns the place. Near enough drags her out of the room. Gripping her arm, wasn't he, Bob?'

'Gripping.' He nodded earnestly, placing his own fingertips around his upper arm to demonstrate.

'And they were outside for nearly ten minutes. We got ourselves right over to the door so we could hear snatches and he sounded ready to blow. Latin, he was. Black hair. Fernando, he called himself, or Fernandez. Written on his name badge.'

'Miguel Fernandez?' said Rachel. 'Are you sure?'

'Sounds about right,' Robert said. 'Definitely Fernandez.'

'But that's who we saw this morning,' Jess jumped in. 'And he was miles downstairs shouting at me.'

'Shouting at you?' Robert's usually placid expression was dismayed.

'Don't worry, Grandad,' Jake said. 'I had it covered.'

'We'll explain later,' Rachel snapped, 'but going back to the man you saw, could this have been him?' She slid her phone across the table, the image of Danielle and her hitherto unknown Vigo companion edited to the clearest quality she could make it.

'That's the one – would you say, Barb?'

'Affirmative,' she said, in a strange American-twang. Everyone looked at her. 'Sorry. I've just heard them say that, you know, in this sort of undercover business.'

The conversation was halted by the waiter bringing more drinks. Aware of the time, they asked, in halting googled Portuguese, for a selection of petiscos dishes to share.

The restaurant was filling up, a buzz in the air, snatches of animated language ringing through the chic interior. This was a sizeable step up from the grubby sports bar.

'Top marks for your first assignment, both of you,' Rachel

said, thoughtfully. 'Don't suppose you managed to hear what they were arguing about?'

'Better than that,' Barbara said, looking at Robert again. 'We wrote a couple of phrases down.' She pulled an A4 certificate out of her bag, still bearing the old *Dance with Tyler and Danielle* branding, the reverse covered in careful handwriting, and slid it across the table. 'We could hear him saying *agua* or *aqua*. *Al agua* it sounded like.'

'Jake?' Rachel turned the certificate. 'How long did you pay attention for in Spanish?'

His eyes grew wide. 'Long enough. Means overboard.'

There was a beat of silence at this bombshell.

'How on earth did you know that?' she said, mind racing. 'I'm starting to think your teachers don't know what they're on about.'

'*Pirates of the Caribbean*,' he said evenly, as if this made any sense as a statement on its own. 'Miss says she's not wasting her time planning a lesson while people are hoying glue sticks round the room. So she just puts dubbed DVDs on.'

Barbara tutted and turned to Robert. 'I said we should have looked into private options. This is what you get in an inner-city comp.'

'Don't be such a snob, Gran.' Jess scowled. 'He'll be one of the ones chucking stuff. Anyway,' she said, pointing to another handwritten phrase, 'what about this one, *demasiado caliente*, or however you say it. Any ideas, whizz kid?'

Jake shrugged, but typed it, painfully slowly, into Google while the rest of them waited in tense silence. 'Got it. Probably not important though – means *too hot*. You said he seemed moody.'

'It could be more than that,' Rachel said. 'Questions are being asked about Tyler. Anyone involved could be getting worried.'

Jess clicked her pen, impatiently. 'We need to start pulling all this info together.'

'Good point,' she agreed. 'Can we use your notebook?'

Jess turned to a clean page and looked at the assembled faces, expectantly. 'What first?'

'Always start with the victim,' Rachel said. 'Tyler Tweedy. IC3 male. Professional partner, Danielle Paige aka Dannii Paggot.'

'That's not even her real name?' said Barbara, aggrieved. 'In heaven's name, Bob, is there anything genuine about that woman?'

'Don't get yourself upset, love.'

Rachel glanced at her dad. He looked tired. She still saw him in her mind's eye as he had been, tall and heavy set: a mountain of a man. He was stooped now though, less a mountain and more a hill.

'He was from Croydon,' Barbara blurted out, excitedly, 'and he went to one of those stage schools. That was all in the article.'

'OK. Good knowledge.' Not Essex after all, then. 'There'll be more online. Jake, see if he's got a Wiki page.'

'How old was he?' Jess asked.

'One sec,' said Jake, eyes darting as he scanned his phone screen. 'No Wikipedia, but there's a fan si—'

'Tyleranddanielle.com,' Barbara interrupted, almost shouting.

Everyone's eyes swivelled in her direction. Robert shushed hurriedly, looking round the restaurant to check they weren't exposing high-value intelligence.

'Erm, awkward. Is this *your* fan site, Gran?' said Jess.

'Yeah, if you were his secret stalker, you can tell us. This is a safe space.' Jake and Jess both cracked up, and rather than going on her usual defensive, Barbara seemed to see the funny side.

'Behave yourselves,' she said. 'Of course not. I'm just more au fait with the web these days. That iPad's a game-changer. Do the big shop on click and collect, don't we, Bob?'

'OK, we believe you,' Jess said, in a voice that implied anything but.

'Yeah, yeah,' said Jake. 'We know you've got a membership card at home. OK. There's a fact file here. Date of birth, twelfth of the fifth, nineteen-ninety-seven.'

'So that made him twenty-six,' Jess calculated. 'You OK, Mam?'

Rachel tried to disguise her shock with a cough, but her mum was giving her a funny look. Nine years younger than her. Was that OK? She definitely needed another drink. Trying to distance herself from the unpleasant realisation that she could now legitimately be described as a cougar, she ploughed on. 'Yep, put that down. Keep these points coming. Height approx. six foot, probably weighed about thirteen stone.'

'Do we need all his stats?' Jake asked. 'The guy's dead.'

'It's important to build a profile,' she said. 'Cause of death's unknown, so we can't discount the possibility of involvement by another individual. We always keep an open mind and having his proportions at the forefront is key. Who could have realistically handled the body? Rigor mortis wouldn't have set in, but he was still a canny weight to shift.'

Jake nodded, taking in her words. 'So, Danielle, you mean? She couldn't have done that.'

'Not alone.'

'Well, our suspects are a limited pool, aren't they,' Jess added. 'If there was someone else involved, they'd have been on the ship from Southampton.'

'Right. So, working hypothesis. Tyler was taking something that night, but probably not what he thought it was. Cocaine can have any amount of other substances cut into it, all virtually impossible to trace without a testing kit. Prescription opioids are missing from the ship's locked store. The doctor confirmed that, whatever Miller's now claiming. And Saira says that even a small amount of oxycontin would have been enough to cause a fatal seizure. He'd bitten a chunk out of his tongue so that seems likely as the cause of death. I just don't buy that Tyler was taking that level of risk himself.'

They listened intently to her stream of consciousness, Jess taking quick notes in shorthand. Rachel's case analysis was flowing freely, although this could have been more to do with wine consumption than degree of insight. Whatever the reason, her family's level of focus pissed all over the jaded incident rooms she was used to addressing.

'Persons of interest, then. Have a page for each of these, Jess.'

'Well, Danielle's got to be there. Even taking into account what you said about her relative size,' Barbara said.

'Agreed. And in my limited dealings with her she's got means and the motive to do him serious harm.' She filled them in on Lennon's update on her sizeable record. Eyes popping almost out of their sockets, voices started clamouring at once with outlandish theories.

'Let's keep it focused on what we can corroborate,' Rachel said, trying to restore some order.

'What about the captain?' Jess asked, pen hovering over the next page.

'Hard to read,' Rachel said, frowning. 'On one hand, we've got that cruise couple saying he's got something going on with Danielle. So that needs further exploration. But then, why would he be involved? It doesn't follow. If he had an issue with Tyler, he'd have just dealt with it through HR.'

'The Fernandez fella,' Robert interjected. 'Looked like he could handle himself. And what's he talking about, going *overboard*?'

'Exactly, Dad. He's our priority. Get those Spanish phrases down, Jess. We need to straighten out the timeline – how come he denied being with Danielle in Vigo, when I've got this photo of him?' She tapped her phone. 'And he seems to have been in two places at once this morning. Going off it with Jess *and* Danielle.'

'Evil twin?' Jake said, smirking.

She gave him her best DI death stare. 'Keep it credible. There's still a question mark over Veronica Chase for me, as well. She's desperate to do the dirty on Miller. Could be pulling strings we haven't even seen yet.'

The sound of Jake's stomach rumbling broke the tension. Time was ticking to when they would need to reboard the ship, but

Rachel's focus lingered on Veronica – her intensity was unsettling in front of the scenes, let alone behind them. As the conversation drifted away from suspects and onto the food and a Newcastle goal-by-goal analysis, every inch of the table was soon covered with small plates, cutlery and more drinks.

Rachel minimised the Danielle and Fernandez image, faces unreadable, and finished her fourth glass of wine, wishing she'd just ordered a bottle in the first place. This makeshift investigative unit was gaining momentum.

Relaxation, off; cop mode, on.

Chapter 29

Land

Wednesday 5th April

ON
ON
ON
ON
wot u got
ON
ON
ON
SHOPS OPEN
get me fucked up!!
ON
ON
ON

'Line's back up, ladies and gents!' Tariq was jubilant, after ten long days without deal line activity. In the world of an intelligence analyst, this was his moon landing.

His shout drew everyone to his desk like hyenas around fresh meat. They all watched avidly as the screen popped and whirred with the sheer quantity of bulk messages streaming to the contact list.

Rachel turned to Chambers. 'Cam's gonna be going off it.'

'They might've got wise to that. Still don't know why they killed the 4-3-5, do we?'

'Maybe just covering themselves. Few of the other ROCUs were saying the same.'

'Back in business now, though.' He rubbed his hands together. 'Belter, this!'

The energy uplift within the unit was stark. Even Coates was swept up in collective optimism and seemed content to ride the wave rather than offer his own superior strategy. She could have done with these vibes yesterday when she'd had to update the DCI, but, looking around at the team now, she felt the pressure slacken from around her neck. She took what felt like her first full breath in several days.

Even the trauma of Friday night was receding. The kids had been all over the prospect of a holiday. Jess, unsurprisingly, was a forceful advocate of low-carbon sea travel, and had even researched the much-hyped entertainment, sharing a YouTube link to a dance duo, TyD, in their *Britain's Got Talent* audition. They had watched it together, mesmerised by the speed of the two bodies in a sexually charged Argentine tango.

Jake had sheepishly returned home and was also pro-cruise. She suspected this was because the proposed dates were in term time. Her parents, thrilled at their enthusiasm, had initiated a sniper-like campaign of calls and messages to pin her down to a departure date.

In reality, though, there was no way she could put a request in for annual leave at this stage in the job. Her attitude to a family trip, in general, was thawing, but she was highly reluctant to commit to this High Life Cruises business. No one gave a shit that she got seasick and they would be the youngest people on board by several decades.

Back in the room, only Bradshaw still looked downcast. He'd been off with her since last week, quiet and avoiding eye contact. Normally understated, yes, but this was different. She'd seen him talking to Sanj, one of the Safeguarding team, in the canteen yesterday. He wouldn't have gone behind her back on the Gaby referral, though, surely. Bradshaw wasn't the type.

She moved round the team, still watching the local addicts jump on the new line, until she was next to him.

'See, told you. We'll be up on this in no time.'

He looked at her warily. 'Hope you're right.'

'Come on, it'll be OK.'

'Wasn't you had to update the foster. She's broken.'

'And we'll get Gaby out. We will. Just as long as we get Gallagher in cuffs first.'

She turned to address the whole team. 'Right. Let's get to work. We'll leave Tariq to his civvy stuff while the rest of us do some actual graft.' She winked at him. 'No honestly, you've smashed it here. This gives us a proper chance, but we can't waste a second. They might get cold feet again and kill this number as well, so we need all hands on deck.'

'Maz, that N Reg Range Rover's due up again. What's every Wednesday about? Get me a full background on the keeper.'

'On it,' she replied, already back at her desk.

'Chambers, Rossy – socials first, gauge the reaction. And start copying this feed. We're going to need a full CPS file sharpish – I can feel it in my bones.' She looked around. 'Where's Lennon?'

'Said the DSU had something for him,' Rossy said.

This day was just getting better. She'd sent Lennon over to the Dedicated Source Unit on Monday to dig on Gallagher, but getting payment authorised always took forever. Everyone working the area at street level knew who the informants were, but if you wanted concrete intel you had to suck it up and get in the queue.

'Coates,' she said, with less irritation than usual. 'Door-to-door write-ups?'

He shrugged. 'On Bradders' desk, boss. Thought you'd assigned them to me by mistake.'

She recoiled at *Bradders*. 'Why would you think that?'

He seemed to feel the chill in her voice. 'Er, just thought – more of a uniform task, isn't it?'

She loaded up, ready to fire. Who did this jumped-up little prick think he was? However, by coincidence or design to alleviate a potential bloody massacre, Tariq called out to her at the same moment.

'Boss – you'll want to see this.'

She shot Coates a look that could have melted stone and stalked away. His bollocking would have to wait.

'Looks like the product's shifted,' he said, pointing to the stream of frying-pan emojis racing down his screen.

'They're cooking now?' This was all they needed. Coke was par for the course in a city of Newcastle's size, whether addicts scraping along rock bottom in Byker or affluent office workers and students doing a line or two in the toilets on a night out. Crack was different.

Bailey had wanted a risk assessment yesterday on Dalton Crescent. She'd played it down, muting Bradshaw's concerns. Eyes on the finish line. But the klaxon was blaring now.

Stick or twist? They needed longer to trace the drivers and follow the money higher up the line. If they charged in and found nothing but a teenager with piss-poor taste in boyfriends, Gallagher would go to ground.

But, the priority had to be protection over pursuit. What if Gaby *was* being cuckooed by a crack dealer with crime stamped all over his family tree? A bloodline so toxic that no one with Gallagher genes got away without poison running through their veins. And they'd infect anyone unlucky enough to get too close.

Rachel felt sick; everything was rising to the surface. She'd failed McKenzie. She couldn't fail Gaby too. Just another kid tactically downgraded as collateral damage.

There was only one person who would weigh this up and give her a straight answer. But where the hell was he?

Chapter 30

Land

She cut Lennon off in the car park.

'What's up?' he said. 'You look like shit.'

'Tariq's back up on the line.'

'And that's put five years on your face because …?'

'They're cooking. Buyers are going akka. I think we need to move.'

'Fits with the DSU purchase. That Dalton Crescent flat's where they're cutting it, anyway. One of them seen the lass in the flat. Not in a good way.' He grimaced.

'Smacked out?'

'Bruises. Someone's given her a proper hiding. And recently – this was yesterday their fella was in there.'

Rachel's stomach churned. She'd known this was a risk – they could've had a warrant before the weekend.

The rain had ceased, but the afternoon sky was grey. It threatened more. She shivered, half from the biting north wind, half from him, aware how little her short sleeves offered against both.

'You're frozen,' Lennon said. 'Let's get inside.'

'No. I'm all right.' She wasn't ready. There was more she wanted, needed, to say.

'Have this then.' He pulled off his jacket and draped it round her shoulders. 'No, don't worry – I'll just freeze my arse off instead.' He rolled his eyes and rubbed his hands together, and she noticed the way his tightly fitted jumper clung to his body as he briskly exhaled into his palms.

'It's not the bloody Arctic. In the car then, OK?'

If he thought she'd actually lost it, he didn't comment, and unlocked the Corsa without a word. Rachel looked up at the three storeys overlooking the car park, paranoia or thirteen years' service making her expect to see faces pressed against the glass, ready to shit-stir this into something spicy.

They sat in parallel, a ruler's width apart, both feigning interest in the brick wall ahead, as if sitting in a stationary fleet vehicle was normal behaviour. Lennon turned the key and cranked up the heating. For another moment, the enclosed space was silent save for the roar of air.

'You gonna tell me, then?' he said, barely audible over the heater.

'Tell you what?' She was suddenly huffy. His leather jacket had a soft shearling lining and the combination of his tone and the furry material pressed against her bare arms felt like the sort of intimacy she tried to avoid at all costs.

She could feel him looking at her, but kept her own sightline squarely on the regimented pattern of bricks and mortar. 'Did the source actually see Gallagher on the premises?'

'Jo" Paul? Nah. But he's definitely in and out.'

'Possession with Intent isn't going to be enough. And the other charges are dependent on Gaby talking. That's if the CPS even back it.'

She swallowed. There was something she was missing. Something important. Something just out of reach, drifting in the ether. The brick wall was no longer clearly visible now the glass had started to fog. Beads of condensation dripped down the windscreen and she shifted slightly on the seat.

It was only a feeling, but it was getting stronger.

Maybe she should just say it out loud. He'd listen. He always had before.

'Look at me,' he said, reaching out, brushing her tightly inter-twined hands with the tips of his fingers. 'Please, Rach.' It was only a half-touch, but she could feel him even at distance, pulling her in with magnetic force. If she spoke now, it would all be out in the open. He'd know how to handle it, how to move forward.

Maybe then she'd be able to sleep. And eat. And breathe.

'I've been trying to— Look it's never the right time, but, I want—' His voice was husky, drowned out by the blasting heat. She allowed her head to turn half an inch, but she was hiding beneath her fringe, eyes firmly down, sweaty palms braced on her knees to stop them shaking. As long as she didn't look up, she could hold on, couldn't she?

But the space was becoming a sauna: steam and hair and a crashing desire to grab onto him obscuring any clear vision or thought process. And the second her gaze strayed sideways, she was gone. All resistance futile. Her hand was in his now, their fingers laced together. His eyes on hers were lasers, like he could see into her soul. He let out a low moan of frustration: 'Just tell me what you're thinking.'

She couldn't. Because what if he thought differently of her, once she let him in? This whole *thing* between them only functioned on the basis that some of their history was never acknowledged. What if all this – all the unsaid – needed to be held back too?

It was an invisible line they skirted around, worn and scuffed over time, but still tangible, like the white outline sprayed by scene of crime officers around a body.

They'd crossed its boundary once. Never again. Otherwise, things might never be the same. But if she didn't say it – right here, right now – would she get another chance?

Desperate now, past caring about the consequences, she drew him closer, one hand somehow tangled in his hair so she could –

A sudden noise made her jump. The sliding door of one of the vans slammed with a heavy clang.

'Jesus!' She dropped his hand faster than a match about to singe her fingers and reached for the dial of the heater. Her heart was racing. But the spell was broken. She took two deep breaths and then her voice was firm. 'Maz'll need time to get the warrant.'

He looked at her, searching, confused. 'That's all you're giving me?'

'Yep.' She'd made her decision. All the roaring heat had stilled. Moment of possibility extinguished.

He leaned back against the headrest. Hands in his hair. Eyes tight shut. 'What's Bailey said?'

'Given it the sign-off but sounds even more sick of his life.'

'The Mood Hoover.'

He opened one eye; she made a face. 'Not your best.'

'I know. Needs work.' He sighed heavily. 'Not even gonna ask if you're going in yourself.'

'Of course.' She flipped the visor mirror down, and examined herself, forcing a smile. 'You know me. Any excuse to get my taser out.'

'Thought that was my line.'

'You've got no lines. That's why you're chronically single.'

'Old patter landed quite well on Friday, thank you very much.'

Something swirled in her stomach, and she strained to keep her voice light. 'Glad to hear it.'

She reached for the door, urgently needing fresh air, but Saira's blunt words – *you're mental keeping him in the friend zone* – rang in her ears. She turned back, daring to provoke him. 'Come on, "taser"? Don't flatter yourself. I've heard it's on the small side.'

'You've heard, have you?' He raised an eyebrow. 'Hasn't changed that much in ten years.'

Her cheeks flamed. This was off limits. She needed to backtrack before this conversation skated over the edge.

'Something's wrong with the heating in these fleet cars. You'll be getting this jacket back damp,' she said, voice strangled, too bright.

He shook his head, reading the shift. 'Minger. If you've stained that lining with your rampant BO I'll be sending you the dry-cleaning bill.'

She opened the passenger door, the return to easy nonsense like the cold side of a pillow. 'Wind your neck in. And it's ma'am to you. Show some bloody respect, eh?'

'Apologies, ma'am,' he said. Half playful, half something else. But what?

She had neither the time nor the inclination to probe. He was probably thinking about whoever he'd been chatting up at the weekend – carefree, fun, without baggage.

Apart from anything else, she was his boss, for fuck's sake; professional boundaries mattered. He *should* be getting out there, dating, living his life. They'd still be colleagues. Mates. That line existed for a reason. No need to let him into every part of her mind.

She braced herself. The clock was ticking, the arrest right there, within reach – but so was the part of him she had no right to want.

Chapter 31

Land

Thursday 6th April

Darkness seeped like an oil slick, but Rachel's eyes cut through to Dalton Crescent, stairway seven. Parked around the bend, the red doorway was in clear view.

Lennon, beside her, was drumming his fingers on the dashboard, whilst, unfortunately for all concerned, the presence of Coates wafted around the car. He was sitting in the middle of the back seat, craning forwards like a child eager to be part of the adult conversation. She had been reluctant to bring him on the arrest, but whether by his own persistence or the requirements of the Graduate Detective Programme, here they were.

The Method of Entry team must have made it up the stairs by now, but silence was all that sounded from her radio. They'd seemed capable enough as response teams went. Always luck of the draw who got assigned for a raid at short notice, but she'd recognised the two carrying the Big Red Key.

She checked her watch. Four minutes and counting since the helmeted figures had run in convoy under the brick entranceway. The depressing regularity of incidents in the Wall over the years had necessitated Northumbria Police holding an entry fob, meaning that officers could guarantee exterior entry whilst maintaining cover for as long as possible. Ramming the door of number nine off its hinges would be the easy bit. BRK-holder was always a popular job.

'Site secure,' blared her radio, '10-26. Over.'

'Got that, Collins,' she said to the sergeant, out of the car in less than a second, already sprinting for the entrance. She heard the other two doors slam in quick succession, but didn't look back. Lennon and Coates were just steps behind and their trainers pounded four flights of narrow stairwell. The internal corridors of the building were grey, its architecturally praised miniature windows allowing only a glimpse of the outside world.

As always, the interior of the Wall reeked of chlorine. Clearly, the council were still hosing down the entire premises on the regs and cranking the heating up to the max. Rachel blinked against the acrid, cloying sensation and, on regaining her vision, was drawn to the remnants of a dirty handprint staining the wall.

At a glance, it looked like a child's finger painting, the sort her kids used to bring home from nursery. But this print was different, daubed in either blood or shit.

Rachel barged the heavy fire door. The exterior corridor was still shrouded in darkness, Tyne Bridge just visible in the distance if you knew where to look. She couldn't see the disrepair, the peeling paint, but the air was heavy with neglect. It was hard to believe they'd built ships here once, in Byker, with everything now just sprawling grey squalor. Fine drizzle overhead barely made a sound on the corrugated plastic canopy, but its misty vapour hung in the air with the scent of weed and mildew.

'All OK?' she asked the PC stationed outside flat nine's redundant door, now beyond repair after a battering from the heavy metal tool at his feet.

'Ma'am,' he said, grimacing slightly. 'Grim.'

She manoeuvred round him into the cramped hallway. 'What we expected.'

Her trainers stuck to the dirty lino, ominous dread building with every step. How many bodies would they be scraping off the floor?

The bare plaster had a single nod to home décor – 'Live Laugh Love' on a cheap canvas print. Gaby must have been proud of this home, her first teetering steps away from the foster family and whatever swamp she'd come from before that.

From the hallway, Rachel had the option of three scuffed doors, each ajar. She could hear voices from within the first two.

'You take the bedroom,' she said, over her shoulder to Lennon. Coates could stay at the door and take notes for his training log. No way was he getting near the action.

She stepped into the open-plan living area and the stench of ammonia took her breath away. Stale piss, but on a scale equivalent to a thousand mangy cats having been allowed to fester in their own urine for weeks.

They'd called it on the crack, then.

She scanned the room – pleather sofa, two grubby chairs, glass coffee table covered with cans of Monster and pizza boxes.

One of the officers was muzzling an XL Bully, secure, but growling by the back door to the balcony, an old length of rope around its thick neck. Rachel waved him through. It would either be deposited with a neighbour or there'd be a call to the dog squad in the offing.

The room was beyond dingy, its only window covered by a broken blind. Dawn was still a way off and, with no bulb in the central fitting and frosted glass in the balcony door, the only source of light was the TV. The Xbox home screen – on, but muted – cast a flickering, eerie glow.

A burly figure loomed in the shadows.

Jo" Paul Gallagher raised his eyes slowly, locking onto her own and curling his lip in distaste. 'Rat's back.'

'Feeling's mutual,' she said. 'Nice place you've got yourself.'

She hadn't had eyes on him in person for nearly three years whilst he'd enjoyed a spell at Her Majesty's Pleasure. In for five, out in two. Scum. No surprise he'd floated back to the surface.

His arms bulged beneath his tight V-neck top, but the thickened waist and receding hairline mildly repulsed her. Whatever else he was, Jo" Paul Gallagher had always taken evident pride in his pumped-up frame. Now, with one officer on the bracelets and the other reading his caution, he couldn't have looked less arsed.

Surveying her lazily, with an arrogance that was at odds with his present situation, he made to speak, but changed his mind and hocked up a mouthful of phlegm, which he spat on the floor close to her feet.

'Charming as ever,' she said, turning her head to Sergeant Collins. 'What we got?'

'Take your pick, ma'am. Exhibit A,' he said, nodding to his colleague in the kitchen area, who was photographing pans on the hob, 'and Exhibit B.'

The PC paused his camerawork and gestured to the pile of ziplock bags spread over the table. 'Interrupted your shift, haven't we, Jo" Paul?'

She walked over for a closer look at the evidence haul. There'd be more than this, somewhere in the flat; the uniforms would have the whole place ripped apart in a couple of hours.

'Thought you'd make us work for it a *bit*,' she said, turning back to Gallagher. 'All the trouble of a search warrant and you've left it out – what an absolute div.'

'Not mine,' he sneered. 'You cunts've planted this.'

'All yours, Jo" Paul. Family reunion coming up.' She crossed her arms. 'Shame though, hear your cousin's out of circulation.'

'You don't know shit.' The arrogance in his smirk really was staggering.

She raised her eyebrows. 'Throwing acid? Sounds like classic

Gallagher. So where would one of you shit-for-brains stash the rest?'

Looking around, then gently shifting the uniform away from the hob, she reached down to the sticky oven handle. Gallagher twisted against the grip of the two officers, but couldn't do anything about her hand reaching inside the cavity and emerging with a heavy bin bag.

She scanned the contents nonchalantly, then raised her eyes to meet his darting, swamp-like pupils. Better than any best-case scenario. Wildest-fucking-dreams territory. This, plus the DSU test purchase, meant he'd be off the streets and banged up before breakfast.

'Boss?' Lennon's voice from the other room, sharp and urgent.

Still walking on air, Rachel made for the bedroom. She clocked Coates in the hallway. 'Ambulance on its way,' he called, but she wasn't really listening, thinking she could give him a job back at the station going through the memory card of that Xbox.

She moved faster. Couldn't wait to see Lennon's face when he got a look at the stash. This was twenty years minimum. And there were at least two phones in there. They'd be bound to seize something with a dot-to-dot straight to the line holder. Her mouth was aching with the strain of holding in her mile-wide smile.

One glance into the bedroom ended any euphoria.

Rachel stepped back, vomit rising. She clung to the door. The scene came in flashes – blinding snaps burning the image of Gaby deeper and deeper into her eyeballs.

Gathering herself, she knelt on the floor beside the girl cowering on the mattress. Lennon and the two female officers had sat her up, but this required support from both sides.

The blonde PC's voice was shaky: 'No one's gonna hurt you now, pet.'

Gaby was painfully thin, greasy hair tied high on her lollipop head. Denim skirt and vest top. Both splattered with sick. Her face was a horror show of raw and historic bruises, graduating in colour from red to purple to brown to green to yellow. This visceral trauma was offset, horribly, by lash extensions that protruded from her hollow sockets like spider's legs.

Rachel's composure was almost decimated once more at the sight of Gaby's feet – filthy, but with sparkly blue glitter polish across each toenail. So childish. So like the *Frozen* Nail Studio Jess had been obsessed with when she was eight.

She was kicked in the gut with the realisation that her kids were near enough the same age and postcode, but a million miles away in terms of care. Even failing miserably as a mum most of the time, here and now she could recognise what they had in comparison to Gaby.

'Medically, is she …' Rachel trailed off into nothing. What was she going to ask: *is she OK?* Clearly not. The room was a monument to the Misuse of Drugs Act with Gaby gripping a plastic bottle of rocks the way a baby would cling to its dummy.

She could have had her out of here days ago.

Lennon's voice: 'Is he here? Did we get him?'

The words snapped Rachel out of her shock. 'He's here. Call the foster and have her meet the ambulance at the RVI, OK?'

Oblivious to his reply, she charged back into the main space, squaring up so close to Gallagher that she could almost feel the pulse of the blue vein in his neck.

'Make you feel like a fucking big man, does it? She's a seventeen-year-old child, you piece of shit.'

His lip curled. 'Likes it rough.'

She felt the hairline cracks beneath her feet splinter out of control, forcing her forward. 'You are vile. Fucking animal, just like your dad.'

'The fuck you saying?' He wasn't laughing now. Leering over her. 'Filthy fuckin' tramp.' The PC twisted the cuffs, unleashing a roar. Gallagher's voice was barely audible above the shouts of the uniforms. She heard him though. 'Think you're better than us? I know who you are.'

She felt the globule of phlegm hit her cheek before she realised what had happened, too troubled by the weight of his words to register anything else.

His spit was an ocean on her skin. She was being pulled under.

'You OK, ma'am?' The taller officer looked appalled, whether by the hepatitis risk or how white her face must have gone. He turned to Gallagher. 'You've just added Assault on an Emergency Worker to your rap sheet – section thirty-nine, Criminal Justice Act. Let's get this scrote in the van.'

Rachel's voice was rasping, weak. Burning water raced through her lungs; her head throbbed, blood pounding in her ears. She was drowning, and she knew it. Yet she forced herself upright. 'Give me a couple of minutes with the suspect. Alone.'

The three uniforms exchanged glances, then left. They'd been told: if the officer in charge said do a can-can on an arrest, you did it. No questions asked.

But Rachel didn't speak. Not yet. They'd be pressed against the other side of that door, listening intently.

She had to get him out. More and more water was rushing in with force; the dam had burst. Fuck the risk assessment. She killed her BWV and dragged Jo" Paul onto the balcony. No one needed to see this.

Slamming him against the barrier, bending back his fingers until he yelped, gave her the surge she needed to continue.

She wasn't drowning. She was stable: a police officer, a grown woman, not a damaged child. 'What the fuck did you mean by that – *I know who you are*?'

He writhed like an animal caught in a trap, but she matched him blow for blow. No thin blue line between them, just two feral figures braying the crap out of each other.

She'd worked too hard to let a Gallagher pull her under.

She refused to drown. Not here. Not now.

Jo" Paul's words were hocked up like globules of infected mucus, rancid with hatred. 'Did a bit digging inside, didn't I?

Things I've been told. Truth always comes out in the end, you fuckin' rat.'

Dizzy, she withdrew her taser as he kicked out, throwing himself around the cramped space with full force. His shoulder slammed into her face, sending her weapon clattering to the ground as the balcony barrier cracked and its wood veneer split in two, exposing a gaping crevice to the elements.

'You're full of shit – truth about what?'

His eyes flashed, green and monstrous. 'About you. Fuckin' bitch – whatever you're calling yourself, *Harlow*?'

Paralysed, torn between wanting to hear more and silencing his lies, Rachel felt hot blood in her hands. She struggled to regain control of the cuffs.

Another voice – close, but not Gallagher's – cut through. Familiar. Steady. Her grip loosened, just enough.

Then, slow motion: the sour tang of breath in her face as Jo" Paul mouthed something, lost on the wind, then his legs flailing, arms trapped, face registering the imminent impact of bone and flesh on concrete.

For a moment, all was calm.

The pounding in her head subsided; the constant panic ceased. Strong arms wrapped around her, warmth and weight like a cocoon. Then reality hit like a tsunami.

'What the hell was that?' Lennon breathed the words into her ear as she swayed, anchored only by the sensation of his heartbeat. 'Listen, Rach, get your story straight and do not deviate. You're in deep shit now. IOPC'll be all over this.'

Then firmer, the last thing she heard before blacking out: 'I've got you. And I won't let go.'

Chapter 32

Sea

Monday 24th April

Rachel woke with a lurch. No groggy transition: a switch had been flicked and she was immediately alert. As a pre-hangover, this shift from off to on was unwelcome, but not unfamiliar. There was an urgency, though, which she couldn't reconcile with the normal after-effects of a few too many.

The cabin was filled to the brim with the sort of infinite blackness that only a windowless room could contain, and, from their sporadic snores, Jess and Jake were still fast asleep. She groped for her phone and brought its soft glow to her face. What had made her wake so suddenly at three a.m.?

She'd been somewhere else. Wind in her hair. Spit against her cheek. It had felt real, but the eyes she'd faced were hundreds of miles away in intensive care. Her heartbeat accelerated. The bleak flat, reeking of weed. Bare feet and glittery toenails. Water seeping under the door and gathering momentum, threatening to drag her under.

Stop now. Breathe.

It was just a dream.

Trying to refocus her spiralling mind, she reached for the remote. With one button, the virtual balcony transformed into a window on the promenade and endless sea. She let her eyes submerge into the hypnotic movement, sure that she'd soon sink back into slumber.

The feed on the screen was dim and shadowy. Only a sliver of pale moon illuminating the ship's starboard side as it carved through the water effortlessly, leaving a single ridge of white-crested spray in its wake. Her eyes adapted to the predictable churning path.

It was comforting to stare at nothingness, to be reminded what existed out there – beyond this cabin, beyond this ship.

When she saw the two figures, she thought, at first, she had drifted back into the shadows of her dream. They were blurry, but this was different to before.

She blinked.

Still there.

They were at the extreme left, just at the edge of the camera's reach. Sitting up, she gazed deeper, eyes boring into the screen.

It was not a dream.

She shivered, despite the stifling temperature of the cabin. Why would people be wandering around the ship, outside on the promenade, in the dead of night?

Rubbing her tired eyes, she rationalised the scene. There would be a perfectly normal explanation. No need to be suspicious. Holidaymakers stumbling out of one of the late bars, or the Poseidon club, trying to sober up.

They looked strangely co-ordinated, though. Uniform. So, crew members? There'd be plenty of them working night shifts. She squinted. Their features were almost impossible to decipher; just two standing shapes, facing each other as if in a duel. Even blurred, their postures screamed aggression. Hands raised, movements wild.

An argument?

Rachel shifted forwards on the bed, aware that she'd been holding her breath. The animation was increasing – one stepped closer, gesticulating with unheard emotion.

What the fuck was going on?

A wave of exhaustion engulfed her. Could she just close her eyes? This was meant to be annual leave. A holiday from ABH and GBH and all the other bloody acronyms. Surely, she was entitled to turn away and leave them to it.

And yet, she stared, unable to ignore the rising threat of violence.

They'd shifted, central on the screen now. They looked the same. Men. Heavy set. Both dark-haired. Could one be Fernandez? She squinted again, trying to make out more from pixellated shapes in the pitch-black of the cabin.

Reaching out, she snapped the bedside light on, but it didn't help. Just glare hitting the screen now, masking one corner of the scene entirely. It couldn't be Fernandez, could it? There were over four thousand people on board. It was hardly likely to be someone she'd seen or spoken to.

She gasped as one arm swung back and crashed into the other, sending him careering out of shot, into the unknown. Almost immediately, he returned to view and now the two were indistinguishable as separate figures, just a thrashing mesh of blows.

Rachel was off the bed now. Tense and alert.

The footage was disjointed, jumpy. Would there be a delay? She looked to the phone on Jake's side of the cabin. Who should she call? 999 meant nothing here.

The day had been good. Sitting in that restaurant, they'd been *together*. It was a batshit jigsaw they were working on, no doubt, with a fair few of the pieces missing, but there'd been flashes of the overall picture.

So why had she woken into this? Why now?

The brawl was suddenly punctuated by a glint of metal in

the moonlight. Her heart quickened, pulse racing. A knife. The blade was frenzied in its movement – in and out of the blur on screen, then in again.

She had to act. One man was slumped over the barrier now, something dark seeping from his chest. The other figure showed no sign of ceasing his attack, heaving the bloodied man up, higher and higher, almost over the rail.

This needed more than a call to Guest Services. Rachel threw the cabin door open and slammed her fist down on the red emergency alarm.

A high-pitched siren ripped through the silence. Strips of strobe where the walls met the floor burst into a blaze of light, pulsing to the rapid heartbeat of the alarm. She let the door slam.

'What's going on?' Jake's eyes were wide, face pale in the strobing glare.

Jess had pulled the pillow over her head and was mumbling something incoherent.

'Emergency alarm – get up right now – we need to go.'

She looked back at the screen.

The figures were gone.

Chapter 33

Sea

They raced down the stairway towards Deck Seven, bumping against hordes of passengers clutching life vests. Some were already scrambling for the lifeboats. Chaos. She could barely believe that the briefing for this sort of emergency action had taken place a mere four days ago.

The air, as they burst onto the promenade, was horribly cold. Rachel sprinted along the starboard side, dragging Jess and Jake to avoid getting separated in the scrum. It was imperative to locate the virtual balcony camera and ensure that the scene was taped off before thousands of trudging footprints trampled the evidence away.

Her eyes raced, looking for Fernandez, or anyone who would fit the description of the figures she'd witnessed. But it was useless.

She had no fucking tape. No scene of crime officers. And it all looked the same. Rachel gripped the rail, searching to pinpoint the exact field of vision of the live feed.

Railings, deck, sky and sea.

There was nothing here to help her. Any trace of the argument or its cause was gone.

What about the blood? They'd only have had moments at

most to clean the area. She'd seen it. A pool. A body's worth, not a splash. And now – nothing.

The whole place was packed with people being shepherded like livestock into pens. Huge printed letters on the walls, which she'd walked past blindly for four days, now made sense as muster points.

She allowed herself to be herded back to the port side where they were electronically marked on the manifest and handed replacement life vests after failing to arrive with the required equipment.

With increasing urgency, Rachel tried to relay her information, but with the siren continuing to scream its insistent warning, it was impossible to make herself understood. The army of stewards in high-vis vests appeared to have clicked into autopilot, their unscheduled wake-up call recalibrating to ultra-efficiency mode.

Amongst the near-hysteria at Muster Point D, they found Barbara and Robert and huddled together for warmth. Speculation was at fever pitch amongst the groups around them. Stewards swerved and volleyed the onslaught of questions, reassuring guests with lines seemingly read from an autocue. They were in no danger. They would be informed via Tannoy when it was safe to return to their cabins.

Her parents' shock at her having pushed the button was palpable. And the timeline hardly sounded credible even to herself as she laid it out in a hushed whisper: 'A fight – two people – barely make it out – a blade – then gone.' She struggled to convey her panic to stop the violence in its tracks. Barbara's raised eyebrows and sideways look at Robert suggested incredulity, but at least the kids were on her side.

Jess hugged her arms around herself, teeth chattering. 'I don't like this.'

'Yeah. Proper gangster shit,' said Jake, sinking somewhat under Barbara's sharp look. 'Soz, Gran.'

She had to break out of this holding pen and report what she'd seen. The old nausea rose in her throat, knowing that she would soon have to stand in front of the captain again, relaying another unwelcome statement. But with the ship's CCTV sure to have caught her hand on the alarm, there was no way to minimise her role.

'There's Oksana,' her dad said, pointing to the smooth platinum chignon bobbing ahead of them in the crowd. 'Report it to her.' His voice was firm, faith in the HLC juggernaut unshakeable.

Jess's face was white and her fingers gripped Rachel's arm tightly. 'Shouldn't we stay with you?' In the darkness, she looked like a little girl again, wanting Mum to check for monsters under the bed.

But real monsters didn't hide under beds; they walked amongst us and stabbed people in cold blood.

Gently, Rachel un-prised her hand, pushing her back towards her grandparents. Her duty here had to be to the victim.

From the frenzy of the blade's incisions, there were only two possible scenarios. Someone on board was either hiding in a dark red pool as their chances of survival dwindled. Or they'd been discarded – over the railing into the water. Whichever was true, this period in the immediate aftermath was critical. A life could still be saved.

Pushing against the flow of passengers still emerging from the aft stairwell, Rachel pressed forward and called out to their steward. She didn't turn so she called again, raising her voice against the insistent wail of the siren and the hubbub of voices. Though a few metres away and still being buffeted by the current of pyjamas and hastily chosen footwear, Oksana stopped in her tracks and faced her. Her eyes were startlingly blue in the dim light, pinpoints of reassurance as Rachel struggled to reach her.

Her words came out in a rush. 'This alarm, tonight, it was me. I saw something ten minutes ago, on the virtual balcony.'

Oksana's eyes crinkled in confusion. '*Vir-tule?*'

Rachel struggled for another way to describe it. In desperation, she drew a rectangle in the air, then circled her fist frantically in the universal charade for 'movie'. 'The screen, in the cabin, to see out here. On the promenade?' Her voice rose, thinking of the blade, the blood. 'Two men, a fight, a knife.'

Oksana assessed her with piercing eyes. 'We must to go. Now.'

She was urged upwards, step by step, Oksana's hand on her shoulder, as they moved against the tide on the crowded stairwell.

'Where are we going?' she asked, craning her head backwards.

'My husband. Deck Twelve. He is know what to do.'

They emerged into a similar scene of ordered pandemonium: guests in disarray, crew armed with bottles of water and textbook platitudes. Andre was stationed at an exit point, unsmiling and alert, one hand to his earpiece, the other at his hip.

Rachel swept her fringe from her eyes and attempted to get her breath back as Oksana unleashed a torrent of unfamiliar language. Andre barked a few questions, reaching out to shake his wife's shoulder and point aggressively at the CCTV camera above their heads.

From his disapproving glances towards her, she gathered that his view of her story was, at best, sceptical and at worst, hostile. Without addressing her or offering reassurance, he relayed staccato bursts into his earpiece. Finally, with a terse nod, he gestured for them both to follow.

Miller was waiting this time as the lift doors opened. His face was puce, upper-class charm all gone.

'Inspector Harlow,' he barked. 'I have been informed that you are responsible for the current situation on board my vessel.'

'If you mean, that I followed the emergency procedure, then yes.'

'And may I ask, what precisely this *emergency* consisted of?' His voice dripped with scorn.

She stood to her full height, albeit a foot smaller than him.

She'd encountered plenty of men in the police force who had tried to intimidate her with their height, weight, volume. Every sort of dick-swinging swagger.

Her voice was cold as she set out the timeline of events. 'I observed a violent altercation between two men on the live feed of the virtual balcony in my cabin. I believe one of them was Miguel Fernandez, but they were both black-haired, medium height and build. I'm certain that one of them was stabbed. Obviously, I was unable to intervene, so my only option was the emergency alarm. You'll have the area under CCTV, so you need to examine the footage immediately and confirm the whereabouts of both men.'

Miller looked at Andre and shooed him forcefully towards the computer screens. 'Set up the night tape for replay. Now.' He turned back. 'If you have no further information, I must insist you leave.' He looked at Oksana. 'Escort the guest back to her cabin.'

'I'm going nowhere.' Rachel crossed her arms and waited for his next attempt to cut her down to size.

Miller's face had gone an even deeper shade of purple. Clearly, he was not used to being spoken to in this manner, but it was unclear whether it was her words, her gender, her accent or her insubordination that was causing his eyes to bulge in his head like overfilled water balloons.

The inevitable pop was narrowly averted by the arrival of Simon Van der Wyk, looking well rested and calm by comparison. The security chief was shower-fresh, in a crisp white shirt, his shadow of light stubble the only sign that this was an unscheduled night shift.

'You again?' He smiled. 'Joining the crew?'

'Certainly not,' Miller snapped. 'Inspector Harlow was just leaving.'

'All crew and passengers accounted for, Captain. Passenger alarm activated on Deck Ten at three fourteen a.m. No discernible fault. Looks like a false alarm, but we'll check the footage.'

'Andre has already been instructed to examine the night feed. Claims of a serious nature have been made, which will require further investigation. But—' he looked at Rachel with disdain '—your presence is not required.'

'Best get to it, Captain,' Van der Wyk said with a nod that loosened his glasses from the bridge of his nose. His manner was, as with Tyler's death, as relaxed as Miller's was tightly wound.

'Take me to the doctor, then,' she said to Miller. 'Let's see if Larson's had anyone banging on her door with a stab wound in the last half hour.'

'Dr Larson has reported to her muster station and returned to her cabin. I will not be disturbing her again tonight. You have no authority, either to interfere with my crew or to stray out of the guest facilities. We have the matter under control.'

'I've got serious concerns about that,' she said, eyeing him defiantly. 'There are clearly drugs on board and now also weapons. You need to locate Fernandez! And identify the other man as a matter of urgency.' Her voice rose. 'This was a violent assault, and quite possibly murder. Not to mention the previous as-yet unexplained death of a crew mem—'

He advanced towards her, all pretence of courtesy gone. 'Now, listen here—'

'Captain, can I suggest we hear Inspector Harlow out?' Van der Wyk inserted himself between them, calming the waters with an impressive level of diplomacy. 'If a critical incident has occurred, her professional expertise may be invaluable.'

'At least someone's taking this seriously.' Rachel glanced at the security chief, but immediately focused her attention back to Miller. 'I may not have authority at sea, but I'm UK police and I'm not going to let this go. The deep-clean of Tyler's cabin, removing all physical evidence, still needs to be investigated. My CID colleague has run a background check on one of your other employees and uncovered an absolute shitshow. And now this?' She braced her legs to stop them from shaking. 'To be frank,

Captain, no, I don't think you have the matter under control in any way whatsoever.'

There was a tense silence, eventually broken by Van der Wyk clearing his throat. 'Captain, I can see from the manifest that Miguel Fernandez has been overseeing the night shift in the Waste Management Centre. No reported absence from duty.'

Rachel and the captain both made to speak, but Van der Wyk continued, gently. 'I'd be happy to meet with Inspector Harlow at a more agreeable time tomorrow and we can go through any outstanding concerns? I'll review the footage now and trace any movement on Deck Seven. I'm sure we can put your mind at rest.'

She looked from man to man. This was such an obvious attempt to fob her off, but realistically, what was her alternative? As much as she despised his arrogance, Miller's words were unfortunately true. She had no power here. Her badge and her warrant card meant nothing.

'That would be a start,' she grudgingly conceded.

Miller looked down his nose, as if she was something nasty he needed to scrape off his shoe. He spoke with words clipped from a cactus. 'If you sign the company NDA immediately, tonight, I am prepared to allow you a brief interview with my chief security officer as a follow-up to your, frankly, outlandish claims. The matter will then be officially closed.'

'Fine,' she said, her tone equally prickly. 'I'll need a new form.'

Still in her sightline, Andre was communicating a terse string of information to Van der Wyk. 'No film. Tape stop 2.57.'

'Must be a system error,' Van der Wyk said, moving away from Rachel and tapping a string of letters. 'Try rebooting it from the C-drive.'

Andre's hard eyes met hers. His lips moved – one word, maybe two – but she couldn't make it out.

It didn't feel like reassurance. It felt like a warning.

'Ten a.m. then.' Van der Wyk was back, stretching his hand in a conciliatory shake. 'I'll collect you from Guest Services and we can discuss the details in my office.'

She stared at the initials she'd scrawled on the NDA, her signature trapped in Miller's fist. On land, she would have been leading this investigation. At sea, she'd just signed herself into silence.

Chapter 34

Sea

Rachel didn't even attempt to get back to sleep. The virtual balcony feed had been terminated and she was left with nothing but the minutes ticking by until dawn eventually broke.

Another morning, another Mediterranean city. Was this really only day five? Rather than her stresses and strains melting away in the promised indulgence, Rachel was dizzy now from the consecutive curveballs, and longed for the cold formality of a case review meeting.

Instead, what she had as they docked in Porto, was a ragtag group of amateur teenage sleuths and opinionated OAPs. Barbara was giving it her best CSI chat over breakfast as Rachel filled them in. Possibly, her dad had had a word, as her scepticism at Rachel's version of events seemed to have lessened. At least Jess had regained some colour and was taking what looked like professional-standard minutes.

'It's a classic case of evidence tampering,' Barbara said, lips pursed, looking around shrewdly, everyone now a suspect.

Jon and the Gorgeous Kevin waved from across the restaurant, their table stacked with far more plates than two diners justified. From their tripod and Jon's animated gestures, they were clearly filming the *Synergy*'s breakfast experience. The Gorgeous Kevin seemed to have adopted a directorial role, standing regularly to adjust the angles. He was also wearing dark glasses and appeared to be limping.

'Let's wait and see what Van der Wyk says this morning,' she said. 'He's alarmingly relaxed, but at least he seems willing to hear me out.'

'If no one's disappeared or needed medical treatment, it won't be high up his list of concerns in terms of security,' said Jess, chewing on the end of her pen.

'Not being funny, Mam, but are you sure you saw it?' Jake piped up. 'You'd had a few, and we all know what happened after your last proper sesh.' He mimed a dramatic vomit motion all over the table.

She gave him a look. 'Too soon. And, yes, I'm certain I saw two people fighting, then a blade. The image was shit – I mean poor quality – but it was GBH minimum.'

'What's the plan, then?' Barbara said. 'We're ready for our instructions. Your dad and I were saying – we got quite into that undercover business. We could question someone else? Or follow one of the suspects?'

'What for though?' Rachel said, frustrated. 'I'm glad you had fun, but really, Jess's right. We've got an OD and a stabbing that never happened, no body and no blood. It's not a lot to go on.'

'You've got an instinct, though, haven't you, love, that there's been foul play.' Her dad's gentle tone was a balm to her heavy mental load.

'I have.'

'Well, that's enough for us.'

'We need to give it a name,' Jake said. 'Y'know, like Operation *Something*.'

The reaction was heated; everyone had an opinion. *Excalibur* was suggested by Robert and quickly dismissed. Barbara tried vociferously to get the simple *Synergy* over the line. 'It just makes sense.'

'Too obvious, Gran. It's got to be something random. But, like, with power.' Jess punctuated this with a punch to Jake's solar plexus.

Rachel swiftly blocked his retaliation. 'This isn't a priority. You know our operation codes just get spat off a computer programme, right? No one sits round like this, brainstorming.'

'What about JC?' Jake said, rubbing his chest.

Jess screwed up her face. 'As in Jesus Christ? What Would Jesus Do?'

'No,' he continued hurriedly, presumably trying to steer his sister away from a diatribe on the perils of religion. 'As in *Just Cruisin*, y'know, from the T-shirts?'

Surprisingly, heads were nodding around the table. 'I like it,' said Jess.

'Perfect,' said Barbara, 'and an ideal opportunity to get some more wear out of them, if we treat them now as uniforms.'

Rachel gulped. There were a limited number of places she could have left that top, but searching for it now across eighteen decks and four thousand passengers, on top of everything else, seemed insurmountable.

'Right,' she said. 'It's almost half nine – I'll have to go and meet Van der Wyk soon. Hopefully something's shown up on the CCTV and there's a clear explanation. If not, we need to get the Portuguese police involved.'

'Didn't you say something about maritime law being different?' Robert asked.

'That's what I got from the doctor. Something about flagged countries. The ship's registered in Panama so, officially, it would be their police force who'd be responsible for investigating any criminal activity. I'm not a hundred per cent on her though, or the explanation she gave.'

'I could do some research,' Jess said.

'And we could at least get a foot in the door with the Portuguese police,' Barbara added. 'We're not in international waters now, are we? Surely now we're docked, it's on their turf?'

Rachel's phone burst into life on the table. That bastard unknown number again. She pressed red and turned it over. 'Sounds like a plan. Are you sure you don't mind, though? Spending your holiday doing admin or sitting in a foreign police station wasn't what you signed up for.'

They brushed off her concerns and seemed genuinely enthusiastic to be picking up their roles under her management. Dismayed to feel a lump in her throat, and touched by their faith, she quickly swallowed it down. Becoming an emotional wreck was absolutely out of the question.

'Can we grab you two, at some point?' a voice called. It was Jon. 'Views for the latest TikTok upload have dropped off a cliff. We *need* to get some Whisper content up five minutes ago.' He had a hand on each of the twins' shoulders, gripping with the desperation of a man on the edge.

'Heavy night?' Rachel nodded across at Kevin's incognito attire and tentative movements as he packed up the equipment.

'A fall,' Jon said, in a hushed tone. 'Deck Fourteen aft staircase. Liquid all over the marble. We could sue.'

'From the muster stations? Last night?'

Jon winced. 'Don't mention it to him. A hard floor isn't a kind surface for the larger man, and he's oversensitive at the best of times. Went down heavily on his right side.'

Barbara launched into an irrelevant story about Pam from the bowls club, who had tripped on a paving stone three years ago and broken her hip. 'Still has trouble with it when it rains even now, doesn't she, Bob?'

'Bad business,' he agreed. 'Not a penny from the council. And her forehand delivery's never been what it was.'

'Has he seen the doctor?' Rachel said, shutting down the bowls chat.

'No appointments all day,' Jon said, hand on hip. 'Either backlogged with injuries or she's off duty. Not strictly speaking allowed, if she is. Should be a medic available at all times.'

'We can do it, no bother,' Jake cut in. 'Whisper's pretty straightforward, once you know your way round the platform.'

'I've got a job for you too,' Rachel said. 'Something on the laptop. I'll show you quickly in the cabin, then I'll have to go and meet the security guy.'

They said their goodbyes to Jon before he hurried away to support the Gorgeous Kevin's hobble towards the lifts. She could see livid purple bruising emerging around his left eye, visible despite the oversized shades. Must have been some fall, to have injured both his face and body.

Time was ticking and she needed to give Jake some legal parameters before she let him loose on his task. Casting off her doubts, she reasoned that if assault wasn't being treated as a serious infringement to HLC's legislation, then surely a bit of light-fingered tech adjustment wasn't going to be an issue either. She recalled Bailey's weary words on her shift in management responsibility in Operation Fever. *Play to their strengths,* he'd said. *Give them a clear job and keep on comms.*

'Mum, Dad,' she said. 'If you get anywhere with the Portuguese police, stay there and call it in to me. Jess, stick with Gran and Grandad and try to get some concrete guidelines of what policing protocol should be at sea and in port. You'll get faster internet when you're off the ship. And Jake, come with me, OK? Better if the rest of you don't know the details at the moment.'

They looked at her with wide eyes: shiny new recruits lined up in front of the super for their passing-out parade. The Operation JC day shift had begun.

Simon Van der Wyk was waiting for Rachel as she hurried across the shiny floor to Guest Services. He had been speaking to the reception staff and she noted the respectful way he ended his conversation before greeting her.

Unlike other senior crew, he didn't bark or belittle. A marked contrast from what she'd seen from management so far on board. Or back home.

'Thanks for meeting me,' she said.

'Not a problem. Rare treat for me to be out of the surveillance office and get some natural light. If we make our way down there, I can show you the footage.'

She appraised him as they exited through the CREW ONLY door. 'Has the captain calmed down since last night?'

He gave an exaggerated grimace. 'I couldn't possibly comment.'

'How'd you come to work here? If you don't mind me asking.'

'Not at all. HLC likes to employ ex-service personnel into security roles wherever possible. I did two years' basic training back home, but – well – private security seems to suit me better.'

'Any particular reason?' She paused on the staircase, feeling she'd overstepped the mark. 'Just being nosy. The police's got its challenges, but I guess the South African military's another level.'

He adjusted his glasses. 'Sight test. I fall below the 6/6 minimum level even with these.'

'Oh right,' she said. 'Hard to take.'

'I like the control on board, so it's worked out for the best.' He continued down the stairs to Deck One. 'Whether that's a spreadsheet or a key card system, security on a cruise ship's fully containable, right? Can't say that in Mzansi.'

'Fair enough,' she said, thinking of her own normalised chaos, every plate spinning at a hundred miles an hour.

'This is me.' He unlocked a door marked *Security Operations* and put a steady hand on her back for her to enter first, his touch courteous, not sleazy. Quite the gentleman.

He hadn't been joking about the lack of daylight. It was dark and oppressively stuffy, with a repetitive clanking sound suggesting they were somewhere near the engines. Van der Wyk shut the heavy door, lowering the background noise to a muffled bass vibration. The small office was dominated by fifty-plus screens, all simultaneously showing grainy activity from different positions across the ship.

'Wow. Big Brother's watching.'

He shrugged. 'You must be used to this sort of set-up, in your day job?'

Overseeing the Byker surveillance felt like an alternative universe. It had seemed so important, just a couple of weeks ago, so meaningful. Reclaiming the streets. But really, hadn't it all just been a waste of time? A few shitty cameras squatting in dusty squalor, spying on kids riding around on bikes with a few quid in their back pockets.

'Bit different to this scale,' she said. 'So, did you manage to retrieve last night's CCTV?'

'Yes. Full system reboot. It's not great quality, as you'd expect, but it does give a decent image of the area. I've been through it twice, and—' he frowned '—sorry to disappoint, but no altercation on Deck Seven at all.'

'You're kidding.'

'Afraid not.' He gave her a sympathetic look, but she could see beads of sweat forming at his temples. 'It's easy enough to get carried away in the middle of the night. Unfamiliar bed. And, obviously, you've had a shock already on this trip.'

Her phone burst into an insistent ring. The unknown number again. Fuck's sake. This was getting ridiculous.

'Sorry, I'll just take this quickly.' She moved into the corridor as she answered the call. 'Harlow.'

'DI Rachel Harlow?' An unfamiliar voice. 'Andy Robinson. I've been assigned as your Police Federation representative for the Professional Standards hearing you'll be attending on the twenty-eighth. I've left several messages.'

'Oh. OK,' she said, struggling to hear him above the mechanical background thrum. 'I'm not in the country, I'm afraid, so I must have missed those.'

'I see.'

She cringed. 'Erm, now isn't actually a good time. Can I ring you back? In about half an hour?'

'I have to say, DI Harlow, this is highly irregular. Officers approaching a disciplinary are usually extremely keen to speak to us.'

'Right. Yes. I just need to deal with a minor situation and I'll call you straight back.'

'As you wish, Inspector. I'll be available until noon.'

'Of course, thanks. Sorry for the confusion.' She hung up, returning to Van der Wyk who was focused on his laptop. Refusing to allow her mind to leave the confines of the ship and veer towards home, she sat to face him.

'It was definitely there,' she said, shaking her head. 'Two figures – would have been about five past three. Are you sure?'

'You're welcome to view the footage for yourself.' He turned the laptop so she could see the screen. The same grey sky. The same hypnotic propulsion forwards through dark water. The only variables from the shadowy palette were the churning white foam and the moon.

Rachel stared at the huge round orb as the seconds in the bottom right-hand corner climbed to fifty-nine and dropped to one again. The time progressed from 3.04 a.m. to 3.07 a.m. and the moon remained a perfect circle.

A narrow ray of clarity shone down like a laser beam. It was a tiny spark, but enough.

'As I said, it's amazing what the mind can conjure up in the middle of the night. Don't dwell on it. No harm done.'

She remained alert, all senses heightened, not wanting to lose the sudden light in the gloom.

'Was there anything else I can help you with? You mentioned a concern with a crew member. A background check?' He'd raised his voice to counteract the engine noise.

She lifted her eyes from the screen. 'Danielle Paige, yes. We had a – how can I put it? – "heated exchange" following Tyler Tweedy's death. I asked one of my CID colleagues to run her through our system. Turns out she's using a stage name on board, maybe you're already aware. Her real name flagged up a long list of youth convictions.'

'I wasn't aware,' he said, frowning. 'All public-facing crew members are required to have DBS clearance, so that's something HR should have found.' He minimised the CCTV footage and pulled up an Excel document. 'I'll certainly follow that up – Paggot, was it?'

She looked at him, skin prickling with an icy chill, despite the stifling air. She hadn't given the name.

Reading people – cutting through bullshit – had always been her primary skill set. But she'd got him all wrong.

Who was this man? Efficient. Professional. Too professional – the type who never made a mistake, except for the one he just had.

She should quit now while she was ahead. Get back above the water line. Back to her family. But would there be another chance to question him alone? Determined, she pressed on, the urge to uncover more too strong to resist. 'Do you have much to do with the crew in your role?'

'Rarely. I don't tend to get involved behind the scenes.'

'Best way. Once in a blue moon, sort of thing?'

He raised one eyebrow and she held her breath. The tension was excruciating. It felt like her insides and her outsides were mirroring each other in a sensory overload. Was the grinding of machinery she could hear just the cogs in her brain turning?

Abruptly, he stood and moved to the open door. She hadn't shut it after taking the call. Rachel was suddenly aware of how far they were from the busy passenger areas of the ship. They hadn't seen another soul below deck. Had he told the crew members upstairs where he was taking her?

Being here, all the way down beside the engine room, now felt loaded with danger. A trap. The vibrations were enough to drown out anything she could shout. Or scream.

Holy shit.

Her instinct to get the hell out could not be ignored any longer. She'd have to extricate herself without raising alarm – but had she left it too late?

'Well, I won't keep you.' Quickly, she rose and held out a hand, willing it not to shake. 'Thank you for sharing the footage. And apologies for my apparently overactive imagination.'

He smiled. 'Easily done, right?'

A bottle of saline solution on a shelf near the door caught her eye as she brushed past, but she forced her face to stay impassive. He wore contact lenses? Her mind lurched back to the safety briefing – no glasses then. Clearly, he did.

She was through the doorway now, machinery noise outside louder than ever. 'I can get myself back upstairs.' The dark corridor stretched ahead – foreboding and endless. Anyone who knew her would hear the brittle tension in her voice. He mustn't see her demeanour crack. Should she start running?

Suddenly, the whole ship seemed to surge and she stumbled, precariously close to falling. Van der Wyk steadied her in the narrow space and smiled politely as she righted her balance. His expression was fixed. Practised.

She recognised that look. Had delivered it herself hundreds of times to members of the public. The interferers. Nosy neighbours. Paranoid conspiracy theorists.

Was she losing it? His role, like hers, was to keep people safe. He was qualified. Skilled. Perhaps she was reading too much into the meagre takeaways of this 'interview', this 'case' – racking up random exhibits to build a narrative against an innocent man. Without a warrant, she had zero power to seize anything down here.

But something in her held firm. Despite the danger and the

doubt, letting this drop felt like a betrayal of the Police and Criminal Evidence Act.

The footage was a fraud. That much was certain.

What was that line in Jess's *1984* book, something about truth and untruth? She had to cling to her DI instinct. Her experience. Her sanity. If she had that, even against the HLC machine, she was not mad.

Chapter 35

Sea

Rachel was gobsmacked with Jake's efforts, when she returned to the cabin. In the hour she'd left him with his laptop and the extortionate Wi-Fi booster, he'd managed to bypass several encrypted passwords and access the HLC intranet.

'Won't this be traced?' she asked, still unsettled by the meeting with Van der Wyk.

'Shouldn't be. I've set up the configuration to hide our device and IP location. The coding's pretty similar to the school SIMs system.'

'I only understood about five of those words.'

'Bless.' He patted her arm. 'Imagine using a skeleton key to get into a building. The lock's not broken so we can come and go like this without leaving footprints.'

'Amazing! Can you alter our access privileges from here?'

'I think I've done it,' he said, holding up the key card. 'We'll only know when we test it out, though. I've set it to all areas, like you said. It was literally just unchecking one box and checking another.'

'And the crew directory?'

He started tapping a string of numbers across the black screen.

'Coming to that now. We'll have to see what records they carry, but it should give us the basics.'

There was a knock at the door. They looked at each other and Jake snapped the laptop shut.

'Room turn-down,' came a female voice.

'Oh, I was expecting Oksana,' Rachel said, opening the door to an unfamiliar, dark-haired woman, holding an armful of towels.

'Different corridor now,' said the woman, whose name badge read *Maria*. 'I come back later?'

'We didn't request new towels. Honestly, there's plenty here. And the room's immaculate.'

'New towels every day. HLC standard.'

'Is everything OK, with Oksana?' Rachel said, remembering her solemn silence as she'd escorted her back to the cabin following Miller's abrasive instructions.

'Yes. Is no problem. I take care of you.' Maria bowed her head slightly and passed the pristine bale through the doorway. 'I collect old ones later. You want towel like swan on bed?'

'I think we're fine, thanks. Bye for now.' She managed a smile, but the exchange left a bitter taste. Everything on this ship was for show. Nothing was ever just what it seemed.

At least Jess hadn't been here to witness the extravagant waste of perfectly clean, unused towels. She probably would have imploded.

Her phone buzzed. The implosion queen herself.

Got nowhere with police. some info though. on our way back to base.

She gave it a thumbs up and turned back to Jake. 'Right, where were we?'

He grinned, the screen showing the HLC logo with SYNERGY OF THE SEAS CREW DIRECTORY at the top. 'Look, there's a search bar. Who did you want?'

'Fernandez,' she said, leaning in.

'There's two. Miguel Fernandez, Environmental Services Manager. He's the one who had a go at Jess, right?'

'Yep. We know him.'

'And Estavo Fernandez, Procurement Officer. What's that?'

'Not sure, but click on it.'

A professional headshot loaded: black swept-back hair, dark eyes and a brooding expression stared back at them. 'No, that's Miguel,' she said. 'You must be on the wrong one.'

'I'm not. It's definitely Estavo, look, his details are here. Date of birth, address, date of HLC induction—'

'Wait, go back to the other one. I'm confused.'

Obediently, Jake switched between the two Fernandez entries. 'Different dates of birth. Estavo's three years older, but they must be related?'

'That explains why your gran and grandad saw him at *Dance with Danielle* while we were in the recycling. Two different guys.' She stared at the near-identical faces, her stomach knotting. Two men. But which was the suspect and which was the victim? If they'd had an evidence board, these pictures would be pinned at the centre, circled in red. 'Screenshot them and send me the images. We need to update everyone.'

'What d'you think's going on?'

'I've got a theory,' she said, 'but we need confirmation. And it takes the threat level significantly higher.'

'Like, bring out the big guns?' He smirked, throwing Hollywood dialogue around like confetti. 'FBI! Freeze!'

'Wrong continent,' she said, grimly. 'But if I'm right, we're in stab-vest territory.'

'They weren't the least bit interested, Rachel,' Barbara said, as she, Robert and Jess hurried back into the Columbus café and took their seats around the circular table.

'The police? Not surprising, but might have helped if they'd at least come on board. If they're anything like Northumbria they just won't have the resources.'

The afternoon sun was low in the sky, casting long shadows

across the dual vista. To the port side she could see Leixões' dock, fancier than other terminals they'd visited, the passenger walkway a white ribbon curling round on itself like a bandage. Through the starboard window was the sea: flat and still, with no sign of its hidden world beneath.

Which way held the answers? Putting their faith in dry land today seemed to have yielded nothing, but treading water on board until something surfaced didn't seem like a good option either.

'We've always said, haven't we, Bob?' Barbara said, tutting. 'Those Portuguese police are a law unto themselves. I mean, you only have to look at that poor McCann family. Mishandled from the start that was, needle in a haystack.'

'Very difficult to deal with,' Robert agreed, coughing into a handkerchief. 'Took a few cursory notes, but they left us waiting at the front desk for over an hour.'

'We weren't even offered a cup of tea. Unsavoury characters being brought in throughout the morning.'

'*Nenhum crime*,' Robert said weakly. 'That's what he said. *Nenhum crime*. We had to look it up. "No crime".'

Rachel turned to Jess, who had been lost in her notebook since sitting down; she was flicking back through the pages, searching for something. Small rectangular Post-its had been attached to the edges of the book in various colours.

'What's your coding system?'

'Cross-referencing for each crew member,' she said, eyes still flicking back through her small, cursive words. 'And I'm going through everything we already know about the captain's version of maritime police procedure.'

'He didn't go into details,' Rachel said, thinking back to her first conversation with Miller on the bridge following her discovery of Tyler. 'It was hands off once he knew I was CID. Adamant on the NDA and confidentiality. I got more from the doctor. Why? What did you manage to find?'

'In general terms, maritime crime's policed by Interpol, but that's focused on international piracy and trafficking. Like, the big stuff. Cruise lines seem like they're exempt. All authority for crime on board tourist ships lies with the flagged country.'

'Yeah, we keep hearing that's Panama.' Rachel shook her head. 'Just seems mental. Hard enough to allocate uniform responders to 999 callouts at home – we've got no chance of getting a couple of Panama officers on a flight to investigate anything here.'

'Tell them what you got from the security guy,' said Jake. 'This is big. Proper mic drop.'

They looked at her expectantly, and she cleared her throat.

Until this point, even with last night's drama, they'd been splashing around in fairly shallow water, playing at their investigative roles, but remaining within their depth. By sharing her suspicions regarding Simon Van der Wyk and authorisation of Jake's semi-legal tech skills, they would collectively be crossing a line. And once they'd taken that leap, it was unclear just how murky the expanse of water beneath them actually was. They could be overboard. Out of their depth. With no rope or life vests.

'He showed me the footage,' she said, gathering the weight of each word on her tongue before continuing. 'The playback feed of the virtual balcony camera.'

'Go on.' Barbara leaned forwards.

'Nothing untoward. No dark figures. No knife.'

'But …' Jess's eyes were wide, voice wavering.

She glanced around. Two waitresses were cleaning behind the counter, but they were metres away. Too far to catch this and report back. 'It wasn't the same night. The moon in the footage was wrong – a full moon, not a crescent. I don't know if he's sliced it together with last night's or just played me a totally different recording, but it was fake. He knows what happened and for some reason he's covering it up.'

A beat of silence hit the table.

'So, you were right, Rachel. Your instinct was right.' Her dad's voice was raspy but his faith glowed like a beacon in the dark.

'Seems like it,' she said. They'd always had her back. Rachel Harlow nee Wilde nee who-the-hell-knew. Even when she was the ragged, squawking toddler they'd taken in. They'd given her a nest and somehow, despite everything, she'd flown back to it.

Her dad's breathing was definitely worsening, though. She swallowed. They didn't even have the oxygen mask.

'We need to know why,' she continued, carefully. 'And how far they're prepared to go. Criminal action without intent just won't wash, unfortunately.'

'D'you think this is getting a bit too much for us?' Jess's voice was small, eyes pleading. 'Maybe we should just, like … stop.'

In contrast, Barbara's face was shining with resolve. 'We'll get to the bottom of it, you mark my words.' Her turnaround was unexpected. If they weren't currently balls deep in this situation, Rachel would have marvelled at her mother's transformation into maverick PI. Miss Marple had nothing on Barbara Wilde, it seemed.

'I know it's scary, Jess. I'm scared too. But there's no reason to think anything else is going to happen.' Rachel reached for her hand, squeezing it tight. 'We'd only be investigating what's already occurred. Creating an evidence base for the police back home.'

Jess nodded, slowly, staring at her notebook, Post-its and pen. From her clenched jaw, though, her stationery haul wasn't offering much solace.

'We've worked out why that Fernandez guy was in two places at once,' Jake said, turning to his sister. 'You can update that in your notes. There's two of them. One's in recycling, one's procurement.'

'Like, supplies?' Jess looked around for confirmation.

'It's a fairly generic term,' Robert said. 'I suppose the HLC procurement staff oversee anything coming onto the ship, other than passengers.'

Jess's eyes widened. 'So, one's loading stuff on, the other's getting rid of the packaging.'

'Sounds like a classic combo,' Rachel said. 'And I'm ninety-five per cent it was those two I saw last night. I'll get Lennon to run the Fernandez names through the database. They must be related. Probably won't come up if they're non-UK, but you never know.'

'But the security guy told you no one's missing?' Jess asked, biting the end of her pen. 'Passengers or crew?'

'Exactly. Which might still be true. If you want to keep this strictly official, we could take it all back to Miller, but I doubt we'll get anywhere if it brings HLC into disrepute. And Van der Wyk needs to be handled with care until we've eliminated him from the enquiry.'

'So two more days,' Jess said. 'Where are we tomorrow, A Coruña? Then a day at sea, then back?'

'Right. Urgent priority is re-examining Tyler's cabin. I can't help thinking this all goes back to him and there's something we're missing.'

'Tonight then?' Jake said. 'You've got the snide key card. Set an alarm and do it when everyone's asleep. I'll keep watch.'

'That's lush,' she said, putting an arm round him, 'but no. Me doing this is one thing, but I'm not putting any of you in a potentially dangerous situation.'

'Key card?' Barbara raised an eyebrow. 'Do we want to know?'

'Probably not, but it's the only way to get onto the restricted decks. We can't go to any of the crew directly – they're all hiding stuff.'

There was a crack as Jess's pen snapped between her teeth. Rachel could see fear in all their faces now. She could feel it in herself. This wasn't fun anymore.

'We are quite vulnerable, out here,' Barbara said, glancing over at Jess. 'In open water, I mean. Never felt like this on cruise before, have we, Bob?'

'Far from it. Ultimate relaxation, that's what HLC's always been sold as.' Her dad looked physically pained to be let down by a reputable company. 'They've won awards.'

'Should we get in touch with Jenny at Destinations?' Barbara looked around, wringing her hands. 'She's ABTA registered … ever so good—'

'She won't be able to help, Gran.' Jess's voice was flat. 'We're on our own.'

'But we've got each other,' Jake said. 'That's the main thing. Isn't it?'

Rachel wanted to agree. They did have each other. They'd just have to keep swimming, slow things down a bit for her dad, and not draw attention to themselves. It was all they could do. Continue to log everything, update Jess's notes and report all the concerns officially through the proper UK channels once they made it back.

She gulped.

If they made it back.

Chapter 36

Sea

In the relative calm of the day's progress, buoyed by her family's confidence, Rachel had seen a path ahead. But now, as the horn sounded and they departed Porto, she felt more out of her depth than ever. Tyler's corpse was still locked in the freezer, making an accurate toxicology report less and less viable. And the bloodied man – whoever he was – gone without trace.

With Google a poor replacement for her usual CID processes, she nevertheless tried to settle her suspicions about the Fernandez brothers. It was a common surname, prevalent in this region and beyond. But with a few more clicks it seemed Fernandez was also the name of a notorious criminal family. Nothing specific to say the two were connected, but still. Wikipedia had reams of information about Fernandez involvement in the Galician mafia. There was even a bloody Netflix documentary.

Thousands of returning passengers piled pressure upon their previous plan and she couldn't help resenting the recharged batteries of the clueless hordes. Smug smiles and bronzed bodies were everywhere. Surely the honeymooners were shagged out by now? But no, here they came, still holding hands and revelling in the dopamine highs from all their goddamn orgasms.

The Operation JC unit had spent a surreal hour in the pool on the top deck as the tourists had trickled back on board, craving a brief slice of normality amidst the rapid deterioration of this trip from holiday to headfuck. But even the water in the hot tub had been tepid. The chill in the air unmistakable.

Her parents had agreed to chaperone Jess and Jake's meeting with the influencers while she tried to beat the odds of the fluctuating Wi-Fi and make contact with Lennon.

She lingered for a moment, at the edge of the Poolside Grill, watching overweight children chow down on hotdogs and copy the entertainers' moves in the Macarena. A conga line starting was her cue to leave. Everyone had a limit and she was achieving nothing lurking here, on the periphery of the action.

Her corridor was deserted and she found the cabin, as always, polished and preened to perfection. Every print removed. Neither Oksana, nor the new replacement steward, were anywhere to be seen.

Rachel stood still, savouring this rare moment of solitude, spoiled only by the cloying scent of chlorine from the pool. She could spare five minutes for a shower.

The force of the water, powering her skin with its touch, was a much-needed distraction from the task ahead, until a sudden draught cut across the steam, raising goose bumps on her arms. Her eyes snapped open and she rubbed at the glass door, already opaque with condensation.

'Hello?' she called, half expecting one of the twins to burst in.

But nothing. Only silence.

Warmth enveloped her again like a cocoon. The HLC shampoo smelled of cloves as she brought her long hair into a lather, hands tangled in its soapy strands.

She closed her eyes and was immediately transported back to another steamy interior – that unmarked Corsa, of all places. With Lennon.

Why had that moment imprinted itself in her mind? OK, it

had been unexpectedly intense. Charged, even. She'd had her fingers laced tightly with his, their faces centimetres apart, moving slowly towards the point of no return. There'd been a spark. A magnetic connection she couldn't control. And something pulsed inside her now. An urgent pull.

She couldn't, though. Not here.

And yet, the room was empty; the voices and laughing and arguments momentarily gone.

She stopped fighting.

Her hand brushed her thigh, and she let her fingers swap the warmth of the running water for the heat of her body. She could feel him, as if he was right in front of her, his mouth pressed into her neck. Holding her tight and whispering into her ear.

The line separating them was washed away. And she was sinking down, deeper within the image of him and his smell and his burning touch. She melted into his arms like water overflowing from an infinity pool and her hand slowed to a stop.

She took a breath.

Finding herself back in reality, water still blasting from above, she reached out and turned the shower off. One thing she knew for sure: he would never, ever know. Not that the person she took the piss out of constantly and relied on for backup in every situation was also the one who privately made her feel like this.

Wrapped in a towel, she followed the steam billowing from the en suite to the wardrobe for something suitable to wear for dinner. A piece of paper on the desk caught her eye. The next day's schedule. She tried to remember where the *Synergy* was docking for the final time before their non-stop voyage to Southampton.

There was no clock in the cabin, but it felt early for the itinerary to have been delivered. Over the week they'd been getting the next day's information at eight or nine. The replacement steward must have a different system.

She stopped in her tracks – almost certain that A4 sheet hadn't been there before. The towel felt too small, damp against her skin.

A prickle ran up her spine. She felt herself reddening, vulnerability exposed in every naked inch of skin.

But the room was empty. Nothing untoward had happened. Fair enough, the stewards had a job to do, and maybe they'd knocked and she hadn't heard. She'd been occupied, after all.

Her skin turned clammy. Unclean. She couldn't shake this off.

Someone had been in here. While she was showering. While she was—

She snatched up the paper.

STOP DIGGING OR YOU ALL GO UNDER

She turned it over. Nothing. Read it again. Fuck.

Blood pounded in her ears. This was as anonymous as it got. White paper. Black capital letters. No marks or smudges. Not that she had the means for forensic checks or handwriting samples.

And yet … A new resolve flooded through her veins.

She was holding legitimate evidence now. As batshit as this note was, here, finally, was concrete proof of criminal intent. It wasn't coincidence or in her mind. This was an unequivocal call to action. The ship's shiny surface had just cracked and she held the jagged edges in her hands.

Quickly throwing on some clothes, she took stock. This was screaming out for law enforcement, not just the sure-to-be dramatic reactions of her temporary sleuthing ensemble.

It was Monday. Early evening. Where would Lennon be? Any lingering thoughts of his former imagined actions disappeared as she sat on the bed and called his mobile. No answer.

She left a hurried voicemail, briefing him on Fernandez and Van der Wyk's names to run through the database, then took a photo of the note and sent it along with the HLC headshots.

The immediate priority had to be locating the others and sticking to them like glue. Whilst she had absolutely no intention of abandoning the hole she'd started digging, a threat was a threat.

She ran through the potential messengers. Who, realistically, knew about her actions so far and had motive to make her stop?

The captain flashed first into her line-up. Regardless of the truth behind the incidents on board, he had made it clear that brand reputation was paramount. The casual vernacular, though? She struggled to see his polish producing this.

Danielle. In contrast, the wording was too polite. A threatening note from Danielle would surely have been a raging assault of C-bombs raining down like heavy artillery fire.

Veronica Chase. Contrary to her charming demeanour, from the feedback of her former colleagues she had a harder side. The digging though – she'd practically handed Rachel the shovel. Could she just have been feeding her a false trail for some ulterior motive of her own?

Simon Van der Wyk. He was a long way from the squeaky-clean professional she'd taken him for, but she'd swallowed his fake footage and given him no reason to suspect that she'd seen it for what it was. He was most likely just following the captain's misguided corporate instructions.

The potential Fernandez cartel connections were the most serious level of risk. But, surely, High Life Cruises must have a tight HR screening process. Even if they had been duped by Dannii bloody Paggot. She had no proof that the marks on the manifest, categorising each brother as alive and well, weren't authentic. And Google didn't lie, did it? It had listed Fernandez as a popular Hispanic surname. She was probably getting carried away – a reputable company just wouldn't be employing members of a known criminal organisation.

So, someone else. Her mind swam with the sheer number of crew and passengers she'd interacted with in the past five days. Waiters, stewards, the doctor, security staff, Jon and the Gorgeous Kevin …

She froze. It couldn't be.

But, they knew their way round the complex systems of a

cruise ship. They knew which cabin was theirs. With hindsight, had their desperation, from almost the first day of the crossing, to involve them in Crewz Secrets been suspicious? That mysterious injury, apparently sustained during the commotion in the early hours, took on a new significance.

And, holy shit – they were with her family right now.

She tried Lennon again. This time it didn't even go to voicemail, just a click and an error message. Her phone needed charging – two per cent battery. But there was no time.

She had to find them. Now.

Chapter 37

Sea

Rachel burst through the double doors onto the top deck, narrowly avoiding a collision with a white-haired woman. Slamming her palm against the vestibule to steady herself, she apologised to the pensioner, who clutched her handbag in shock.

'Have you seen a couple, your sort of age, with two teenagers, a boy and a girl?'

The woman didn't reply, but shook her head and backed away.

Rachel circled the open deck, eyes darting, heart thudding in her chest. From that reaction, she must look wild. Unhinged. Her plan had been to start at Deck Eighteen and work downwards, port to starboard, fore to aft, passenger to crew levels, until she found them.

But, already, she felt hideously overwhelmed. There were people everywhere, obstructing her view in all directions. Her breath was ragged, lungs screaming for oxygen. Every muscle was taut, braced for the need to restrain. To disarm. To fight.

The pool she'd been in, only hours earlier, had emptied – only one solitary swimmer remained, face submerged, still pushing through the waves created by the ship's relentless motion.

That would have to be her. Pressing forward, alone.

She knew, despite the one-line threat, there was no rational need to assume the worst. No incriminating evidence to suspect the two men they had befriended on the trip, who had only been friendly and enthusiastic.

But that meant nothing.

She'd locked up plenty of unlikely perpetrators. Means and motive were paramount. And they had both. They could be hiding in plain sight aboard this ship. Acting upon a grudge, committing violence with impunity. Panic streamed through her like sand in an egg timer, every grain another possibility of violence. By the time she'd circled the loungers and bar, she could already see her mum at gunpoint, screaming for mercy.

She gripped her phone, willing it to ring. WhatsApp wouldn't connect, and her battery was running on fumes now, dwindling second by second to nothing.

A group shoved past, jolting her. The phone slid from her hand, hitting the deck, and skidding out of reach. Before she could react, a shuffleboard player's heel finished it. She could hear the crack from ten paces.

Scrambling to retrieve it, holding the useless handset in her shaking hand, she tried to steady her racing heartbeat. The hairline fracture she'd been nursing for months had lost all prognosis for recovery.

This was the last straw. She had no phone. No plan. No Fucking Idea.

Should she change tactic? Almost eight o'clock; surely, they'd have come back. Her dad always had a lie-down before dinner. Manifesting a miracle, she heaved the doors and tore down the eight flights to Deck Ten and her corridor.

But both cabins were still unoccupied. Silent. Untouched. No more threatening messages had been left, but she was absolutely no further forward.

Where now? Running round the whole ship would take hours. It was a maze. And she'd be bound to be stumbling down one staircase whilst they were making their way up another.

Think. Treat it like a response call.

Her current approach was hopeless. Unprofessional. She had to take command.

Guest Services.

She'd find out where the Crewz Secrets high-end suite was and intercept them at source. Best-case scenario, their harmless marketing meeting would have finished, the influencers preparing to party all the way to A Coruña. The alternative: her family were being held somewhere against their will. Or worse.

The worst could have already happened. On her watch. While she'd been—

She gulped. Control over every aspect of her life was spinning out of orbit. And, as she raced down more steps, she was slapped in the face by yet another way she was failing: she'd completely forgotten to ring that union rep back from this morning.

This was a whirlpool. Work, family, safety, security. Not just one high-risk misper to report, but four. It was all slipping away. Everything teetered on the edge, perilously close to disaster.

She fought the urge to let emotion overtake action. Falling apart now just wasn't an option.

The bland familiarity of Guest Services, with its maroon logo and smiling crew members was an absurd relief. Hysteria bubbled within her, the last dregs of an air tank.

'Two guests,' she said, gasping for breath. 'I need to know their cabin number urgently. I've lost my family and they were with these people.'

'That shouldn't be a problem.' The receptionist looked at her, head tilted at just the right angle to appear empathetic, yet efficient. 'Surname?'

Bollocks. She had no idea what either of their full names were, but suspected that 'the Gorgeous' was not going to elicit any results.

'I don't know,' she said, palm to forehead, not even caring

about the complete meltdown she was now having in public. Her voice was too loud, manic. 'I only know their first names, Jon and Kevin. They're working on board though, as influencers – they might be booked under their brand name? Crewz Secrets, with a z. They mentioned something about having a suite?'

The receptionist tapped the keys. 'Nothing coming up. Are you sure you have the details correct?'

'I don't know,' she said, desperately, knuckles white against the polished wood.

'Would you like me to put out a Tannoy call?'

'Yes. For my parents, Barbara and Robert Wilde and my children, Jake and Jessica Harlow. Can you ask them to come to this desk urgently?'

Rachel was left, pale and sweaty, almost gouging finger marks in the desk from the strain of holding herself still.

She would take anything at this point. One of Barbara's trade-marked tutting-eyeroll combos. She'd embrace her dad from his shuffling walk like it was the finish line of the Great North Run. Even refereeing the twins in full MMA mode would be welcome.

But the figures moving through the endless space were all strangers – smiling and buzzing around, revelling in their holiday honeypot, oblivious to the five-star façade.

Rachel scanned the area, paranoia growing. Her eyes flitted upwards, counting three surveillance cameras in her immediate vicinity. They were extremely discreet: small robot eyes placed at regular intervals where the wall met the ceiling. One of the cameras shifted, almost imperceptibly, its lens angled straight at her.

Heat rose to her face. She blinked.

The lighting suddenly seemed too harsh – a spotlight. These CCTV cameras must be Simon Van der Wyk's domain. But why would he, or anyone, be tracking her now?

The possible interpretation of her being here to report the note in her cabin hit her with a wallop. If someone was using the surveillance cameras to track movement, her arrival at the *Synergy*'s help desk would surely be a red flag that, far from heeding the warning, she was upgrading from a shovel to a fucking excavator.

Goose bumps flared. The pleasant breeze of the afternoon had picked up and her teeth chattered in the draught whistling invisibly through the air. Through the storm-force glass to her left, she could see that the sky was darkening. The day had turned.

Promises and bargains collided in her brain.

Things were going to change from now on.

Once she'd found them, she was cutting every ounce of drama loose, stepping off the ship a changed woman. Gone were the one-night stands and binge drinking.

She'd be a consummate policing professional, straight as a line. A rock.

No sexual encounter would ever derail her life like this again. She'd be asexual. An amoeba. A nurturing, calm and collected amoeba.

Please. Let me find them.

Chapter 38

Sea

And then, all at once, they were there.

Barbara was moving swiftly through the crowd, leading their group, with the Gorgeous Kevin hobbling as fast as last night's injuries could accommodate. Rachel almost sobbed with relief.

She bashed through the mass of people, knocking experienced cruisers out of the way like skittles.

'Thank God,' she said, grabbing her mum in a hug.

'What's the matter? We heard the Tannoy and came straight here.'

'Where've you been?' she called to the rest.

'They're brilliant,' said Jon. 'We've filmed so much new content – this is going to revolutionise the BTS cruise influencer market!'

'Uploaded the first Whisper posts – thousands of likes already. They're gonna go viral!' said Jake, beaming.

'You all right, Jess? Dad?' He was pale, but still standing and Rachel registered her own lungs inhaling a proper breath for the first time in hours.

Robert was jubilant. 'Oh, we're on the pulse, now. Got our own profiles and everything. Building up quite a follo—'

'I've been so worried.' She cut across him. 'My phone's smashed and Guest Services couldn't find a Crewz Secrets booking.' She looked pointedly at the two flamboyant figures, dressed in gold monogrammed tracksuits.

'Whole trip's fully comp, Queen!' Jon laughed. 'There's no money changing hands. And on the manifest we'll just be plain old Mr and Mr Williams.'

The Gorgeous Kevin nodded, sagely. 'So important not to overpromote the brand whilst on board.'

'All too easy for *influencers* to become *outfluencers*,' Jon added. 'We always maintain a dignified level of anonymity throughout each voyage.'

Rachel took in their outfits, encrusted with enough diamantes to render them visible from space.

Jess was first to fully register her frazzled state. 'What's wrong, Mam? Is it—'

'There's been an incident,' she said, hesitating slightly and glancing at the non-members of the newly established Operation JC unit.

'I think we should tell them.' Jess read her pause and continued, firmly. 'They know so much about cruising. They can help.'

Jon and the Gorgeous Kevin looked at each other, evidently curious. 'Go on,' said Jon. 'We're extremely discreet.'

Could she trust them? Not five minutes ago she'd lumped them in with the rest of the dubious suspects on this floating labyrinth of lies. Bringing them into the inner circle was a risk. But risk was all she had.

Squashed into her cabin, Rachel briefed the expanded team, their six faces as attentive as an elite command force. Reactions to the note varied from stoic acceptance (her dad), through outrage and vows of vengeance (the twins and her mum), to wild theories of corporate espionage and international skullduggery (Jon). Only the Gorgeous Kevin remained silent, just nodding occasionally at her explanation of events to date. Finally, he spoke.

'The way I see it, Rachel, it's imperative that you get back into Tyler's cabin ASAP and examine it for any residual evidence. You've been here five days and witnessed ABH; two probable murders; an attempt at perverting the course of justice; and a document falling slap bang under the Malicious Communications Act. All this and we're still NFI on the primary offender. There must be a reason you were given this warning. Someone's rattled.'

Everyone's attention lasered on him, draped in velour and glitter, weighing up the charges with the gravitas of a senior investigating officer. Rachel tried, with difficulty, to lift her jaw off the floor.

'You're police? Since when?'

'Another lifetime,' he said, almost shyly. 'It's been a while, but it comes back quick.'

'But how? When? Which force?' She felt a hot prickle of shame at the way she'd judged him by sparkle, not substance.

'The Met,' Jon cut in. 'He was shattered when I met him. Shattered.'

'This was the early Noughties,' the Gorgeous Kevin conceded. 'Met police and a camp-as-Christmas gay officer. We weren't a good match. Off the beat and onto the *Princess* and I've never looked back.'

'But you agree?' she said, elated at his overview. 'You think it's got legs?'

'Absolutely,' he said, nodding earnestly. 'Tyler had a reputation, and senior crew always keep a lid on negative publicity, but withholding a body on board for seven days certainly isn't standard practice. Not at all.'

'Miller's always had rumours flying around about his behaviour,' Jon said, 'but this is another level. I still can't take it in that Tyler Tweedy's dead.'

The Gorgeous Kevin looked grave. 'Extremely concerning, never mind the Fernandez situation.'

'And the CCTV cover-up,' Jon continued. 'Why go to the trouble of concealing it if Van der Wyk knows what happened?'

'Exactly,' Rachel agreed. She looked round at her family. 'I really wanted us to keep investigating. You've been amazing, all of you. But that threat changes everything.'

All eyes swivelled to the innocuous sheet of A4 still lying where she'd found it on the desk. They'd already shuffled over to inspect its seven heavily weighted words from behind her strict perimeter, in case it could still be used as evidence.

'I'm not pretending everything's OK, threat or no threat,' Jess said. 'We have to get to the truth.'

'Well, *I'm* not putting you at risk,' Rachel replied firmly, in the voice she normally reserved for excessive overtime requests. 'You're more important than any case, whatever's happened. I'll search Tyler's cabin, but you guys can't be moving around the ship from now on. You'll have to completely lock down until Southampton. No exceptions.'

''Til Thursday?' Jake said, ashen-faced. 'Have you seen the room service menu? We won't survive.'

Jake's dramatic response to the prospect of limited food for fifty-odd hours was quashed by a loud buzzing from his phone. 'It's Lennon. What's he ringing me for?'

'I left him a voice note when I found that,' Rachel said, nodding to the paper on the desk. 'Before my phone got trashed.'

'Who's this one?' Her mum leaned over to her dad, lost now in the tangled web. 'Is this the colleague? The handsome one?' She'd changed her tune. They'd only met for five excruciating minutes on Boxing Day, but Barbara's disapproval of his accent and appearance had shone ten times brighter than the Christmas lights.

'Well, officially, he works with her,' Jess called over, 'but really, he *lurves* her.'

Rachel rolled her eyes, holding her hand out impatiently for Jake's phone. 'He really doesn't.'

Jake joined in, eagerly, concern about imminent starvation forgotten. 'Yeah, he does. You should see his face when he's looking at her. It's rank.' He didn't look disgusted though. Neither of them did, even though they'd clearly completely misinterpreted Lennon's feelings.

Rachel made a cut-throat motion to them both as she answered. 'Lenn, everything's blown up here—'

'Fuck's sake, man,' he said. 'You can't drop a bomb like that then go dark for hours.' He sounded angry. She could picture him: foot tapping, hands balled into fists. For someone so laid-back, in the rare moments she'd seen him stressed his pent-up energy made every limb a coiled spring.

'Look, my phone's dead,' she said, pulling the useless handset from her pocket, 'as in, rigor mortis. And I've been running round the ship trying to make sure this lot don't go the same way.'

'What d'you mean? Have you got an ID on who wrote it?' His voice had risen to a level where everyone could hear. 'Did you say you were actually in the cabin at the time?'

She looked around at the tense faces, his concern a wake-up call. Someone wanted to silence them and who knew how far they would go to turn words into reality?

'OK, calm down,' she said. 'I might as well put you on speaker. We're all safe. In my cabin and the door's locked.'

'That means nothing,' he said, ignoring his transition to a wider audience. 'Whoever left the note's already got a method of entry. Has the door got a chain? Or a deadbolt?'

Jake jumped up to check. 'No, just one of those Do Not Disturb signs.'

'Awesome,' Rachel said, trying to lighten the mood. 'That'll do the trick.'

'This isn't funny,' Lennon said sharply. 'You've pissed off the wrong people. This Fernandez family make the Gallaghers look like the Brady Bunch. I've had a source check out your pictures. They're bad news.'

'Who's done that for you?'

'Don't ask. Owed me a favour. We shouldn't be doing this verbally, though. Cabin's probably bugged.'

All eyes in the room were suddenly wide, scouting for potential listening devices. Barbara clasped her handbag tighter and Jon fanned the air theatrically as if to dissipate the sound waves.

'He's right,' her dad said, standing up. 'We're not safe in here.'

She took a deep breath, assessing their tactical options. It was after ten o'clock, with nine hours of non-stop motion ahead until they docked for the penultimate time. If anyone wanted to act on their previous threat of harm, this no-man's land of international waters would be the ideal time to go for the jugular. And with Van der Wyk's editing skills, the evidence could be deleted at the push of a button.

'OK, Lenn. We're going to need backup,' she conceded. 'Can you get a steer from the NCA?'

'NCA?' Her mum looked confused. Miss Marple hadn't used all these acronyms.

The Gorgeous Kevin leaned over. 'National Crime Agency,' he whispered. 'Handle anything on a big scale, cross-region.'

Barbara nodded, shrewdly.

'On it,' Lennon said, 'but for God's sake be careful, Rach. Please. No one's expecting you to solve this single-handed. And you all need to get out of that cabin.'

'We could relocate somewhere busy?' Jon said, every other word disguised with a fake cough. 'The Poseidon'll be heaving. No one's going to overhear us in there.'

Rachel opened her mouth to disagree, but closed it again. It was testament to the batshit nature of this whole affair that no one, not even the serving police officers, questioned the logic of moving their tactical planning to a nightclub. With no better ideas, and hysteria rising, the dance floor was, once again, calling her name.

Chapter 39

Sea

Rachel raced out of the still-pounding Poseidon club, alone. They'd debated the pros and cons of searching Tyler's cabin for the past hour. The Gorgeous Kevin had offered to assist, but – if they were being tracked – his eye-catching ensemble wouldn't do them any favours. And, with his injuries, he wouldn't be capable of outrunning an assailant.

To assuage Lennon's concerns, they'd settled on swapping cabins: the Crewz Secrets duo would sleep in her parents' room and the rest of them transfer to the suite.

She would rather have carried out this task in the very dead of night, with a guarantee that almost everyone on board would be asleep, but by half eleven, after Lennon's further attempts at caution had failed, she had to go for it.

The time was now.

At her mum's insistence, she'd borrowed Jake's cap and pulled it down as far as she could over her brow. She paused at the CREW ONLY doorway and took a deep breath. If this key card failed, they had no method of entry; the search would be over before it started.

A faint click. The light turned green. He'd done it.

Despite the stakes, Rachel's heart lifted for a second until she faced the next hurdle: lift or service stairs?

Her momentary hesitation was answered with a ping and she dived to the left, crashing through the door, onto the dark stairway. Had she been seen? She bit down on her bottom lip, tasting blood. Had she responded quickly enough?

A staccato exchange of raised voices rattled through her brain like gunshots. She couldn't make out the words – except three, slicing through the air like a blade: *whatever it takes*.

A door closing, then silence. Her pulse thudded. That accent – familiar, foreign. Van der Wyk? Maybe. Or an American drawl. Whoever it was, the message was ominous. That had been far too close.

She pressed further into shadows, close to the wall, straining for the slightest sound.

The crew could access these service stairs at any point. This was their domain: a far cry from the guests' decadent marble staircase. Something cheap and hard was underfoot here. All expense spared.

The exit was almost in sight, but, descending in the gloom, she lost her footing. Her stomach dropped.

Stay upright. Do not fall now.

The hinges groaned as she opened the heavy door, just a crack. Harsh strip lighting immediately cut into her shadowy refuge, the glare making her eyes sting.

Deck Two's corridor stretched forever, the far end shimmering like a mirage. And, for a second, she faltered. She'd run this way before, hand in hand with Tyler. Back then it had felt like a game. An escape.

Now it felt like a dead end. But she had to try –

Head down. Cap low. Keep moving. Doors on either side. Too many. Any of them could open. A bassline leaked through thin walls. A sudden laugh ripped the air. She jolted, heart slamming.

How much further?

Every step was risk. If she was stopped down here, it was finished.

She sped up, feet pounding the threadbare carpet until she reached H656. Key card ready, she pushed down on the handle.

It was pitch-black.

One switch flooded the cabin from the bare overhead bulb. Still empty.

Moving quickly, Rachel assessed the scene with fresh eyes.

She thought of her colleagues – the skills, the qualities they brought to an investigation. Rossy, tenacious and stubborn. A pit bull with a bloody bone. Lennon's authenticity, that ability to get people on side and bring out information they didn't even know they had. Even Coates. Insufferable as he was, his desire to turn over every single stone, double-bag and label it in his neatest handwriting, had been an undeniable asset.

Operating alone like this, she would have to rely on what had made her fall in love with policing in the first place: finding the missing piece. That elusive something that made all the chaos make sense.

The four walls of the cabin were almost within touching distance, bunk beds to her left and wardrobe to her right. Without the costumes that had covered the floor during her time here with Tyler, she could clearly see the worn patches – gaping flaws on show. Far below the gleaming polish of the guest decks, the foundations of this ship were rotten to the core.

She needed to leave with something. A scrap, however small. She pulled open the wardrobe and yanked each drawer. Just a few sets of clothes, neatly folded. Nothing of evidential value.

Fuck. Tyler had to hold the key.

Losing patience, she ransacked the contents. But no break. No lead.

Rachel's shoulders slumped, the airless room sapping all energy. What the hell was she doing here rummaging through a dead man's clothes? A man she'd known for a matter of hours. A man who'd built a reputation on shagging his way around the ship, using his relative fame to entice women back to his bunk beds.

Had any of his patter been genuine? Or was he just throwing out lines the way he had with hundreds of others? His complaints about Danielle and the set-up on board were probably just cynical attempts to get her knickers off faster.

She'd now been through every piece of clothing. From this capsule wardrobe, he'd had money to burn. Burberry, Stone Island – most of it still with tags on.

She grabbed his TAG Heuer watch. Still ticking. Trying to focus, she stared at its face, her breath ragged as the fine line jerked its way round the circle. There had to be answers somewhere here.

Frantic now, she dropped to the floor and stretched an arm under the bunk, groping blindly. She hit the torch on Jake's phone, dying to see a clue fire up in the darkness.

There was nothing under the bed, but as she rose, she was knocked sideways by a visceral flashback to Tyler. His naked arse cheeks. The tinny blast of his backing track. He had reached up, touching a gridded tile to reveal his songwriting stash –

She jumped, arm outstretched, but got nowhere near the ceiling. Dragging the bedside table, she clambered up, pushing the tile free, immediately swearing in triumph at her pink polyester top.

Of course it was here. She could picture him now, laughing as he'd lifted it over her head, saying he'd sign it as a souvenir. It was just as hideous as she'd remembered, but as she pulled it out of the dark cavity, a folded bundle of paper hit the floor.

One word on the front: *SHERLOCK.*

A sudden noise sliced through the silence. A creak of footsteps? More likely another shriek of laughter from down the corridor. She forced herself to hold her nerve. In here, surely, she was invisible. The CCTV couldn't extend this far.

Please let it be something relevant, not just more of his

God-awful lyrics. She stepped down, paper gripped tightly in both hands, and began to read.

His writing was sprawling with no punctuation or paragraphs. A spidery stream of consciousness, the pen pressed so hard into the page she could probably have read it from the other side. It smacked of a heady rush, a frenzy – words spilling out of him like an unstoppable tsunami.

Rachel held her breath, skimming the rest of the page: come on, Tyler, get to the point. Impatient for the bull's-eye, she almost ripped the second sheet, pulling it to the front to continue.

to hide it in the costumes sewed the bags into the lining
but then he finds out and wants in as well

Her lungs were screaming for air. It was taking all her energy
to decipher his train of thought. There was a reason they took
this part of the process off witnesses and suspects. Transcribing
a frightened person's garbled words into a clear account was a
skill that many of her CID colleagues saw as beneath them, but
having it down in black and white was imperative.

He starts getting greedy wants to fuckin push it more
even Danielle was scared of him he says if we upped it we
wouldn't need to do the cruises no more we'd have it made
and now it's just out of control with the fuckin Vigo cartel
and theyre telling me I can't get out cos I know too much
about the deal I put in for a transfer but

Rachel's stomach flipped. She could feel herself getting within
touching distance of the hierarchy of this narcotics empire he was
trapped in. Jesus. No wonder he'd been petrified. 'Give me the
fucking names, Tyler,' she said aloud, searching ahead on the page.

But at that moment, her eyes were yanked as if on a piece of
string to the door handle which was, ever so slowly, descending.
There was no time to move. Not a second to hide herself or the
sheets of paper.

The door creaked wide. Beige chinos. Brown belt. A gut that
blocked the light.

Dark eyes locked on hers – and everything stopped.

Chapter 40

Land

Thursday 6th April

Rachel couldn't look over the edge after Gallagher hit the ground. In her mind, he'd shattered the concrete, smashed through the surface of the earth. But she heard his screams and, soon afterwards, the wail of the ambulance.

In the aftermath, once Lennon released his grip, she reverted to SIO mode. He followed her closely, not letting her get more than a metre in front. Was he worried she was going to launch herself off the balcony as well? Or was it more of a professional concern, that she might tamper with the evidence as well as the suspect?

Whichever it was, it was wearing thin. She'd got hold of herself now, wiped the spit trail from her cheek and stemmed the blood from the wound on her hand. Gallagher's words were no longer ringing at quite the same decibel in her ears.

The faces of the uniform officers were pale. Gloves snapped, evidence bagged, eyes averted. Pretending the arrest hadn't just flatlined.

She collared Coates as he ran back into the flat from directing the ambulance. 'Bag the electronics up, OK? I want you all over that Xbox this afternoon.'

He nodded mutely, eyes flitting to Lennon, who was still hovering. Why the fuck was everyone tiptoeing around her?

'Have we got confirmation that Gaby's reached A&E?' she asked him. 'Who went with her in the ambulance?'

Lennon cleared his throat and she spun round. 'What?'

'You need to go.' His tone was harsh. She started to object, but he grasped her shoulders. 'It's blown up down there. Just kids at the moment, but they've filmed him straight after the – the incident – shouting and bawling your name. Saying you've pushed him.'

Fuck. Now it made sense. Content like this would be all over social media within minutes. Taking on a life of its own. It didn't take much round here for animosity towards law enforcement to escalate. They'd all heard the stories about the Meadow Well riots in the Nineties – and that was before TikTok and #fuckthepolice.

'Right.' She swallowed. 'Does Bailey know?'

'Wants you in his office ASAP.' Lennon was pale and clammy. 'Look, I'll go down and have a word. There's some we know from Safeguarding. Might be able to calm it down.'

'Be careful,' she said. 'Not by yourself.'

He nodded. 'Coatesy, you're driving. Get her back in one piece or you've got me to deal with, all right? I'll follow in the van.' He leaned in, voice firm in her ear. Each word a lit match in the darkness. 'Do not deviate. He jumped.'

DCI Bailey's office crackled with tension. She perched opposite him in his small, functional cubbyhole. Light was flooding the room from the window to the car park, but it only drew more attention to the dusty surfaces and scraggy lever arch files.

She'd seen the footage. First in the car with Coates and now in another excruciating screening with her line manager. It was already gaining traction on Facebook within the East End community groups and the views and shares were only going to build in the cold light of day. Even at this time, barely an hour since he'd hit the ground, the shaky, twenty-second clip had gone far beyond its teenage makers.

On screen, Jo" Paul was a car crash. Still cuffed, sprawled face down on the concrete, both shoulders collapsed at sickening angles. Head twisted to one side, he howled directly to camera.

Most of it came out slurred while he struggled to expunge teeth and cartilage from what remained of his mouth – just a few jagged sounds landed: 'Polis rat. Harlow. Fuckin missed 'er. Pushed.'

Rachel strained at the distortion. Missed her? Mister? The sense was garbled, syllables sliding away before she could pin them down. The only word anyone would latch onto was the one screamed with absolute clarity. *'Pushed.'*

Then the siren swelled, a clamour of younger voices and all went black.

Bailey stabbed a finger at the blank screen where the clip had ended. 'I don't need to tell you what this means. On so many levels, an absolute bloody PR disaster.'

She swallowed, mouth suddenly dry. 'I think – he could have said—'

'This isn't about what he said, Harlow,' he barked. 'It's about what people heard. And right now, every kid with a phone down there thinks you pushed him. That's the headline, that's the problem. The rest is just noise.'

She stared at her shoes, flecked with blood. 'Sir.'

His baggy eyes were incredulous. 'What possessed you to take him out on the balcony?'

She braced herself. This was the worst part. She couldn't give him the truth of what had been said, couldn't explain the creeping dread or the nightmare intensity of Gallagher's gaze.

'Events were escalating, sir. We were losing control. He'd spat on me – it was in my mouth.' She couldn't look at him, but she forced herself to get this out. 'I wanted to de-escalate. I've got previous with him so … I thought … I could talk him down.'

Bailey exhaled loudly. 'Moving him from a contained situation with three other officers to a high-risk area by yourself. It doesn't make sense.' He leaned over the desk. 'It's career suicide, Harlow.'

'I know, sir. I can see that now.'

'And the fall itself, his accusation?'

She heard Lennon's voice in her ear. 'Pure fabrication. Resisting arrest and he jumped.'

'Your BWV?'

'Cuts in and out. Not a clear recording.'

He shook his head, wearily, like it weighed a ton. 'Probably the one thing in your favour. Get your statement down in full. Every detail.'

'What are you going to do about the clip, sir?'

'It's being taken down as we speak. Media team are drafting a short statement.'

She had visions of Gallagher repeating his character assassination, in more detail, to whoever would listen at the RVI. 'Has he said anything else? Maybe I could talk to him.'

Bailey snapped. He was scarlet now. Steaming. 'Talk to him? Last I heard they've put him in an induced coma while they try and assess the internal organ damage. You won't be talking to anyone; let's get that clear right now.'

'Sir, the case – there's evidence to work through and someone needs to get a statement from the girl. I should be briefing the—'

'I don't think you've registered the severity of this situation.' His voice had turned icy hot. 'Professional Standards are going to be breathing down my neck. There'll be a full PIP. You're looking at a misconduct charge, minimum.'

Her chest clenched, every breath useless.

Bailey only pressed harder. 'The IOPC are all over use of force since Carlisle. You've compromised the whole operation.'

'I can put it right, sir—'

'You can't put it right!' he thundered. 'I should never have signed you off as SIO. You're emotional. Unpredictable. You never just toe the line!'

Her own anger surged. 'Then why did you?'

The reply was bitter and low. 'Commissioner's instructions. National directive. More female officers in senior roles.' Then, rising to his full height, his voice slammed into her. 'You fit the bloody quota, Harlow. Tick a box. And, look where that's got us.'

She forced her head to stay high although it burned her neck. This assessment of her professional capability was salt rubbed deep into raw flesh.

'Get out of my sight. Restricted duties pending investigation.'

Her legs were weak, but she spoke one syllable with as much strength as she could muster. 'Sir.'

His final words were tossed like rubbish. 'Custody nurse. Now. You're a mess. Only thing you've got us this morning is a probable hep C diagnosis.'

Chapter 41

Land

The custody nurse was kind, her motherly care making a heavy lump form in Rachel's throat. She was a locum, Nigerian, with a warm smile and soothing voice. The last nurse had quit and they'd struggled to backfill. With the rate of self-harming incidents in the cells usually outnumbering the occupants, it wasn't hard to see why applicants weren't queueing up.

'Disgraceful,' she said, cleaning the deep wound on her hand. 'Spitting at a police officer. Ought to throw away the key.'

Rachel said nothing – couldn't trust herself to speak. How had it all gone so wrong?

'Lovely-looking lady like you, as well.' A tut as she applied the dressing. 'Nasty bruise you'll have on that eye tomorrow. You can't have been in the force long?'

Rachel nodded with numb agreement. She hadn't even registered the throbbing right side of her face. And, compared to the lifers who'd been on this patch for twenty years or more, she was a rookie. She'd climbed fast, relishing each role and promotion.

Now, she sat in the rubble. A fraud.

'Sharp scratch,' said the nurse, tightening a tourniquet around her arm. Rachel could see her blood filling the vial, and felt a rush of panic.

The nurse leaned in, conspiratorial, misunderstanding her reaction. 'No need to fret. Chance of infection's low. Anything untoward, we'll be testing him as well, of course. And you'll get the results by email.'

She sat silently, afraid that if she opened her mouth, all the cracks inside her would shatter to dust.

Afterwards, she stood, frozen, in the corridor. Statement done. Same version she'd given to Bailey. There was a missed call notification on her phone screen from Lennon, probably back in the building, but she couldn't bear to hear his voice. Couldn't face him. Couldn't stand in the office with Rossy, Chambers, Tariq, knowing that she'd lost it all up there on the balcony.

She typed slowly, each movement making her hand throb.

Bailey's cut me loose. RD pending investigation.

Seeing the words made it real. She wanted to apologise, promise Lennon she'd fix it, but how, when she didn't even know who she was anymore? Let alone the next steps of Operation Fever.

With some latent muscle memory of competence, she added one more line.

Get Rossy to go through the comments on the JPG video and cross-check evidence board.

But what was the point? Everything was crumbling. If she lost this version of herself – professional, capable – who was the part that remained?

Shoulder charging the door to the car park, she felt a pulse of possibility in her hand. Her phone's spiderweb of cracks cut across the lock screen image of Jess and Jake, years ago, in matching Halloween costumes. They grinned up at her, brother and sister, side by side. Painted faces and gappy teeth. These days she could barely get them in the same room. No way they'd pose for a photo.

Right now, there was no one by her side. No path ahead. So

should she stop running forwards? Go back – alone – instead? Back to whatever was missing?

Heart pounding, she googled Newcastle City Council and slipped into her car's bubble. The children's services receptionist on the phone was polite, but uninterested in the specifics. It wasn't unusual to make a Subject Access Request. She'd need to bring two forms of ID and could access her record in electronic form or have the physical files delivered to her home address.

She'd teetered on the edge of this decision for two decades. Coming to the North East hadn't been coincidence or a random tick box on the UCAS form. She'd known only two facts: Newcastle Upon Tyne, date of birth. And she'd bargained with herself ever since.

Foot down, she powered along the Coast Road, grabbed her passport, then into the city's heart. Now she'd located the rock she was going to overturn, she didn't care what scuttled out. One way or another, after this morning, she had to know.

At the council office, she handed over her ID. No police badge. No trace.

'I'm Rachel. I called earlier. I need to know who I am.'

Chapter 42

Sea

Tuesday 25th April

Andre shut the door and strode towards her, every step a heavy-footed threat. The tiny cabin seemed to shrink even further, walls closing in. Rachel scrambled, looking around desperately for something she could use as a weapon.

'You can't read?' he said, jabbing a finger. 'I tell you stop.'

Her mind raced, thoughts hurdling over each other. 'It was you? You left the note in my cabin?'

'I already try. On bridge. I say this. I say stop.' His dark eyes flashed with rage.

She tried to breathe, but the air was almost solid. 'I can't stop. I'm a police officer. I knew there was something more. I knew Tyler wasn't an overdose.' She had to keep him talking. Make him think of her as a human being, not an expendable obstacle. A thing to silence. 'My family know I'm down here. They'll come looking for me.'

He stared at her, sweat dripping from his craggy features. Could he see the blood accelerating through her veins? The blind panic she was trying so hard to disguise?

Still, he said nothing, just watched as her heart hammered in her chest. She stared back, trying to stop her legs from shaking.

Finally, he spoke. 'You are wrong. You see, but you do not understand.'

This was better. At least there was some impulse to engage rather than cut straight to violence. She swallowed. 'So tell me. Explain what your role is. Make me understand.'

'Yes, I leave you warning in cabin. After my wife, I try to keep you safe.'

She was halted in her tracks. Safe? A message to warn, not to threaten.

But his manner had been rude and obstructive from the get-go. He'd shown no desire to prevent harm, beyond the perfunctory role he had played in escorting her to the captain and swiping her off and on the ship. The tangents in her mind were colliding. Nothing made sense.

'Oksana? Are you talking about her being redeployed?' Her words came out in a rush. 'I assumed she'd requested the move – away from the trouble?'

'They try to bring my wife into … their business. They tell her, do this, do not ask questions, we give you cash. But she say no. We want quiet life, job, money to send home. We want no part in this.'

'Who did? Who asked her to do these things?' Her voice cracked. She was shaking in earnest now.

'You are not safe. I track you tonight on the cameras. I follow you. But they see everything. They will find you.'

Rachel looked at him, an angry stranger, standing before her offering help. Andre would have been the last person on board she would have put her faith in. She hadn't even finished Tyler's letter, but right now she had two options: get on his lifeboat or take her chances with the sharks.

Making her choice, she held out the lined paper. 'I've got this.

He was wanting me to help him, the night he died. But it was too late.'

He scanned the top sheet, then glared at her, hands shifting to rip the paper apart. 'You need to destroy. It is dangerous to know even half of this information.'

'No—' She grabbed it, just in time. 'If drugs are being smuggled on the ship, we need to involve the authorities. They can't get away with this. A man has died.'

'Two men!' Andre's face was pale and clammy. 'One in the mortuary – the other, no one will find, gone to the sea. What you saw, last night – he makes the tape disappear, but what you saw was true.'

'But who did it?' Her mind was hurtling, about to crash and burn. She'd known about Van der Wyk's footage. She'd known the tape was fake, so why hadn't she acted immediately?

Andre was frantic now. 'Fernandez. They are brothers, but they fight. Estavo says to cut shipment loose. Too hot. Van der Wyk tells Miguel he must do it – Estavo overboard – he must end him.'

'Miguel Fernandez killed his own brother? There'll be evidence. Blood splatter, the knife?'

'This is nothing. Van der Wyk makes it disappear. Tyler's cabin. Evidence. Anything they want to hide—'

Rachel reread Tyler's unpunctuated scrawl until the letters steadied: They get the coke on in Vigo search the oyster crates its all there its van der wyk you need to go after but be careful

The words were a flurry of blows. Oyster crates. Vigo. Van der Wyk.

'Waste storage,' she said before she could stop herself. 'The recycling. They hide shipments there, in the packaging. That's how—'

The last line was almost illegible, letters colliding. She struggled to decipher the words or their meaning: watch out for danielle

What had he wanted her to do? Was this a warning or a plea to help her?

She watched Andre pace, trapped in his own storm. He'd risked everything tonight. She couldn't fall apart now – not with Tyler dead, Andre breaking ranks, her family still out there. Someone had to take control. And it was going to be her.

Rachel sprinted up the corridor, prioritising speed over silence. If what Andre had said was true, her most vulnerable point was now.

The strip lights seemed to pulse above her. Though her lungs were burning in the airless, windowless passage, she couldn't stop. Not for a second. She clung to the evidence, gripping the paper so hard the ink was smudging on her skin. But there was no option of letting go.

Two deaths at night, in open water.

A rogue vessel floating outside the rule of law.

This cruise ship – any cruise ship – was a criminal's wet dream.

Van der Wyk had already crossed the tipping point from narcotics to murder, so what would stop him from killing her as well?

They could say anything. No one would question them. They held the authority out here, not her. Bailey's evaluation of her recent CID performance could probably be used at the fucking inquest. Unpredictable. Emotional. Two and two would become five. Just a tragic suicide at sea.

A heavy thud. This was it.

She snapped her head back. Someone coming. Or just the pounding motion of the engine room?

No one in pursuit, but a sudden flash of red in her peripheral vision. A faint whir. Barely there at all.

Andre had said they'd be watching. They'd see her on the cameras. Could they zoom in and see the evidence in her hand? She rammed the cap down further, but they'd already know. There was nowhere to hide.

She had to get higher up. To the passenger decks. To witnesses. It was only metres above, but down here she was screaming out to be silenced.

Should she risk the stairs? Too many flights to the suite. Too many exits. Too easy to push her down, watch as she tumbled over and over. Then a sickening smash of bone on metal.

Almost at the lift, every rasping breath burning her throat, she chanced one more look over her shoulder – was that a shape in the distance? A flash of forward motion?

So far away. Impossible to be sure.

Slamming into cold steel, she hit the button again and again. Why wasn't it opening? She couldn't breathe. Her reflection warped in the sheet metal – distorted, stretched, a blur …

But behind that, something else. Something moving.

Rachel spun as the doors slid wide. Not something, but someone. In the corridor. Running towards her. Closing the gap with every step.

She dived inside – her only chance. But the lift doors stayed stubbornly open. She'd be trapped here – on a metal plate. A fucking wipe-clean surface.

Deck Fourteen. Come on. She had to hold on.

Rachel tightened her grip on the crumpled paper, on the proof Tyler had left.

This was for her family. Her anchor.

Whoever was coming, whatever they tried – she would fight for them with everything she had.

Chapter 43

Sea

Bursting into the suite, Rachel found them all focused on a video call with Lennon. The sight of his face, brow furrowed, hair in his eyes, made the tension in her shoulders immediately subside. From the fluorescent glow, he must be in the office, but at this moment, he shone like the bloody North Star.

'She's back,' Jake said, grabbing her in a hug.

'I said I'd be back,' she choked, struggling to speak. 'It's OK. I've got what we need.'

Suddenly everyone was talking over each other, on their feet, crowding around. She pushed through, taking in the opulent décor of their temporary refuge. It was huge.

'Where's this come from?' she said, facing the gleaming MacBook. 'How've we got a clear signal?'

'The boys,' her mum said, voice melting. 'They've been a Godsend – should've involved them straight away. Though goodness knows what they'll be making of our cabin, Bob.' She wrung her hands. 'Must be a third of this size. They'll be used to a much higher standard of—'

'Never mind that,' her dad said, turning to Rachel. 'Tell us what happened.'

She took in the anxious faces, Lennon's blazing eyes urging her on. 'It's worse than we thought,' she said. 'Three of them. Van der Wyk, Fernandez and Danielle. They've been using this as a regular importation route for cocaine they're loading onto the ship in Vigo and getting off in Southampton.'

'How d'you know the details?' Lennon's voice was husky. She glanced at the clock in the corner of the screen and added an hour – almost three a.m. where he was.

'I found a statement Tyler had written.' She held out the paper to Jess, who unfolded it and immediately started reading. 'He knew I was police. He wanted out and he's written it all down.'

'You need to get off the ship,' Lennon said. 'Enough's enough. First thing in the morning, you're gone.'

'Agreed,' she said, 'but we've got someone we can trust now inside the crew. He's going to help—'

'You can't trust anyone.' Lennon's voice cracked. 'This Fernandez lot, they're ruthless. Pack your bags and be ready to go as soon as you dock. It'll be much harder to touch you if you're all together, in public.'

'We're not packing any bags,' she said firmly, looking at each of them in turn. 'Andre'll be manning the kiosk. He's going to check us out and keep our key cards, then swipe them back just before the ship sails. We have to let them think we're still on board or they'll know we're onto them and the drugs are never going to make it into the UK.'

'But our clothes, Rachel!' Her mum gaped, mouth open like a fish.

'We can do without a change of outfit.' Her dad was firm. 'Let me get this straight, though. We're disembarking in A Coruña tomorrow with everyone else, but we're not getting back on board?'

'That's the plan.' She held his gaze, steady and unblinking.

He nodded. 'We're with you, love.'

She turned to the twins. Jake shrugged, casually. 'I'm in.'

'Jess? You OK with this?'

Jess glanced up from her intense scrutiny of Tyler's statement. Her hands were steady. 'Try and stop me. I'm just trying to decipher this crime against punctuation. Had he never considered the impact of a full stop?'

'Don't speak ill of the dead,' Rachel said, half-smiling. 'He'd committed far bigger crimes than that, even if he did try to blow the whistle in the end.'

'I'll feel ever so much better with you organising things from the other side,' her mum said to Lennon. Was she blushing? 'Someone with authority to get us home.'

Rachel thought she saw him sit up a little straighter at this description. 'Of course I will, Barbara. I've already made contact with the National Crime Agency. Send me that statement through, Rach, and I'll bring them up to date on everything we have. What did you say the security guard's called?'

'Andre Rucɑo,' she said. 'He and his wife are both crew. Van der Wyk tried to involve Oksana, but she refused, so he gave some cock-and-bull story to Veronica Chase and she's been withdrawn from service. They're terrified they're going to be targeted by the Fernandez cartel. The NCA need to keep their names out of it and give them protection.'

'On it.' Lennon was typing furiously. 'Waiting on the Interpol request for Van der Wyk, but that might take days. Bastard Brexit. I'll book all your travel now, though – first flight out of A Coruña.'

'It'll make all the difference,' her mum fawned, not even blinking at Lennon's language, 'having the UK police involved.'

'I've always told you he's all right,' Rachel said, elbowing Barbara. 'Brains, brawn. Just a shame he's physically repellent or he'd have the full package.'

'Shut it,' said Lennon. 'Or I'll book four seats and leave you stranded at the airport.'

'OK, not repellent, just bang average. *Dreadful tattoos.* You're a solid six out of ten.'

'Have a word, pet. I'm a twelve.'

She locked eyes with her DS. Her best friend. Her—

He'd know what she was doing. The twins might be acting cool, but they were only fifteen. She could see the truth in their pale faces, the way they edged closer to the laptop, basking in Lennon's smile. That was his gift: even across oceans, he lit up the dark.

So much could go wrong. But for the first time, she wasn't facing it alone. Her family. Her partner in crime. All of them, bound together.

Maybe this was worth more than a haul of cocaine and three suspects in cuffs.

She knew who she was now. *Emotional*, sometimes. *Unpredictable*, always.

A daughter. A friend. A mum. All this and more.

She was DI Rachel fucking Harlow.

Chapter 44

Sea

The mood over breakfast as the ship approached A Coruña was bright and breezy, but brittle. The family blended in, almost perfect replicas of every other group. Nothing to see here. Rachel carefully adjusted her Ray-Bans: no sudden movements, nothing to attract attention.

Inside though, every cell in her body was screaming.

Land was tantalisingly close. But not yet close enough.

Seated on the starboard side, they'd made one stilted trip to the buffet, primarily to maintain cover, but, as Jake kept reminding them, who knew when they'd get a chance to eat again today?

Forcing a croissant down her clenched throat, Rachel assessed the crowded area, searching for anything that could jeopardise their escape. This would have been the ideal spot to relax and enjoy the smooth glide along Galicia's coastline and into the sun-drenched port. The ship's movement had coated the rocks in white spray, while the stone lighthouse, the Torre de Hércules, stood proudly observing their safe arrival into the transatlantic dock.

This morning, though, the view was tinged with tension.

'That's it, we've docked. Let's move,' hissed Barbara, gripping her bulging Radley bag. She'd been the hardest to rein in this morning, campaigning to return to their cabin to sort through their 'smalls' herself rather than leave it to Jon and the Gorgeous Kevin.

But Rachel had put an absolute ban on moving away from the protection of thousands of passengers to gather belongings.

'Not yet,' said Robert, putting a hand on Barbara's arm and looking over at Rachel. 'We've never disembarked this early.'

She nodded, still scanning the buffet. 'If we're first in the queue for the gangway, we'll immediately draw attention.'

As if demonstrating what this would be like, Jake's phone started to ring – a piercing screech, all the more conspicuous without the usual white noise of the engine.

'Call yourself a tech whizz,' Jess said, grabbing the handset and killing the volume. 'She told you to keep it on silent.'

He looked aggrieved. 'I did. I've set the notifications just for Lennon. For emergencies.'

'Maybe you should take it?' Barbara leaned forwards, tapping Rachel's knee and pointing to her left. 'Those restrooms are very well proportioned. For privacy, I mean.'

'No – the plan's in place.' She paused her sweep of the area and focused on the four of them. 'Let's commence phase one. Togeth—'

The word was halted on her lips by a booming chime: the Tannoy. Rachel shrank back, expecting to hear her name ring out in a request to approach the Guest Services desk.

They couldn't splinter off or separate. One family. One unit.

But the announcement only carried the smooth timbre of Veronica Chase, officially welcoming them to A Coruña where they would be docked until five forty-five p.m. Ample time, apparently, for guests to dine, enjoy the beaches of Orzán and Riazor or hop on the local train for the short ride to Santiago de Compostela.

Barbara gave a solemn salute across the tables to their allies in the task ahead. The Crewz Secrets camera was aloft on its tripod, documenting each phase of the operation. They'd agreed to track the family, from a subtle distance, until disembarkation. Every moment recorded for extra security. Or, if their worst nightmares were realised, for evidence.

She checked her watch: 8.16. The flight was in just under two hours. This was tight.

The buffet had begun to empty. Rachel glanced at her dad, whose foot was tapping under the table. He stopped. Both resumed neutral expressions and sipped their cappuccinos. The pretence of relaxation had to be maintained.

Veronica Chase's announcement drew to a close with a reminder to keep hold of all key cards in order to reboard for the final crossing. The *Synergy* was scheduled to arrive back in Southampton, as they had begun, on Thursday at six a.m.

Less than forty-eight hours on the clock.

Whilst everyone on board soaked up the last of the sun, their own looming itinerary cast a heavy shadow: escape the ship, reach the airport without being followed, depart A Coruña, arrive at Heathrow, co-ordinate with the NCA team, travel to Southampton, share evidence with the Border Force, formalise an arrest plan. Not to mention make it back to Newcastle in time for Friday's disciplinary hearing.

Rachel put her coffee cup down to disguise her shaking hand and picked up her bag. Every member of the unit snapped to attention as she mouthed one word. '*Ready?*'

This was it.

An overwhelming urge to protect these four people, at what-ever cost to the overall operation, bubbled within her. To bundle them off the ship as fast as possible. To shield them from harm. But, she forced her feet to move at a regular pace, leading them slowly, step by step, towards Midship Deck Five.

The queue stretched almost to the atrium with twitching pensioners jostling for space.

Rachel took in the red carpet, the polished handrails, the heavy crystal chandelier for, what she prayed would be, the last time. The shine of the ship's Swarovski sparkle had well and truly dulled. Never again.

They stood, rigid and alert, heels immediately clipped by more and more passengers joining the crush for the gangway.

A sudden jolt made Rachel jump, clutching Jess's arm.

'Could we just – so sorry—' a woman in an oversized sunhat was elbowing in, dragging her husband like a dog on a lead. 'Rest of our party made it here before us, backlog on the aft stairs – could we just …'

Rachel smiled tightly, ignoring the tutting eye-roll of her mother, to whom queue-jumping was almost equivalent to murder.

Just breathe.

Focus on the timeline. Phases two to four. Taxi. Check in. Make the flight.

It was going to go to the wire. And that was without being followed or stopped.

Barbara inhaled sharply as a maroon-skirt-suited figure circled in the distance, meeting and greeting with her usual tepid charm. Rachel still couldn't get a handle on how much Veronica Chase knew. Was she part of the criminal activity on board? Or, fishing, professionally or otherwise, for the truth?

They braced for impact. Chase was close now. Only a few dozen passengers away. Rachel could almost feel the temperature chill. Surely, she'd use this opportunity to question them. Push for information. Scupper their escape.

'Mam,' hissed Jake, holding out his phone. It was on silent, but the faint vibration felt as conspicuous as a klaxon. Lennon. 'This is the third call this morning. Just answer.'

Rachel glanced up, counting three cameras in the immediate vicinity, every one swivelled towards their group. 'I can't be seen talking on a mobile. It's too obvious.'

She swallowed and rechecked the contents of her bag – passports, broken phone, the single bagged contact lens and Tyler's statement – for the fifteenth time. Gripped their five key cards. Almost there.

'Shit.' Jake was white, turning his screen to show a text from Lennon in caps lock.

INTERPOL. VAN DER WYK DISHONOURABLY DISCHARGED FROM ARMY. SA WARRANT OUT FOR HIS ARREST FOR VIOLENT OFFENCES. FFS BE CAREFUL.

A crashing wave engulfed her.

A warrant? Previous for *violent offences?* This was a red alert. Should they abort? What if he got to them and something happened to her mum or dad? Jess or Jake?

She forced herself to stand tall. To withstand the tide.

'It's OK,' she said, putting a steadying hand on Jake's arm. 'You're with me. We'll make it.' She'd faced more overt threats of violence than this on a Bank Holiday Monday as a uniform response officer. Handy with the pepper spray, she'd built her reputation on the quality of her peripheral vision.

Never caught unawares. Never letting her unit down. Never taking a step back.

What was it Lennon had said last night, after everyone else had fallen asleep? Just the two of them, in the stillness of the rising light, planning every aspect of this urgent departure.

You know who you are, Rach. Think of Fever. Even when you fuck it up, you're still all over the detail. Still running the show.

Through a screen, over a thousand miles apart, he believed in her. They'd been connected. A burning in his eyes. A fire in her heart. She'd felt it.

She could do this.

They were in touching distance of the kiosk now, but – all at once – Veronica Chase was upon them, embracing Jess in a vice-like hold. 'My little environmentalist! I do hope Miguel was able to show you exactly what we do so well below deck!' Jess twisted in the cruise director's grip. 'HLC takes such pride in the way we make all our garbage disappear.' She released Jess and clicked her fingers. 'Anything surplus to requirements – gone! Whatever it takes.'

Rachel shuddered. *Whatever it takes.* She tried to assume a neutral expression, but could only manage a grimace. 'It was very interesting. Thanks so much.'

'Oh, my pleasure. It's not often we get such a specific request.' She stepped closer to Rachel, beaming, though her eyes were glassy and shoulders tense. This close, the cloying scent of hairspray that hung around her was bitter. Rachel held her breath. Hands sweaty – her grip on the key cards precarious. 'I've been hoping to catch you again. A little bird's been telling me all about your private meeting with our chief security officer.' She let the words hang in the air, pushing for more.

'Just a quick chat.' Rachel looked around, eyes darting, desperate for an excuse to leave – other passengers had started to push past. Her voice was strangled. 'Nothing to report.'

'Well, I must say, I'm disappointed you didn't come directly to me with any further concerns. In fact—' Chase hooked Rachel's arm, faux charm almost dripping onto the carpet '—would it be too much trouble to borrow you now for a few minutes?'

Robert broke in, gesturing to his watch. 'I'm afraid we've booked an excursion – you know what they're like on coach trips—' His response had started assertively, but was quickly undermined by rasping coughs.

Veronica Chase ignored him and drew Rachel closer, voice lowered to a hiss. 'Only yesterday, I had to remove your steward, Ms Ruc□o, from duty due to serious allegations. The captain's employment of these Ukrainians has been in breach of all HR processes.' Her nails were sharp, clawing. 'I need the information you passed to Simon Van der Wyk.'

Rachel forced a level stare, even though her throat was burning. 'No issues with Oksana. We can talk later.'

'Later won't do.' Veronica Chase's tone was cut-throat. 'Do I need to involve security?'

They were trapped: Robert still wheezing, Jess deathly pale.

And Rachel could see ice behind Chase's eyes. She wasn't going to be shaken off here, or side-lined.

Then suddenly, behind them, a booming call to arms. 'And five, four—'

Rachel spun: two warriors had been unleashed.

The remaining numbers were signalled by sharp finger motions as they stormed forwards, parting the pensioner pile-up with ease, armed with tripod and mic, jingle blasting at a thousand decibels: '*We'll take you all across the seas, show you all the balconies, the gourmet meals, the VIPs, exceptional facilities, Crewz Secrets!*'

Jon raised the boom like a spear, Kevin already corralling Chase into shot.

'The lady herself! We promised you more senior crew content here on TikTok Live and … here she is!' The Gorgeous Kevin's authority was pure custody sergeant. All cop, no camp.

Chase looked dazed, but professionalism in a live-stream PR situation evidently superseded interrogation.

Rachel grabbed their chance and dived forwards.

Her pupils met Andre's for a split second as she released her grip on the key cards, but it was only a cursory glance, nothing to arouse suspicion. Five quick beeps and they were through.

She clenched her empty fists, pulse racing.

Speed was imperative now. Could her dad manage the pace?

She wanted to look back, to check whose eyes were following their descent, but forced herself to keep moving, slicing a path through the crush.

Someone was shouting. Texan vowels. A command to stop.

There was no going back. No other way.

Jake was at her shoulder, voice fearless and firm. 'We've got you, Grandad. Lean on me.'

And then – hard ground. Concrete underfoot. They were off. Running. Free.

For now.

Chapter 45

Sea

Thursday 27th April

Rachel stood on the edge of land and sea, poised in anticipation. Solid ground sprawled behind, but in two strides she could be in freefall. One wrong move and she would be under the water line, sinking into the English Channel.

She'd spent the past twenty-four hours in the Border Police incident room, barely seeing daylight, going over and over the evidence with the NCA Near Europe Task Force. They'd retrieved the images from her phone. Mapped the crime scenes. DNA testing was underway.

The ship was so close now. Half an hour ago, when the vans had deposited her and the twenty armed officers at the Mayflower terminal, it had been a dot on the misty horizon; now it loomed, large and clear, only metres from shore.

'Are you ready?' The SIO's voice cut through her adrenaline, bringing her back with a bang. He had the aura of the Terminator: a man of few words and flexing muscles. Tim McFarlane. As NCA operations manager, he'd be leading this multi-arrest. Despite his intimidating physical presence, he'd treated her with refreshing professional respect since the five of them had been collected from Gatwick and taken straight to the Task Force HQ.

She'd been issued with a replacement phone; her pending disciplinary dismissed as a minor inconvenience. As the key witness to events on board, her inclusion within the operational team was the immediate priority.

This was it. No option now, but to bring her A-game.

And yet, visions of impending failure flashed through her mind. So many ways an operation of this scale could crash and burn before they even gained entry. This dawn raid made her previous arrest CV look like child's play. There was no Big Red Key big enough to batter the door of the *Synergy* off its hinges. And how exactly were they going to isolate the suspects amongst thousands of high-risk, elderly passengers?

Rachel held firm to Lennon's parting words this morning. His faith in her.

She focused on the three targets: Fernandez, Van der Wyk, Paige. What would their mindsets be at this moment, shoreline in sight and only a few steps before the money transfer? Surely, high alert. At least there'd been five of them previously to share the tense wait for the product to be unloaded and hushed away, out of the port and up the capillaries of the UK distribution network.

Today was different. Only three remained. They had the blood of two men on their hands and not even an ocean was going to wash that away. The NCA tactical team were clear: this was a smash and grab. As soon as any of the three suspects realised they'd been scuppered, their MO would quickly shift from getting the drugs off the ship to cutting the whole batch loose.

Rachel gulped as the gangway was secured to the familiar embarkation point at Midship Deck Five. Any second now.

At least the people who mattered were safe: her mum, her dad and the kids were holed up in the Premier Inn, eager for news. She felt their presence like a second skin – the once-despised pink polo shirt, invisible beneath her jacket and stab vest, was pressed close to her heart. Jess and Jake had been desperate to be part of this: to swarm onto the ship like avenging pirates, taking possession of treasure and hostages.

But this wasn't a game.

In strict adherence to the HLC schedule, the anchor had been lowered at precisely six a.m. The ship was tethered securely now; the dock, a swarm of port workers in high-vis and hard hats. Lorries were already starting to arrive with fresh provisions. Rachel winced. Border Force would be embargoing anything moving from ship to shore and vice versa until the whole scene was cleared. Passengers rocking up for this afternoon's scheduled voyage were going to be making furious calls to their insurance companies in a few hours.

She glanced at the officers assembled behind her. Their body language said *standard operation* whilst hers screamed *fish out of water*, but fuck it, she'd been schooled with Bank Holiday shifts in the Bigg Market. She could handle hostile environments.

The radio at her hip crackled, launching the Terminator into action. He gestured to the gangway, one eyebrow raised. 'After you?'

Rachel led the charge, hitting the security checkpoint at speed. 'Police – stand aside!'

The slippery concept of international waters was gone. The end of contingency and the beginning of consequence.

She was back on board.

Only two figures observed their dramatic entrance. One security guard's eyes popped out of his head as she flashed her warrant card; as planned, the other was Andre.

She addressed him as a stranger, tone curt. 'We have a Section 23 warrant under the *Misuse of Drugs Act 1971* to search these premises. Take us to the captain immediately.'

Although, by now, she had reasonable confidence in the intelligence they had compiled, it was impossible to know for sure how many other crew members could potentially be involved. For Andre's safety, it was crucial that his cover be maintained.

Stationing two armed officers at the bulkhead, Rachel and the NCA squad, complete with two narcotic detection dogs, raced forward. Andre lumbered beside them, playing his role to perfection.

She felt power build within her, relishing the adrenaline coursing through her veins. Fuck desk duty or five-star relaxation. She was DI Harlow. This was where she belonged.

At this hour, the ship's vast spaces were almost deserted. Only a few cleaners could be seen hoovering the already-spotless carpets. They looked up, alarmed. One stepped forward, brandishing his Henry like a battering ram, but he was immediately pushed to the side, vacuum silenced as the plug was ripped from its socket.

A scattering of passengers observed the thundering approach of twenty uniformed intruders, NCA stamped across every black jacket. One white-haired pensioner, seemingly on the way to the promenade, froze mid-footstep. A woman pushing a buggy flattened herself and her baby against the wall as the unit tore past.

'What's going on?' she screamed, gripping the buggy handles and looking around desperately for a crew member. 'Are we safe?'

Holiday time was officially over.

Now in the atrium, the unit closed ranks before their imminent dispatch to tactical positions. 'Target A team, down to Deck Zero. Target B, security ops. Target C, we head for the bridge,' the Terminator barked, gripping his iPad like a battle map.

Every member of the team was alert. Even the two spaniels appeared to be listening intently, ready for their handler's cue. Jesus – the NCA ops force had a reputation and a half, not all of it complimentary. She'd heard the term *wankers* thrown around back home, but this lot were making the SAS look like amateurs.

The Terminator nodded to Rachel. 'This is who you need to listen to. DI Harlow has been close to these individuals and knows the particular challenges we face this morning.'

She fired through her key messages: 'Fernandez is volatile – approach with caution. Van der Wyk's ex-military. And record says he'll use it. Keep constant comms with the divers. Product must be secured.'

On her left, an officer tapped twice at the screen in his hands. A blank window blinked on the deck plan: *No feed available.* He raised it to signal the fault, but Rachel cut in before the distraction grew. 'Eyes up. Assume surveillance is compromised. Move.'

Hands tightened on weapons. Radios clicked.

But before she'd taken a step, a pulsing alarm ripped through the quiet of the ship. The NCA had pre-empted this. Of course the HLC's premier cruise liner wasn't going down without a fight.

A Tannoy announcement broke through the siren. Miller's clipped, cut-glass tone: '*Crew Announcement. Code Charlie Charlie Charlie. Repeat Charlie Charlie Charlie. Over.*'

Rachel locked eyes with the Terminator. *Charlie* – the captain, in on it after all?

He sounded like he was reading Tariq's Byker line feed announcing the shop as open for business. Surely, to reveal his knowledge of the drug hoard at this stage over a loudspeaker was brazen.

Andre read her expression. 'Not drugs. Code for serious security alert. My access will now be cut.'

'Who can get us into the bridge?' the Terminator said.

Andre made to speak, but was drowned out by another Tannoy blast: '*Doors will be automatically locked in one minute due to a security breach. All passengers must remain in cabins.*'

For a split second, Rachel saw not suspects, but the woman with the buggy, about to be trapped behind an auto-locked cabin door. A baby in lockdown, while killers roamed free.

Could they make it to the bridge in time? Pulling her stab vest tighter, Rachel broke into a run.

'What is the meaning of this?' A frantic American voice rang out from behind them. 'Who gave you clearance to board?'

Veronica Chase was struggling to match their pace in her stiletto heels. Spotting Rachel at the front of the group, in NCA uniform, she gaped. 'You? But how?'

The cruise director regarded her and Andre with the same shrewd gaze she had employed throughout the sailing, albeit significantly more sweaty and less poised here. For whatever reason, Veronica had had her own pre-existing suspicions as to Miller's captaincy of the vessel. She could prove to be a useful ally, once they'd ruled her out of any personal culpability.

But the clock was ticking. Lockdown imminent. No time for shrewd gazes or useful allies. 'UK Police have reason to believe that crew have been using this ship to import controlled drugs into the country,' said Rachel. 'We need access to the bridge immediately.'

Veronica stared, dumbfounded. Genuine surprise? Possibly. But Rachel filed it as inconclusive – shock could be faked, and this woman had made a career of stage-managed appearances.

A sudden crackle from the radio. 'We have Target A. Repeat: Target A in cuffs. Over.' The voice from Deck Zero was firm and steady. All in a day's work.

For Rachel, however, this was the tipping point. They may have apprehended Fernandez, but that meant they were also likely to be at the site of the drugs. Absolutely everything rested on what was inside that packaging.

'Have you located the product? Over.'

She held her breath: this was the line between everything and nothing.

'Not yet, ma'am. Suspect has required significant restraint. One officer injured. Medic required. Over.'

Rachel turned to Veronica. 'Will your security clearance override the lockdown?'

She nodded, feebly. 'Only Miller, myself, the first officer and Simon Van der Wyk. He's not one of your suspects though, is he?'

'Just get us to the bridge. And hurry.'

Chapter 46

Sea

If Rachel thought she had witnessed Miller's rage over the events of the previous week, she was very much mistaken. The captain strode towards them as they burst into the bright space, the vast expanse of sea and sky still visible behind him across the glass panorama. Officers moved quickly to the engineers manning the navigation equipment, each needing to be discounted as a threat in order to focus attention on the known assailants.

Veronica Chase, galvanised by her elite security privileges, had pushed herself to the front of the group, the chance to land a sucker punch seemingly outweighing her former professionalism. 'On your watch, Dick?' she drawled. 'You've either been in on this or turned a blind eye. So, which is it?'

'You have no place in the tec"ical area – get back to hostessing or whatever it is that you're paid for.' He turned dismissively and faced the officers with his public-school, pompous pedigree dialled up to the max. 'I am the commander of this vessel and I demand an explanation.'

The cruise director was clearly not going to be demeaned so easily, however, and she stepped forward, jabbing a maroon-manicured talon.

'Not this time.' She was nose to nose with him now, nostrils flaring. 'You don't get to call the shots. Your reputation's in tatters.'

Miller's hiss was full of menace. '*Reputation*, Veronica? You speak to me of *reputation*?'

Rachel had had enough. 'You two clearly have issues; however, criminal activity on board takes precedence over whatever soap opera you're playing out.' She nodded to one of the officers. 'Could you escort Ms Chase off the ship for questioning. I'm sure she has a wealth of useful information.'

Veronica hit Miller with a haughty stare, but allowed the officer to lead her away. She spun back as the doors opened and landed a final zinger, brimming with Texan charm: 'I always faked it, Dick. Every. Single. Time.' And with that she strutted into the lift and was gone from view.

Rachel flashed her warrant card to the captain. 'Let's get on with this, shall we? I'm on board now purely in a professional capacity. We've got evidence that members of your crew are part of an established drug-running operation. And the incidents I reported to you are all directly related. Start talking.'

He started to do something, but it was more akin to splutter than speech. His face was as white as the powder she hoped she'd soon be receiving confirmation of. She caught bursts of vitriol, '*ideas above your station … Northern lower-class mentality*', but quickly tired of his attempts to assert control.

'Pack it in,' she snapped. 'We'll be pulling this place apart: personal phone, tablets, laptops. If there's a speck on your shoe I'm going to find it.'

The Terminator leaned in. 'Dogs got the drugs. Two tonnes at least. Biggest haul we've had since Covid.'

Amongst the intensity playing out on the bridge, Rachel hadn't registered that her radio was out. The sheer volume of feeds and receivers in this area must have saturated the police network.

'Excellent. Let's share the news with the captain, shall we?' She was buzzing as she returned to him. 'Now confirmed. A huge quantity of narcotics. On board your ship. So, I'll start you off with an easy one. Where's Danielle?'

'I'm here.'

Everyone swivelled. The voice was soft, nothing like the off-stage screaming banshee. Danielle was leaning in the doorway to the captain's office, dressed in a silk robe, her hair arranged in loose curls over one shoulder, drawing deliberate attention to the V where the material crossed low, leaving nothing to the imagination. This tallied with Andre's information on her sleeping arrangements – the captain's accommodation directly accessible from the bridge.

Danielle had a champagne flute in one hand. With the other, she dabbed a tissue to her dry cheeks, eyes cast downwards. A bargain-basement Princess Di.

Rachel didn't buy it for a second. 'A little premature for your cele-bratory toast I'm afraid, Dannii. I'm arresting you on suspicion of importing controlled drugs into the United Kingdom. Furthermore, on suspicion for your role in the conspiracy to murder Tyler Tweedy and Estavo Fernandez. Let's get you dressed and banged up, OK?'

She nodded at a female officer, who duly disappeared through the office into the captain's private quarters to fetch Danielle some clothes. It wouldn't bother Rachel to march her down the gangway and into the van half-naked, but protocols concerning public decency had to be obeyed. 'Any report on Target B, sergeant?' she asked the dark-haired officer to her right.

'Nothing yet, ma'am. Security office was clear,' he said, unclip-ping his cuffs from his belt and taking a step towards Danielle, who seemed to be crying in earnest now. Rachel wondered if she'd poked herself in the eye to get some crocodile tears going.

'Richard,' Danielle sobbed. 'Are you going to let them tell lies about me? They can't put me in handcuffs like a common criminal.'

Rachel raised her eyebrows. 'From your PNC list, you must've got pretty used to our bracelets? At least until you hit the reality TV jackpot. Then you upgraded to some proper sparkle.' She cocked her head, evaluating her suspect. 'According to Tyler, though, you got greedy. Back to your old ways. Scrotes like you never really change their spots, do they, Dannii?'

'I object to this *woman* being present in the strongest possible terms,' Miller barked, blocking Danielle from the handcuffs and appealing to the officers behind. 'DI Harlow has subjected Miss Paige to a campaign of harassment – desperate to cause trouble since she boarded.' He approached the Terminator, palm outstretched. 'Now look. I'm sure there must be something we can do to straighten this whole business out, man to man?'

The Terminator frowned. 'I'm afraid not, Captain. At the National Crime Agency we take any attempt at bribery and corruption extremely seriously. And I'd suggest that you show my colleague the respect her rank demands.'

'I swear to you, Rich, I don't know what they're talking about. First, I lose my professional partner …' Danielle let out an exaggerated sob and dabbed her eyes '… and now *this*.'

'Of course you're not involved.' Miller looked around the room wildly, a politician mid-*Panorama* exposé. 'Ms Paige is the victim here.' He embraced the still-weeping Danielle, tenderly. The sight of Miller so obviously fawning over a tarted-up low-life, barely half his age, was enough to make Rachel retch. She suspected a heavy reliance on Viagra in this 'relationship'.

But her queasiness was halted by the sound of glass shattering. The champagne flute.

Everyone's attention swerved to Danielle, the change in her demeanour a rapid curveball. One second, she'd been giving it her best doe-eyed, Bambi performance and the next she was holding her jagged glass stem to Miller's throat.

Now, her voice was ragged and coarse, a primal return to her backstage persona. 'You can all fuck off. I'm walking or this cunt hits the deck.'

Miller's face fell. 'But no,' he stuttered, straining his neck away from the glass blade. 'You said – I've told my wife – we were—'

'You were convenient,' she said, eyes hard, staring straight ahead, assessing her possible exit route. 'Simon said we needed you distracted. I know your type. What you'd want.'

'Put the weapon down,' Rachel said firmly. 'This ship is full of armed officers. There's no way you're walking.'

'Simon'll get me out,' she said, tone manic, as if expecting Van der Wyk to abseil through the window at any moment and whisk her away.

'Sorry to disappoint you, Danielle,' Rachel said, lying smoothly, 'but we've got him. And Fernandez. They've both confirmed you're the brains in this operation. You set it up. You brought the cartel into the mix.'

'You're a fuckin liar,' Danielle spat. But her hand trembled and the glass glinted in the early morning sun. Her eyes had lost their steely focus.

'Drop the weapon!' shouted Rachel, stepping forward. The officers next to her had fingers poised on triggers, arms outstretched.

Time seemed to slow.

Miller's flesh had turned white. His eyes were wet with terror, all captaincy gone. A slowly expanding shadow at his groin told Rachel he'd pissed himself. For a split second Danielle looked like the woman Rachel had seen on stage – strong, elegant. Then the jagged shard in her fingers flashed. And she tore it across the captain's throat.

The world sped up again. Blood sprayed across the white shirt. Miller's knees buckled; his face contorted in pain.

Rachel lunged. 'Drop the weapon!' The command filled the bridge. The female officer who'd gone to fetch clothes launched herself across the doorway and tackled Danielle as the blade clattered free.

'Medic to the bridge!' Rachel choked, pressing her hand to the captain's neck, which was gushing blood. 'We need a medic now!' She wrenched her earpiece and heard nothing. 'Someone make contact – quick.'

The scene was frantic. It took two officers to cuff Danielle – still shouting abuse and resisting arrest for all she was worth. Rachel tried to concentrate on Miller. His laboured breathing. The pool of crimson collecting under her hands. The whites of his eyes as she tried desperately to stop him from slipping away.

'Just hold on,' she said, attempting calm. And then: 'How long?' to the officer at her side.

'On board, ma'am,' he said. 'Two minutes, tops.'

Two minutes was too long. Every second could be his last breath.

'Update on Target B?' Rachel called to the Terminator. He was in close communication with the HLC first officer, formerly second in command and now officially in charge of the ship. She hoped that he, unlike the captain, would take closer heed of the signage on the wall. Miller's Danielle-shaped blind spot had certainly put his *constant vigilance* mantra to shame.

'Still at large,' he said, returning to her side. 'And passengers are starting to push back against the lockdown. They're banging on doors, shouting from balconies. There's going to be trouble if we leave them like this much longer.'

'Let's make another Tannoy announcement appealing directly to Van der Wyk to turn himself in,' Rachel said. 'We need to locate him and fast.'

The lift doors opened and two paramedics quickly relieved Rachel of her blood-soaked watch over the captain's dwindling pulse. 'Is he going to make it?'

'He's lost a lot of blood,' the younger medic said, applying an oxygen mask, 'but you've given him the best chance.'

She glanced down at the bright red hands at the ends of her arms, barely registering them as her own. They looked like they'd been amputating limbs in trench warfare. Floaters darted across her retinas and a sharp pain made it impossible to get a full breath. She dragged both palms down the side of her black jeans, quelling the rising panic she could feel within.

'You should get checked out too,' the Terminator said. 'We'll keep you informed of every development.'

'No way,' she said, forcing oxygen into her lungs. 'I've come this far. Finding Van der Wyk's too important.'

The Terminator assembled the remaining officers not dealing with Danielle. 'Border Force have reported objects being launched from one of the upper decks. They think Fifteen. They've recovered a laptop from the water.'

'How many officers still operational?' the dark-haired sergeant said.

'Two still at the entry point, twelve in total.'

'We need to split up,' Rachel said, 'and approach Deck Fifteen from above and below. There are three stairways – we'll have to cover every possible exit route.'

'Is your radio back on comms?' the Terminator asked.

'No,' she said. 'But I'll be fine.'

'OK. Approach with caution. Let's finish this.'

Save for the officers stationed periodically with guns, the whole place was a ghost ship. Rachel's heart hammered as she sprinted the length of Deck Fourteen, making for the aft stairway. The volume rose as she raced down the passenger corridor. Rattling doors. Shouts. Pounding fists. Further instructions had been issued, but there was a limit to how long thousands of paying customers could be detained behind locked doors.

The air fizzed with unrest.

As the corridor opened out into the vestibule and grand staircase, she forced herself upwards, two steps at a time. Feet pounding marble. She ignored the burn in the back of her throat, professional pride obliterating her pain threshold. Then she was out through the heavy doors. Weapon in hand. Eyes everywhere.

She barely needed to search, though, for there he stood. Simon

Van der Wyk – one foot astride the barrier.

She'd had the right staircase, or the wrong one.

He was going to go. And she had no means of calling for backup. He surveyed her for a moment, teetering on the edge.

Flashes of Gallagher assaulted her senses: his eyes, his words, his fall.

Not this time. Not again.

Without words, in one instinctive motion, she grabbed the chief security officer and dragged him down from his summit. He landed with a thud on the hard floor, glasses skittering across the deck.

'You're done.' She coughed, breathless. 'It's over.'

He panted, accent still harsh. 'You can't prove anything. You've got nothing on me.'

'That's where you're wrong.' She fought to keep him on the deck. 'Divers have retrieved the laptop. We'll get what we need.' Her voice cracked, but she continued, needing him to hear this. 'I've told them all about your director's cut CCTV footage.' She could hear footsteps now; black figures were approaching from the midship, radios blaring.

'All Fernandez,' he said, still wheezing. 'I never touched the bodies.'

The sight of NCA officers running towards them gave her voice power. 'Wrong again. Unfortunately for you, you left a crucial piece of evidence in Tyler's cabin.'

He looked at her, sceptical. Convinced he'd covered his tracks.

'You can look at me however you want, but your eyesight's shite – you said so yourself. And you weren't wearing glasses in that first muster drill.' She smiled, as if in sympathy. 'It's a right ball ache at home, never mind at sea, when you lose a contact lens, isn't it?'

His face froze. Arrogance gone.

There were strong hands on her now, pulling her to her feet. But she wanted him to know. To hear it from her. 'It found me, you know, the evidence, not the other way round. Just a single piece of plastic, but that'll be enough. You killed Tyler and you ordered Fernandez dead as well. The NCA forensics team have got it right now – DNA lasts longer than you'd think, you shady fuck.'

He was cuffed. Just another criminal facing justice. No longer a threat.

She nodded at the Terminator, who still looked disarmingly Teflon, and shook hands with the other officers, though her skin was stained with blood.

Her phone buzzed: Jon and the Gorgeous Kevin confirming they'd got the footage they needed, having been stationed on their portside balcony since sunrise, camera trained patiently on the gangway.

She was aching now to give her family the good news, but it was Lennon, more than anyone else, who she wanted. He'd inhale all the details – intricacies that only another detective would understand.

True, he'd probably just be piss-taking again within a few moments, but she'd grasped concern in his voice earlier when he'd wanted specifics about firearms officers and PPE. He'd made her promise not to approach any of the suspects alone. Maybe she'd have to go light with some of the details after all.

She could leave the ship now. Right on time.

Her journey aboard the *Synergy of the Seas* was over.

Chapter 47

Land

Thursday 27th April

More than a dozen reporters were clamouring with questions as the NCA Terminator approached the lectern. The press conference was being held at the Border Force's evidence confiscation facility at Southampton International Dock. It was a glorified shipping container with a concrete floor and corrugated walls; however, the main focus was the stack of polystyrene crates housing bag upon bag of white powder.

Rachel stood to one side, flanked by NCA officers, breathing through her mouth to mitigate the sharp tang of diesel in the air. She was dead on her feet. Now that the suspects had been remanded in custody and she'd had her debrief, the come-down from this morning's adrenaline surge was intense. The last few days had been a whirlwind and she'd barely slept or eaten, but due to the minor celebrity involvement and the quantity of drugs seized, the whole operation had garnered significant media attention.

'Is it true that Danielle Paige has been arrested as part of this operation?'

'Can you confirm that Tyler Tweedy's death is being treated as murder?'

'What's the street value of the drugs seized on board this morning?'

'Will you be using sonar equipment to search for the missing crew member?'

The Terminator raised his hand for quiet and the barrage of noise fell to a hush. Rachel looked past the Sky and BBC camera crews to the quartet at the back of the room. Her mum gave an overexcited wave while her dad sat, still and watchful, clearly impressed with the calibre of news outlets in attendance.

Barbara held up her phone to record, flipping the leather wallet case back and forth as if the camera might be hiding from her. She leaned across to Jess, who tapped something and handed it back. Jake had taken his AirPods out for the occasion and was trying to get a good angle of the drugs haul through the gaps in the melee of reporters.

'Thank you for attending this short press conference.' The Terminator was predictably monotonous in his tone. Did *anything* raise his heart rate? 'We have today made four arrests relating to the seizure of a substantial quantity of cocaine on board a UK cruise ship. Three of these individuals were crew members, whilst one further arrest was made of a port security guard.

'The National Crime Agency is dedicated to tackling harmful Organised Crime Groups that have strands overseas. Our Near Europe Task Force has worked in collaboration with Border Force and port authorities to make this seizure. We are particularly grateful to the dedicated professionalism of an off-duty CID officer, on holiday aboard the ship, who provided us with invaluable intelligence relating to this operation at significant risk to herself and her family.'

She could see Jake and Jess giving each other a high five, with her dad nodding and leaning over to say something to Barbara. She shushed him, pointing at her phone, which was still outstretched, intent on capturing this moment of fame for posterity.

The NCA Terminator continued in his gravelly bass: 'The UK domestic cocaine market is dominated by criminal gangs who the NCA believe to be making in excess of four billion pounds a year. This particular network was an attempt to flood UK streets with cocaine. It has been stopped in its tracks. Today's seizure not only reduces the harm illegal drugs cause within our communities, but also makes a huge dent in the profits of smugglers.

'We will continue to work with the UK Border Force to target these international gangs upstream and overseas, disrupting and dismantling them at every step. Today's successful operation sends a clear message to criminals that they will be caught. No further questions will be answered at this time regarding the ongoing investigation. Thank you.'

Lights flashed and voices soared, but the Terminator's resolution was final. Rachel manoeuvred past the press pack to the four figures in the back row.

'That was awesome – are you gonna be on the news?' Jake was breathless with excitement.

'If you get an OBE, you've got to turn it down, OK?' Jess's eyes were wide, considering the possibilities. 'No curtseying.'

Rachel grinned. 'Let's not get carried away.' She looked at her mum and dad, now deep in conversation with a Sky news reporter who seemed to have made a beeline for them after realising that his questions about Tyler and Danielle were going to be met with a firm *no comment* by anyone official.

'Yes, she had it under control from a very early stage,' her mum was saying, breezily, 'but that's our Rachel all over, really. She takes all aspects of the job in her stride.'

'Er, Mum,' she interrupted, putting a hand gently on her arm. 'The NCA were really clear we shouldn't discuss the details.'

'Quite right, Barbara,' Robert said, zipping an imaginary fastening across his mouth. 'Mustn't jeopardise the case.'

'Oh, yes!' Her mum was suddenly flustered. 'Ever so sorry,' she said to the eager reporter, obviously intent on getting a personal angle.

Rachel's phone beeped. Lennon.

Selling your story to the Sun, then? They'll pay double if you get your baps out.

She stepped away, whispering to Jess in an undertone, 'Get ready to put a gag on your gran.'

He answered in one ring. 'All done?'

'Yeah, just an NCA statement. They set up a photo op with the drugs haul, but a PR exercise more than anything else.'

'Everyone here's buzzing for you. Even Bailey's cracked a smile. Been in the office, taking credit.'

That figured. At least it was an improvement from his last appraisal of her. What was it he'd said? *Emotional and unpredictable.* Pretty accurate. She smiled, imagining Bailey's downbeat tone and baggy eyes: *Northumbria Police provides a thorough grounding in all elements of investigative tec"ique.*

'Tell him to go for it,' she said. 'Might boost my chances of not getting sacked.' The NCA had already been in contact with Northumbria directly – her disciplinary pushed back three days. Nevertheless, it hovered in the back of her mind: a dull throb of tension.

'You'll smash it. And if not, there's always the kiss and tell to fall back on.'

'Solid plan B,' she said, yawning. 'What I really need before then's a seven-hour drive.'

'I said I'll come and get you – it's no bother.'

'We'd have to listen to your music all the way back though, right?'

'Absolutely.'

'And I'm not allowed any Girls Aloud? Come on, they've got some bangers in their back catalogue.'

'Have a word with yourself. First you turn your children's

holiday into a criminal investigation, then you try to poison their eardrums? Come on, pet. Be reasonable.'

She smiled, torn between wanting to hug him and give him the finger. 'Thanks for the offer, but I'll just get my head down and set off in the morning.'

'You sure? I don't mind.' He paused. 'All right, we can take it in turns. Your shite and my actual music.'

She laughed. 'No, you're OK. The NCA guy said something about taking us for a pizza tonight, anyway. Then I just need to sleep.'

'Oh right. That the Robocop wannabe?' There was something strangled about his voice. She was about to correct him – *Terminator actually* – when he continued, 'Didn't realise you'd hit it off.'

She couldn't quite read his tone: banter or something else? 'We haven't really. Tim just mentioned it – as a thank you.'

'Of course he's called Tim.' Lennon's voice was suddenly Geordied up to the max. 'Some things never change, eh? Keep it classy, Rach.'

She turned back to her family, who had thankfully managed to shake off the reporter. Had she detected a dig in Lennon's final words? She was probably overthinking it. He'd be glad she'd saved him from an entire day of travel. The last thing anyone would want to do at three p.m. would be sit on a train down the length of the country and then drive straight back.

Barbara checked her watch, anxiously. 'The parking's due to expire, Bob. We should probably be making a move.' They'd been granted access to the *Synergy* one final time to collect their luggage, accompanied by a woman with a high-up-sounding executive role in High Life Cruises Ltd. The ship was still swarming with police and scene of crime officers, searching for whatever forensic traces could be recovered from Tyler's cabin and the site of Estavo Fernandez's stabbing.

The HLC exec had been gushing in her gratitude for their assistance in bringing the conspiracy to light, although evidently desperate to avoid further bad publicity. An all-expenses-paid repeat trip had been mooted, along with assurances that lessons would be learned. Rachel had suggested that they might want to start by looking at the HLC whistleblowing procedure and paying Andre and Oksana a sizeable bonus.

She stopped short of saying she'd rather cut her own arm off than endure another cruise. It had been the trip she'd needed, after all, if not the one she'd wanted.

'We're going to miss you,' she said to her parents.

'Yeah, who's going to tut when we start swearing?' Jake said, smiling.

'We should do it again,' Jess added. 'I mean, not a cruise, but, like, go away together.'

'Somewhere quieter next time.' Barbara's eyes twinkled.

'I've heard there are some good deals to Beirut,' her dad said, straight-faced.

Rachel grinned. 'Get Jenny from Destinations on it. I'd be up for another try – on dry land, obviously.'

'Well.' Barbara turned to Robert and took his arm. 'We should …'

'Yes,' he agreed. 'Been caught out before at that port car park. Five pounds they wanted last year, wasn't it?' For going over by less than—'

'Unless, you need us to stay?' Her mum's voice was hopeful. 'We could always top it up on the app?'

'We'll be fine, Mum. Honestly.' She stepped forward and pulled her into a hug. 'Thanks for everything.'

'We're only a phone call away,' Robert said, giving her a bristly kiss on the cheek and speaking softly into her ear. 'Your mum was right about the oxygen mask. I want to be on all the future holidays so I'll be giving it a proper go.'

She squeezed his hand and watched as they walked out into the warmth of the afternoon, her mum supporting her dad's shuffling steps. Jess and Jake stood on either side, catching the extra bits of information Barbara kept turning round to dispatch.

'I've sent the press conference video to the chat,' she called. 'Thought you'd want a copy even if we do end up watching it on the news!' Her eyes flashed, probably already mentally organising a screening at the bowls club.

Jess duly opened the WhatsApp group, recently renamed *Just Cruisin'*, and the three of them watched in increasingly uncontrollable hysterics as the video played a three-minute close-up of Barbara, with a slice of Robert's ear, in selfie-mode, shushing and commenting over the entire NCA statement.

Rachel didn't know whether the lump in her throat had been lodged there through laughter or some other emotion as she heard her mum's undiluted praise, pride brimming with every syllable. She'd waited a long time to hear that sound.

Chapter 48

Land

Friday 28th April

The sun was low as Rachel turned off the Central Motorway and crossed Byker Bridge. She fiddled with the seatbelt, its hard edge cutting into her shoulder. Jutting blocks of the Wall loomed over the side of the car, casting their usual shadows over the city, but with her foot on the accelerator, in seconds they were past, heading towards the welcome ordinariness of home.

Rachel parallel-parked at her first attempt, without any new dents to the paintwork, and turned to Jake, beside her in the front seat. Jess had been asleep since Scotch Corner, her snores still audible over Sam Fender's 'Seventeen Going Under', which Jake had cranked up to max volume for the last leg of the journey. She cut the engine and they sat for a moment, deafened by the sudden silence. Jake reached back, through the gap between their seats, to prod his sister.

'We're back, Jizzica.' No response. A harder jab. 'Howay, mutant.'

'Jake, don't,' Rachel intercepted, trying to pre-empt what felt like a sure-fire slide back into domestic disharmony.

'What's he calling me?' Jess mumbled, swamped within her hoodie.

'Nothing,' he said in a sing-song tone, historically extremely effective in provoking her wrath.

Escalation was halted by Jess's phone, ringing with an insistent buzz.

'It's Dad,' she said, looking at Jake, surprised. 'Hey. Yeah just pulled up.' She snorted and rolled her eyes. 'Well, Mam is, kind of. I know, mental. Erm, yeah, I guess. I'll ask him.' She took her hood down, phone away from her ear. 'Asking if he can pick us up to sleep there tonight?'

Jake shrugged. 'We're playing Southampton at home this weekend – ask him if it's tomorrow or Sunday?'

Jess rolled her eyes. 'I'm not your secretary – ask him yourself.' She looked at Rachel. 'Is that all right, Mam. You don't need us to do anything?'

'You offering to help with the laundry?' She gave Jess an encouraging smile. 'Get yourselves over there. You can fill him in on all the drama.'

Jake turned as Jess spoke into the phone again. 'Why's he ringing her? They don't normally speak.' He looked put out, position destabilised in the fragile, divorced-parents ecosystem.

'Dunno. But it's good, I think. You need to start planning how you're going to tell him about your IT exploits anyway.'

He looked shocked. 'You're really gonna grass?'

She considered for a moment. No harm done, really. So far.

'Well …' She paused, making him sweat a little longer. 'If you *swear* you'll pack in any more unauthorised access, I guess I could just let it go.' Her voice hardened. 'No more calls from the school though. You've shown what an absolute genius you are on a laptop – apply it to something constructive, OK?'

He fist-bumped her, solemnly. 'Deal.'

'Right, he's coming in half an hour,' Jess said, half-smiling at the unexpected paternal olive branch. Her focus was still on her phone, rapidly swiping, in full efficiency mode. 'Switch your roaming settings back on, by the way, if you haven't already.'

'Roaming?' Rachel asked, picking up her unfamiliar handset.

The twins looked at each other. 'For God's sake, Mam,' Jess said, not unkindly. 'How do you actually manage day-to-day life?'

She shrugged, deciding not to dwell on the hundreds of pounds of EU data charges she had probably accrued over the last week. Perhaps she could add it to the compensation package they'd been offered by HLC since the press conference.

Jake had been giving them a running commentary for most of the drive home on how much traffic Crewz Secrets' latest content had attracted. They were up to two million hits for their footage of Danielle screaming, 'Do you know who I am?' as she was marched off the ship, overlaid with flashing images from *Titanic*, and Britney Spears' 'Toxic' as the pounding soundtrack.

The twins had already had payment for their consultancy services transferred to their bank accounts and were now sitting pretty on a sizeable nest egg, their social media benefactors promising to book a reunion trip to the Toon as soon as their cruising schedule allowed.

'At least put that to the right time,' Jess said, looking up from her screen to the dashboard, clock still running an hour behind.

Jake leaned forward and, in less than five seconds, had altered the display. 'Sorted. *JC*, right?'

Scott dutifully pitched up half an hour later, bearing two giant pizza boxes.

'Thought you wouldn't have much in, food-wise.'

Rachel could have actually kissed him. This was, bar none, the most thoughtful thing he had ever done in the seventeen years she'd known him. 'You,' she said, 'are an absolute legend.'

'No bother. Done all right on that drugs seizure, mind. Front page of the *Mirror*.' He whistled through his teeth. 'What was the street value? Twenty-two mill?'

'Yeah, well. Never really off duty in this job, are you? I got loads of help from these two. Coppers in the making.'

Jake and Jess looked low-key chuffed and they all managed to sit, as a foursome, around the kitchen table for a pleasant fifteen minutes, stuffing slices of pizza into their mouths, without a shot being fired in any direction.

'Right,' Scott, said, wiping his mouth with kitchen roll. 'I'll drop them back first thing – got a CrossFit comp in Middlesborough at eleven.'

Of course you do, she thought, but let it wash over her.

'What about the match?' Jake said.

'Sunday, mate,' Scott replied, 'and I've got an extra ticket, actually. Barnsey's in Tenerife so I was gonna see if you fancied it, Jessie. I know it's not really your thing – I can see if Holly's lad wants it. Corrupt Saudi blood money and all tha—'

'No, I'll come,' Jess said, in a rush. 'I mean,' she slowed, catching herself, 'we watched the Spurs game – maybe I'm a lucky charm.'

Jake looked across at her, sharply. 'Don't think you're shooting your mouth off, though, with all your shite. St James' is a sacred space.'

She held her hands up. 'I can play dumb for ninety minutes, or whatever it is. You can help me with my IT homework later, then, OK? We all know you've got skills in that department.'

Jake stood up hurriedly from the table. 'Let's get going.'

Rachel saw the two of them exchange meaningful stares as they made for the front door. 'Bye then,' she called. 'Do I not even get a hug, after all that?'

Two sets of feet charged back down the corridor and her breath was almost extinguished in the force of their arms wrapped tight, squeezing her into submission.

She could vividly remember being handed her twins for the first time, by Scott, in the delivery suite: Jess first, red and angry-looking, limbs twisting in perpetual discomfort; then Jake, long-legged and sleepy, nestling straight into the crook of her arm. She looked at their dad and smiled, something like affection passing between them.

It was peaceful in the house, once the front door had slammed. No blaring TV noise, no shouts of 'Mam – where's my …' bouncing off the walls. Just quiet.

She emptied the cases, put a dark wash on, started unpacking her shoes and make-up. Mind wandering, she sank into the sofa and dipped her toe into the wreckage of her professional life. Despite the out-of-office, her inbox was heaving with unread updates and briefings.

Lennon had done well, acting up. The DDTRO application was in and communication with the CPS lawyers looked promising. Her heart raced at the subject line of one email from NHS England: *Results*.

Impulsively, she clicked and scanned the first paragraph. *Negative*.

Pouring herself a large glass of wine, she silently toasted this confirmation that she wasn't riddled with hepatitis. Not really the sort of celebration she could share more widely, but hopefully this streak of luck was a good omen for the hearing. Good fortune came in threes and all that.

She'd taken Jess's copy of *1984* out of the suitcase, one corner still folded from the morning she'd found Tyler. Her attempt at relaxation had come to a crashing halt almost immediately on their 'trip of a lifetime'; maybe she should have a bath and see how it all turned out?

But, she was restless. Something had been happening in her stomach all day as they'd bombed it up the M1. A pulsing beat, getting stronger as they drew closer and closer to home. She picked up her phone: eight forty. Should she ring him, or just call round?

Trying not to overthink it, she pulled on her Uggs. He'd offered to get the train down to Southampton and drive them back. That had to mean something – didn't it?

Chapter 49

Land

In fifteen minutes, she was shivering on Lennon's doorstep, holding a bottle of red and a big Toblerone she'd grabbed on the short drive to the other side of the Coast Road.

Potential scenarios flew through her mind as she waited, shifting from foot to foot, peering into the glass panel of his front door.

He was taking a while.

She turned to check – maybe he'd popped in on his dad – but his car was definitely there on the drive. What would it be like to just throw herself over this threshold, rather than spend any longer arsing around? Years they'd wasted, skirting their feelings, bantering each other into banality, never actually admitting how it could be if they just took that leap into the un—

'Rach? What you doing here?'

Lennon sounded shocked, and she spun back around, unable to hide the beaming smile from her face. She felt all her inhibitions dissolve. They didn't need that line anymore; it had been scuffed away to dust. Almost invisible. He'd been there through everything – she could take the mask off now.

He looked bedraggled, like he'd just got out of the shower and thrown on those shorts. Bare-chested; skin glistening in the night air. The pulsing beat had become a pounding rhythm inside her. Louder and louder. Impossible to ignore. She could see he was flustered, as if he could also sense that this was going to be the start of something new. Hair was bone-dry though.

'Erm, ok – always answer the door half naked? These are for you,' she said, gabbling, holding out her gifts. 'Been catching up on the job. You've – yeah – done well.'

He stood awkwardly, pushing his hair back, avoiding her gaze.

She laughed, suddenly shy. 'Too weird when I'm nice?'

'Erm, it's not a good time. I wish you'd called.'

A sound came from behind him, another voice. 'Adam? Everything all right?'

Holy shit.

Desperate to retreat, Rachel instead found herself rooted to the paving stones. Smile still frozen on her lips, she couldn't turn, couldn't move from her spot in the half-open doorway. She tried to lift one boot, but only managed to scuff her toe across the join between the grey slabs.

He'd only moved into this place a year ago. A new build. It had looked pristine last time she was here, but now there was a small cluster of weeds poking through the paving. In mortifying slow motion, they both endured the pained silence while the female voice approached.

A blonde woman stood in the doorway now, one hand on the PVC frame, the other draped round his waist. She was wearing a man's shirt, which Rachel recognised as one of four items she'd approved on Vinted after telling Lennon his wardrobe was tragic and needed updating.

Louise from the work canteen. Of course it was. Big pouty lips, blonde waves tumbling effortlessly like Rapunzel.

Rachel felt the comparison shining like a spotlight between the two of them: even in this state of rumpled undress, she looked perfect. Boobs so fucking pert the shirt was hoisted forwards, barely covering her arse. From this distance Rachel could see she wasn't even wearing a bra. They'd be fake, but the effect was impressive. What a cow.

'Hey,' said Louise, looking her up and down with a coy bat of her thick lashes.

'Hey.' Rachel struggled to move her lips, jaw so tense it felt like her chin might snap off. 'Just dropping these.' But now she'd started talking, she couldn't judge how to stop. 'Got them for all the team, you know, take advantage of the duty free. Little thank you.'

'Awww, Ads, isn't that cute?' *Ads?* He wasn't Ads. He was Lennon. Her Lennon.

His eyes stayed firmly on the ground, but she could see the flush of crimson rising up his neck.

'Right then,' she said, as brightly as she could fake. 'Have a … nice night.'

'Byee,' trilled Louise. She giggled, but as Rachel had already lurched to escape, it was impossible to tell at what. Better not to know, she told herself, forcing her head to stay high and continue walking rather than shrivel up and die.

She thought she might have heard Lennon's voice once more, softly, calling something that sounded like *wait*. But she was hurtling away from him now, drum beat deafening in her ears, racing to put more distance between them. Away from what might have been.

Then, louder, unmistakable: 'Wait,' and he'd grabbed her hand.

She shook him off, breath rasping in her throat. 'Just leave it.'

The door was shut behind him. No audience.

'It's not what it looks like.'

The tears were so close, but she refused to cry. 'Right. You don't have to explain.'

'I want to. She's just – look, it's not … I thought maybe—'

She forced a hollow laugh, clinging to the only dignity left. 'I said she'd be your type.'

'It's not like that.' He stepped forward, so close she could almost hear his heart thudding. 'Honest, just listen for a—'

'I feel so stupid.' She was welling up now. Oh God.

He lifted his hand – hesitantly, like she might push it away. 'I've been going crazy, Rach.' His thumb grazed her cheek, smearing away the tear. Heat flared where he touched, and she hated how much she felt it. 'For so long. Waiting for you.'

'You could have had me, though.' Her voice cracked. 'Years ago … But you just—'

'It was all wrong. Back then. You were still married.' His hand was in her hair now, stroking a loose strand behind her ear. 'I didn't want to be—'

'To be what?'

'Be the one to blame.' He was choking on his words. She'd never seen him like this. 'I thought it was just after a few drinks and you'd change your mind. Or I'd lose you.' His hands were clasping her shoulders, and she could feel the warmth through her denim jacket. 'You needed a friend.'

The heat from his skin was blazing and she shoved him away. If he touched her again, she'd burn.

'Well, cheers for being my *friend*. What a bloody hero. You'd better get back in to Louise.'

His face crumpled. 'I don't want Louise.'

'Milk Tray Man, right?' Her laugh was bitter. 'In and out. Man of mystery.'

'You know that's not me.'

'None of my business.' Her eyes flashed, mask firmly back in place. 'Wouldn't touch you with a bargepole. Once was more than enough.'

He stepped back, throat bobbing with a hard swallow. 'Touch every other fucker though, won't you?'

'What's that supposed to mean?'

'Always someone else. On duty. Off duty. But never—'

'Tyler? You were laughing a few days ago. *Please come back with more of these stories,* wasn't it?' Her impression of his voice was harsh, exaggerating every vowel.

He shifted. 'Afterwards. The NCA one. Robocop or whatever.'

'Terminator.' Him repeatedly getting this wrong was pushing a button she didn't even know she had. She spoke through gritted teeth. 'That was a joke. And nothing happened.'

He didn't reply, eyes unblinking.

'It didn't!' Why was she justifying herself to him here? 'What the fuck, Lennon?'

He stepped forward. 'You don't hear what they say, around the station. I do. That Matthews wanker, calls you *Whorelow.* I should've knocked him out—'

Anger overtook her now. The double fucking standards. 'All right for you though, isn't it?' She jabbed towards the house. To Louise, wearing his shirt. 'Bet you're getting all the banter. Shagging the canteen staff's all part of your charm, right?'

'You know I'd never do that. You know me.'

'I thought I did.'

'Yeah, well. I thought so too. Guess I was wrong.'

'Just get back inside. Give the lads something to talk about next week.'

His voice reverberated halfway down the street. 'Next week I'm at your fucking hearing, remember? Trying to save your job.'

'Don't do me any favours.' She was shouting now too and she didn't care. 'I don't need your help.'

She strode away, not looking back, a red mist in front of her eyes. What the fuck had she been thinking? He'd literally had his dick in someone else when she knocked on the door. Whatever she'd thought was building between them was a lie. She'd been kidding herself.

I've got you and I won't let go.

Of course he'd let go. Seen who she really was and dropped her like a stone.

He didn't chase her this time. Didn't call out. The only sound was the slam of the door.

Driving away, rage and shame curdling in her stomach, Rachel cursed the hypocrisy of the organisation she worked in. Jess was right. The fucking patriarchy. The world was stacked against them.

Even worse, now she was going to have to buy everyone in the unit a bloody holiday present to show Lennon he was nothing special and her heart hadn't been ripped out and stamped into the pavement. Prick.

Chapter 50

Land

Tuesday 2nd May

Rachel looked at her watch: 9.05 a.m.. A sensible person would have left five minutes ago. It was only a short drive to the Forth Banks police station on the quayside, but the last thing she needed was a sweaty dash before facing the panel who were to decide her professional future.

The kids had left in a tangle of noise, approaching their first day back at school with a pitch-perfect duet of apathy and indignation. It was just like old times. They'd been weirdly in sync since they'd returned, buzzing, from the Newcastle–Southampton game, after smashing the southerners 3–0. The mood of the whole city seemed to be sky high over the bank holiday weekend, a Champions League place for next season almost within spitting distance.

As Rachel did a last sweep of the kitchen, she noticed that the bread and Nutella had been put away and someone had actually run a cloth over the bench. True, the toast crumbs had just been brushed onto the floor, leaving a crunchy residue underfoot, but it was a novelty nonetheless.

The doorbell rang. Clattering to the door, heels probably puncturing the floorboards, she yanked it open. A courier stood on the step.

'Mrs Harlow?' He held out a clipboard. 'Signature and ID, please.'

'No bother,' she said, wondering what had been ordered already with the proceeds of the kids' new consultancy income. Probably Jake. This must be something questionable, though, if he'd used her name for the delivery. She reached for her passport, still in a pile with the others on the radiator, yet to be put away.

'Needs to be the same as when you made the request.' The man nodded at the passport. 'That right?'

She faltered, looking properly now at the package: Newcastle City Council. Children's Services.

Fumbling with the pen, she scrawled something in the two places marked with an X and took the heavy box.

Her mouth was dry. She really needed to leave now. She could read it later.

Or not at all.

Just because they'd sent the information, it didn't mean she had to open it. Things were looking up – she'd just brought down an international drugs cartel. Half her head had been in shot on the nine o'clock news. This was not the time to delve into the past.

She'd just take it with her. For safekeeping.

The fifteen minutes from Heaton to the quayside passed in a blur, her eyes on the package more than the road. She turned the engine off and sat, rigid with indecision, in the car park. The clock on the dashboard seemed to pulse: 9.41 a.m.. Instinctively, she went to brush her fringe out of her eyes, forgetting that Jess had cut it for her at the weekend and she no longer even had that to hide behind.

And then, as she'd known she would, she tore off the tape and began to pull out the contents of her case file. Stacks of stapled documents fell into her lap, smelling of dust and old offices. She scanned the first sheet, but the text blurred, and she could only take in fragments.

Profound evidence of neglect … living conditions are dirty and the children's hygiene needs are not being met adequately … they have been left alone for long periods in the property.

The words detonated: *left alone,* for how long? It was dated February 1990 so she would've been – what – two and a half? And why did it say *they*?

She could just stop reading – lock it in the boot and pretend it wasn't there.

But her chest was tight. Her lungs were burning. She had to know.

9.52 a.m.. Not caring about the time, she grabbed the next document, almost ripping it. A report from the emergency foster placement where she had been taken following removal from her birth family. It was messy. Handwritten. Words redacted.

Rachel is timid. She stores food in her pockets during mealtimes which she then hides. She does not form attachments easily and relies on xxxxxxxxxxx to speak for her. He is fiercely protective of his sister. We hope the twins can remain together in their long-term placement as their bond is remarkable given the trauma they have experienced.

She slapped the pile back together and tasted metal.

It couldn't be true. But with a sickening wave of realisation, she knew it was.

She had a brother. More than that – a twin.

How could she not have known?

Her focus snapped to the impending hearing and she threw the stack of paper onto the passenger seat. She needed to get out of this car. Far away from—

To what, though? Only judgement. Exposure. Humiliation.

She already felt raw and exposed following the excruciating doorstep exchange with Lennon on Friday night. He probably wouldn't turn up. Why would anyone want to defend her – *dirty, timid, alone?*

Her eyes crept left. The new top sheet on the upturned pile was different to the rest – an original, not a photocopy. With shaky hands, Rachel turned it over and felt an unexpected wave of serenity. The dots that had been bouncing around her brain for so long joined together with a thick red line.

She'd been anxious about the questions she was about to be asked in the hearing. Her statement was murky, like she'd borrowed someone else's notes and couldn't read their writing. Now, everything on that balcony made sense.

Even if Lennon was there, even if he heard the full extent, it would be a relief. Everything laid bare. No gaping holes in her history.

Sliding the single piece of paper into her bag seemed to increase its weight a hundred-fold, as if she had stones in her pockets. There was no doubt this decision would drag her straight under: a heavy descent, but one of her choosing.

9.58 a.m..

Take it. Show them. This is who you are.

Reaching for the door handle, she withdrew the birth certificate one more time, rereading the words which had shadowed her for weeks, months, years – a whole lifetime.

PLACE OF BIRTH: Newcastle Upon Tyne

NAME AND SURNAME: Rachel Ann GALLAGHER

Chapter 51

Land

'Thank you all for attending this postponed hearing in relation to Detective Inspector Rachel Harlow's professional conduct on Thursday 6th April of this year.'

The chief commissioner for Northumbria Police, Julia Ferguson, offered a tight upturn of her thin lips, before continuing. 'As is customary following any death or serious injury in police contact, a post-incident procedure was initiated. Detective Sergeant James Harrison has acted as post incident manager and will guide us through the evidence gathered, including the complainant's recorded statement.'

As papers shuffled around the table, Rachel let her eyes creep up from the pointed toe of her black shoe. The horseshoe of attendees stretched the length of the bland conference room, royal-blue décor echoing the Northumbria Police crest.

Lennon was there, eyes downcast, uncommonly smart in a charcoal suit. The Police Federation rep, Andy Robinson, was to her right. He'd looked at her with disdain when she'd shaken his hand, five minutes ago. She never had returned that call.

The chief commissioner cleared her throat, instantly commanding the room. Flanked by a stern IOPC representative on one side and the Northumbria post-incident manager on the other, she said, 'DS Harrison. Shall we begin?'

Rachel's gaze thudded back to the floor as Harrison gave a monotone overview of the raid on Flat Nine, Dalton Crescent. Words and phrases broke through the wall of self-protection she had constructed around herself in this airless room: *vulnerable care leaver, mismanaged risk assessment, history of violence, defective BWV, third-floor balcony, fall of twenty-two feet, broken femur, two dislocated shoulders, fractured wrist, ruptured spleen, concussion, induced coma.*

She swayed in her chair, gripping the table as though the gradient had tilted beneath her. But she was not adrift anymore.

Raising her focus, she looked straight ahead, through the gap between the seats, out of the broad window, onto the free-flowing river at the bottom of the bank. With no heavy fringe obscuring her vision, she could see clearly.

The DS introduced two expert witnesses. First to speak was the consultant, Mr Ahmed, who had been treating Gallagher at the RVI. He spoke calmly and at length about the life-changing nature of Jo" Paul's injuries. Although his condition had improved markedly in the last week, he remained in critical care, and at such a point he could be discharged, this would be to the hospital wing of Durham Prison whilst he was retained on remand for the number of offences for which he was arrested.

'In your view, Mr Ahmed, did the complainant have injuries that would correlate with excessive force, prior to his fall from the balcony?' the chief commissioner asked.

'As Mr Gallagher landed on his front, thereby receiving significant trauma to his face and body, it would only be speculative for me to offer a view on the lead-up to the catastrophic fall.' The doctor shook his head. 'In my opinion, however, I would judge the scale of the injuries as most likely to have been exacerbated by the force of another person's momentum at height.'

The chief commissioner frowned. 'For the benefit of the

minutes, doctor, could you clarify your position?'

He paused for a moment and glanced at Rachel, before continuing. 'A push,' he said. 'A push would have increased the velocity of his fall and therefore the severity of the injuries sustained on impact.'

The IOPC representative's eyebrows shot up. He tapped the tablet in front of him and began making notes on its screen, presumably preparing her imminent P45.

The second witness, a Policing Standards use-of-force expert, Liam Fitzpatrick, was next to give his testimony. He was Northern Irish, softly spoken and took time to consider each question before answering.

'Mr Fitzpatrick,' said DS Harrison. 'Having read DI Harlow's statement, would you say that her actions in dealing with Mr Gallagher on the sixth of April *prior* to the balcony location were proportionate and reasonable in the circumstances?'

His pause stretched out like a void in the room and Rachel held her breath. 'Whilst the aim should always be to use as minimum force necessary, officers do need to *read* situations and act accordingly. In the specific circumstances laid out in Inspector Harlow's statement and that of the three officers also present, I believe that it was reasonable to take hold of the complainant in order to manage a volatile scenario.'

'And afterwards, Mr Fitzpatrick? Would you say that it was reasonable for DI Harlow to move Mr Gallagher to a higher-risk area of the residence, an action that ultimately resulted in him sustaining the injuries Mr Ahmed has already outlined?' DS Harrison's voice was more urgent now, and the tension within the room seemed to crank up another gear.

'Having assessed DI Harlow's statement on the reasoning for this move, to de-escalate an assault, I would suggest that this, again, was a proportionate strategic tactic. Northumbria Police have acknowledged that a marker should have previously been added to Mr Gallagher's record, warning of previous resistance to arrest and the need for a spit guard as PPE.' Rachel let out the breath she had been holding.

'Thank you, Mr Fitzpatrick,' said the chief commissioner. 'Your testimony has been most useful. However, the fact remains that DI Harlow's deviation from the arrest plan on the sixth of April directly led to this critical incident and the subsequent reputational damage to Northumbria Police. Quite apart from Mr Gallagher's injuries, his allegations have put significant strain on wider community trust in the force.'

'Indeed, ma'am,' added DS Harrison. 'If we could now hear from the key police witness, DS Adam Lennon, who witnessed the latter part of the interaction between DI Harlow and Mr Gallagher.'

Lennon shuffled the agenda and his typed statement, stacking the sheets of paper together as though he needed something to do with his hands, but his voice was steady in confirming his rank, role and involvement in Operation Fever.

'What exactly did you see as you approached the doorway to the balcony, DS Lennon?' the chief commissioner asked.

'I saw Jo" Paul Gallagher kick out at the balcony perimeter and I heard him shout something in DI Harlow's face. I then saw DI Harlow try to pull Jo" Paul Gallagher back. I reached to open the door to assist, but by that point it was too late and Jo" Paul Gallagher had jumped from the ledge.'

'Would you say that DI Harlow used a reasonable amount of force in her dealings with the complainant on the balcony, DS Lennon?'

He nodded. 'I would. The size difference between the two was considerable and I would say that DI Harlow used force in a wholly proportionate manner in her attempt to stop Mr Gallagher causing injury to himself or others.'

'And finally, DS Lennon, you state that you have worked with DI Harlow for over a decade, both as response officers and in CID. Would you say that she is an officer who upholds the professional standards of the force more generally, in respect to her behaviour towards colleagues and the general public?'

Lennon looked directly at Rachel and spoke firmly. 'The best officer I've come across. We need her back, ma'am.'

'Thank you, Detective Sergeant Lennon,' DS Harrison said, whilst the commissioner made a series of quick notes. 'Before we move to DI Harlow herself and commence the final stage of the hearing, I would like to read some extracts from the other testimonials in your document packs. Several of the officers from the North East Regional Organised Crime Unit have specifically requested for their statements to be included as part of this hearing.'

Rachel bit her lip and focused on the water in the distance, the current pulling the Tyne upstream effortlessly, wind rippling its surface into irregular patterns. Who would have wanted to add their weight to her downfall?

She listened, however, in rapt silence as she heard the words of Bradshaw and Rossy: statements steeped in solidarity, without a mention of unsigned overtime requests, or the wrath she regularly inflicted when she assessed they needed a good kick up the arse.

The last statement, even more surprisingly, was from Coates.

Jesus. She'd barely muttered two civil words consecutively to him during his placement in the unit. He'd been useful solely in making satisfactory cups of tea, and she'd even refused one of those when he'd handed her the Sports Direct mug, which she despised with a passion.

The senior officer he described seemed to be someone else entirely.

'DI Harlow has a sharp intellect and razor focus on the operation. No question is deemed too insignificant, and my confidence as a member of Northumbria Police has grown since working under her leadership.'

'She has taken time, often after hours, to explain elements of investigative procedure to me. Even after the incident on the sixth of April, she directed me to a crucial piece of evidence that has enabled progress in our work to prevent, prepare, protect and pursue leads within Operation Fever.'

'It is typical of DI Harlow's dedication that, despite the personal impact of the incident, her focus remained on the wider investigation. I sincerely hope to keep learning from her as soon as she is reinstated.'

Rachel felt something wet escape from her eye. She quickly brushed its trail away, but – horrifyingly – more drops burst their bank and before she could get a hold of herself mascara was flooding down her face. She sniffed loudly, not caring anymore. The damage was done.

'It is not standard that we receive testimonies of this nature, or quantity, DI Harlow,' the commissioner said. She reminded her of a brisk World War Two hospital matron, running a tight ship with limited resources and brooking no nonsense.

The commissioner reached into her handbag and, for a second, Rachel thought she might be about to receive her papers and be marched from the room. However, a tissue was all that had been withdrawn and it was passed, person to person, along the royal blue chairs until it reached her hand.

'We have, of course, taken your prepared statement into consideration, DI Harlow,' said the commissioner, 'and this has been supported by the testimony of DS Lennon. And we are aware of the significant progress made in county lines policing, due in large part to evidence recovered during the raid on the address in question. Under your management, Operation Fever has successfully identified the route of Class-A drugs into this region and has an application pending to dismantle the associated telecommunication network. Is there anything else you would like to say in relation to the incident?'

Rachel pressed the tissue, one more time, under each eye. 'Yes, ma'am. I do.' Her hand was steady. If she was the person of integrity whom her colleagues had just described, it was time to be honest.

She looked to the Police Federation rep. 'I can present documentation to the hearing that hasn't been previously disclosed, is that right?'

He nodded, eyeing her quizzically. Lennon coughed. The commissioner sat up straighter in her chair and looked at DS Harrison for confirmation of this deviance from the agenda, but he shrugged. Rachel smoothed her single sheet of A4 and took a deep breath.

Suddenly, there was a noise from the other end of the room. The double doors had opened with a bang and a uniformed officer strode purposefully across the carpeted floor. He was holding a manila folder, which he set down on the table in front of the commissioner and spoke in a hushed voice into her ear. She looked from him, to Rachel, and opened the file.

After examining the document in silence for a few moments, the commissioner pointed to a highlighted passage, turning first to DS Harrison, and then the IOPC representative. His long neck was craned to better peruse the typed page in front of them.

'This is most unusual,' the IOPC official said, beady eyes on stalks.

'Unusual, indeed,' the commissioner agreed, 'and yet, timely. I thank you, Constable, for bringing this new information to our attention.'

Rachel tracked the ripple of unease around the table. Lennon was pale, his dark hair sticking to his forehead in clumps, tie strangling at his throat. Nails near-puncturing her own sheet of paper, she held herself still, waiting for the interruption to be explained.

'We have a late addition to the document pack.' The

commissioner pressed her thin lips together, tightly, as if preparing them for the impact of her subsequent words. 'I will, of course, ensure that this is properly itemised within the appendix of your electronic copy. However, rather than adjourn and necessitate a further postponement, I propose that we incorporate this new evidence.

'Mr Gallagher discharged himself from the Royal Victoria Infirmary in the early hours of this morning and presented at Byker Police Station, wishing to give a revised statement regarding the serious injury sustained on the sixth of April. Mr Gallagher now states that his fall was caused entirely of his own making and wishes to withdraw any accusation of excessive force or misconduct against Detective Inspector Harlow. He requests to have it on record that the fall was an attempt to evade capture by Northumbria Police and, as such, had no correlation to DI Harlow's actions.'

Rachel's eyes snapped to Lennon.

Gone was her focus on the fast-flowing river. What the fuck?

He averted his gaze, but a slight movement at the corners of his mouth and the immediate reddening of his neck told their own story. This had his name written all over it, but what was the deal? She forced her face to stay neutral, but the possibilities Jo" Paul could have demanded were exploding in her mind – deliveries to his cell? A contact? A quiet promise of a get-out when the trial came?

The chief commissioner's wrap-up jolted her back into the room. 'In this case, DI Harlow, with no misconduct accusation to answer, I can draw this hearing to a close. Unless, of course, you still have information that you wanted to bring to our attention?'

Rachel's hand hovered, before she slipped the paper back into her bag. 'I'm ready to let the matter lie.' She heard her own voice: crisp, professional. Like she meant it. Like this was over. But the name Gallagher still dragged behind her, an anchor she couldn't cut loose.

Chapter 52

Land

The sun was warm on the back of Rachel's neck as she walked down the steep bank towards the quayside. Lennon had been loitering outside the station entrance as she'd left. He'd said nothing, only leaned in for a hug. For a moment she ached to melt into him, to give him everything she'd been holding back. But she stiffened. He felt different. Cooler. The usual blaze of his skin had dulled to something tepid, and she pulled the ache tight, locking it inside.

They'd let go at the same time. That line between eroded for good. And she suddenly understood what it had always been. It had held them together, not kept them apart – for all these years.

Now it was gone.

They'd have to speak, sooner or later. She'd have to uncover what he knew. The deal he'd made. And the cost.

The Gallagher she'd encountered on arrest after arrest wouldn't have added years to his sentence without the promise of something sizeable. He respected no one: could barely look at a woman without knocking fifty shades of shit out of her.

She stopped still on the slope. Had she ever known Jo" Paul

at all? Her mind was reeling from the contents of the file on her passenger seat. *Fiercely protective of his sister.* And those mangled words up on the balcony, the bitter howl in the video clip – had she missed his meaning in the chaos?

She was one of them. A Gallagher.

Thoughts of the rest of the family made her skin crawl. The things they'd done. If Jo" Paul knew, surely he would have been shouting it from the rooftops. He could have used their connection for his own gain, time and time again, rather than keep her submerged beneath the surface.

Rachel couldn't stand still with this going round in her head. She needed to move.

As she reached the level ground of pavement, river and bridges, she pulled out her phone. The two hours she'd had it on silent had been eventful. Missed calls from the DCI, Byker station and Bradshaw; a fingers-crossed emoji from Jake; a rainbow positivity glitter cloud GIF from Jess; and an unrelated, ecstatic message from Saira:

Lola off the boob & sleeping through! Let's get on the tequilas.

There was also a voice note from her mum. Unable to recall a time when either of her parents had utilised such a modern mode of communication, she put it on speaker.

'*Is it recording, Bob? I can't tell if it's recording. No, that's it, it's working. Rachel, it's us.*' Barbara's voice was maddeningly loud, every syllable defined as if she anticipated a need for the message to be interpreted by a non-English speaker. '*We just wanted to wish you the best of British for this morning.*'

Her dad's voice now, raspy, farther away from the phone. '*Give 'em what for, love. We're proud of you whatever the outcome.*'

Barbara, again: '*They can't believe all this down at the bowls club, honest to goodness. That Danielle! I mean, I said to Pam – you know, makes the teas – what a piece of work! And our Rachel, stopped it all, had her in handcuffs! Saved the captain. And her*

*barely five-two in flat shoes – such a worry all these years, with the
teenage pregnancy and the divorce and … well, you've come good
in the end, haven't you, love?*

Her dad, cutting in, firmly: '*Don't be dragging all that up again,
Barbara. This must be costing a fortune – it won't be in our price
plan. Let the girl go, she'll be in the hearing. Just let us know how
it goes. We'll be here.*'

She smiled, despite the many points of potential irritation in the two-minute recording. Soon, she'd ring back and
deliver the good news, but, just for a while longer, she wanted
to hold the glow of relief to herself. Nowhere to be and no
clock ticking.

Her stiletto heels picked their way, step by step, under the
shadow of the Tyne Bridge and onwards along the quayside path.
The sun was mild, in comparison to the scorching heat of Galicia
and Portugal, but it was a welcome change from the driving rain
and icy wind they'd endured in the year so far.

Rachel paused and leaned against the barrier, looking down
into the murky water. She took hold of the momentous piece of
paper for what she knew would be the last time.

I know who you are.

Her mum had been right. Not the past, not the future – she
was grounded in the here and now.

Tearing the page in two, and then in half again and again, she
watched the pieces fall away from the fading scar in the palm
of her hand, down to the river. Almost immediately, they were
submerged, then pulled along, carried off towards the sea.

She lingered, watching the sun's rays dance on the rippling
surface of the Tyne, twisting and twirling effortlessly in the breeze.
Time stretched out ahead of her and, for once, she was comfortable with the unknown.

A beautiful mess. Maybe that much was true.

She knew who she was now.

It didn't matter how she'd started; the past could be dissolved.

She might have stood there for a minute or an hour, letting thoughts drift like waves, but – eventually – Rachel turned from the water and walked inland, towards home.

THE END

**Read on for the next instalment following
DI Rachel Harlow!**

**Read on for the next instalment following
DI Rachel Harlow!**

Prologue

'Control to DI Harlow, are you receiving?'

Static, then the worst words imaginable: 'IC1 male, looks fifteen or sixteen. Dark hair, grey hoodie. Stab wounds. Critical.'

Jake. Her throat clenches.

Rachel floors the accelerator, the CID Astra rattling as she forces a path through Byker traffic. Sirens wail somewhere else. Closer. Not hers. No blues, no kit, just the weight in her chest and a mother's panic.

Concrete blocks rise around her, balconies stacked like cages. Every window a witness. Every shadow a threat.

Radio chatter crackles: *scene preserved, cordon up, suspect outstanding.* Too many voices, none of them saying the one thing she needs – *it isn't him.*

The estate tightens as she skids to a halt. Narrow walkways, graffiti warnings carved into walls. Phones glowing in the darkness. Kids in hoods filming, circling. Blood on the pavement.

Uniforms push the crowd back. 'Keep clear. Police scene.'

Her ID shakes in her hand: the card means nothing when your own child fits the description. Every step past the cordon drags, weighted, endless.

She doesn't want to look. She has to.

Because if it's Jake …
The job, the rank, the results – none of it matters.
The world ends here.

Chapter 1

Away

Sunday 16th July

The top line flashed in red across the departure board: KL955 AMSTERDAM FINAL CALL.

Rachel's trainers slammed against the tiled concourse, hand luggage thumping against her hip, each breath tearing at her throat. Gate 26. Missing this flight wasn't an option – not when she was presenting tomorrow, the North East Regional Organised Crime Unit's name on the line.

How the fuck had it come to this? She should have been here an hour ago.

Swerving around a family – the dad pulling a toddler on a blue Trunki, the mum with a newborn asleep in a BabyBjörn – she felt a sting hit harder than the stitch in her ribs.

A sharp-suited businesswoman breezed out of duty free, Clinique package in one hand, laptop bag in the other. Sleek. Composed. Rachel caught herself in the shopfront glass: Jake's cap barely disguising her wild hair, dark shadows under her eyes, top sticking to her back. Frazzled. Late.

Her phone buzzed. Another missed call. Rossy. No time to

listen to the voicemail. She pictured DS Natalie Ross at the gate already, impatient, extra-hot-oat-decaf order nailed. Always planning ahead. Always in control.

Rachel, by contrast, had been firefighting all afternoon – instructions for her parents, dinner money, school forms, Jake slamming the door after she'd taken half his wages.

They'd parted in another blazing argument. Her mum and dad hovering, last-minute cavalry after Scott had let them down again. And Jess, head in the bloody College of Policing manual since her stint at HQ, convinced she knew procedure better than Rachel herself.

All of it pulled at her as she sprinted through Departures. Too many lives depending on her being everything at once: mother, daughter, detective inspector.

She banged down the escalator. Lungs burning. Every step a jolt. If she missed this flight, she could kiss goodbye to the leg-up from Tim, her NCA contact – her first teetering chance in an international setting. The conference would be packed with senior officers from across the continent. Europol. Three days of intelligence sharing, case studies, networking. She needed to be there. Needed to show she belonged in the room.

The gate shimmered ahead. Seconds left. She risked a glance behind, confirming she was the very last—

And slammed into someone solid.

The collision knocked the air out of her. Papers slid from her bag. Her ankle went, sending one trainer flying over the empty seats at Gate 26. Strong hands caught her before she hit the floor. And she was engulfed by something hotter than the sun, hotter than nuclear fission.

Her head snapped up.

Lennon.

For a second, the world stilled. Just his face – the dark eyes, the cut of his jaw, the smell of him, sharp and maddeningly familiar.

Her mouth moved before her brain caught up. 'What the fuck are you doing here?'

His mouth twisted. 'Change of plan. *Ma'am.*'

'Not a chance.' Her pulse hammered. 'Rossy's—'

'They're in hospital.' His tone was flat, guarded. 'Hayley's gone into early labour. I'm covering.'

Rachel blinked and words tangled in her throat. Rossy. Hayley. Baby. Shit. She should've known. Should've answered.

'Nope.' Her head shook before she could stop it. 'No way. This isn't happening. I'll get Bradshaw. Tariq.' Fuck it – even Coates would be preferable.

'Not exactly ideal for me either,' he said, low and biting. 'Bailey's call. I'm your number two whether you like it or not.'

Heat flared in her chest, anger sparking through exhaustion, through the sweat sticking her top to her back. 'Don't play the martyr. You wanted this.'

His eyes narrowed. 'Believe me, Rachel, I didn't.'

Her full name in his mouth was too much – cold, jagged. She could feel her cheeks flame. 'Look, we're not doing this here.'

'Fine by me.' He shifted, broad shoulders brushing hers, the burn of him unbearable. Then, under his breath: 'Least I've got both shoes on.'

Her jaw clenched. She hated the way his calmness only made her pulse race faster, hated that her body remembered things her mind wanted to bury.

'Excuse me?' a sharp voice cut in. One of the cabin crew, neat bun, lipstick immaculate, stood in front of them. 'Gate's closing. You're the final passengers.'

Rachel's fingers shook as she pressed her phone to the scanner. Even the beep felt judgemental. Lennon was close behind, presence heavy at the back of her neck. He bent, retrieved her stray Adidas Samba, and passed it to her with the faintest smirk before striding a pace ahead. As if she wouldn't clock it.

A WhatsApp from Jake flashed on her home screen like a raised middle finger. She rammed the phone into her bag, not ready for round two, or twenty-two, or whatever number they were up to now. A hundred quid for glass collecting? She was in the wrong bloody job. No way was he blowing it on cheap cider in Heaton Park with these new charver mates.

Shoving on her shoe with as much dignity as she could muster, she stalked down the jet bridge. Her hands were still trembling. Her heart still hammering – from fury, from something stronger than rage.

And the worst part was knowing she had three days of this.

Three days worrying about Jake.

Three days with Lennon.

Chapter 2

Away

The plane door sealed behind them, and Rachel shuffled down the narrow aisle, clattering against armrests, Lennon just a half-step ahead. Too close. Always too close.

Every seat she passed was full of scowls, raised eyebrows, irritated sighs. Delayed now. All eyes on them. The humiliation prickled across her skin.

Their row came into view – aisle seat already occupied by a woman with a grizzly baby. The empty seats looked impossibly cramped. She might as well be sitting on his lap.

Brilliant.

Rachel barged past Lennon, hip brushing his thigh as she slid into the window seat. She caught her reflection in the dark glass: cap shadowing tired eyes, black top wrinkled. A mess. Yet beneath it, unavoidably, she saw what he must still see – the sharp cheekbones, the full curve of her mouth. Attractive. Sexy, even. Against her will, her pulse quickened at the thought.

He was squashed into the middle now, shoulder pressed firmly against hers. The smell of him – clean, warm, infuriatingly familiar – filled her lungs.

She set her jaw and picked up her phone, removing all

notifications with a decisive swipe. She'd go back to Jake later, when they'd both had time to cool down. For now, she had to focus. Professional detachment was the only way through this shitstorm.

'We'll be going over Europol updates on OCG activity first thing,' she said stiffly, reading from the itinerary, trying to block out the wails of the baby only inches away. 'Then the panel discussion on supply chains. Afternoon workshops on cross-border comms protocols. I'm presenting at two p.m. Then the regional case study sessions.'

'Right.' His reply was neutral, eyes forward, but the sharp click and tug of his seatbelt undercut the single word.

'And the intelligence brief. We'll need to—'

'I know the schedule.'

The bluntness shut her down, left her staring at her own face in the glass again. Eyes too tired to hide their anger.

Silence stretched. The baby had stopped screaming. She side-eyed right, swerving Lennon, and saw the mum, flat out, baby moulded into her chest. Rachel tried to swallow, but something had lodged in her throat. Jake had been petrified, flying as a toddler – Scott as helpful as a chocolate teapot. He would've been on the other side of the aisle, headphones on, Heineken in hand, while she struggled with the twins. Jess, trying to wrestle out of her seatbelt; Jake white, bottom lip wobbling as he gripped her hand.

She sat up straighter, trying to concentrate on the here and now. The rhythmic chomp of the baby on its dummy. The rustle of a stranger's newspaper – probably *The Chronicle*, yet another headline screaming about knife crime stats despite the Connelly arrest. She forced her mind to focus on something else. The warmth of Lennon at her side. Unbearable, unignorable. The closest they'd been in months.

'You're canny quiet,' he said eventually, voice pitched lower. Blunt edge gone.

'Lot on my mind.' She didn't look at him. Couldn't.

'Don't worry,' he said. 'I'll keep my distance.'

She willed herself not to say it. Not to give the impression she cared. But the words formed of their own accord. 'Instructions from *Louise*?'

He shifted slightly, thigh brushing hers. Didn't reply. No sharp retort. No banter. Just let the void deepen, with his silence cutting sharper than words.

Her thoughts wrenched her homeward whether she liked it or not. Jess on the sofa, devouring the case files she'd wheedled out of the admin team during her week's work experience, her fascination with forensic detail both impressive and unsettling.

Jake on the periphery, eyes on his phone. Tapping. Shielding the screen from view.

Guilt lodged deep in her chest. A break-up at fifteen could hit hard. She should've been more patient, sat with him properly. Not flown off the fucking handle. Again.

Worst of all, her own secrets. Her own shame. The box she'd sealed and shoved out of sight – names, dates, all still undisclosed. A ticking time bomb under the bed.

The minutes blurred in the cabin air and every small movement from Lennon – his elbow grazing hers as he stirred his coffee – sent fresh sparks through her blood. She clenched her hands in her lap, furious with herself. Furious with him.

By the time the wheels screeched down onto Amsterdam's runway, her whole body felt wired, tight as a cordon line with a baying crowd behind it.

Rain hit hard against the taxi windows, soaking them even in the dash from car to hotel entrance. As they stumbled through the glass doors, clothes saturated, it was nearly midnight. Rachel shoved her cap – Jake's cap – in her bag. The lobby gleamed, bright and indifferent, polished floors echoing their footsteps.

She braced her palm on the reception desk, pushing clumps of fringe from her eyes. 'Two reservations for Northumbria Police.

Harlow and—' she dragged her eyes to the completely wrong DS beside her '—should be Ross.'

The receptionist clicked the mouse, then smiled, contrasting the smoking train wreck of her words. 'One standard double. Three nights.'

Rachel's stomach dropped. 'Erm, no. That won't work. There should be two—'

'Definitely one room.' The woman typed and clicked and shook her head. 'And we're at full capacity with conference delegates.'

'That's impossible.' Her voice rose, desperate now. 'There must be—'

'Rach.' Lennon cut across her. Calm. Even. He leaned closer, resting a steadying hand on her arm. Heat seeped through the thin cotton of her top, slowing her breath. 'Travel team's cock-up. We're wet through and knackered. Let's just take the room.'

The way he said it – gentle, unflustered, like he could shoulder her anger as easily as her luggage – made her throat tighten. For a moment she wanted to lean into him, let him take some of the weight.

She forced herself to sign the form instead.

The lift was tiny. Mirrored walls crowded them even closer, different versions playing out in every direction: trainee response officers, one-time lovers, CID partners, best mates. And all for what? Now just cold colleagues. Strangers. Enemies. Rachel pressed herself into the corner, clutching the room key. Lennon leaned against the opposite wall, expression unreadable.

She shoved damp strands of hair out of her eyes, but her hand shook. He noticed. Of course he noticed.

Leisurely, he stepped forward, slow, unthreatening. Brushed her fringe gently aside with the backs of his fingers. The tenderness of it undid her – made her chest ache in ways anger couldn't cover.

For a moment, she almost let her forehead rest against his chest. Almost.

She tried not to look at him. Fought it for a second, maybe two

– wrestling with the way this affected her. But his hand cupped her chin. And she lifted her gaze. Slowly, excruciatingly slowly.

No words.

For one dizzy second, she thought he might kiss her.

But the lift pinged. They jolted apart.

The corridor smelled aggressively of carpet shampoo, lights low and humming. Lennon opened the door, let her step in first.

And there it was.

One bed.

Wide. Immaculate. Waiting.

Rachel froze in the doorway, pulse hammering, emotions colliding – fury, frustration, desire, dread.

Beside her, Lennon's jaw tightened. His eyes flicked to hers, but still, he said nothing.

The bed said it all.

Rachel's throat was dry. 'Don't get any ideas,' she muttered, trying to alleviate the tension, but her voice cracked.

Lennon dropped his bag onto the chair, slow, deliberate. He looked at her, a faint smile tugging at the corner of his mouth. Then he spoke, but so low she almost thought she'd imagined it.

'Yeah. That might be a problem.'

A Letter from Elle Blair

Dear Reader

Thank you so much for getting on board with DI Rachel Harlow – I really hope you've enjoyed the story. In my 'day job', teaching English to students who have been excluded, I've worked with many young people facing challenges similar to McKenzie's and Gaby's. It's been a privilege to bring a little bit of this context to my book.

If you're interested in finding out more about services supporting teenagers at risk of exploitation, this is an amazing local charity who generously helped me with research: https://www.streetwisenorth.org.uk.

I love hearing from readers – it means the absolute world that people are reading this book and taking the characters to their hearts. You can find me on Instagram @elleblairwriter, where I'll keep you updated on the DI Rachel Harlow series.

Personal recommendations make such a difference to debut writers, so if you enjoyed *In Deep Water*, I'd be enormously grateful if you could tell your friends and/or leave a review. Your support is so truly appreciated.

Happy reading!

Elle

Acknowledgements

It feels surreal to be writing the acknowledgements for my debut novel, having always loved reading these pages at the back of books. Firstly, huge thanks to my agent, Hannah Ferguson. I'm so happy to have you in my corner. Also, to the Hardman & Swainson team for the support, especially Lucy.

Thank you to everyone at HQ. George – thanks for seeing something special in my police-smut manuscript. To Ellie for explaining every part of the process so patiently. To Sophia for your support. To Cari for your meticulous edits. To Helena for copy-editing and Eldes for proofreading. To Anna for the cover. To Lisa for the warm welcome. Thanks to the sales, marketing and PR teams, especially Becci, Georgia and Lou.

Despite harbouring quiet dreams of being a writer since childhood, I never had the confidence or discipline to see a project through to the end – until I turned forty. The same day my youngest son started Reception, I began the life-changing Crime Fiction MA at the University of East Anglia.

Big thanks to the exceptional writers I was lucky enough to learn from at UEA: Richard, Kate, Sheena, Elaine, Brian, Jess, Vic, Gerry, Ben, Valerie, Clare and Austen. Also, to Rebecca and Rebecca from the cohort above for their advice after graduating. I'm forever grateful to the tutors – Nathan, Tom, Julianne – who helped me shape my DI Rachel Harlow character. But most of all, thank you to Henry Sutton who has been a brilliant and inspiring friend and mentor, on the course and afterwards.

I feel immensely grateful to the friends who have supported me to keep writing. To Vicky and Anna, by my side in good times and bad, you were my first readers and made me think it was worth carrying on. Emma and Charlie, your enthusiasm after reading gave me the biggest boost. To Ben, for setting me straight on authentic East-End vocab. Janet, an amazing writer: your detailed feedback was a game-changer. To Amit and Flora, you should really set up a husband-and-wife editorial business – good cop/bad cop in the best possible way!

Next, to the friends who kept asking to read it, but haven't been allowed because I want to actually sell some copies! My uni girls and their families: Julie, Antonia, Caroline and Vic. For everything. The footie mams and dads who asked for updates at every match. Paul, Steph and Becky, for your encouragement. Bea, Jess and Liccie, for inspiring much of the kids/work/life content. And to the incredible English teachers I've worked with over the last twenty years – I've learned so much from you all.

Thank you to those who helped with research. To Vicky, for pharmaceutical matters; Diane, for sharing your expertise in Children's Services; Anna-Lou, who lives in the Byker Wall, and showed me its community spirit; and Graham Bartlett, for your niche expertise as a writer and former police officer. I'm very lucky to have friends who work for Northumbria Police and I'm hugely grateful for your help. Any errors on police procedure in the finished novel are entirely mine. Thank you, Caroline, Steven, Paul, and – the man, the myth, the legend – Doppa the Copper. Apologies for the never-ending questions!

To my family: Mum, Dad, Con. I'll never stop thinking of us as a unit of four and hope one day we will be again. Thank you for all your love and support – for being strong in the hardest of times. Lorna and Billy – your help with the kids while I've been writing to tight deadlines has been invaluable. And to all my North-East family for introducing me to the finer things in life: NUFC, Greggs' cheese pasties and a night out with no coat.

And finally, to the most important ones: David, Isaac, Annie and Ted. I love you. Sorry for all the times I've been locked to the laptop and ignored Yoda barking, tea burning, screen limits extending … Thank you, D, for reading multiple drafts, telling me I could do it and fixating on minuscule details like the car she wouldn't drive. I hope I've made you proud.

Dear Reader,

We hope you enjoyed reading this book. If you did, we'd be so appreciative if you left a review. It really helps us and the author to bring more books like this to you.

Here at HQ Digital we are dedicated to publishing fiction that will keep you turning the pages into the early hours. Don't want to miss a thing? To find out more about our books, promotions, discover exclusive content and enter competitions you can keep in touch in the following ways:

JOIN OUR COMMUNITY:

Sign up to our new email newsletter: http://smarturl.it/SignUpHQ

Read our new blog www.hqstories.co.uk

X: https://twitter.com/HQStories

f: www.facebook.com/HQStories

BUDDING WRITER?

We're also looking for authors to join the HQ Digital family! Find out more here:

https://www.hqstories.co.uk/want-to-write-for-us/

Thanks for reading, from the HQ Digital team